ASBARAN SOLUTIONS

BOOK TWO OF THE REVELATIONS CYCLE

Chris Kennedy

Seventh Seal Press
Virginia Beach, VA

Copyright © 2017 by Chris Kennedy.

All rights reserved. No part of this publication may be reproduced, distributed or transmitted in any form or by any means, including photocopying, recording, or other electronic or mechanical methods, without the prior written permission of the publisher, except in the case of brief quotations embodied in critical reviews and certain other noncommercial uses permitted by copyright law. For permission requests, write to the publisher, addressed "Attention: Permissions Coordinator," at the address below.

Chris Kennedy/Seventh Seal Press
2052 Bierce Dr.
Virginia Beach, VA 23454
http://chriskennedypublishing.com/

Publisher's Note: This is a work of fiction. Names, characters, places, and incidents are a product of the author's imagination. Locales and public names are sometimes used for atmospheric purposes. Any resemblance to actual people, living or dead, or to businesses, companies, events, institutions, or locales is completely coincidental.

Ordering Information:
Quantity sales. Special discounts are available on quantity purchases by corporations, associations, and others. For details, contact the "Special Sales Department" at the address above.

Asbaran Solutions/ Chris Kennedy. -- 1st ed.
ISBN 978-1942936404

I would like to thank Beth and Patty, who took the time to critically read this work and make it better. I would also like to thank my mother, without whose steadfast belief in me, I would not be where I am today. Thank you. This book is dedicated to my wife and children, who sacrificed their time with me so I could write it.

"And there went out another horse that was red: and power was given to him that sat thereon to take peace from the earth, and that they should kill one another: and there was given unto him a great sword."

— *Revelation 6:4*

Chapter One

Planet Moorhouse, Kepler 62 System

"This is bullshit," Sergeant James Wilson grumbled. The tall, dark-haired trooper spat, the betel nut chew making his spittle a bright crimson on the sun-bleached sand.

"What's bullshit?" Private Dave Daniels asked, his pale brows knitting. "This is only my second contract, but it seems like pretty good duty to me. Walk some fence line, guard a mine, and get paid a ton of credits? Seems pretty soft. No one's trying to kill me, and I can go down to the bar after my shift. Sure, the locals look like anteaters, but they pay well enough so I can afford some of the overpriced beer they've imported."

"Naw, that ain't what I'm talking about, at all," the sergeant replied. He spat again. "Don't get me wrong, I enjoy not getting shot at as much as anyone. Having actually been hit a couple of times, I may even enjoy it more. What I'm saying is that this whole contract's fucked up."

"Why's that?"

"Do you see the bird on our crest?" Sergeant Wilson asked, pointing to where the Asbaran Solutions company flag hung limply from the staff in the humid, breezeless air.

Private Daniels nodded his head, then wiped the sweat from his eyes the motion caused. "Yeah. There's a bird with the company's motto, *'Kill Aliens. Get Paid.'*"

"Do you know what kind of bird that is?"

"Nope; it looks like some sort of griffin."

The sergeant stopped and glared at the junior enlisted. "Do they not teach unit history at basic any more, or are you just too fucking stupid to remember? It ain't no damn griffin, boy; it's a huma bird."

"A huma bird?"

"Yeah. It's a type of bird that never lands; it lives its entire life flying above the clouds where you can never see it."

"Wow, that's pretty cool. I've never heard of a bird like that."

"That's because it doesn't exist, you dumbass," the sergeant said, cuffing the private in the back of the head. "It's mythological. The point I'm trying to get through your stupid fucking head is that us Asbaran ain't for sitting around guarding shit. We're mobile; we strike from above and crush our enemies. We don't hang around waiting for them to hit us while we're sitting on the damned toilet in a guardhouse on some godforsaken planet at the ass-end of the galaxy." He spat; another red stain marked his passage. "If the Founder could see us now…"

"What? What would he do?"

"If the Founder could see us now, he'd probably come back and kill every single motherfucker in management. This ain't how we're supposed to be used. It don't play to our strengths…*and it just ain't right!*" He sighed. "It ain't what I signed up for anyway." He spat again, hitting his first mark dead center. "I signed up to be up there," he continued, pointing up to the sky.

Daniels looked where the sergeant pointed and squinted. "Hey, what's that?" he asked. "There's something up there."

Sergeant Wilson looked up. A miniature boomerang shape could just be seen, silhouetted against the clear green sky. "Fuck!" he grunted as he broke into a run back toward the shelter. "*Incoming!* Get under cover *now!*"

He had only covered half the distance to the bunker when he heard the tell-tale shriek of the banshee bombs, and he knew they weren't going to make it.

* * * * *

Chapter Two

Room 117, Neptune Hall, College of the Atlantic, Virginia Beach, Virginia, USA

Nigel Shirazi winced as Mr. Jamison walked toward him with the graded test papers. Reaching Nigel's desk, Jamison paused to inspect the number written on the old-style paper, even though Nigel was sure Jamison knew it by heart. A sneer twitched across Jamison's lips as he slapped the paper on Nigel's desk.

With a "Hmph!" he thrust his nose in the air and proceeded to the next student in the row. "Excellent work, Miss Beach," he praised before continuing down the row.

Nigel's twitching fingers found the page, and he risked a look, but Jamison had put the paper face down. Of course he had.

Bastard.

Jamison would want to make it as demeaning as possible; in fact, he was probably watching from the back of the aisle, just waiting for Nigel to take a look.

Nigel spun around in his seat. Sure enough, he caught Jamison staring back at him from the end of the row. "Is there a problem, Mister *Shirazi*?" He smiled, daring Nigel to reply. "Is your grade not what you expected?" The sneer was back now, in full force.

Always the emphasis on his name, as if he didn't belong. Wasn't it bad enough that the aliens had glassed his home country of Iran into oblivion 100 years ago? When was everyone going to let that go?

Nigel turned back around, more slowly this time, and he glared at the paper as if to read the grade on the opposite side with x-ray vision. Based on Jamison's reaction, Nigel doubted he needed to flip the paper over.

He already knew the grade; he had failed.

It had been a battle all semester. Someone had told Jamison who Nigel was, and Jamison had delighted in making Nigel's life miserable. The son of Sargon Shirazi, Nigel stood to inherit the family business when he graduated from college.

If he graduated from college.

Having been kicked out of his previous three institutions, this was Nigel's last chance. Although they used the polite term, "disenrolled," what they really meant was, "thrown out on his ass" for poor grades and fighting.

Nigel sighed. Waiting wouldn't make it any better. He flipped over the paper aggressively, like ripping off a used stim patch…something he was becoming more and more unlikely to ever do.

At the top of the paper was the number that ended his career as a mercenary before it ever began. 36%. In red pen, Jamison had written, "Never Is Good Enough," underlining the capital letters.

Nigel's pulse throbbed in his ears and temples, and a red haze came across his vision. He'd kill the motherfucker. He exploded from his seat, flinging it into the next student over, and spun toward the back of the classroom to give Jamison the beating he deserved. He made it two steps before the security officers tackled him.

He got in a good elbow strike on one of the officers, whose nose exploded like an overripe melon, but then the other one hit him with a stun wand. Everything went black.

Dean's Office, College of the Atlantic, Virginia Beach, Virginia, USA

"Well, at least you didn't yell, 'I'll kill you!' this time, so they can't bring you up on murder charges," Steve Rath noted with a smile as he walked out of the dean's office with Nigel. His best friend, Steve had shown up to help plead his case, but it had been for naught; as expected, Nigel had been "disenrolled" again. "At least you've got that going for you. It shows you *can* learn, after all."

"Yeah, ha ha," Nigel replied. He put on a pair of sunglasses to hide the black eye one of the guards had given him after he was stun-locked. "I'm sure my father will appreciate the irony. I prove I'm not stupid by getting thrown out of school again. I doubt he'll buy it."

"So what's your plan? Find another school?"

"My plan? I don't know. It was hard enough to get into this school. I think Father promised them a million-credit endowment if they'd take me. I doubt anyone else will give me another chance, or that the company could afford to buy off another school." He sighed. "Besides, this was my last chance. Father told me if I didn't pass this time, I would be ineligible to take over the company."

"Why'd you have to go after Jamison, then? Sure, he's a prick, but that pretty much killed any chance you had of staying here."

"I don't know, sometimes I just…lose control. He baited me into it, almost as if he wanted me to come after him."

"Obviously, he expected you to, or he wouldn't have had the security force present."

"Yeah, that was a nice touch on his part, wasn't it? I end up with a black eye and disenrollment, and he gets a promotion for dealing with 'such an unruly student.' It makes *total* sense."

"I still don't understand why you had to go after him, though."

Nigel shrugged. "I was bullied plenty as a child in Chabahar, New Persia, where I grew up. When I went to tell Father, he told me to take care of it myself. If I couldn't deal with little things like that, how did I expect to deal with something like running one of the Four Horsemen?"

"That's kind of callous. What did you do?"

"I took a bunch of abuse. Even more once the other kids learned that Father wouldn't do anything. They used to say, 'You know what Nigel stands for? Never Is Good Enough Loser.' It built up in me, more and more, and finally one day I'd had enough. We were playing cricket, and I got put out, and one of the other kids said it while I still had the bat in my hand. I snapped, and I beat him down with it. Hard. The kid was a couple years older than me and big as shit, but I took him down with the first swing. Probably would have killed him too, if some of the other kids hadn't tackled me. I don't know. I remember doing it, but I wasn't in control of myself."

"What happened?"

"Dad paid off the kid's parents and took care of all of his hospital bills, and I was brought to America to grow up. That part was okay. I got to spend a lot of time with my grandfather, who was totally cool. I've been back to Chabahar a few times, and it really sucks. The family estate is nice enough, I guess, but the rest of the city isn't much to speak of, despite all the money Asbaran Solutions and my family has put into it."

Nigel shrugged again. "Anyway, that nickname has followed me around ever since, no matter where I go or what I do. I thought I'd finally escaped it, but Jamison wrote it on my paper. No idea how he knew about it, or if he even meant to do it, but I was under a lot of pressure—I needed that class to graduate—and the combination of the bad grade and the note he wrote…I don't know…I just snapped, like I did on the cricket field that day."

"And every other time you've been kicked out of school?"

"Yeah."

A black limo pulled to the curb in front of them, and Nigel sighed. "That's probably for me."

"You don't sound very excited about it. Is it your family?"

"I suspect so. Remember you asked what I'm going to do now? The person in that car is probably coming to tell me what is required of me, now that I've failed them again."

"Well, good luck," Steve said as a short man in a dark, impeccably-tailored suit got out of the car and held the door open for Nigel. "Let me know how it turns out."

Nigel got into the car and saw he was alone with the man. Normally a family member was present to admonish him or make him feel better, or whatever tactic they were using at the moment. He wasn't sure what that meant.

The man took the seat facing him, and the car pulled away from the curb.

"Your father is sorry to see that you have let your temper get the best of you yet again."

"Yeah, well, it was nice of him to send you to tell me that, rather than coming here himself."

"You may not be aware, but your father runs one of the largest and oldest mercenary organizations on this planet. Its yearly budget could buy almost any country on Earth. He should be excused if he has more important matters than seeing to a son who has once again demonstrated his lack of self-control and inability to follow instructions."

"Yeah, everything's more important than me. Always has been, and it always will be."

"Despite your inability to do what he asks of you, he still loves you; however, at this time your father is currently off-planet, so he couldn't have attended this meeting, even if he wanted to. He left instructions for what to do with you before he left."

"*What?* He was so sure I'd fail that he left instructions for what to do with me when it happened? What the *fuck?*"

"Well, sir, I'm sure even you can look at your own track record and see that what happened *was* a possibility."

"Fuck you, too."

"I understand you are having a difficult time at the moment, but there are still some matters that need to be addressed, based on your continued inability to graduate from college." He opened up a briefcase on the seat next to him and pulled out a slate and a stack of papers.

"Like what?"

"There is the matter of disinheritance from the family business which must be attended to."

"*Disinheritance from the family business?*" Nigel fell back into the seat, stunned.

"Yes, sir. As you were previously advised, if you did not graduate college, you would not be given the opportunity to inherit Asbaran Solutions when your father passes." He handed the slate to Nigel. "Please sign at the 'X,' indicating I have advised you of this termination."

"But, but..." Nigel sputtered.

"Come, come, Mr. Shirazi, you have been told repeatedly this day would come if you continued down the path you trod. You have now arrived at your destination."

All emotion drained from Nigel, and his face went pale. Barely aware of what he was doing, he signed his name.

"Very well, thank you." The man put the slate back in his briefcase. "As I mentioned earlier, your father truly does care for you. Although you won't be given the opportunity to receive the company, he has offered you a number of other opportunities with the company. Failing that, he intends to provide funding for you to live a luxurious life, as long as you do not embarrass him, your family, or Asbaran Solutions."

"A luxurious life?"

"Yes, a large sum will be deposited into your account every month, as long as you do not give your father the reason to terminate this benevolence."

"So just stay away, stay out of trouble, and do whatever the hell I want?"

"If that is what you desire." The man handed the stack of papers to Nigel as the car pulled to the curb. "It is all detailed in this document." He opened the door. "This is where you get out."

Unable to talk or think, Nigel stepped out of the car and stood on the sidewalk with his mouth open as the limo drove off. He stood that way for a long time.

* * * * *

Chapter Three

Planet Moorhouse, Kepler 62 System

*"C*olonel Shirazi, we're on final approach, but we're already taking incoming fire. They obviously know we're coming."*

"Understood. We need to retake the facility. Get us down, and we'll take it from there."

"Okay…just so you know, the defenses are…fuck…pretty heavy." The dropship swayed as the pilot maneuvered. *"There's a lot of shit up here."*

"How long 'til touchdown?"

"Fuck! Sorry, sir. Damn it! We just lost one of the dropships. Damn it! There goes another. They're gone. No survivors. 30 seconds. If I make it. The third dropship's hit. I've never seen so much—"

Mexico Mikey's Bar and Grill, Virginia Beach, VA, USA

"I'm sorry about your father," Steve said.

"Thanks, but as you know, we weren't very close," Nigel replied. "The best thing he ever did was leave me alone the last few months." The old-fashioned bartender came by, and Nigel ordered another round. The human bartender was the main reason Nigel frequented Mikey's; all the other bars in the area had converted to robotic bartenders.

"He also bought us these beers, too," Nigel added, "which I appreciate." He toasted with his bottle, and the two men laughed.

"So, is this good-bye? I suspect you're going to be heading to Houston to take over the company, right?" Steve asked. "I mean, you're the eldest; that's how it works, right?"

"For 100 years, that was how it worked." Nigel held up a slate and flashed the screen at his friend. "But not today, according to this."

"What's that say?"

"As discussed previously, I was disinherited, as acknowledged by my signature in Block 43 of the attached document."

"Did you really do that? Sign your rights away?"

"Yeah, I did, the day I failed out of school. Remember the limo? They sent a lawyer to tell me about it. Apparently, all of the family was too busy to come."

"Really?"

"Yep."

"That sucks."

Both men took pulls from their drinks.

"So," Steve asked, "are you going to your dad's funeral? Is that going to be in Houston too?"

"No, the funeral's in Chabahar, which I hate. It may not be hell, but it's close." He noticed two pretty women entering the bar and motioned for the bartender to send them a drink. "And no, I'm not going. Fuck 'em."

"Aren't you worried that whoever takes over the company will cut off your funding?"

"No, my younger brother is taking over, and he'll do whatever it takes to keep me from challenging his right to run the company." He held up the slate. "This letter also says that all of the current arrangements will continue in place, pending appropriate behavior."

"So, basically, if you're a good boy, they'll send you money and if not…"

"I'll get cutoff. Right."

"Doesn't that make you mad, though? Isn't that a lot like bribery or getting bought off?"

"What a *good* friend you are to bring that up," Nigel said, his voice dripping with sarcasm. "And yes, I won't lie, some days it irritates the piss out of me. But other times, I'm pretty okay with it." He held up his beer. "I mean, really, I have enough money to do what I want and no responsibilities. Who wouldn't want that?"

"Judging by the tone of your voice, you."

"Do I think about what it would be like to run one of the most powerful companies on Earth, and maybe in the entire galaxy? To control more war-making power than a lot of countries? Of course I do." He smiled over Steve's shoulder as the two women he had sent drinks approached.

"Hi," one of them said, holding up her drink. "Do we have you to thank for these?"

Nigel winked at Steve. "Other times, I find I don't care quite so much."

* * * * *

Chapter Four

Planet Moorhouse, Kepler 62 System

"Colonel Shirazi, I've never seen defenses like this before. This is way…fuck…way worse than what we were told."

"Well, we've got to get down and complete this contract. We've already failed to retake the plant once, and we can't afford to fuck it up again. We're running out of gear!"

"Gear? Sir, I don't think you know how bad it is up here. Gear is the least of our problems. I don't think I can…damn, damn, damn…there goes one of the other dropships. I recommend we abort; this ain't gonna work."

"Can't you drop faster or something? We need to get down. *The company is going to go under if we don't."*

"The company is going to go under if we all die, too! I'm serious, sir…fuck, we just lost the third dropship…Screw it! I'm aborting. We can't—"

Mexico Mikey's Bar and Grill, Virginia Beach, VA, USA

"Dude, I'm really sorry," Steve said. "First your father, and now your brother. It's been a bad year."

"Yeah, well Farhad was a dick, so don't cry too hard for him. He was always the 'bad cop' when my sister Parisa tried to be nice to me. 'Don't baby him, Parisa, he needs to grow up and take responsibility for his life. Blah, blah, blah.' And besides, being in the mercenary business tends to shorten your lifespan somewhat. He knew what he was getting into."

"Did you get another one of the 'stay away and we'll keep sending you money' messages?"

"No I didn't…not this time."

"What do you suppose that means?"

Nigel smiled. "Seriously? I think it means I'm going to get my shot at running the company after all."

"Really?"

"Yeah. The company is supposed to be passed down through the males in my family, and we're all out of adult ones. Farhad has two little boys and Parisa one, but none of them are old enough to manage the company, and they won't be for at least 15 years. And that pretty much leaves *me*."

"Why haven't you heard anything then?"

"Bah, they're probably trying to decide who has to fly here to ask me to come back. They need me, and they have some serious crow to eat. Ha! They're probably drawing straws, with the loser being the one who gets the job!"

"Well, don't forget the little guys who helped you along the way when you make it to the big time, okay?"

"Hey, who was your first customer when you got your financial planning license?"

"You were, of course, and with your account, I moved past everyone else in the company in the first month."

"Well, don't screw it up, because I'm going to need it; as soon as one of the little brats comes of age, I know they'll want to fire me. I was written out of the will, so I'll only be a steward of the company until they can get 'their person' in…but I'm going to have fun with it while I can."

Open Arms Apartments, Sandbridge, Virginia Beach, Virginia, USA

Four days later, Nigel woke to a banging at the door. "'Bout damn time," he said, shrugging off the arm across his waist. Disentangling himself from the other arms and legs lying across and around him, he slid from the bed. "C'mon ladies, let's go," he said, clapping his hands. "It's time for me to go take my birthright."

"When will we see you again?" the blond asked. Nigel thought her name was Cindy, but was far from positive. That might have been the brunette. He was pretty sure it wasn't the redhead's name.

"I'll give you a call once I get all of the legal stuff squared away," he replied, stepping into last night's pants. "It shouldn't take long." He shuffled them out of the bedroom and to the door.

"Hi, Pari—" Nigel said, opening the door. He had expected his sister, but cut himself off when he found the short man in the dark suit waiting there instead.

He shooed the women out and then asked, "Can I help you?"

"Interesting company you're keeping," the man said. "May I come in?"

"I don't see why not," Nigel replied, moving out of the way, "although I'm not sure what business it is of yours whose company I keep."

"It *is* my business, as my firm is responsible for maintaining Asbaran Solutions' image. I am personally responsible for dealing with the…issues…you cause, like when you attacked your teacher in front of 17 other witnesses. We could probably stay comfortably in business, just in the fees we receive for covering up your…adventures."

"Typical lawyer."

"I am not, 'a typical lawyer;' I am, in fact, *your* lawyer. I am charged with keeping you out of trouble and minimizing the damage you cause to your family's name."

"You must be busy then," Nigel said with a smile. "If the family doesn't want me to be part of the business, I can find other things to hold my attention."

"Indeed," the short man replied. He shifted from foot to foot, looking uncomfortable.

"Well, get on with it," Nigel urged. "We both know why you're here. My brother's dead, and the company needs *me*, the only surviving male heir, to come and take over Asbaran."

"Uh, no, that is *not* why I am here," the man replied. "Well, part of that is true. As you are aware, your brother Farhad is indeed dead."

"Yeah, I heard about it on the Tri-V. I notice I wasn't invited to the funeral."

"The funeral was a private service for close relatives only."

"*Close relatives?* I was his fucking *brother*! How much closer do you want?"

"Be that as it may, you were in no way 'close' to him, nor have you been close to the family since you left school. You have neither come to the company's facility in Houston, nor have you visited the family estate in Chabahar."

"Well fuck you, Mr. High-and-Mighty. The family and the company turned their backs on *me,* not the other way around. Why would

I want to go where I wasn't wanted? I was told to stay away, so I have."

"No, you were decidedly *not* told to stay away. You were in fact offered a position in the administrative section of the company where, it was hoped, you would learn some self-control and a bit about leading others."

"Bullshit."

"I know that to be true; I wrote the letter and personally handed it to you."

"Well, I don't remember the letter having that invitation in it." Nigel shrugged, wondering if he still had the letter. He couldn't remember ever reading it. "If you're not here to invite me back to run the company, what the hell *are* you here for?"

"We need you to come to Houston. There are some contracts that need to be signed…and some other duties."

"Why can't the new president sign the contracts and whatever the hell else is needed?"

"Because the new president is currently off-world, and the contracts must be signed by a member of the Shirazi family."

"So get my sister to sign them. Everyone likes her; they'd probably allow her to sign in my place."

"I'm sure they would. Unfortunately, she is the new president who is off-planet; thus, she is unavailable to sign the contracts."

"*What?*" Nigel exploded. "That's bullshit! She can't be the president! It has to be a male heir. It's in the company charter. How the *fuck* did she get to be president?"

"The Board of Directors made an allowance for her to function as the acting president when your brother left to finish off the contract that killed your father. When your brother got killed too, the

Board decided to retain her as acting president until her son was old enough to take over."

"That is such *bullshit*. I should have been the president, not her. Why didn't the Board call me?"

"Because you were deemed unworthy, based on your past disassociation from both the organization and your family."

"So what makes me worthy enough to come sign the contracts now?"

"As I have already stated, the contracts are financially significant enough that they must be signed by a member of the Shirazi family. At the moment, you are the only adult member of the family available."

Nigel noticed a small emphasis on the word, 'adult,' as if he thought Nigel were not sufficiently 'adult-like.' Well, fuck him. "No," Nigel said. "I'm not coming to sign the contracts. You bastards changed the rules once so Parisa could be president, change them again so someone else can sign."

"We tried; otherwise, I wouldn't be here. This rule was integral to the original charter. In order to change it, we would have to dissolve the company. The people who risk their lives on a daily basis for the company deserve better."

"Better than what? Better than me?"

"Better than losing their jobs and getting thrown out into the street," the man said, starting to lose his cool for the first time. Nigel noticed he hadn't answered the second question.

"And what about me?"

"Yes, they also deserve better than to have the company run by a spoiled brat like you. They deserve someone good enough to run the company like it should be run!"

There it was, out in the open. Nigel stalked to the door and threw it open. "*Get out!*" he screamed. "Not good enough? You're probably the one who talked to my last instructor and sabotaged me in that class. All my life, people have called me 'Nige'—Never Is Good Enough—and now I see how that's being perpetuated. You mother-fucker, get out, and *get out now* or I'll kick your fucking midget ass so hard you won't *need* a plane to fly back to Houston!"

"But the contracts—"

"Can damn well wait until my sister gets back!" Nigel yelled, giving the man a push that sent him stumbling through the door. "Fuck you, fuck her, and fuck Asbaran!" He slammed the door.

* * * * *

Chapter Five

Planet Moorhouse, Kepler 62 System

"Shit! There goes dropship Number Four!"

"Can you get us down?"

"I don't know ma'am…I've never seen defenses like this. Damn it! Dropship Number Two just got hit; they're gone."

"Are we taking fire?"

"No, ma'am. They aren't shooting at us yet. Aw, fuck. Three's gone."

"How long?"

"We'll be down in five seconds…Ramp's coming down…We're here!"

"Asbaran, let's go! Oh, shit—"

Open Arms Apartments, Sandbridge, Virginia Beach, Virginia, USA

Nigel whistled a happy tune as he turned off the car, grabbed the two cases of beer, and sprinted up the stairs to his apartment. He had only made it halfway when he noticed there was someone waiting in front of his door—the same pain-in-the-ass lawyer who had come by a couple of months previously. The whistle stopped mid-note, his cheerful mood evaporating like a mist in full sunlight.

"What the hell do you want?" Nigel asked. "Didn't I make it clear to you the last time you were here I wanted nothing to do with you?"

"Yes, Mr. Shirazi, you made it quite plain," the lawyer said. "I believe there was mention of kicking me hard enough I would fly to Houston on my own."

"And yet here you are again," Nigel said, setting down one of the cases so he could open the door. "Either you're a pretty slow learner or things have really gone to shit. I don't care, either way. Get the hell out of here." He entered the apartment and tried to shut the door, but the lawyer's foot stopped the door from closing all the way.

"If you will hear me out for five minutes, I will leave and never return," the man said. "I believe I possess information you will want to have. If not, you can give me the aforementioned kick you promised."

Nigel opened the door. "C'mon in," he said. "This will be fun. I'll put on some steel-toed boots while you speak. Five minutes. Your time starts now."

The two men walked into the apartment's small kitchen, and Nigel put the beers in the refrigerator, filling it. Pulling one out, Nigel walked over to the table and sat down. "You're wasting a lot of your time."

"May I sit down?" the man asked.

"By all means." Nigel could see the man looking at his beer and knew he was being rude for not offering one to the lawyer. Fuck him.

"There has been…a situation."

Nigel laughed. "A situation? That's what you call the last six months? A situation? You're going to have to do a lot better than that, and your time is running short."

"Your sister has been taken hostage."

"*What?*" Nigel asked, spraying some of the beer in his mouth. "What do you mean?"

"I meant exactly what I said. She tried to complete the same mission that killed your father and brother, but she failed and was captured. The mercs holding her sent us a ransom note. We have a month to come up with the money, or they will kill her and the rest of the troops they are holding."

"Well pay them, damn it!" Nigel exclaimed. "If you need me to come sign the check, I will. I can be on a sub-orbital this afternoon."

"That would be helpful…except that we *can't* send them a check."

"Why not? Don't tell me the Board won't accept my signature. I'll come down there and shove it up their asses!"

"While your enthusiasm is commendable, especially in light of your past history, I'm afraid that isn't the issue. The real problem is that Asbaran Solutions is broke."

"Asbaran? Broke? How can that be? Asbaran is one of the biggest companies in the world!"

"Yes sir, that is true; Asbaran Solutions is one of the five biggest companies on Earth. As many other large companies have found in the past, though, size does not equal financial security or stability. Businesses depend on money coming in to cover the bills they generate. In the case of Asbaran, we have not successfully completed a contract in over a year; therefore, we haven't been paid. During that time, we have lost twelve of our newest KW12 *Huma* dropships, as well as twelve APCs and 150 CASPers. Not to mention almost 200 troops, drivers and pilots. All of those have a substantial cost."

"Well, no fuck they do. People, experienced people, are worth way more than gear; grandfather taught me that as a kid."

"Indeed. Regardless of their individual price tags, all of them were lost without completing the mission. We lost substantial investments and received no income. Between that and our normal operating costs, we are bankrupt. We can start selling off assets, which will bring in a little revenue, but our best assets were lost with your father and siblings. We can put off some of our bills, but before long we will have a situation much like the Cartwrights did last year."

"What are you going to do about it?"

"Me? There's nothing I *can* do about it. We bent the rules to get your sister into the company as CEO, but there's no further bending that can be done. There is no one left in the bloodline to run the company. If you don't do it, the company will fold."

"It's commendable of you not to mention that my monthly stipend will cease if that happens."

The man gave a wan smile. "I thought I would appeal to your sense of family first, but yes, that will indeed happen. In fact, it already *has* happened; the payment you received last month was your last. All discretionary spending has been stopped. Your sister kept your stipend in the budget as long as she could…"

"But now she's gone, and it's been stopped."

"No sir, now she's gone, *and there's nothing left to pay you with.*"

"Then I guess I better get down to Houston and get this figured out."

"Yes sir; that would be helpful."

* * * * *

Chapter Six

Asbaran Solutions, Houston, Texas, USA

"Wow," Steve said, looking up at the massive glass-steel mega-building. It covered two complete city blocks in both directions and rose 57 stories into the muggy Houston sky. "So this is your new office?"

"Yeah, my office is at the top of this monstrosity," Nigel said. "We own it all, although we rent out a number of the floors to some of our subsidiaries and some of the smaller merc firms we have relationships with."

"Impressive."

"What's really impressive is what's underneath. There are a number of weapons laboratories, test beds, ranges, and the like in the basements and sub-basements. We try to keep high explosives out of the building in case something goes wrong, but sometimes that's not possible. And some of the batteries we use are extremely dangerous in their own right."

"And it doesn't worry you to be sitting on top of all that?"

"No more than it did any of the three generations of Shirazis before me."

"Just three?"

"Yeah, my great-grandfather built this structure after our last building blew up. 57 was his favorite number."

"So, you're taking me into in a building that could blow up at any moment?"

"Could? Yeah, but the odds are really, really low. Like I said, it hasn't blown up in 65 years or so; we've got a great safety record."

"But *why* would you want to have all that stuff in the building?"

"Security, mostly. We control everyone and everything that comes and goes, and we have implemented a large number of security procedures to make sure people don't get into spaces they aren't cleared for. There are two security departments, and both of them have procedures the other doesn't know about to keep outsiders from getting a mole into our building and learning our secrets." He shrugged. "Nothing's perfect, but my grandfather was pretty anal-retentive about security and did everything he could to protect the building. Besides, it's in the middle of the city and assaulting it would provoke a reaction among a number of other merc outfits; anyone trying to break in would be faced with some of the best mercs in the galaxy. Once again, nothing's impregnable, but it's as good as we can make it."

"Thanks for coming down to get me."

"Don't worry about it; I *had* to come and get you or you'd have spent all morning and most of the afternoon trying to work your way through security. Remember those security procedures I mentioned? Besides, I need to thank *you* for coming on such short notice. I'm in over my head here, and I need someone who understands finance."

"Finance? I don't know finance. I know *personal financial planning*, like where to put your money on the galactic stock market, and things like that. I don't know *anything* about corporate finance, nor do I want to."

"You can at least do math, and that's the one area I've always struggled with. I don't want to say any more down here. Let's go up to my office where we can talk."

They started walking toward the building, but Steve stopped and pointed at the middle floors of the building. "Is that the Asbaran logo? What is that, a griffin?"

"Yeah, that's our logo, but it's not a griffin. It's a huma bird from Persian mythology. It's kind of like a phoenix, in that it's supposed to rise from its ashes. The way things are going, we may need its spirit guidance…"

"Okay, so what's going on?" Steve asked 90 minutes later after they made it through security and up to Nigel's office.

"Remember what happened to Cartwright's Cavaliers last year?"

"Yeah, they went bankrupt, didn't they? It was all over the Tri-V news shows."

"Correct. It's about to happen again, only this time it's going to happen to us."

"What? Is that how they talked you into coming down here?"

"Pretty much. Here's the story in brief. We took a contract that went bad. My father tried to salvage it but got killed. So my brother tried to salvage it, but he got killed too. So my sister tried to salvage it, but she got taken prisoner, and the mercs that have her want to ransom her back to us. Personally, I think they're scared about what would happen if they just killed her, but now we're in a real bind."

"Why's that?"

"Remember all those failed rescue missions? They used up assets, and none of them actually completed the mission which would have resulted in payment. They're still tallying all the bills, but we are about 11 *billion* credits in debt at this point."

"Holy shit! That's like the gross domestic product of…"

"Most of the planet," Nigel finished. "Yeah, we're pretty screwed."

"So what are you going to do?"

"I'm going to get Parisa back and then let her decide what to sell off. Even after a week here, I still don't have much of a clue how our finances work or any idea how to begin trying to save the company. I'm hoping you can figure out some of that for me while I concentrate on getting my sister back."

"So let me get this straight…you want me—someone with no idea how this company works—to figure out what assets you can sell so you can ransom your sister?"

"Fuck that. I'm going to take her back; I just need you to buy me some time. I want you to make the company's finances work long enough for me to put together a rescue mission."

Steve's brows knit. "Wait a minute," he said. "You're going to *what?*"

"I'm going to get my sister back from the motherfuckers who've taken her."

"And you're going to do that…how?"

"I'm going to put together what I can from our remaining equipment and personnel and go get her. We don't have the funds to pay her ransom, and I can't let them kill her."

Steve shook his head. "Now, admittedly, I'm not a merc," he said, "but I don't see how that has one chance in hell of working."

"I want my sister back," Nigel said, his shoulders set in defiance; "she was the only one of my whole family who was ever nice to me."

"That's fine," Steve replied; "I'm not suggesting you don't do something to get her back. What I do take issue with is that it sounds like you're going to do the same thing your sister did, and your brother and father before her. It didn't work for any of them; why do you think you'll be successful when they weren't?"

"Are you saying I'm not a good leader?"

"Honestly, I have no idea what kind of leader you are. I've never seen you lead a classroom discussion, much less an airborne assault. I'm worried about how you'll do, sure, but it's more than that. What makes you think you can succeed with second-tier equipment and troops, where no one else in your family could with the best stuff money can buy?"

"*Because I have to do it!*" Nigel exclaimed. "Don't you get that?"

"Yes, I do." He paused for a moment and then asked, "Have you ever heard of Albert Einstein?"

"Of course I have," Nigel replied. "I got kicked out of school for fighting, not for my grades."

"Remember, I've seen your grades," Steve said. "Yes, you got kicked out for assault, but you were within a couple of weeks of failing out when it happened."

"Okay, that's true, but I was doing poorly because I was partying too much, not because I was dumb."

"You know, you can be a real asshole when you don't get your way," Steve said, exasperated.

"Yeah, it's one of my more redeeming qualities." Nigel smiled, easing the tension. "Okay, so what are you trying to tell me?"

"Do you know Einstein's definition of insanity?"

"Asking your friends for money?"

"No, legend has it that he said insanity was doing the same thing over and over, and expecting different results."

"Okay, how is that applicable here?"

"Well, to the neutral observer, it looks like you're going to do the same thing the rest of your family did, but that didn't work for any of them, even though they had more training and better equipment. I'm hoping I can dissuade you from throwing your life away like they did."

"My sister isn't dead."

"No, but she will be—and so will you—if you try the same shit."

"Then I guess I will have to try something different."

"Good. In that case, I'll try to figure out how to keep the company solvent long enough for you to rescue your sister."

"You're a good friend, Steve."

"Yeah, and you're a dick. So show me where the company's books are and find me someone who can explain them to me in English."

"Remember that lawyer who showed up at my house?"

"Yeah."

"His name is Jonathan Spivey. He'll be your guide."

* * * * *

Chapter Seven

Asbaran Solutions, Houston, Texas, USA

"Okay, I've made some calls and juggled some accounts," Steve said. "Mr. Spivey and I agree that we can probably keep the company going for about one more month, but then it's going to collapse like a house of cards, and when it goes, it's going to go *fast*. It'll probably fold faster than Cartwright's Cavaliers did."

"Thanks; no pressure there."

"Pressure? If you wanted pressure, I could talk about the thousands of people who work for the company who are about to be out of a job. They're all counting on you."

"Thanks, but I really wanted some reassurance, not more people counting on me."

"Well, I hate to be the voice of reason, but you're about to do something I think is incredibly stupid. Not only are you going to get yourself killed, but everyone else who goes along with you. Those people all have families. And everything that gets destroyed with you has a price tag that will come out of the company's assets when it goes into bankruptcy, which it will when you fail, leaving even less for the people who trusted this company to provide for them."

"Thanks, a third time."

"Have I convinced you to give up this stupid idea yet?"

"No, if anything, you've confirmed it's the right thing to do."

"And how the hell did you come to that conclusion?"

"It's the only way the company can win."

"You're willing to bet everything this company stands for, and everything you own, even your life, on one throw of the dice?"

"I am…or I will be; I'm still shy a number of troops with combat experience, especially at the leadership level, and I'm going to have to use senior enlisted leaders in the company commander and executive officer slots; there just aren't any officers available." Nigel shrugged. "It's a bastardized setup, but it's all I can do at the moment. Even good, experienced senior enlisted are in extremely short supply." Nigel looked at his watch. "I am, however, hoping to fill the company commander position shortly."

"What do you mean?"

"I had someone who called from the Golden Horde who said he wanted to go with me on my 'upcoming trip.' That tells me two things."

"Which are?"

"The first is he may be the experienced leader I need."

"And the second?"

"Our operations security sucks, which is probably why the previous missions failed. We'll have to do better than they did, or we'll come to the same end."

"Mister Shirazi?" Nigel's secretary asked from the door. "There is a Mr. Thomas Mason from the Golden Horde here to speak with you."

"Please send him in."

Mason walked through the doorway, filling it with his bulk. Although the trend was smaller troopers that better fit the current model of CASPer, Mason was huge; he stood at least a couple inches over six feet tall and probably weighed the better part of 250 pounds, all of it muscle, with dark hair and dark eyes.

"I heard you're putting together a mission to recover your sister," the man said. "I want to lead it."

"I've seen your resume," Nigel said. "You look like just the person I need as my second-in-command. You're hired."

"Second? I heard you wanted to lead the mission, but I thought the person who told me that was just bullshitting me. Please tell me that you aren't really planning on leading it."

"I'm not sure where you heard it, but you heard correctly. I *am* leading the mission to recover my sister. I am unaware what concern it is of yours, though. If you don't like it, you don't have to sign on."

"My concern is that you have no combat experience; everyone that goes with you is going to be killed, and the mission is going to fail."

"Once again, though, I still don't see what concern it is of yours."

"Let's face it, you know shit about being a merc, much less leading a group of them, and some of your troops are friends of mine. I'd like them not to get killed unnecessarily." He strode over to the shelves along one wall and pointed to a stuffed teddy bear that sat between a Mark 15 hypervelocity pistol and a Fargahr ceremonial sword. "Do you see this? Tell me what you know about Rule One."

"Rule One?"

"Yeah, Rule One. What do you know about Rule One?"

"I didn't know there *were* a whole lot of rules about being a merc."

"I'm not talking about *being* a merc, I'm talking about *surviving* as a merc. Rule One is simple. It states, 'Danger lurks within cute and cuddly things.' That teddy bear was brought home by your grandfather…after he disconnected the booby trap the Ssselipsssiss had left. The bear was wired to trigger a nuclear weapon; if he'd picked up the cute and cuddly teddy bear, he would have initiated a 42-megaton explosion. If you don't even know about Rule One, you're a liability who's going to get someone killed. Yourself, definitely, but I don't give a shit about that. What I *do* care about is that when you do something stupid, which you will, you're going to either get me or someone else I like killed. I take enough chances just being a merc; bringing you along is nothing more than a death wish, and I don't have one of those. Let's face it, you're just not good enough to lead this."

"*What did you just say?*"

"I said you're not good enough. Maybe with training, someday, but you're pretty old to be a newbie. You may never be good enough."

"That's *it*," Nigel screamed. "I'm going."

"Obviously, you must be deaf as well as stupid," Mason said in a level tone. "Didn't you just hear what I said? I'm not bringing you along. If you're going, you're going to have to find someone else to lead this abortion of a plan. If I were to bring you along, I might as well go out behind the hangar and blow my brains out. It would at least save the company the cost of transporting me there."

"I'm. Going."

"Well, then you're going to have to find someone else to lead it, and as far as I can see, you're flat out of options. I've talked with some of your folks. I'm the only platoon leader you've got, much less company commander."

"Steve, can you write a note that we need to update our nondisclosure training? Obviously, some of our folks need refreshers on keeping their mouths shut."

"So you'll let me lead it?" Mason asked.

"No. I'm leading it. Get out."

"*What?*"

"I said, 'Get out.'" Nigel's voice was stronger now, more sure of himself. "I'm the heir to one of the Four Horsemen. This is *my* company, and *I* say who's going to go on this or any other mission. Now get the hell out of my office before I shoot you myself."

"And how *the fuck* are you going to do that?"

Nigel stood up, revealing the laser pistol in his right hand. "I may not have known Rule One, but my grandfather taught me Rule Two when I was here one day. I was hiding under his desk and asked what the thing was in the leather holster. He told me it was Rule Two. Now get the hell out."

Mason looked back and forth between the pistol and Nigel's eyes. Neither wavered. The look on Nigel's face showed he was mad enough to do it.

"You'll be sorry."

"I'm already sorry I let you waste this much of my time. Now get the fuck out!"

Mason turned and walked to the door. "You haven't heard the last of me." He walked out and slammed the door.

Nigel found he could no longer hold the pistol steady, so he safed it and dropped it on the desk before he accidentally shot someone.

"That could have gone better," Steve remarked. "While you did prove who's boss, you're now out a company commander."

Nigel fell backward into the chair, all of his nerves on fire with the adrenaline rush. He took a couple of deep breaths, shook his hands out, and then took another deep breath. "No, he'll be back once he calms down," Nigel said.

"I doubt he'll *ever* be back."

"Well, you may know a lot more about finance and Einstein than I do, but growing up in one of the Horsemen families, I know a lot more about people than you do."

"What do you mean?"

"Isn't it obvious? He's in love with my sister. He wants her back at any cost, even to the point of losing his job or pissing off the temporary boss. It's the only reason he'd be dumb enough to want to go on this mission. It's certainly not the pay, and this mission is dangerous as all hell. The only reason anyone would show up wanting to go is to save my sister." He chuckled. "It's the only reason I'm going."

"So how are you going to get him back?"

"Easy—all I have to do is wait. Right now, he's probably calling all of his contacts looking for someone with a ready force he can convince to assault Keppler 62 to try and get my sister back."

"What if he finds one?"

"He won't. There's no money in it. As far as they know, there's no contract to be assumed, so no company is going to want to take it on. For him, it's a personal decision to do it, but for everyone else, it's a business decision to *not*. He'll be back, because I've got the same problem."

"What's that?"

"Although it makes sense for *our* company's bottom line, and we *can* complete the contract if it all works out, it's personal for me, too. I have to do it, and once he calms down, he'll realize his best chance to see my sister alive again is to come back and lead the mission so I don't get everyone killed."

"You'd let him lead the assault after that display?"

"Absolutely. If he has enough balls to go up against the head of one of the Horsemen in his own office, even if it's me, he's the one I want in charge." Nigel chuckled. "I certainly don't want to lead the mission. He's right; I don't know shit about leading a company of mercs. I'm learning, but there's no way I can learn everything I need in time. I would have picked up the damned teddy bear as a souvenir."

"Me too," Steve replied. He sighed. "Can I ask you something?"

"Sure."

"What's Rule Two?"

"*Always* have an ace in the hole."

Asbaran Solutions, Houston, Texas, USA

"Sir, Mr. Mason is here and is requesting a moment of your time."

Steve looked up from the report he was briefing and raised an eyebrow.

'Told you so,' Nigel mouthed at his friend. "Please disarm him and send him in."

Mason walked in, much calmer than when he left the day before. He came to a position of attention, his eyes focused somewhere slightly above Nigel's head, his back ramrod straight. "Mr. Shirazi," he said after the briefest of sighs, "I would like—"

"That's enough," Nigel said, cutting him off. "You're hired. Welcome to Asbaran Solutions, Sergeant First Class Mason."

"Just like that? You're not going to make me apologize and tell you I was wrong?"

"Just like that."

"You're not mad?"

"Sure, a little bit, but the truth is, you *weren't* wrong—I'm not qualified to lead the mission."

"So you're going to let me lead it?"

"Of course I am, you're the right person to lead. You're the only one we have with the experience and the skills required to do it successfully, and I don't have time or money to hire someone else to lead it. Nor would I trust them more than I do you. But I'm still going."

"Wait, you're what? I thought you said I was leading the mission."

"You are. You will be in charge, however, I'm going and I will have the overall say-so on certain aspects of the mission. Look at it this way—you're in charge of tactics; I'm in charge of strategy. You're too emotionally involved to lead this operation without an advisor who has a sense of...detachment. That's me; I may like my sister, but I'm emotionally detached from my family. It's something I've had years of practice with."

"And if I still say, 'no way I'm going if you go'?"

"Then I will have you escorted from the building again, only this time I won't let you back in. I appreciate your strength of conviction, but I hoped I had made my point yesterday. *I* am the president of this company, even if I'm only the acting president, and *I alone* get to say who comes and goes. If you can't live with that, I don't have a place for you, on this mission or any of the others I am currently contemplating."

"Others?"

"I'm not at liberty to say, until I have your word you'll respect my position of authority, whether or not you respect my skills."

"No chance of getting you to sit this one out?"

"None."

"Then I'm in. Also, you can remove your hands from under your desk. You won't need the pistol."

"I didn't think I would," Nigel said. "But it's always good—"

"—to have an ace in the hole," Mason finished.

Houston Starport, Houston, Texas, USA

"**D**amn," Nigel said with a sigh. He shaded his eyes from the scorching south Texas sun as he looked down the ramp area of the 9,000-foot-long Runway 17R. In addition to the enormous hangar Mason and Nigel had just walked out of, two more cavernous hangars lay to the south, surrounded by a variety of support buildings and other structures.

Although the field had housed a number of United States military, NASA, and general aviation tenants in its 300 years of continuous operation, all of it now belonged to Asbaran Solutions. At least until the creditors came to take it away.

"What?" Mason asked, coming to stand next to Nigel. He looked in the direction his boss was staring. "I don't see anything."

"Yeah, that's just it. The last time I was here, about 10 years ago, this place was a beehive of activity. The ramp was full of dropships, loaders raced back and forth prepping them for flight, and people covered the entire area like a horde of ants. Now…it's just us." He shook his head as he turned to walk back to the hangar they'd come from. The three aging KX9 *Phoenix* dropships looked forlorn, sitting by themselves in the center of the massive hangar. "And the remains of our fleet."

"What once was, can be again," Mason said philosophically as he caught up to walk alongside him. "Yeah, we lost some equipment and some damn good folks, but if we can pull this off, Asbaran Solutions' name will still mean something."

Nigel noticed Mason had said "we." Apparently, Mason already felt like he was part of the team, but Nigel didn't know if that was because of his love for Parisa or if it was just the way mercs thought. Maybe once you're hired, you're immediately considered to be part of the team. Nigel hoped he survived the mission so he could find out which was true.

"You said 'if we can pull this off,'" Nigel noted. "Are you worried we can't?"

Mason stopped, causing Nigel to stop as well. "I won't lie," Mason said. "Your family had some of the best-trained folks and state-of-the-art equipment available. They were soundly beaten *four times;* our opponents wiped out the initial garrison, killed your father and your brother, and they captured your sister. We have fewer troops, our equipment is shit, and I have a newb who wants to ride shotgun over me. Our odds of pulling this off are damn near zero; it's a testimony to how much I love your sister that I'm even willing to try it at all. *When* we pull this off, hopefully, you'll remember to tell her that."

Nigel chuckled. "Assuming I'm still around, I will."

"Being able to defend yourself will help with that. Have you been to the range yet?"

"Yeah, I went there once. The new personal laser rifles finally arrived, so I went and shot one of those since I've never fired one before. The last time I went shooting before that was with my grandfather." He paused and then asked, "Did we ever find out what caused the delays?"

"Yes, sir. Apparently some nut job named Chris Sommerkorn in Logistics sat on the requisitions. By the time he went to make the purchase, all the contract offers had expired and had to be renegotiated."

"What the hell did he do that for?"

"Well, the guy wrote a pile of reports on various issues…firing rate, stopping power, that kind of stuff…and gods can that guy write! He must write like 10,000 words a day."

"I don't remember ever seeing *any* of those reports," Nigel noted.

"That's because he never sent them up. He wrote them, but then got bogged down in editing. They're all still sitting on his desk."

"Really? How did someone like that get hired?"

Mason shrugged. "He had a good fitness report from Cartwright's Cavaliers. I don't know…they must have written him a good report so he wouldn't fight it when they shit-canned him."

"Do me a favor?"

"Sure thing, boss."

"Write him a similar report and shit-can him."

"With pleasure."

* * * * *

Chapter Eight

Chairman's Office, Asbaran Solutions, Houston, Texas, USA

Steven looked up from the report he was reading. "Have you seen the estimates on selling off some of our F11 stores?" he asked.

"No," Nigel replied. "Was I supposed to do something with it?"

"No, I didn't mean, 'Did you look at it?' I meant, 'Have you seen it?' It was here earlier, but now it isn't. I was wondering if you had taken it."

"No, I haven't seen it, but I was curious how much we could get for the F11. Do you remember what it said?"

"No, I don't; I hadn't had a chance to read it yet."

"When did it go missing?"

"Hmm…I had it right before the meeting we had with Mason and Spivey, but after that, it was gone."

"One of them must have accidentally picked it up."

"Maybe…" Steve said, his head cocked to the side in thought, "but are you sure it was an accident?"

"What are you saying?"

"I'm asking if you're *sure* it was accident. When I first got here, I noticed some of my files seemed to go missing for a while. They would always show back up, but they were definitely gone for a time. At first, I thought I had just misplaced them, but then you mentioned you thought we had a mole. After that, I started watching my files, and I noticed some of them *were* disappearing."

"And you think it's either Mason or Spivey?"

"No, it can't be Mason; the files were disappearing before he got here. It has to be Spivey."

"It can't be Spivey. He's been working for Asbaran longer than I've been alive; he would have been found out long before this. Maybe he was just using them for projects he was completing."

"You know, I'd be tempted to believe that, but the last two files that disappeared detailed financial opportunities we were pursuing, and before we could act on their contents, the markets turned, and we lost out."

"Markets turn sometimes," Nigel noted.

"I think the quote is, 'Once is an accident. Twice is coincidence. Three times is enemy action.' If someone floods the market with F11 fuel tomorrow and drives the price down before we can sell ours, I think we've found our mole."

Chairman's Office, Asbaran Solutions, Houston, Texas, USA

"I'll kill the motherfucker," Nigel said, throwing a copy of the morning newspaper on the sofa next to Steve. In lurid letters, the headline screamed, "Price of F11 tanks in overnight trading."

"Spoken like a true spoiled brat who didn't get his way."

"What do you mean?" Nigel asked.

"I mean that killing him would be easy, especially with all the mercs and weapons you have access to…it might even feel satisfying for a brief time…but then what? Once he's dead, what do you get from him?"

Nigel drew back, his brows knitting. "Uh, nothing, I guess, but I'll know we plugged our information leak."

"See Nigel, that's the problem you've always had; you're too short-sighted. If you'd *read* the paperwork you got when your father died, you might have come here and learned the trade. You might even have been named chairman when your brother got killed. But instead, you got mad and threw the invitation into the garbage. You're doing the same here."

"I don't understand."

"I can see that. You're missing the point; Spivey is your invitation."

"My invitation to what?"

"To find out who's behind all this. Spivey might be your leak, but he's a link to *someone* somewhere else. If you kill him, it's going to be awfully difficult to find out who's paying him…and why."

"But it will close the leak."

"God, you can be frustrating sometimes." Steve flipped through his papers for a moment, then he sighed. "Okay, let me try this again. You have someone who is passing on information about the company. This person is responsible for getting two of your family members killed, at least indirectly, and another one captured. He's also brought this company to the edge of ruin. Killing him may be satisfying, but it won't solve the problem—there's someone or something out there that has a serious grudge against either your family or your company. If it's the company, they may be satisfied when it goes under next month. If it's *you* they're after, though, killing Spivey isn't going to get you any closer to the truth. In fact, you'll just be making it easier for them to kill you too, if that's what they're after, because you won't have any idea where the next attack is going to come from."

"But, I…" Nigel started, but then ground to a halt, his mouth hanging open as he contemplated his friend's words. "Oh," he finally said.

"How eloquent. At least I think you finally understand what I'm trying to tell you."

"Yeah, I do." Nigel shook his head. "You've obviously given this a lot more thought than I have. What do we do?"

"I think the first thing we need to do is get Mason involved, because we're going to need some muscle."

"So you trust him? I mean, *I* trust him, but I think the current situation shows I may not read people as well as I thought."

"I do trust Mason, and I think you were right about why he's here. We're going to have to trust someone, and he's at least an outsider. If our adversary has suborned Spivey, they may have other moles as well."

"And what if Mason is a plant too?"

Steve shrugged, "If he's working for the enemy, your first trip into combat with him isn't going to go very well. Happily, I will be back here, far from it. Regardless, I doubt he's been corrupted—he has too much of a personal nature invested in this endeavor."

"I think he's out at the field working with the troops," Nigel said. "Let's go talk with him out there…away from any prying eyes."

Houston Starport, Houston, Texas, USA

Unlike his earlier trip, this time the hangar was alive with activity, and Nigel, Steve, and Mason had to watch where they were going as they walked through the enormous structure. Forklifts carried pallets and crates from place to place at breakneck speed, larger vehicles brought in new equipment and machinery, and more people than Nigel had ever seen raced between the various piles, unloading and assembling a variety of maintenance and analysis systems. Weaponry was stacked along the north wall of the hangar, in close proximity to the firing range just outside. Next to the weapons, 10 Binnig MK 6 Combat Assault System, Personal (CASPer), suits stood silently in their maintenance harnesses, waiting for the technicians to service and arm them. Nigel could feel the draw of the suits—nearly 10 feet tall and almost 1,000 pounds of death and destruction.

Mason sighed, bringing him back to the present. "So, the bottom line is we have at least one mole and potentially more?" Mason asked.

"Yeah," Nigel replied. "We're pretty sure that at least Spivey is working for someone else. There may be more."

"Well, that's just fucking great. I didn't think it was possible for this operation to have a smaller chance of success. Thanks for proving me wrong." He paused, obviously considering his options, then asked, "Before I decide whether or not I want to leave this organization, what are your intentions for dealing with the leak?"

"Steve and I have been talking about it, and I think he's right—finding out that Spivey's a mole may actually be a good thing for a couple of reasons. First, now that we know there's a leak, we can be very careful about what information we give out beyond the three of us."

"That might help us a little, but it isn't going to alter the fact that the forces on Moorhouse will know we're coming…and what crappy equipment and poorly trained troops we'll be bringing."

"I thought you'd been training the troops," Nigel said. "Aren't they coming around?"

"Yeah, they're doing okay," Mason replied, "but the equipment we have is still crap, and the enemy is still going to know we're coming."

"Perhaps not. I have a plan."

"Great. *You* have a plan. I feel safer already."

"It was actually my plan," Steve said, "if that's worth anything."

"Maybe a little more," Mason replied grudgingly. "Before you tell me about it, what's the other reason having a leak is good?"

"The other reason is it lets us give our enemy a little misdirection."

"Uh huh," Mason said, sounding unimpressed. "Misdirection. Let me guess, now you two are going to give me tactical advice? The success meter has now completely hit rock bottom."

"Wait a minute," Nigel said. "At least hear me out. If you don't like what we've come up with, then you can leave or whatever else you want to do."

"Okay, what's your plan?"

"We're going to make Spivey an offer he can't refuse."

* * * * *

Chapter Nine

Montrose Neighborhood, Houston, Texas, USA

"This is stupid," Private TJ 'Thunder' Allen said. He put down the scope and rubbed his eyes, then stretched in the darkened vehicle. "Why are we doing this?"

"Because I told you to, dumbass," Mason replied. "Look at this as special operations training—something you're totally unprepared for. The guy in that house has special information we think he's going to pass on to his bosses. We need to find out who the bosses are and where they're located." He raised his own scope to look at the massive house on Waugh Drive. "Fuck! The light's out. When did that happen?"

"A couple of minutes ago," Private Dave Parker replied. "The guy went up to his bedroom, turned out the light, and went to bed."

"How the fuck do you know he went to bed?"

"The lights went out."

"All that means is the lights went out, you dumb fuck! He could have gone back downstairs and snuck out. Fuck! Parker, get out and go around behind the house. Allen, go up Waugh to the north. Epard, go down Welch Street. I'll take a little cruise around the neighborhood. Look around and make sure he isn't getting away. We'll meet back here in 15 minutes. And whatever you do, you imbeciles, *don't* let him see you."

Mason put the car in gear once they were clear and pulled away from the curb, leaving the headlights off. He drove up Waugh and turned right on Willard Street, coming to a quick stop when he saw movement in front of him.

A man in dark clothes crossed one of the enormous lawns, walking down a row of shrubbery. He stooped down so as not to silhouette himself, but Mason could see him from where he sat. He couldn't be sure, but the man looked like Spivey's shape. The man reached the street and walked 50 feet to the east to where a dark hovercar stood idling. He looked both ways as he got in and Mason saw the face. Spivey. Damn it.

The door shut, and the hovercar accelerated down the street. Mason gave the car a little room and pulled out to follow, nearly knocking over Private 'Thunder' Allen who stepped in front of the vehicle.

"Get in, you fucking moron," Mason yelled, jumping on the brakes.

"What'd I do?" Thunder asked as he climbed in.

"You're going to let him get away by getting run over."

Mason raced after the other car, sighting it as it suddenly did a U-turn back toward them. "Down!" Mason exclaimed as he slammed on the brakes. The two soldiers ducked as the car roared past them and headed north on Waugh, barely slowing for the stop sign.

"What about the other guys?" Thunder asked as Mason sped off after them. "Are we going to go back and get them?"

"Give them a call and let them know they'll have to find their own way home," Mason replied, dodging a parked car he hadn't seen with the lights off. "I'm kinda busy at the moment."

The car they were following took the cloverleaf onto Memorial Drive and headed west, alternately speeding up and slowing down.

Mason hung far enough back that he didn't *think* he'd been seen. The car continued west until it reached the Memorial Park Golf Course, and then the driver braked hard and swerved off the road onto the golf course.

"Damn it!" Mason exclaimed. He continued past where the car had turned off and stopped the car. "Let's go," he said, springing out the door.

By the time Thunder made it to the back of the car, Mason was already pulling weapons from the trunk. "C'mon," Mason said. "We've got to hurry, or we're going to miss it."

"Miss what?" Thunder asked as he took the rifle Mason handed him.

"Whatever the hell they came here to do."

Mason also gave the private a pistol, a night visor, and a large knife. He armed himself similarly, then he pulled out a large crossbow with strangely shaped bolts.

"Holy shit!" Thunder exclaimed. "What're those for?"

"Silent action," Mason replied, gently closing the trunk. He placed the night visor over his eyes, lighting up the landscape in shades of white and gray and jogged back in the direction of the golf course. The hovercar didn't leave any ruts in the ground, but Mason had marked where the vehicle had gone off-road and followed it onto the golf course, listening intently for any sign he was catching up with Spivey.

"Hey Top, wait up," Thunder whispered, and Mason spun and put a finger over his lips.

"Shut up, you idiot," Mason murmured into the soldier's ear. "If you can't keep up, go home. I don't want to get killed because you can't keep your damn mouth shut."

Thunder's eyes grew, and Mason could see that the enormity of the situation hadn't dawned on the junior trooper. The situation could easily become life or death. Thunder didn't reply, but nodded his head slowly.

Certain the trooper now understood, Mason turned and stalked in the direction the car had taken, staying in the shrubbery that lined the hole. They had only walked for a couple of minutes when Mason saw a glow in front of them. He motioned Thunder to wait and continued by himself, careful not to make any noise.

His caution saved his life; he slowly spread the top of a bush to find a small ship resting in the clearing beyond, with sentries on the ground nearby. He watched for 30 seconds, chewing his lip, before returning to where Thunder waited.

"Do you remember what a Tortantula is?" Mason asked.

"Yeah, big spider-looking thing, right?"

"Correct, but it's *really* big, like five feet across, and it has 10 legs, not 8. It also has a ring of eyes all the way around its head, so it's damn hard to sneak up on them."

"Are there some of them there?"

"Just one, but it's got a Flatar rider. Have you seen them?"

"Uhh…" Thunder said, thinking hard. "I think I saw a picture, but I don't remember what they are."

"Flatar look like oversize chipmunks that ride in a saddle on the Tortantulas. They usually carry hypervelocity pistols to finish whatever the Tortantulas they're riding take down. The Tortantulas are tough, even without armor, and like I said, they are hard to surprise. They aren't that smart, though, and can be fooled. The Flatar aren't as tough, but they're smart. Putting a Flatar on a Tortantula lets an employer get the best out of both. A Tortantula/Flatar pair makes an excellent guard combination."

"And there are some in front of us?"

"Just one, but that's enough. They're close enough to stop us from getting in the ship that's sitting there, but not so close that the light coming from the ship will blind them. We'll have to kill them or take them prisoner if we're going to find out what's happening on the ship."

"Kill them? Here? On Earth? Are we allowed to do that?"

"Not really…but then again, I'll bet they aren't supposed to be here in the first place. No one is officially going to miss them. And we need to get into that ship."

Mason didn't think the trooper's eyes could get any bigger, but they did. He knew the young merc had been tested, and the company had verified his ability to handle stress, but he knew the unexpected nature of the situation was threatening to surpass the trooper's limits.

Mason punched Thunder on the shoulder. "Don't worry," he said, "all you have to do is talk to them. I'll take care of the rest."

"What? Talk to them? What would I say to them?"

"Here's how it's going to work. You're going to give me a two-minute head start, then you're going to go crashing through the forest like you don't have a care in the world. Call out your girlfriend's name a few times like you're looking for a late-night booty call. When you stumble into them, just look shocked and scared, and talk to them for a minute. I'll take care of everything else."

"Looking scared won't be a problem…"

"Good. Oh, and leave all of your weapons and night vision gear here. If you have it, they won't buy your story."

"What? *Go unarmed?*"

"Yeah. Unless you want them to shoot you on sight?"

"No, that's okay," Thunder said, laying down his weapons. "I can leave my gear here."

"Okay. Give me two minutes before you move."

Memorial Park Golf Course, Houston, Texas, USA

Thunder crashed through the underbrush, pretending not to notice the noise he was making. He had decided to act like he was drunk, and he called out the name, "Anna!" in a slurred tone as he stumbled toward the ship.

"Don't move!" the Flatar ordered through its communicator as the soldier approached.

Thunder jumped back in surprise, tripped, and fell on his back. The Tortantula took two steps toward the soldier, and Thunder could smell a musty fragrance from it. He scrabbled backward away from the aliens, looking at the Tortantula and shrieking, "Spider! Big spider!" It was no longer an act; he had never been this close to an alien before, and the clicking noise the Tortantula's front pincers made as it approached terrified him.

"Get up, human," the Flatar said, pointing an oversized pistol at him. "Who are you and what are you doing here?"

Thunder climbed to his feet, edging away from the Tortantula. "My…my name…my name is Bob," he stuttered. "I'm just…just…trying to find my girlfriend—"

With the sound of a cleaver striking a watermelon, a crossbow bolt struck the Tortantula in the back of its head and detonated on impact. The alien fell forward toward Thunder, its rider flying free to land at Thunder's feet.

The Flatar had lost its pistol during its brief flight, and it met Thunder's eyes before spinning around and scampering off toward the ship on all fours.

"Get it!" Mason yelled from the side. "Don't let it get back to the ship!"

Startled into action, Thunder chased after the alien. The soldier made up some ground on the Flatar, but he could see the alien was going to beat him to the boarding ramp. He dove forward at the last second, and his outstretched arms were just able to grab the fleeing creature.

"Got it!" he cried, holding up the squirming alien as he rose to his feet.

"Watch out—" Mason yelled.

"Fuck!" Thunder screamed as the Flatar sunk its teeth into the skin between his thumb and pointer finger. He flung his arm into the air, and the Flatar got its second flight of the night.

"—for its teeth," Mason finished as the alien spun through the air to strike a nearby tree. The creature fell to the ground, and Mason raced over and picked it up by the nape of its neck. The Flatar hung lifeless in his grasp as Mason strode over to Thunder.

"Is it dead?" the soldier asked.

"No," Mason replied. "They've got a similar reflex to kittens. They go limp when you pick them up this way. You never want to grab them around the waist. They'll bite the shit out of you if you do it that way."

"I see that," Thunder replied. His hand throbbed, and blood trickled out from where he held it.

"You'll want to get that looked at," Mason added. "They've got some funky alien bacteria in their mouth you *don't* want in your system. It'll mutate and mess you up pretty bad. I've got antibiotics for it back at the hangar."

Mason walked over to the Tortantula and nudged its head with the toe of his boot. "This one, however, *is* dead. About the only weak spot they have is just below the eyes in the back of their head. They're darn hard to damage anywhere else."

"You sound like you've fought them before."

"Yeah, they're pretty good shock troopers." Apparently satisfied with what he saw, he added, "C'mon, let's go. Hopefully everyone onboard hasn't heard all your screaming."

Thunder followed Mason to the ramp, holding his bleeding hand. He could almost *feel* the alien bacteria swimming in his veins and wondered when the mutation process would start. "Do we have time?" Thunder asked. "How long…how long have I got before I start turning into a…a whatever it is I'm going to turn into?"

"Oh, don't be such a baby," Mason whispered. "It'll hurt so much you'll *wish* you were dead, but you're not going to turn into a werewolf or anything like that. You have to get bit by a dumfuk for that."

"Wha…what's a dumfuk?"

"You're a dumb fuck, now shut the hell up and guard the top of the ramp while I go find our target."

"Umm, Top, I don't have any weapons. You made me leave them all behind. What am I supposed to guard the ramp with?"

"Oh, for fuck's sake," Mason said, shaking his head. "Do I need to change your diapers for you too? Here, take this." He handed Thunder a large knife with a bend in the middle.

"What's this?"

"It's a kirpan. A Sikh gave it to me for saving his life. Don't lose it; it means a lot to me." He started to leave then turned back around. "Hold this too," he added, handing the limp Flatar over to the junior soldier. "And, *don't* let it get away again."

Without another word, Mason drew his pistol and snuck off down the hallway. He went around a corner and was gone.

Thunder looked at the alien. It did look a lot like a chipmunk, except for the sharp teeth in the front of its mouth. Its eyes were closed, and it almost looked cute…except for the blood stains on its fur where Thunder had bled onto it. It's not cute, he reminded himself; it's an alien that bites like a son of a bitch.

He looked up and down the passageway, feeling tremendously under-armed with only a knife (even if it *was* a big one) in one hand and a small, furry alien in the other.

Worse, he realized he wasn't even really under contract. Actions on Earth were definitely *not* part of his contract. When he got back, he would have to see about a contract mod, or a combat bonus, or something, for having to fight an alien force. *Oh my god!* He was fighting aliens! He'd have to call his brother; Tom would never believe it. Well, he'd have to call his brother *after* he got the bite treated.

With a whine of hydraulics, the ramp started to close.

What? Thunder looked up and down the passageway. There was no one…human *or* alien…in either direction. Who was raising the ramp?

Additional noises joined the hydraulic sounds of the ramp. Fluid flowing, machinery cycling, and a large motor lighting off. *What?* A motor lighting off? Something was wrong—they weren't supposed to go to space, were they?

Someone had to stop the pilot from taking off. Thunder was sure Mason would be back to handle that like he handled everything else, and he watched expectantly down the corridor for Mason's return…but no Mason. A second motor lit off.

Crap. Still no Mason.

Thunder knew he didn't want to go to space with nothing but a large knife and a fuzzy alien. If Mason wasn't coming, he would have to do something about it. The pilot had to be in the cockpit, he reasoned, which must be toward the front of the craft. Leading with the knife, he stalked up the passageway toward the bow of the craft.

The urge to *go faster* warred with the need to *go quietly*; he compromised with a quick walk, keeping to the right side of the passageway. He passed several doors, deciding to leave them until later, then heard voices from further forward. He could see a glow and scurried forward, finding himself at the back of a cockpit.

The space was illuminated by the phosphorescent glow of the dials and other gadgets on the instrument panel and side consoles; two giant millipedes appeared to be preparing the ship for flight.

Dumbstruck, he stared for a couple of seconds. Yes, two very black millipedes were operating the ship's controls. Almost four feet long, claws reached out in a number of directions simultaneously, each grasping or manipulating various instruments. The one on the right advanced a collection of levers that rose from the floor between them, and the engines rose in pitch. *They were taking off!*

"Hey!" Thunder yelled. "Stop that!"

The creature on the right pulled the levers back and both aliens turned to look at him. "Grchip blxer tg zhebl," the one on the right said.

Thunder pointed the knife at the one on the right. "We're not leaving."

The millipedes looked at each other and turned back to the instruments. The one on the right advanced the levers again.

"Hey!" Thunder yelled again. He slapped the alien's…claw?…from the levers with the flat of the knife and pulled them back again. Both aliens turned to look at him again.

"Grchip blxer tg zhebl," the alien on the right repeated, louder this time.

Thunder held the knife to the throat area of the creature he was holding. "Do that again and the Fleetar gets it!" he threatened, mispronouncing the alien's race.

The aliens looked at each other again and went back to what they were doing. The one on the right reached for the levers.

"I fucking mean it!" Thunder yelled. "Get your hands off that!" He poked the millipede's arm with the point of the knife.

The creature on the right screamed something as it pulled its arm away from the levers. It bent over to the right and turned, a pistol now in one of its claws. "Grchip. Blxer. Tg Zhebl," it yelled back, motioning for Thunder to leave.

The freaking millipedes were armed? What the hell? Thunder looked at the knife. It didn't seem quite as big as it had before the alien pulled the pistol. Definitely not big enough to go up against the alien's pistol. A drop of blood ran down the blade from the wound in his hand.

That's it!

Without thinking, he lobbed the Flatar in his other hand toward the millipede with the pistol. Halfway along its route of travel the creature regained its senses and began moving. The millipede caught the Flatar in several of its claws…just in time for the alien to erupt into a ball of claws and teeth.

The millipede dropped the pistol with a scream and swatted at the Flatar with its other appendages, trying to get the creature off it. Green fluid spotted the cockpit as it flung its arms around, bleeding from a number of wounds. It finally succeeded in pushing the Flatar away, and the chipmunk dropped to the deck of the spaceship next to the pistol.

Thunder sprang forward to retrieve it, but the Flatar scooped it up and pointed it at the human. "Step back!" it ordered. "And drop the knife."

"Umm, it's an important knife to a friend of mine; he'll kill me if I lose it."

"As much as I don't want to have to clean up the mess, if you don't drop it, right now, I *will* kill you."

The knife clattered on the metal deck.

"Move," the Flatar said, motioning with the pistol for Thunder to go aft. The alien said something to the pilots, and they went back to what they had been doing.

"Down the ramp," the Flatar said when they reached it. "I don't want your blood on the ship."

"My blood?" Thunder asked.

"Yes. You've seen us. I'm afraid I'll have to kill—" His voice ceased and Thunder heard a plastic on metal sound.

He turned to find Mason picking up the pistol, with the Flatar limp in his other hand. Mason was a mess. He was bleeding in at least three places, had claw marks across his face, and had been shot in the side.

"Thought I…told you…*not*…let Flatar go," he said. He staggered down the ramp and handed the alien to Thunder then gave him the pistol. "Call for…backup," he ordered, before slumping to the ground.

* * * * *

Chapter Ten

16th Hole, Memorial Park Golf Course, Houston, Texas, USA

Nigel, Steve, and a small group of mercs arrived at the golf course to find a medic attending to Mason and another trooper lying unconscious in front of an alien ship. A fourth merc stood guard over a group that included Spivey, a giant bipedal badger, two oversized millipedes, and a chipmunk. Only the millipedes weren't zip-tied; the chipmunk had both its hands *and* feet zip-tied. A dead Tortantula lay on the other side of the tee box.

Nigel directed the troops he had brought to take charge of the prisoners and walked over to the trooper who was administering first aid.

"You guys have been busy," Nigel said to the medic. "What's your name, trooper?"

"Corporal Cindy Epard, sir!" she exclaimed, springing to attention. "They call me 'Shrewlet,' sir!"

"My name's Nigel," he replied, feeling embarrassed. "You don't need to 'sir' me."

"I know who you are, sir, and with all due respect, the use of 'sir' is quite appropriate. You're the boss, sir."

That didn't make him feel any more comfortable. In fact, the way her shouted answers attracted attention just made it worse; everyone was now staring at him. All of a sudden, what he was doing became very real. He wasn't just playing at running the company, he was making decisions that could very well send troops like Epard to their death.

Holy shit.

"Well, uh, corporal, can you tell us what's going on here?" he asked, indicating the three other people who had come with him. "I got a call saying I needed to bring two pilots and a bunch of troops and came as quickly as I could find them."

"I recognize the pilots with you, but is the other person you brought cleared for this, sir? I've got a lot of things to report that are somewhat…less than fully legal, sir."

"Yes, this is Steve Rath, my principal assistant. He is cleared for anything I am."

"Yes, sir. Well, First Sergeant Mason and three of us were sur-veilling the target," she said, nodding toward the group that held Spivey, "when Top noticed the target had left his residence. Top and Private Allen here," she nodded to the other unconscious soldier, "chased them down to this spaceship here and captured all of them."

"And then they passed out?"

"Well, Top was already passed out when we got here, but he had caught and zip-tied most of the…enemies? Adversaries? Whatever they are, and Private Allen had them under guard. He is the one who called us after the fight, but he got bit by the chipmunk-looking thing—"

"The Flatar," Nigel interjected.

"Yeah, the Flatar," Epard continued. "He got bit by it, and they've got some nasty bugs in their mouth. I had to knock him out as the pain was pretty bad. Anyway, most of them beside the Flatar and the giant badger are noncombatants, so they didn't give him a lot of trouble. I wouldn't let the Flatar go; he's a nasty little critter. And the mouth on him? Wow. We had to duct tape his mouth shut because we got tired of his threats. We warned him first, though."

"Well, that dead Tortantula over there is probably his partner," Nigel replied nodding in the direction of the corpse, "so I guess he's pretty pissed."

"Apparently, he also didn't like being carried around by the nape of his neck," Epard added.

"No, they're sensitive about that. You probably would be too if someone had you totally at their mercy just by grabbing you in a certain...vulnerable place."

"No, sir, I can't say I would like that, sir."

The company's executive officer, Sergeant First Class Robert 'Turk' Kirkland, jogged up. "We've got the prisoners under control, sir, and we've swept the ship. It's clean. What do you want us to do with the detainees, sir?"

"Take them back to the airfield and hold them until we determine what to do with them," Nigel ordered, "and get rid of the corpse and as much evidence here as you can."

"Yes sir!" Turk turned and began issuing orders.

Nigel looked at the sky and saw it was starting to turn gray in the east. He turned to the pilots. "We need to get the ship under wraps before anyone sees it and starts asking questions," he added. "Can you get it back to the airfield without being seen?"

"We've been trained to fly most small craft," the pilot said, "so we can probably fly it, but I doubt we can get it back without being seen. Heck, anyone who looks up can see it. But we can fly it low and get it back to the field. It's pretty stealthy, which is how the aliens got it here in the first place. I don't think air traffic control will see us."

"Good; do it. Get it under wraps in a hangar as soon as you can and keep people away from it."

"Yes sir!" The two pilots raced off, trying to beat the rising sun. It would be close.

"All right," Nigel said to Steve, "we better get out of here too, before the grounds maintenance people get here."

"How did you know what all of those aliens were called?" Steve asked as they walked back to the road.

"My grandfather. Remember I told you he used to bring me to the office? I would sit under his desk playing my game-slate while he conducted business. He always gave me the latest combat games and had them modified to show real aliens, with accurate abilities. These are the first aliens I've seen in real life, but they look just like they did in the game…they act the same way, too, apparently. He also made sure I knew what the MinSha looked like. He used to say, 'Someday, we're going to pay them back for what they did to our country.'" He shrugged. "They were some pretty realistic games."

"You know this isn't a game, right?"

"Yeah." He sighed. "It just got pretty real."

Houston Starport, Houston, Texas, USA

Mason lay on the bed, unmoving. Half of his face was covered in bandages where he had taken a blow to the face, but Nigel had been told he wouldn't lose the eye.

"Can you wake him up?" Nigel asked. "I need to ask him some questions before I decide how to deal with the rest of our captives."

"I wouldn't recommend it, sir," Corporal Epard replied. "He needs time to rest and recover from his wounds. The laser hit in particular was pretty serious. If we didn't have the alien med tech, he would have been in critical condition by the time we got him back."

"Understood," Nigel said. "The fact remains, I need to talk to him, and I need to do so now."

"Yes sir."

The medic pulled out an old-fashioned hypodermic needle and injected the soldier. After 30 seconds, he began to move. After another 30 seconds, his eye opened. "How loooong have I been out?" he asked with a bit of a slur.

"Just a few hours," Nigel replied. "We'll put you back to sleep to recover, but I need to know what happened in the ship."

"Ship…hmmm…oh yeah, the ship." He paused and Nigel wondered if he was going to pass out again, but then he continued, his voice a little stronger. "I went into the ship with the new guy. Allen. Needs works but a good heart. Not sure how bright he is."

"So you went into the ship…"

"We went into the ship. I left Allen at the ramp and went to find the target. Came up on them. The Cochkala was interrogating your guy."

"Cochkala?" Steve asked.

"The thing that looked like a giant walking badger," Nigel replied. "Then what?" he asked.

"Something…supposed to happen tomorrow that is going to financially break you, but I didn't catch what it was. Sounded like the Cochkala was threatening…the target. I attacked when I heard the engines start up…was too close to the Cochkala, and it caught me with a claw. Think I won…may have zip-tied them…don't remember…anything else." His head rolled to the side.

"That's it, sir," the medic said. "He really needs to rest."

"Got it," Nigel said, and he motioned Steve and Turk to follow him into the hall. "What do you think?"

"Interesting," Steve replied. "We can guess what they were talking about; it's the information we planted."

"What information is that?" Turk asked.

"We knew we had a mole," Nigel replied, "so we fed him the information we were going to sell off almost all of our remaining F11 stores to pay our bills. We already had to do it once before, so we were pretty sure they would believe it and assume it was their chance to break us once and for all."

"But you're not actually going to sell it off?"

"Hell no. Actually, we need to buy some more, so we were hoping the rumor would drive the price way down for us. We've liquidated some of our other investments, and we're going to buy all the F11 we can once the bottom drops out of the market, courtesy of our friend the mole. Hopefully, we'll make a killing when the price rebounds."

"So what now, boss?"

"Now we need to talk to Spivey; he's the human you brought back."

"Follow me, sir." The enlisted man led them to a different corridor with several guarded doors. He stopped at one and motioned the guard to step aside.

"This one's the human. He's handcuffed to the chair, so you don't have to worry about him."

"Wait for us here, please," Nigel said. He opened the door. "C'mon, Steve, let's see what the scumbag has to say."

The two men walked into the cell room to find Spivey with his head in his hands, leaning forward on the table to which he was handcuffed. He looked up as the men entered the room, and Nigel could see the man had been crying.

"Yeah, boo hoo, we caught you," Nigel said. "Did you think I was too stupid to notice what you were doing?"

"No," Spivey replied. "There are many things you may accurately be called, but people who take you for stupid are destined to be unpleasantly surprised. I tried to tell them that, but they wouldn't listen. They could only see the lazy, spoiled brat; they couldn't see what lay beneath. Although you don't have your grandfather's work ethic, you have his brains and mental agility."

"So why did you betray my family? My grandfather gave your career a huge boost when he hired you; he must have seen something in you. My father must have seen it too, or he would have fired you a long time before now."

"Does it matter why I did it? Just kill me and be done with it."

"Oh, I don't think your death will happen for quite some time. There are a lot of folks around here who have lost friends and relatives who would love to have a private 'talk' with you first. Unfortunately for you, there aren't many people who know we have you, and they're the ones looking forward to speaking with you." Nigel shrugged. "I've got better things to do than beat up a helpless man, but they apparently don't."

Spivey seemed to wilt into himself. "I was afraid of that. I always knew and feared it would end this way."

"Then why did you do it?"

"They paid well. I wanted the money."

"Bullshit! My family paid you well for everything you did. I'm sure you are one of the wealthiest lawyers on the planet."

"Maybe…but their offer would have made me wealthy compared to even *your* family."

"I'm still not buying it," Nigel said.

"Fine. You really want to know why? Because I didn't want to work for you. I have always despised you and how your family put up with your sloth. I just couldn't work for you, so when they offered me the money, I took it. I couldn't make them see the light about you, but I *could* bring you down all by myself."

"That's probably closer to the truth," Nigel said, "especially knowing the nature of our past dealings, but I'm still not buying it. You had to have been involved long before I took over. My father was too good a leader to get killed the way he did, and my brother and sister wouldn't have blindly followed him into an ambush they knew existed. They would have tried some other strategy, and probably something that was very creatively different. With a galaxy of equipment and possibilities, they could have found any number of ways to attack Moorhouse. "Death from above" isn't just a slogan the company bandies about lightly; we do airborne assault better than anyone else in the galaxy. It's the reason we survived our first contract. You had a hand in getting my brother and my father killed, along with a lot of good men and women who deserved a hell of a lot better than to be betrayed by someone integral to the company. My father and brother *trusted* you and you got them killed. *How the fuck could you do that?*"

Spivey's face fell forward into his hands, and he began sobbing; he didn't just cry, he wailed and bawled, crying harder than anyone

Nigel had ever seen before. But Nigel didn't care; he was far too angry. The man had killed his relatives, gotten his sister captured, and was actively plotting against Nigel as he tried to rescue her.

"I'm going to ask you one last time before I walk out of here. *Why the fuck did you betray us?*"

The sobbing slowed, but didn't stop, as Spivey tried to talk. He had cried so hard that he had developed a case of the hiccups, which further complicated his speech.

"They...*sob*...they have...*hic*...they have my...*hic*...they've got my daughter."

"They've got your daughter?" Nigel asked.

"*Yes!*" Spivey replied, his voice the wail of a dead man.

"Well why the fuck didn't you say something? My family would have gotten her back."

"I did tell them! The only reason your father took the Moorhouse contract was that was what the people holding my daughter wanted. I was supposed to convince him to take the garrison contract there, and he took it to gain some time to figure out who was holding my daughter. When the garrison fell, he had to go take it back in order to satisfy the contract. They knew he was coming, and he knew they knew," Spivey wailed, "yet he went ahead with the assault, anyway. That's how much he valued my service; *enough to throw away his life for me!* He thought he could do it, but now he's dead *and it's all my fault!*" He buried his face and began sobbing again.

Nigel's anger evaporated. His father *would* have done exactly that. He would have taken a garrison contract for Spivey, even though holding territory wasn't one of Asbaran Solutions' specialties. They didn't have the experience or the equipment to do it as well as they should if resistance was expected.

Damn it, Father!

As much as he hated his father for taking the mission, Nigel knew it was exactly the sort of thing his father had been brought up to do, because it was the way Nigel had been raised as well. The family had descended from knights who fought for the Sasanian Emperor, and when the empire fell to the Muslim advance, his family had fled to the area around Chabahar. Although they'd lost their noble status during the intervening centuries, they had never given up their code of ethics and beliefs. His father would have done whatever he could to help one of his retainers, just like Nigel's brother and sister would.

In fact, viewing it through that lens, he would have done the same, had he known.

"I take it both my brother and sister were also aware of all of this?"

Spivey replied with a muffled, "Yes."

"Why didn't you tell me?"

Spivey raised his head and sniffed a couple of times, trying to get himself under control. "Two reasons," he said finally. "First, it was all I could do to save the family, and I didn't want to see the entire family destroyed trying to save my daughter. I thought that if I told you, you would also have felt obligated to retrieve my daughter, despite having no training or adequate equipment."

"I would."

"Like I thought." He sniffed, then continued, "Your sister was quite the gifted leader and tactician, and her assault almost succeeded. That really scared them, and they were worried another attack might actually succeed in retaking Moorhouse. I convinced them I could financially ruin the company without them having to face another assault, and they accepted that plan. It was all I could do to save you. Yes, your inheritance would be gone, but I knew you would land on your feet somehow; you are too smart not to. And at least you would be alive."

"Too smart? I'm the one that didn't get to take over the company because I couldn't graduate from university."

"It was never that you weren't smart enough; you absolutely are. What I think is that you were too afraid you couldn't measure up to your grandfather's standards. I used to watch how you followed him around, taking in everything he did and said. When he died and you started to face up to the fact that you would someday have his place in the company, you got scared. I could see it in how you carried yourself. Your whole bearing changed. You didn't want to be compared with him, so you did everything you could to prove you *weren't* him. You became lazy. You got into fights. Anything so people wouldn't say, 'He's almost as good as his grandfather.' You idolized your grandfather and didn't think you could do the job he did."

"Maybe," Nigel said, although a tiny voice deep inside him heard the truth in Spivey's words. He had been crushed when his grandfather died, and it had been the start of his downward spiral. He would never have recognized it if Spivey hadn't said it…but it was true. His eyes started to mist over as he remembered his grandfather and how he had always said Nigel would be the best leader Asbaran Solutions had ever had.

Nigel cleared his throat to get rid of the lump that had suddenly appeared. "What was the other reason?" he asked gruffly.

"The second reason is personal," Spivey replied. "As good as your sister was, she was only the second best in your generation; you are far brighter and far wilier than either of your siblings. Your standardized tests were off the charts; that's why your family was so disappointed in you—you had more potential than anyone, and you squandered it on alcohol and women."

"I don't understand what you're saying."

"The other reason I didn't tell you is I truly believed you would succeed. I knew that somehow you'd find a way to retake Moorhouse…and then they'd kill my daughter, when I was so close to getting her back."

"So close to getting her back?"

"Yes, they promised me I would get her back when your company was ruined."

"So this was never about your daughter, this was always about destroying Asbaran Solutions."

"I didn't realize that until after your sister was captured, but yes, I believe that is true."

Nigel turned and walked toward the door.

"Where are you going?" Spivey asked.

"I'm going to take back Moorhouse," Nigel said over his shoulder, "but first I'm going to get your daughter."

* * * * *

Chapter Eleven

Houston Starport, Houston, Texas, USA

"Did you get what you needed from him?" Turk asked as Nigel burst from the cell.

"Yes and no," said Nigel, brushing past him to walk quickly down the hall. He stopped suddenly, looking around with a puzzled expression. Finally, he took a deep breath, released it slowly, and let out a chuckle.

"Can I help you?" Turk asked as he and Steve caught up to Nigel.

"Yeah, you can," Nigel said. He smiled ruefully at Steve. "Spivey was right; I'm going to have to break the spoiled brat mindset at some point. I busted out of there, intent on beating the answers out of the Cochkala. It's the way I've acted for a while now; fighting is how I solved problems. There's two problems with that."

"Oh?" Steve asked. "Do tell."

"Well, I don't know where the damned Cochkala is, for one thing."

Steve laughed. "And the other?"

"Did you see the thing? It would kick my ass if I got into a fight with it."

All three men laughed this time, and a wan smile crossed Nigel's face.

"So what are you going to do?" Steve asked.

"I'm going to stop and think a few minutes before doing anything rash."

"Wow…" Steve replied. "How unlike you."

"Yeah, isn't it?" Nigel smiled ruefully. "I do need to talk to the Cochkala, though, as well as the Flatar and the Jehas."

"The Jehas?"

"They're the things that looked like giant millipedes. They're great shipbuilders and engineers. They're also pretty good pilots when you can get them out of the engine room."

"So, you need to talk to a bunch of aliens," Steve said. "What are you going to talk to them about?"

"I'm going to ask them where they're holding Spivey's daughter."

"And you think they're going to tell you?"

"Probably not. Especially not the badger. He's in charge, and he's the one I'm least likely to get anything out of."

"Which are you going to start with?"

"The badger."

"But I thought he's the least likely to talk."

"He is…but maybe he'll give us something we can use on the rest of them." Nigel turned to Turk. "Can you show me where the Cochkala is?"

"Yes sir, he's just a couple of doors down." He led the group to a blank door; unlike the rest of the doors, there were no guards.

"You're not guarding him?" Nigel asked.

"Yes sir, we absolutely are." He opened the door, and they walked into a room similar in size to the first one, but the only furniture in it was a bed, to which the Cochkala was handcuffed, both 'hand' and 'foot.' Since there were no chairs, the two guards were forced to stand on the opposite side of the room, with rifles at the ready. "There's no leaving this one alone," Turk added. "He almost broke out when we first got him here. Put two soldiers in the infirmary, too, the bastard."

"Can he understand us?"

"Yes, he has a translator. He may act like he can't, but he can."

Nigel walked over to the bed.

"Sir, please don't stand so close," Turk said. "I'm not sure the cuffs can hold him, and you're standing in the line of fire."

Nigel and Steve moved to the end of the bed, out of the way.

"How long do you intend to hold me here?" the Cochkala asked. "We both know it's against a number of treaties and accords."

"Interesting," Nigel said. "You're not going to pretend you don't know how to speak English?"

"You know I have a translator; what would be the point? Besides, you're violating my rights and if you don't release me, I will be forced to bring charges."

"Oh, you're going to bring charges, are you? I'm not aware that we are actually members of the Union yet, so I'm pretty sure any of the Union's treaties and accords aren't binding on us. What *is* binding are the rules on unregistered travel to Earth, which I'm pretty sure *you* are in violation of. Maybe I should just turn you over to the authorities and see what they have to say."

"Obviously you aren't going to, or you would have done it at the start. Now that you've held me here, you are as guilty as I am."

"Perhaps I'm just waiting to hear what you have to say. I may kill you if your information isn't useful."

"You're not going to kill me. I'm worth an awful lot; my ransom would be substantial."

"That's probably true, but maybe we don't want word of your capture to get out. Maybe we don't want it to *ever* get out." The temperature in the room seemed to drop several degrees with the pronouncement.

"And why would that be?"

"Because maybe we already know where she's being held, and we're mounting a rescue mission. Of course, once she's safe, maybe we'll let your people know that you told us where she was being held…and *then* we'll let you go. That might be fun, too." Nigel turned to Steve. "C'mon, let's go."

Nigel took two steps, then turned around suddenly and went back to the alien's bed. In a sudden move, he grabbed the Cochkala's translation pendant and pulled it over the creature's head. "Thanks," Nigel said; "I always wanted one of these."

The two men walked out of the cell with Turk. "That was…odd," Steve said once they were out in the passage. "I'm not entirely sure who won that discussion."

"Won it?" Nigel asked. "No one won it. That was just the opening arguments. I wanted to give him something to think about while he lies there. I'm pretty sure he knows we don't know where the girl is."

"How would he know that?"

"If we knew where the girl was, we'd have no use for him. We'd have either killed him or ransomed him. Obviously, we still need him for some reason…we'll just let him stew on what that is for a while."

"Either Spivey was right, and you're a lot smarter than I thought, or I'm a lot dumber, because I didn't get *any* of that from the conversation."

"Which do you suppose it is?"

"I'm not sure," Steve replied. "I'll let you know when I figure it out. I hope it's the first."

"Me too. Otherwise, we're screwed."

Houston Starport, Houston, Texas, USA

"So, who's next?" Turk asked. "The chipmunk or the bugs?"

"Let's go see the bugs; they'll probably be the simplest, although they'll know the least."

Turk led the two men to another guarded door. "Oh, shit," Nigel said as he opened the door. The Jehas had disassembled the bunk bed and were using the pieces to tunnel through the wall of the cell. It looked like they were halfway through. The two millipedes turned around with makeshift hammers and awls in their hands.

"Did I mention they were outstanding engineers?" Nigel asked.

"*What the hell?*" Turk exploded. "Allen, get in here!"

The private ran into the room, rifle at the ready.

"What the fuck is this?" Turk asked. "They're halfway through the wall, and you're standing next to the door. *How the fuck did you let this happen?*"

"Gosh, Sergeant Kirkland, I never heard a thing. I had no idea they were doing it."

Turk drew his pistol and pointed it at the Jehas. "Before you folks get any ideas with those pointy things, why don't you drop them and step away from the wall?"

The Jehas dropped their tools and moved away from them. The equipment barely made a sound as it hit the floor of the cell. Nigel could see that both the hammers and awls had been covered with the padding from the pillows.

"Allen, why aren't these prisoners shackled?" Turk asked.

"Well, uh, look at them, Sergeant Kirkland! They've got like 50 pairs of hands! We didn't have enough zip-ties to tie them all up, so I tied the top and bottom pairs of arms to the bed. I guess they, uh, got out."

"You think? Get the hell out of here and get some of the foam from the armory."

"Foam, Sergeant Kirkland?"

"Yeah, we must have some of the anti-mob foam. You spray it on things, and it hardens into an almost-concrete. If they're going to try to break out, we can hold them with that."

"Aw…shit," one of the Jehas said, its pincers clacking loudly as the translation pendant rendered its speech into English. "What if we promise not to try to get out? I hate that stuff. I've been sprayed with it twice, and it gets down into my carapace. It took me years to get rid of it all the last time. Imagine having gravel in your joints; it hurts like getting your *grten* cut off without anesthetic."

"You promise not to try to escape?" Nigel asked.

"Yes, we will," both Jehas said.

"Okay," Nigel agreed. "We won't use the foam *this time*, but I'm going to keep someone in here with a canister of it, just in case."

"Thank you," they both replied.

"So, let's talk," Nigel said. "Where did you come from?"

"An egg."

"No, seriously, what planet did you come from?"

"We were hatched on XDSP-81DR."

"I don't care where you were hatched, I want to know where you came from, when you came here."

"We came down from space."

"And where did you come from before that?"

"Hyperspace."

"Where were you before you went into hyperspace?"

"The stargate."

"And where did you come from before that?"

"In space."

"In space around which planet?"

"XWTP-29SJ."

"What did you do there?"

"Refueled."

"Are you getting anywhere with this?" Steve asked. "I thought you said this would be easy."

"I said it would be simple; I never said it would be easy. They're answering the questions; unfortunately, I forgot how literal they were."

"Can I ask one?"

"Sure."

"Okay, Jehas. There was a Cochkala onboard your ship. On what planet did it board your ship?"

"Unknown."

"What do you mean?"

"The ship was the Cochkala's."

"What?"

"We don't know where it got on. It was on the ship when we came onboard."

"Where did you board it?"

"GrBatch."

Steve looked at Nigel and raised an eyebrow.

"It's the home world of the Cochkala."

"So boarding it there?"

"Probably a dead end."

"We're getting nowhere fast with them."

"No, we're not."

"Should we go speak to the chipmunk?"

"Yes, let's."

Nigel turned back to the Jehas. "Don't forget; if you try to escape, you'll get the foam."

Shaking their heads, Nigel, Steve, and Turk left the room.

"I don't know about you," Turk said, "but they made my head hurt."

"Mine too," Nigel replied. "We need to find someone who speaks engineer. In the meantime, let's go see the Flatar."

Turk led them to another unguarded door, and they walked in to find a soldier standing guard over the Flatar, who had been confined to a small cage.

"Really?" it asked as the men walked in. "A dog cage? Couldn't you come up with something a little better than this? How humiliating, to be caged like a simple, non-thinking animal."

"He's put two troopers into the infirmary with that bite of his, sir," Turk advised. "We thought it safer for the long-term health of the company if we just went ahead and caged him for the time being."

Nigel nodded and approached the cage. "Dogs *can* think," he said, "and in most cases they don't bite unless they're trained to do so. What's your problem?"

"I don't like to be touched," the creature replied, "and I definitely don't like to be put to sleep."

"I see," Nigel said. "We'll see what we can do. The real question, though, is what we're going to do with you. You see, you're in a pretty bad spot. Your partner's dead, your boss doesn't want to tell us what he's doing here, and your pilots don't want to tell us where you came from or where you're heading. We don't know anything about you except that whatever contract you signed when you hired on with the Cochkala, you've failed to complete it. Your principal has been captured, you've been captured, and the whole stealth aspect of this mission has been blown. And that's something you can never get back."

"I told him it was asking for trouble for him to come down to the planet," the Flatar said. "He should have just sent me; I could have blended in."

"You probably could have, but now you're caught and our options for what to do with you are pretty slim. We can't turn you in to the authorities as you might rat us out to them."

"Pun intended?" Steve asked.

"Yes," Nigel replied with a smile. "Even though he does look more like a chipmunk than a rat." He turned back to the Flatar. "So, we can't give you to the police, we definitely can't let you go, and we can't ransom you back to your company, for a number of similar reasons. About the only thing we *can* do is kill you, which would solve all of our security problems."

"But if you killed me, you'd have to kill all of us, including the Cochkala, to ensure the word doesn't get out."

"That's true. When we decide it has to be done, we will have to kill all of you."

"What if there were another way?"

"And what way would that be?"

"What if I were to tell you that, with my capture, I have effectively terminated my employment with the Cochkala. How about if you hire me, and I come work for you?"

"And why, pray tell, would I want to hire you?"

"Because your off-planet knowledge is limited, where it exists at all. You have little idea how to run a mercenary unit, much less how to conduct an airborne assault. I could help you hire some specialists, where needed, so that your mission will be successful."

"So successful you'd come along with us?"

"Uh, no, sorry. You see, airborne assault isn't my thing. Too many opportunities to go 'splat' or get blown up in the sky where I can't do anything to prevent it. I don't like putting my life in someone else's hands."

"What about the Tortantula you were riding? Isn't that putting your life in someone else's hands?"

"Nah, not really. I could always jump out of the saddle any time I wanted. It's hard to jump out of a dropship that's taking fire. No thanks."

"Well, in that case, I think we have a problem of trust," Nigel noted. "I'm not sure how we can trust you to work for us and not betray us to your current employer at the first opportunity in order to try to satisfy that contract."

"I see," the alien replied, "and there might be some merit to your argument, *if I was still employed by him*. But like I told you, getting captured results in a 'mission fail' termination of the contract, with no further payment due either me or my unit. Right now, I'm without transportation back to my home planet, and it's an awfully long walk.

Assuming you let me go at some point, and I haven't given you any reason not to, I'll need to hire on somewhere in order to get a ticket home."

"Uh huh. Well, that's all nice and everything, but it really doesn't make you any more trustworthy at the moment. You might say anything to get out of that cage. Perhaps if you told me where the Cochkala is holding my associate's daughter, we might be able to come to a mutually beneficial solution to this impasse."

"You see, I'd really like to do that, but I can't."

"Why not?"

"I'm not entirely sure where she's being held, for one thing, and I couldn't tell you if I did, as it would violate the non-disclosure terms of my last contract."

"Do you have a death wish?"

"What do you mean?"

"I mean that the only reason you're still alive is you *might* have information I need, and then you tell me that not only don't you have it, but you also wouldn't give it to me if you did. I'm struggling to understand why I'm keeping someone here to watch you when it would be easier to just shoot you and be done with it."

"Death wish? No, I don't have one…and I might be able to provide some information that makes my care and feeding a little more worthwhile to you."

"Oh? Do tell."

"Sure. When I said I didn't know for sure where she was being held, that was true; however, I'm pretty sure I can narrow it down to two places, and I have a good idea of which one it really is."

"What about not being able to tell me which one it is? That would still seem to be a problem."

"Well, I couldn't tell you where it was, but maybe you'd want to give me a ride home for my troubles in lieu of hiring me. It *is* on the way, and I wouldn't mind a brief stopover to refuel the ship or pick up additional passengers…like, say, Amanda Spivey…"

"What's your name?"

"Breetar."

"Well, Breetar, how would you like to come work for Asbaran Solutions?"

* * * * *

Chapter Twelve

Chairman's Office, Asbaran Solutions, Houston, Texas, USA

Nigel looked up from the report he was reading as Steve entered the room. "Hey, did we get the contract from the Winged Hussars yet?"

"Yeah, it just came in," Steve said, holding up a thin stack of papers. "'Standard Contract for the Employment of Xenomorphs.' I couldn't get their president, so I talked to the Hussars' personnel manager."

"I'm not surprised. I don't think Alexis Cromwell has been to Earth in her life."

"Really? So no chance to meet her? She's gorgeous as hell."

Nigel smiled. "She is indeed; however, she's way out of your league."

"Well thanks, I appreciate your vote of confidence. You don't think I'm good enough for the chairman of one of the Horsemen?"

"Good enough? Sure. Exotic enough? Nope. I hear she has a thing for one of those…what did you call them? Xenomorphs?"

"Yeah, xenomorphs. Extra-terrestrial creatures…really? A thing for one? Well, damn. Her loss." He shrugged. "In any event, the Hussars sent the contract." He sprawled on the couch and flipped through the papers.

"Anything interesting in it?" Nigel asked.

"Nah. Pretty standard stuff. It just goes into more detail about how and where the employee will be paid and where the remains will sent if the employee should fail to survive the contract." He looked up sharply. "Does that happen often?"

"Look at the last four groups we sent to Moorhouse."

"Good point. With that in mind, can I ask why you're still planning to go there?"

"I'm not. Well not right away, anyway."

"*What?* When did that change?"

"Today. That's why I asked for the contract you're holding."

"You're going to recruit the chipmunk?"

"His name is Breetar, and yeah, I'm hoping to hire him. The millipedes, too, if I can."

"Why's that?"

"What can I say? I got tired of you and Mason telling me how stupid it was to assault Moorhouse directly. Maybe we can get some leads from them and get an edge on whoever is doing this and why."

"'Bout time you started using your head," Mason said from the doorway. "Sir," he added as an afterthought.

"You look like shit," Nigel noted. The soldier still had a patch over one eye, and his left arm was in a sling. The half of his face that could be seen was a mass of pink flesh where the nano meds had repaired the Cochkala's slashes.

"Thanks. Despite how I look, I'm actually feeling surprisingly well. The miracles of alien science, I guess. What did I miss?"

"You captured the spaceship before you passed out, and then the private was able to defend it until help arrived. We've got a Cochkala, a Flatar, and two Jehas in custody at the field. More importantly, we've got the Cochkala's ship and a window of opportunity to go find out more about who's behind this."

"But sir, I thought you were focused on getting your sister back."

"I *am* focused on getting my sister back, and I'd like to leave to do so as soon as possible. Let's look at what we've accomplished so far." Nigel picked up a piece of paper and held it up; it was blank. "Unless I miss my guess, this is about the sum total of what we know about the enemy so far. Can you add anything to it?"

"Frankly, sir, no I can't." Mason shook his head slowly. "And that's probably why the previous missions failed. Honestly, that's why we're probably destined to fail, too."

"You don't have any optimism at all?"

"No, sir, I don't. I've recruited a company of troopers. Are they the best? No. Some are friends of mine, and they're pretty good, but the rest aren't. We barely have enough CASPers for everyone, and the ones we have are ancient. The dropships we have don't have the latest electronics. I'm hoping you have some advantage you haven't revealed yet that is going to turn the tide for us. Gods, I hope you do."

"I'm sorry," Nigel said. "I wish I had one too…but I don't."

"Well, failing that," Mason continued, "we'll have to find or make an opportunity the other groups missed. Otherwise, we're dead."

Nigel smiled. "Thank you very much; you just encapsulated all of my arguments for why we need to go after the people in charge of this first, rather than directly into the strength of their defenses with marginal troops and equipment."

"Okay," Mason replied, "so what's the plan?"

"The plan? I don't know…yet. But I do have some ideas, and I'm working to refine them. We've got assets we're holding at the airfield as well as a ship we can use to exploit them. If we can put all these assets to their best uses, then maybe we'll get that edge you're looking for and be successful where the rest of my family failed."

"Sir, that's the best thing I've heard you say, and for the first time I have a glimmer of hope we might actually be able to pull this off."

"Thanks, but I *don't* have a plan yet."

"Not yet, but you're working on it, and that's worth putting off our attack on Moorhouse for a few days. What's next?"

"Next, we go and see if Asbaran Solutions can hire its first alien. If so, we're well on our way to a plan."

"And if we can't?"

"There's always the direct assault on Moorhouse approach."

"I really hate working with aliens, sir, but I'd love it if you'd do me a favor."

"What's that?"

"Go hire the damn alien."

Houston Starport, Houston, Texas, USA

"I've got it from here," Nigel said, shooing out the guard. He pulled the guard's chair over to the cage holding Breetar, pulled out a key, and opened the cage door. Smiling, he sat down on the chair and looked expectantly at the alien.

Breetar's eyes moved back and forth from Nigel to the open door. "What's the catch?" Breetar finally asked. "Is this where I get shot escaping?"

"I hope not," Nigel replied. "I rather thought we could have a conversation." Nigel held up his hands. Besides a few sheets of paper in one, they were empty. "I'm not armed."

"Of course not," the Flatar replied, "but I'll bet there are armed guards outside the door."

"There are. Still, I thought you might like to stretch your legs for a bit while we talked." He started to get up. "I can shut the cage if it makes you more comfortable…"

"No, no, that's fine." Breetar walked out of the cage, looked around, then sprinted around the room several times. Nigel would have had a difficult time catching him.

"That *did* feel good," the alien said as he slowed. He took a couple of quick steps and jumped onto the roof of the cage so he could almost look Nigel in the eye. "So, what's the offer?"

"The offer?"

"Well, I'm still alive, so I must have some value. The head of one of the Horsemen comes to see you, not once, but twice; he obviously wants to cash in on that value. In order to do that, an offer has to be made and accepted. I just wanted to cut through the crap and see if it's something worth talking about or if I'm going to have to do something more…radical to ensure my release."

"I don't believe you need to do anything that might damage our relationship at the moment. As it turns out, I *do* want to discuss your employment with the company."

"Under what terms?"

"We'll get to that, but I want to mention something else first." He paused and then said, "It appears someone is out to get me."

"Really? How could you tell? The fact that we're all here?"

"You know, you were a lot less of a smartass when you were in the cage. You can always go back…"

"Oh, don't be such a—" The translator buzzed as it encountered an untranslatable word.

"A what?"

"Someone who can't take a joke."

"Oh. Can I continue?"

"By all means."

"So, someone's out to get me, and potentially, all of my family. I want to find out who."

"I'm sorry, but I don't know who it is."

"You don't know who hired you? Weren't you working for the Cochkala we captured you with?"

"Well, yes, but I get the feeling he is an employee also. I think he was contracted to run the operation, but I don't think he's behind it."

"Why not?"

"When my partner and I got hired, we were told to meet an individual at a certain time and place. When we went there, he was waiting."

"I don't see how that makes the Cochkala an employee."

"When I asked who we were supposed to meet, the individual who hired me couldn't tell me the race of the person we were meeting; he said he didn't know."

"Maybe he really didn't know. Maybe there were several layers of intermediaries between them."

"Perhaps…but if you were trying to do something secret, wouldn't you want to include only the minimum number of people? The more folks that know what's going on, the greater the chance the secret gets out. An entire clan can keep a secret, but only if they are all dead."

"That makes some sense. Anything else?"

"Yeah, and this is what clinched it for me. When we got there, the Cochkala didn't know what race we'd be, nor did he know who the pilots were going to be. He's not in charge."

"So the pilots are a dead end, too?"

"Probably. They said they were picked up there, too, so I doubt they know any more than I do."

"Well, if none of you know anything, why should I bother hiring you? Why should I even bother keeping you alive?"

"I didn't say I didn't know anything; I said the Jehas probably didn't know anything more than me. I may not know who is pulling the strings, but I know who hired me. If you take me to the transfer station at Karma VI, I can point him out to you."

"Why would I want to hire you instead of the Jehas? It would seem the two of them could do a better job than you in identifying who hired them. They also could pilot the ship on the way."

"Maybe so, but have you talked to them? They're super-hard to work with. I'm easy, as long as you don't mind a little sarcasm from time to time."

"Well, that's true."

"So it's settled; you're hiring me?"

"Against my better judgment, yes."

"Good. Then let's go talk to So'Kla."

"Who's that?"

"The Cochkala. I think it's time for me to let him know I'm working for you."

Houston Starport, Houston, Texas, USA

Nigel led Breetar into the Cochkala's cell. Not much had changed since his last visit, although the alien was now only handcuffed to the bed by one arm.

"You can leave," Nigel said to the guard stationed in the room.

"Yes, sir," the guard said. "Please be careful, sir. He's already ripped the bolts out of the bed once."

"Thank you," Nigel said with a nod. The guard left.

So'Kla stared at Breetar for a moment before asking, "Can I infer from the fact you aren't shackled that you have gone over to the other side?"

"Well, I didn't think our employers would be coming forward to ransom me anytime soon, so I figured it was the only way off this rock. I would like to get back to civilization sometime." He paused and then added, "By the way, I consider our contract terminated."

"Yes, I figured."

"Just wanted to give you formal notification, in case there was any doubt. By the way, we're going to see if I can identify your employers for my new boss." He patted Nigel on the leg. "Mr. Horseman here would like to have a few words with them."

So'Kla's eyes traveled up to meet Nigel's. "In that case," the alien said, "please kill me before you go."

"Kill you? Why would I want to do that?"

"Because part of my mission tasking was to kill everyone if it looked like we were going to be captured. I was, obviously, unsuccessful in that endeavor. If you're going to go looking for our employers, then you might as well kill me, because *they* certainly will when they find out I failed...and they won't be so nice about it—I will be a long time dying. If you kill me, hopefully it will at least be quick. I'll tell you everything I know if you will but promise me a quick death."

"I still don't know why I'd want to do that," Nigel said. "You seem to have considerable skills with economics and market manipulation, and I need someone with those skills. It turns out that Asbaran Solutions could be doing a lot better financially at the moment—"

"Sorry about that," So'Kla interrupted.

Nigel shrugged. "No worries; you were only doing your job. I want your boss."

"Me too," Breetar added.

"Why's that?" Nigel asked.

"The motherless whores wanted me killed while I was under contract to them? If I wasn't going to help you before, I surely would now. My motto has always been, 'Do unto others as they try to do unto you.' They tried to kill me? I'd like to repay them the favor…with interest."

* * * * *

Chapter Thirteen

Chairman's Office, Asbaran Solutions, Houston, Texas, USA

"Where are the creepy crawly things?" Steve asked, nodding in the direction of So'Kla and Breetar. "It looks like you've purchased the contracts of everyone else sent to kill you."

Nigel smiled. "Mason neglected to tell me which alien to hire, so I picked up all of them." The smile faded. "Seriously, though, I only picked up Breetar's contract and the Jehas. Breetar is hopefully going to point out who hired him, and the creepy crawlies as you call them are going to pilot the ship that's going to get us there. So'Kla here is a free agent, although it is likely he will soon have a price on his head. And…since economics and market manipulation are his specialties, I told him you probably wouldn't mind if he gave you a hand undoing what he did, and he volunteered to stay here and help you. If he does a good job, we'll work out a payment plan for him that will let him disappear. Until that time, though, I would watch him closely."

"You don't trust me?" So'Kla asked. The translator even managed to put a hurt tone on his voice.

"It's not so much I don't trust you as I hope Steve will learn everything he can from such an expert. The truth be known, I *don't* completely trust you, but if you make good on your word, I'll make good on mine."

"If you survive to do so."

"That's true. If you know anything else that might ensure my success, I'd be happy to hear it."

"Unfortunately, I do not."

"Well, I'm happy to have his support," Steve said. "Certainly, he knows better than anyone else what needs to be undone."

"If that's all agreed, I'd like to talk about the trip to Karma," Mason said. "Do we have time to go there?"

"Yes," Nigel replied, "although time is rapidly running out to save my sister. But then again, we really don't have time *not* to follow up on this lead. You convinced me hitting Moorhouse by ourselves was a bad idea so I'm trying to find another way. If we're fast, we ought to be able to get to Karma and then on to Moorhouse with several weeks to spare...hopefully, with an edge in hand."

"What's the edge?"

"I don't know yet; that'll have to wait until we find the people who hired So'Kla and Breetar. Hopefully, we can find them and, in doing that, get the edge we need. I also kind of promised to find Spivey's daughter and free her."

"Do you know where she is?"

"Nope. But if we can find her, she may turn out to be the edge we're looking for."

"I hope so, because we don't have a lot of support at the moment. We've got So'Kla's ship, two piece of shit dropships, and a company of raw troops. Some of them show potential, but they're all pretty much newbies. Hell, we don't even have CASPers for all of them."

"What's a CASPer?" Steve asked.

"The Combat Assault System, Personal, is the armor we wear in combat that makes us the equals of whatever we're taking on. In the early days of off-planet combat, humans got creamed. We didn't have the offensive firepower necessary to put the enemy down, nor could we take a hit from anything the other merc units had. Just like Samuel Colt made all men equal, Dr. Mauser made us equal with the alien troops when he introduced the CASPer. Well, not equal with the first version of the suit, but at least we were closer. We could at least damage the enemy and take a glancing blow or two before going down, and each new generation of the suit has given us additional offensive and defensive capabilities. What's the latest version, Mason?"

"The Mark 8, sir. It's got great haptic feedback controls, although they keep making the damn suits smaller and smaller, so they aren't such big targets. Before too long, you'll need a damn midget to operate one of them."

"Haptic controls?" Steve asked.

"That's the marketing spiel," Nigel replied; "it just means the suit has a sense-of-touch user interface." He turned back to Mason. "I may not have any 8s lying around, but I'm pretty sure I can round up a platoon's worth of 6s from our museum and maybe even some 7s. I'll try to call in some favors and see what else I can come up with." Nigel laughed. "I learned how to operate a 6 when I was younger; hopefully, it will all come back to me."

"It's like riding a bike, sir…except one you can kill yourself in it if you fuck it up. Needless to say, you can kill a lot of other people with it, too, so hopefully we'll have time to get you reacquainted with it before you actually have to use it."

"Understood. Mason, I want you to go back to the field and start getting the troops ready to leave."

"We're going to take them with us to Karma? The only thing worse than having to take you there would be letting a bunch of newbies run around unsupervised on the station. Those that don't get killed for offending an alien will probably end up into some of the extraterrestrial drugs you can get there. One time, we had a new guy that passed out for three weeks after drinking a cup of that Axanarian blue milk they serve there. We had to leave him when we deployed."

"We don't know where the trail is going to lead, and we may need the company to back us up. I agree, though; we'll have to cancel shore leave while we're there. I don't want word of what we're doing to get around. It's going to be tight on the ship with everyone onboard, and mounting the dropships to it is going to be a bitch, but the Jehas have a reputation for being great engineers; hopefully, they can figure something out."

Houston Starport, Houston, Texas, USA

Nigel and Steve arrived at the hangar to see Mason talking with the Jehas. After a few moments, they left, leaving Mason shaking his head as he watched them go. Nigel sympathized with Mason; he knew the level of frustration the Jehas could cause.

"Hey, Top," Nigel called. "Got some extra time?"

"I've got a little," Mason allowed. "What's up?"

"I heard the first load of extra CASPers arrived, and I thought I might start getting reacquainted with them."

"Yeah," Mason said, "they're the older Mark 6s, so they're going to be a couple of steps backward for most of the troops. They aren't as smooth as the current models, but they've got a hell of a lot of armor and don't chafe as much."

"Mark 6s?" Nigel asked. "Cool. Like I mentioned at the office, that shouldn't be too much of a problem for me; that was what grandpa let me play with when I came here with him."

"Your grandfather let you *play* with one of those?" Steve asked, wonder in his voice.

"Yeah, I guess 'play' is the right word for it. They had the weapons removed, and he let me do pretty much anything I wanted with them as long as I stayed out of the way of the people working here." He gave Steve a crooked smile. "I used to play 'Humans and Aliens' with the trees on the airfield. Even without weapons, the suits are still pretty powerful. There were a lot fewer trees here when I was finished than when I started."

"So you've got some experience with suits?" Mason asked. "You've also probably had the nanite treatment too, right?"

Nigel nodded.

"Awesome," Mason said. "That'll help the process considerably. We'll still have to do the laser measurements to get your suit set up for you, but you're not too far from the default setting; we could probably take out a pair of them right now if you wanted."

"That'd be great!"

"I'm going to head back to the office then," Steve said. "I haven't had the treatment, nor do I want it. I understand it hurts like hell."

"Pretty much," Nigel agreed. Mason nodded. Every trooper remembered coming out from under sedation when they received the nanite treatment to strengthen their bodies in preparation for using a CASPer; the pain was legendary. "I'll see you back at the office."

Steve departed, and Nigel and Mason walked toward the line of CASPers.

"What do you remember about using them?" Mason asked.

Nigel stopped and closed his eyes, thinking back through the years. "I think I could still put one on." He pantomimed placing his feet into the legs of the suit, including snapping them into place, then went through the motions of connecting the haptic links and interface cables.

"One more on the right side," Mason said as Nigel inserted his right arm into the phantom suit.

"What?"

"You missed one of the cables on the right side," Mason said. "Other than that, pretty good." He sounded impressed, Nigel thought. Finally, he had done something right! Nigel tried to impress Mason by completing the rest of the sequence without making another error.

Nigel made the motion of connecting the cable he had missed. He knew immediately which one he had forgotten; it was the same one he had forgotten a couple times when he was younger. Both times it had caused him to fall, and he had amassed an impressive collection of bruises in the process.

The rest was easy. Put on the helmet, make the last few connections, and flex his arms to insert them into the arms of the suit. He paused as he mentally waited for the phantom technician to turn the power on, and then he made the "okay" signal with both hands, pinching his index finger and thumb together, which would bring the suit to an operational state.

"Close canopy," he said. He opened his eyes. "How'd I do?"

"Pretty good for someone who doesn't do it every day," Mason said. He flagged down a passing technician. "Hey, Oscar, can you take the boss and get him suited up? We're going to take a couple of the CASPers out to the range."

"Sure," the technician replied, leading Nigel in the direction of the nearby locker room.

When Nigel returned 15 minutes later, dressed in a combat uniform and helmet, Mason was already waiting for him in one of the CASPers. As Nigel approached, the soldier fired the suit's jumpjets and launched himself in a low arc across the assembly area. Nigel stood his ground as the suit rocketed toward him.

Less than a second before it would have squashed him to paste, the jets fired again and Mason slowed it enough to come down in a controlled landing, flexing the suit's mechanical knees to absorb the shock of landing. He opened the canopy and smiled. "Ready?"

"You bet," Nigel said, ignoring the dangerous maneuver the trooper had just performed. "Which one's mine?"

"This one," a technician said, pushing a boarding ladder into place at the third one in line. "It's checked out and ready to go."

Nigel climbed the ladder, careful not to snag any of the cables he was carrying. He reached the platform and found the Mark 6 suit to be the same as the ones he had played in—old and worn. The suit was probably older than he was; at least, it looked it. The paint was worn off across most of the suit's skin, and the interior padding had more places where it was patched than where it wasn't. But it was home, and wearing one was his birthright. It looked beautiful to him.

Careful not to go too fast, Nigel turned around and backed into the frame. Kneeling down, he slid first one leg and then the other into the suit, pointing his toes and wiggling his leg to get it all the way into the unyielding plastic. It had been a little easier when he was younger and more flexible, but he managed, finally snapping his legs into place. He stood up and found one of the leg splints rode too high into his crotch. He knew from experience the first time he jumped it would slam him in the groin and incapacitate him for several minutes. He adjusted the setting to a more comfortable level and plugged in all of his cables, careful not to miss the one he had forgotten earlier.

After checking to make sure there weren't any unconnected cables dangling or in places where they would get hung up, he put on his helmet, activating the haptic skin sensors built into it. Everything in place, he rotated his shoulders and flexed his arms backwards into the arm holes. These were easier to get into, as the suits were designed with a little more space in the arms.

Nigel nodded down to the technician. "Ready."

"Roger," the technician said. "Standby for startup."

Nigel watched the power indicator switch from blue to yellow as the suit's motor started. The hydrogen-powered generator came to life, and the suit vibrated slightly.

"Clean board," the technician advised. "Good start."

Nigel made the okay sign with both hands, and the suit's status indicator switched to the green 'operate' symbol. "Close canopy," Nigel said, and the canopy rotated down and sealed with a small thump. The suit pressurized as it came to life, and he stretched his jaw to pop his ears. All of the suit's systems came online, including the cameras which gave him the same exterior view he would have had if the canopy had been glass and not hardened steel.

He checked the monitors that showed his suit's status. No warning or caution lights on the indicator panel. Power output, backup battery, and life support were all in the green section of their bar indicators, and his fuel status was at 98%. The only thing he was missing was the weapons status, which was grayed out as no weapons were loaded. *Yet*, he thought with a grin. He turned on the exterior speakers with a finger motion and reported, "Good start. All systems green."

"I want you to move all of your extremities and get used to the suit again," Mason said, stepping up in front of Nigel's suit. "Take it slowly, though. If you haven't done it in a while, it will come back pretty quickly, but I don't want you to hurt yourself by doing too much too fast."

Even though Nigel felt ready to run an obstacle course, he knew Mason was correct and tempered his desire. Before he had donned his first suit, his grandfather had told him a story about how a new recruit had mistimed his first step. The man had fallen forward on his face, given himself a concussion, and then had a blood clot cause a stroke that killed him. Nigel didn't know if it were true or urban legend, but he remembered how easy it was to fall when you were first learning to operate a suit, and he knew from personal experience that really painful injuries could result, even if death did not.

He spent the first few minutes moving his arms and legs then practiced marching in place to make sure his timing was correct. His suit's left leg was a little slow to follow the motion of his own leg, and he had the technician calibrate the controls until it worked flawlessly. Finally, he felt he was ready.

"Ready for release," he said.

The technician looked again at his status display and nodded. "All systems operational on my board. Releasing."

Nigel felt the straps holding him back release, and he dropped forward into his favorite superhero's pose, on one knee with a raised fist. "Let's rock!" he roared, his external speakers set to max as he mimicked MechaMan's battle cry.

"Easy, sir," Mason said, stepping in front of him. "You won't do anyone any good if you hurt yourself the first time out."

"I know," Nigel said with a mental sigh. Old people never get it. "I was just playing."

"Yeah, well play time is over. We need to get you checked out in the suit and up to speed, including the weapons system, which you said you haven't used. We don't have the weapons systems installed yet, so you'll have to come back for that, but we can at least get you up and, hopefully, running."

"Got it," Nigel said, trying to sound more chastised than he really felt. "What do you want me to do first?"

Mason ran him through a variety of start-up maneuvers designed to assist the suit in making its final internal calibrations. Nigel handled most of them fairly well, although some of them were things he had never attempted before, like lying on his back and raising his torso while supporting himself by his hands and feet in a an upward-bowed 'bridge' position. That one took him a while to get right, and his inability to do it correctly left him feeling a little bit…well, not chastised so much as annoyed.

"Good operators can use that position to spring to their feet, just by pushing off," Mason noted.

"Bullshit," Nigel said. After many failed attempts at performing the maneuver, he didn't see how it was possible.

Mason lay down on the hangar's concrete floor, bridged himself, and flipped up to a standing position.

"Any questions?" Mason asked, sarcasm audible even through the speakers.

Nigel stood looking at the other CASPer, his mouth hanging open inside his suit. He would have bet an awful lot of money Mason couldn't do it.

"Now, are you ready to do what I tell you?"

"Yes." Nigel hoped he didn't sound as sheepish as he felt.

With Nigel's attention now riveted on every word and movement, Mason led him through the rest of the basic maneuvers. Nigel completed them within 10 minutes and was quickly moving around without having to think about it anymore.

"Ready for something a little more challenging?" Mason asked.

"Yes!" Nigel replied.

Mason led him through another series of drills, including running, jumping, and picking up and manipulating small objects. These were things Nigel had done before; even though he hadn't done them recently, he was familiar with them and picked them back up fairly quickly. He was pretty happy with his performance; he only had one bad fall, and that was during the jumpjet practice. Using the jumpjets had been frowned upon when he was growing up, so he only had a little prior experience with them, gained when his grandfather wasn't looking. It didn't make his horizontal landing feel any better—it hurt like hell and caused some minor damage to the suit—but at least he understood why it had happened.

"Had enough?" Mason asked two hours later.

"Shit!" Nigel said, looking at his suit's chronometer. "Is that really the time? I've got a meeting I'm going to be late for."

"Yeah, time flies when you're having fun or driving a CASPer, which amounts to about the same thing."

The pair ran back to the hangar at full speed. Although Nigel was close, Mason beat him by two seconds. They secured the suits to the maintenance harnesses, opened the canopies and climbed down the egress handholds. Mason was already down and drinking a bottle of water when Nigel reached the floor.

"Nice run," Mason said. "You're a lot further along than I feared you would be."

"Was that your top speed?"

"Honestly? No. I slacked off a little bit so you wouldn't give up. Still, that was better than any of the recruits did on their first time in the suits, so you're ahead of schedule. Next time we'll try one with weapons and see what you can do."

"Really?" Nigel asked. "I'll be back as soon as I can!"

Cell Block, Planet Moorhouse, Kepler 62 System

"I don't think your brother likes you very much," Commander Tranayl noted, his carapace clicking in amusement. "I'm told he is going somewhere else rather than coming here to rescue you."

"Maybe he's just smarter than you," Parisa Shirazi said to the MinSha. The creature looked like an oversize praying mantis, with a blue sheen to its chitin. "Maybe he knows something you don't. Wouldn't be too hard; you're obviously not very smart." She was tired of the creature coming down to taunt her every few days, and she knew it was starting to show.

"The results suggest otherwise," the giant insectoid said, one claw indicating the prison in which Parisa was being held. "I am on the outside of the cell; you, however, are in it."

"For now."

"I do not believe our positions are likely to change. This strategy is the culmination of years of preparation. Our spies are everywhere; we know all. Everything has been foreseen, and is taking place as it should."

"You should have finished my civilization when you had a chance. You know what we do with bugs in Chabahar? We step on them. My brother is going to do the same thing to you, you oversized insect."

"Are you trying to bait me?"

"Isn't that what you're supposed to do with pests? Bait them with poison and kill them?"

"Perhaps you're hoping I will become angry and kill you prematurely, but you're wrong. You will die at your appointed time. No sooner and no later. Besides, you don't even like your brother. Our investigation into your family revealed that, while your brother feels a familial relationship to you, you feel nothing toward him."

"There's really no reason for me to explain the dynamics of my family to you. Do bugs even have families? I'll bet you eat your young, don't you?"

"Killing *all* of our children is hardly something that would ensure the longevity of our race, but defective ones are often destroyed, yes. It is the way things always have been, and why our race is so much stronger than yours. Yours allows genetic aberrations to continue unabated; ours gets rid of them. We are stronger because of it, as indicated by our present circumstances."

"So what *are* you planning on doing with me? Why haven't you killed me like you did my father and brother?"

"I'll bet you'd like to know, wouldn't you?"

"Well, it's obvious I won't be allowed to leave. I know you used banshee bombs to capture the outpost here. Those bombs are illegal; I doubt you're going to let me tell everyone about it."

"Aren't you the smart one?" Tranayl asked. "Of course you're to be killed, but right now, *you* are the bait we need to get your brother to come."

"But why? Why do you have to kill him here? Can't you just shoot him back in Houston and be done with it?"

"Ah, nothing is ever as simple as it seems, and the answer to your question is no different. The point of this isn't just to have your family dead."

"Could have fooled me. It looks like you're doing a pretty good job of it."

"Oh, we want you dead, make no mistake about that, but that is only part of the plan. We want your family totally discredited first. Not only are you all going to die, but you're going to do so while failing to complete this contract. It is perfectly timed for him to die as the contract expires. Not only are you discredited, but we get paid for the contract in your place. The officer who thought up this plan was a genius."

"My family isn't finished yet."

"From what I hear about your brother's ineptitude, it soon will be."

* * * * *

Chapter Fourteen

Houston Starport, Houston, Texas, USA

Nigel slid into the CASPer shell, finding it easier to don this time. The only problem—he couldn't stop staring at the suit's armament while he mated his leads to the suit. An autocannon hung from the outside of his left arm and a coil gun from his right. A giant knife blade, bigger than the blade on a medieval polearm was also mounted to his left arm, but was retracted back into its sheath. Every time his eyes strayed to the missile pack on his right shoulder, a grin split his face. Nigel had seen armed soldiers go off to war a number of times, and off to the firing range more times than he could count, but this was the first time he had strapped on an armed suit. He had to fight the urge to giggle.

"How's it fit, sir?" Sergeant First Class William Mackenzie called up. Nigel couldn't remember a time the tall, broad-shouldered armorer hadn't worked for the company, first as a trooper and then, after losing his legs during a mission, as the chief armorer. "I had a couple of minutes to update the interior of the suit after you left last time."

"Like a glove," Nigel replied. The CASPer suit interior was adjusted via moveable padding and straps after a detailed laser scan; Mackenzie had set his up perfectly.

Nigel finished strapping in and closed the canopy. This time, as his reticles came alive, the weapons' status readouts were different;

not only were there weapons attached, but the ammo indicators were green and showed 100%. Cool.

"Check all weapons safe?" Mason asked from the cockpit of his CASPer.

"All green and safe," Nigel agreed, checking his readouts.

"That's more weapons than you're likely to ever have mounted on your suit at one time, especially with the autocannon," Mason added, "but we wanted you to get the feel for as many as possible today, since our time is short."

"Ready to release?" Mackenzie asked.

Nigel flexed all of his extremities; he had a full range of motion. "Ready."

The suit fell to the ground and Nigel flexed his knees to absorb the shock, foregoing the superhero landing. If Mason didn't understand it the first time, Nigel doubted that most of the old-timers standing around would appreciate it now that the suit was armed. Too bad; he really *was* ready to rock.

Nigel went through the rest of his checks and nodded. After a couple of seconds he realized Mason couldn't see him. "I'm ready."

Mason led him to the end of the runway then down the path to the weapons range. The area was a square 1,000 feet per side that had been dug 20 feet down into the ground, with all the excavated earth pushed up to the sides in a massive berm that encircled the range. A variety of targets were scattered throughout the pit, with the hulk of an ancient Jivool tank at the far end.

"Initiate range mode," Mason said.

'Range mode enabled' scrawled across Nigel's head's-up display for three seconds, indicating the suit's safety interlocks would prevent its weapons from firing if the suit calculated the rounds would leave the confines of the training grounds.

"Range mode confirmed," Nigel said.

"Good," Mason replied. "The Houston officials get pissy if you start lobbing missiles into the city. Okay, one at a time, we're going to cycle through your weapons and try them out. Chain gun first. Let me know when you're ready."

"Chain gun first," Nigel repeated, arming the 25mm autocannon. A derivative of the venerable M242 Bushmaster, the weapon was mounted to his left arm with a metallic link belt that ran back to the storage drum mounted on his back. General purpose in nature, the gun was hell on troops in the open and could also be used on lightly-armored vehicles and aerial targets. Although it could also fire high-explosive incendiary rounds, Nigel's suit was currently armed with armor-piercing shells.

"Arm chain gun," Nigel said inside the suit, and the targeting reticle in front of his left eye switched to red, indicating the weapon was ready to be fired. "Normal rate of fire." An 'N' appeared next to the symbol for his left arm weapon, signaling that the cannon would fire at 500 rounds per minute rather than its lower rate of 200.

"I'm ready," Nigel reported over the external speaker. "Chain gun armed, normal rate of fire."

Mason surveyed the range to make sure it was clear. "Clear to fire!"

Nigel picked an old hovercar in the center of the range and enabled the laser rangefinder. Holding the reticle on a hole in the driver's door, he flexed his index finger as if pulling a trigger.

"Brrrrrrp!" The suit safed itself as Nigel was thrown over onto his back. "What the hell?" Nigel asked as Mason helped him back to his feet.

"That's a lot of gun for a suit," Mason advised with a chuckle, "especially at its normal rate of fire. You've really got to lean into the shot or it's going to…well, as you saw, it's going to knock you on your ass."

"Thanks for the warning," Nigel muttered inside his suit. "Asshole." He bent his knees and leaned into the shot. *"Brrrrrrp!"*

Holy crap! Even though he only held the trigger for a little more than a second, the ammo remaining dropped by nine. 1,500 rounds seemed like a lot…until you realized it could be expended in three minutes. And his rounds had hit two feet low and to the left.

"Low rate of fire," Nigel said as he made the adjustment necessary to the targeting system. An 'L' appeared briefly. "Firing," he broadcast.

Nigel fired at the hovercar again and the rounds hit where he had aimed. He shifted his aim and put five rounds into the control section of a large, unmanned aerial vehicle. He switched again and hit just outside the bullseye of a target at the far end of the range. Although 1,000 feet away, it was well within the weapon's 10,000 foot effective range. He used the suit's optical zoom and put the next three rounds into the target's bullseye.

"This is fun," Nigel said, cycling between targets as fast as he could. Once it was adjusted, the laser targeting system made it deadly accurate.

"All right," Mason said. "Let's see the MAC."

"You got it," Nigel said, arming the magnetic accelerator cannon on his right arm. His right reticle turned red as the coil gun powered up. The weapon used magnetic force to accelerate a projectile down its barrel by switching 17 electromagnetic coils on and off in a pre-cisely-timed sequence. As the ammo had no need for propellant, more rounds could be stored in a magazine the size of the autocan-non's; however, the MAC fired at a substantially slower rate. Its 2,100 rounds could only be delivered at 150 rounds per minute.

"*Pop, pop, pop, pop,*" The rounds fired with much less noise, and slowly enough that Nigel could count the individual shots. He ad-justed the targeting system then began plinking the objects on the range. Although it didn't have the same visceral thrill of firing a 25mm autocannon, the MAC was a good weapon for extended bat-tles where you didn't need the overwhelming force of a rapid-fire rifle.

"Ok, safe up," Mason said after a few minutes. "Mackenzie and I wanted you to get the feel for the autocannon and the MAC, but I also want to at least show you the laser. This is the other main weap-on that can be mounted to your arms. It's a 13.7 megawatt laser that gets its energy from a chemical reaction, so the magazines work by injecting the active materials. Set your suit to show lasers."

"Show all lasers," Nigel said inside his suit and received the 'Show Lasers – All' message on his heads-up display. Although a laser beam travelled faster than a human could see, the suit registered laser fire and could slow the image down, allowing the user to 'see' the laser beam's path.

"These work better in space, where they aren't attenuated by air, humidity, and smoke, but they can also have applications in atmos-phere. Watch."

Mason fired the laser several times, cutting through some of the thinner skinned vehicles where it left a burning metal hole in its passing. He fired at the Jivool tank several times; the weapon was far less effective against it.

"The laser's good for people and thin-skinned vehicles," Mason said, "but that's about it. You're just wasting your charge if you shoot it at a tank, especially a main battle tank. On the good side, it's a technology we can shrink down enough to give you as a personal weapon for when you're not in the suit."

Mason moved back behind Nigel. "Okay, enough standing around," Mason added. "Try firing your weapons while you're moving around. You're going to have to get used to doing it that way; standing still in battle is a good way to eat an incoming round and get yourself killed."

Nigel ran sideways across the end of the range, firing at the hovercar. Although he succeeded in hitting it a few times, any time he went faster than a slow walk he also hit everything around it. When he ran, he mostly succeeded in hitting things that weren't even particularly close to the intended target, and several times the suit automatically safed itself.

"Fuck, that's hard!" Nigel exclaimed.

"It just comes with practice. It's a matter of judging how fast to move your arms, based on your speed and how close the target is. Sometimes, you can get by with spraying bullets everywhere, but generally you don't want to waste ammo like that. Once your ammo is gone, you'll be down to fighting with your knife…and there are few things worse than bringing a knife to a gun fight."

Nigel commanded his knife blade to extend and it locked into place with a loud snapping noise. With the blade fully extended, he could reach out at least seven feet…but bullets, lasers, and autocannon rounds could travel much farther. He retracted the knife back to its stowed position. Gotta watch my ammo, he admonished himself.

"Okay, I sucked at that," Nigel said. "How about showing me how it's done?"

"Sure," Mason said.

He walked 150 feet to the left, turned, and sprinted back toward Nigel. Mason's laser and MAC fired nearly continuously, and Nigel could see hits on all of the targets he passed, with strikes on targets at the other end of the range in between. As he got within 30 feet of Nigel, he threw himself forward into a roll. He came out of the roll firing downrange, and as he went vertical, he triggered his suit's jets, launching himself over Nigel, somersaulting in midair as he passed. Nigel turned around to find Mason behind him with his sword blade extended. It rested on the joint where his neck armor was fastened to the suit's torso.

Nigel reached up and pushed the blade off to the side with a metal finger. "Okay," he said; "You've made your point; I've got some work to do."

"A bit," Mason agreed, "but you have to remember I've been doing it a lot longer than you. Take your time, practice, and you'll be able to do all that, too, eventually. It's really not as hard as it looks."

"Riiiiight."

"Last thing," Mason instructed. "You've got three missiles in your launcher; take out the tank."

"Really?"

"Yes, sir. Kill it."

Nigel activated the missile system. Unlike the rifles, where the targeting reticle moved depending on where he pointed his arm, the reticle for the missiles followed wherever *he* looked. The missiles had two settings, IR and Video. If a target had a heat source, you used the infrared system; if not, the video system worked pretty well by grabbing onto a piece of digital video and homing in on it all the way to the target.

The Jivool tank didn't have an operating engine, so Nigel didn't have an IR heat source to lock the missiles onto. He switched to video mode, and designated spots in the front, center and aft section of the tank.

"Ready," Nigel noted when his targeting was complete.

"Fire!" Mason ordered.

The missiles streaked across the 'battlefield' and struck the Jivool tank. The center missile blew off the turret, while the other two missiles ripped jagged holes in its main body. The turret slammed to the ground on the far side of the vehicle while several small fires danced around it.

Mason slapped him on the back. "Not bad," Mason said. "What do you think? Still ready to rock?"

"*Hell*, yeah!" Nigel exclaimed. "Even more so!" Maybe old folks did get it, after all.

Houston Starport, Houston, Texas, USA

"**D**id your mother have any children who *weren't* born brain-dead?" Mason roared, his voice augmented by the speakers in his Mark 6 CASPer as he helped lift Private Parker from the concrete floor. "What are you trying to do? Commit suicide in *my* combat suit?"

"No, sir, I—"

"*I'm not a fucking 'sir!' I work for a living!*"

"Yes, Top! I mean, no Top, I'm not trying to commit suicide! I just mis-timed my landing."

"If you do that in combat, you're going to be dead! Now try that again, and don't mis-time the landing!"

Mason stomped away from the trooper and saw the Jehas approaching. Great, now what?

"We have figured out how to mount two dropships to the ship," one of them announced. "It will not be pretty, but it should be functional. We do not believe it will affect our performance in hyperspace."

"You don't believe it will, or it won't?"

"We have never attempted something of this design before," the other replied, "so we don't believe it will. The only way to know for sure is to try it. We will either survive or we won't."

"But you think it will work?"

"Our calculations indicate a 97.2% likelihood of success," the first replied.

"Which leaves a 2.8% chance of total gravitic separation," the other concluded.

"What the hell is that?" Mason hated talking to the Jehas. They gave him an almost-immediate headache.

"It's a complete reversal of gravity," the first replied.

"Imagine if the forces holding your body together immediately switched and start pushing it apart," added the second. "Your body will explode at nearly the speed of light."

"But it's a really small chance?"

"2.8%, which is unlikely."

"But not insignificant."

"Good, go ahead and do it," Mason ordered. And get the hell away from me, he added to himself.

"Oh, one other thing," the first Jeha said. "Several of the troops will have to live in each of the dropships while we are enroute to Karma."

"There isn't enough room in the ship, otherwise," the second added.

"Of course there isn't. Just. Fucking. Do. It!"

Mason thought about living in one of the tiny dropships for a week. It was going to suck for those troopers, but at least they'd be away from the Jehas. On second thought, maybe he'd volunteer for the duty, just to be away from them. He shook his head. Stupid bugs.

Chairman's Office, Asbaran Solutions, Houston, Texas, USA

"**T**he platoon is getting the last few pieces of gear stowed as we speak," Mason said as he entered the office with a man and woman in tow. "It was tough getting all the suits in, but we made them fit. We will be ready to leave this afternoon as planned."

"Good," Nigel replied. "We've taken longer than I wanted getting everything assembled and loaded; our time is running short."

"Well, the only thing worse than getting there late is getting there early without the right equipment. Then we'd be dead too, and would have done their work for them."

"Intellectually, I know that," Nigel said, "but here," he tapped his chest over his heart, "I want to go *now*, do something *now*, and save my sister *now*."

"One of the hardest skills for youth to learn is patience," Mason replied, "but being prepared for battle is halfway toward winning it. Speaking of which, I wanted to bring by the new lead dropship pilots so you had a chance to meet them."

He nodded to the woman. Nigel had never seen someone who was able to pull off looking both tough and sexy at the same time; she did. Just the way she stood said, "badass." "This is Lieutenant KC 'Mama' Seville," Mason said. "She will be the senior dropship pilot and will be flying with Lieutenant Junior Grade (LTJG) Jonny 'Dark' Minion." He nodded to the man, who stood almost a foot taller than the diminutive lead pilot. "This is Lieutenant Tom 'Harv' Walsh. He'll be piloting the second dropship, with LTJG Michael 'Salty' Morton as his copilot."

"Welcome aboard," Nigel said. "Mama?"

"It's short for Mama Bear, sir," LT Seville said. "Excuse my language, but some of my contemporaries learned the hard way that you just don't fuck with the mama bear." She smiled. "Thanks for picking up our contracts. Top filled us in on the mission, but he didn't have many details. Do we know anything else about our enemies or their capabilities?"

"Unfortunately, no. I think our new allies are being straight with us—that they don't know anything beyond what they've already told us."

"That isn't a hell of a lot, sir."

"No, it's not, but we'll have to follow the trail and see what we can find. And fast."

"Well, I like fast. I'll take Harv and we'll go get our gear stowed. I understand we leave later today?"

"That's correct."

The two aviators left and Nigel turned to Steve with a raised eyebrow. "Where did you find them?"

"Mason recommended them; he knew them from the Golden Horde. Apparently they took one of the Horde's dropships joyriding one night."

"And?"

"And they were doing some low-altitude stuff. Apparently the Uzbeckis had just put up some cabling to distribute power from their new fusion reactor. It hadn't been added to the chart system yet, so they didn't know it was there and flew right through it. I'm told there are still about a million people in Tashkent who are without power, and the authorities would really like to talk to LT Seville. She jumped at the chance to go off-world for a little while and brought the rest of the pilots with her."

"There going to be any problems with the Horde if we take them with us?"

"No, I talked to Sansar Enkh, the head of the Horde. She said she'd appreciate it if we took Mama and Harv with us. The other two pilots weren't with the Horde; they were just people LT Seville knew and could get here quickly."

"Was Sansar happy to be getting rid of them or was she trying to keep them out of trouble?"

"A little of both, I think. Seville and Walsh are apparently rather colorful, and she was looking forward to a little 'quiet time' with them gone." Mason looked at his watch. "Speaking of being gone, it's time for us to head over and load up."

"Indeed it is," Nigel said, rising and heading toward the door. "Good luck, Steve. Watch the store while we're gone."

"You got it, boss," Steve said from the couch. "Have fun storming the castle!"

So'Kla's Ship, Approaching the Orbital Transfer Station, Karma VI

Mason floated in front of Nigel, who was cocooned to the bulkhead of the ship. They'd been coasting in null gravity for almost a week, and he had almost adjusted to the weightlessness. Almost. At least he didn't want to throw up *all* the time now.

"Have you ever been to Karma before?" the merc asked.

"No," Nigel replied, "but my grandfather talked about it a lot. He said the transfer station is…interesting. Especially Peepo's Pit."

"Interesting is an understatement. It's an explosion of color and noise that can be overwhelming the first time you experience it. Just seeing all the different aliens in one spot can be disconcerting. One thing you don't want to do? Don't stare. Ever."

"Why? Some races don't want to be watched?"

"Yeah, there are some that consider staring an insult, but more importantly, if you're staring, you run the risk of walking into other aliens, and that can be fatal. Whether they have toxins on their skins or they decide bumping into them is an insult worth dueling over…it just ain't worth it."

"That makes sense."

"But the worst thing about staring—"

"There's something worse than toxic aliens?"

"Yeah, the worst thing about staring is you lose your situational awareness. Remember, there are probably entities on the station who want you dead. If you get hyper-focused on something, you're not fulfilling your most important duty—you're not watching my back."

"Your back? Shouldn't I be watching my own?"

"No, that's my job."

Nigel raised an eyebrow.

"Can you see behind yourself? How about doing it without walking into what's in front of you? I've got your back; you've got mine."

Orbital Transfer Station, Karma VI

Nigel, Mason, and Breetar entered the orbital transfer station, and Nigel was immediately struck by how much larger it was than he had expected. Corridors ran off into the distance in both directions, only starting to curve upward at the far horizons.

"Fuuuuu…uck," he mumbled, his mouth agape as his eyes scanned his new surroundings looking for something—anything—that would help him make sense of what he was seeing.

"It does have that effect the first time you're here," Mason noted. "Remember, this is the merc guild headquarters for this entire arm of the galaxy. If you want to hire a merc unit, this is where you do it."

The group took the first glideway they came to down to the gravity ring. An oversized pneumatic pressure tube, it gently blew its occupants along until gravity was strong enough for them to walk/crawl/fly (or whatever else they did) on their own.

Mason and Breetar turned right at the gravity ring like they knew where they were going, and Nigel hurried to catch up.

"I see what you mean," Nigel said as a caterpillar crawled by. It was the seventh race he had seen that he was completely unable to identify. "It *would* be easy to stare."

"Just stay at my side," Mason said, "but not so close you block my gun arm."

"Or mine," added Breetar. Against Mason's better judgment, Nigel had given the Flatar his gun back.

"You think someone will take a shot at me here?"

"Not if it looks like we're on guard. If it looks like they could take us unaware, though…you never know. I don't want to give anyone any ideas."

Nigel's eyes scanned the crowded tube, his eyes continually in motion. The constant need for vigilance made the journey to Peepo's far less fun than his 15-year-old self had imagined it would be while listening to his grandfather relate the station's sights and sounds.

"I just can't believe there are so many races I don't recognize. I memorized every single one in the games I used to play."

Mason snorted. "There are thousands of races in the Union. The ones you probably saw were the mercs, of which there are only 37, counting us, and the ones who hire mercs, of which there are more, but probably not more than a few hundred. Most races are happy to keep to themselves or engage in honest trade with a few partners. It's the ones who are more…active…that keep us in business."

"All right, we're here," Mason said, stopping in front of an otherwise nondescript door after about a 10-minute walk.

"Doesn't look like much," Nigel noted.

"Yeah, well, if you have to ask, then you don't belong here." He nodded to Breetar. "Why don't you go in first, so you can judge everyone's reactions when we walk in."

"Sure, but what if my former employers are there, and they recognize me?"

"Pretend you're someone else. All you rodents look the same to us. Now go, before we're seen together."

"Sheesh," the Flatar muttered as it stalked to the door. "Stupid humans look the same to us too. Especially lying dead on the ground with hypervelocity rounds through their big, stupid foreheads." Breetar entered the establishment, using what looked like a small doggie door at the base of the main door.

"You ready?" Mason asked after counting to twenty.

Nigel nodded.

"Good. Keep your head on a swivel. Let's go."

Mason opened the door and walked in ahead of Nigel. Even though Nigel had known what to expect, the wall of random noise hit him as he entered, and he was forced to pause and take it all in before hurrying to catch up with Mason. Peepo's Pit looked *almost* like any of the huge sports bars he frequented back home. The place was packed, with patrons filling most of the space at the central bar and nearly all of the tables. Serving robots rolled back and forth across the floor, taking and filling orders, and hundreds of flat-panel Tri-V displays lined the walls.

There were two main differences that made it obvious he wasn't back in Houston. First, humans were a small minority in the establishment. The Pit was a microcosm of everything he had seen so far at the station; a huge variety of aliens talked and gestured in an assortment of languages, roaring their displeasure or agreement…it was hard to tell which in some cases. A number of individuals ran away from the tenants of one of the tables; that one looked like a disagreement. Nigel watched for a moment as the two individuals, both of whom looked like eight-foot-tall purple bears, screamed in an alien language and gestured at each other.

Mason elbowed him in the stomach, not too gently. "Stop staring at the Oogar," he ordered in a stage whisper. "Head on a swivel."

Nigel turned away as the two bears fell into each other's arms and began licking and stroking their pelts, argument resolved. Nigel shook his head; that was an unwanted mental image he would be a long time getting rid of.

The other difference Nigel noticed as he followed Mason was that the furniture was all wrong. The 'chairs' at each of the tables were a variety of sizes and styles to accommodate the multitude of clients; some were no more than posts to roost on or lean against. Some tables had no furniture next to them at all. There also weren't any live-action sporting events on the screens on the walls; all of them had data scrolling across their faces in various directions and at differing speeds. Due to his eclectic childhood upbringing, Nigel recognized the lettering on a number of them, even if he couldn't read the words.

Mason led them to a table beneath a screen with English, the official language of Earth, running across it. Four human-sized and -shaped chairs sat around it. Nigel took a second to check out the data on the screen—merc contracts, as expected; some groups were paying exorbitant amounts of credits for successful completion. If the mercs survived.

"I see new humans in my pit," Nigel's translator announced.

Glancing down from the display, Nigel saw the speaker was a Veetanho, a female alien that looked like a giant albino mole and stood as tall as a fully-grown human. She had short arms and legs for her long body, and a huge pair of sunglasses hid her eyes. "I do not recognize one of these humans," she continued, sniffing the air with her large, flared nose, "although the other I know. Welcome back to Peepo's Pit, Sergeant Mason."

"Hi Peepo," Mason replied. "That's First Sergeant Mason now."

"Oooh…congratulations are in order. You have come a long way from when I saw you last as a guard for Sansar Enkh. Your first beverage is on the house."

"Thank you, Peepo; that is most kind of you. We are testing the waters to see what's available."

"Who is testing the waters with you? I do not recognize him, and we have select clients here."

"I am very much aware of that," Nigel said, reaching over to hand the Veetanho a coin. "My grandfather spoke very highly of you. I am Nigel Shirazi."

The alien held the coin close to her sunglasses to study it, then handed it back to Nigel. "I heard about your grandfather, and it saddened me…and your father and brother as well. The latter were not my favorite clients, perhaps, but your grandfather and I fought together once, a long time ago."

"He told me," Nigel replied. "He said you were the only one to ever best him."

"Best him? I do not remember it that way. I believe we fought to a draw that made neither of our employers happy, but satisfied the terms of our contracts so we were both able to walk away with our honor intact. We never fought each other again, and that is probably fortunate for both of us."

The Veetanho put a hand on her chest, and reached out to put the other on Nigel's chest. "Our fates are shared," she intoned.

"I mourn for our loss," Nigel added, completing the ritual.

"Peepo's Pit will always welcome you, and I shall offer a toast to his memory."

"Thank you," Nigel replied with a bow.

"Will you be negotiating today?" Peepo asked, bring the conversation back to the present.

"Perhaps," Nigel said, his eyes sweeping the pit. "We are looking for a little more information first."

"Clients come to Peepo's for information more often than contracts," the alien noted, "but both come at a price."

"I understand."

"Good luck, grandson of my respected enemy. I hope you find what you are looking for, at a price you are willing to pay."

With that, the alien gave a small bow, turned, and left.

"That went well," Mason said.

"Did it? I nearly wet my pants," Nigel replied, "and I can't remember half of what I said. Talking with Peepo in Peepo's Pit? It's déjà vu from my childhood. Grandfather said the only way to talk to Peepo was with confidence…but if only half of the stories Grandfather told me about Peepo were true…"

"Probably all of them," Mason replied. "She was one of the greatest merc commanders ever. Still is. The battlefield got a lot safer for everyone else when she retired. Employers have offered her a shitload of credits to come out of retirement and lead their troops, but she has always refused."

"Why is that?"

"No one knows," Mason replied, his eyes continuing to move about the room. "I'm sure she has her reasons, but she has never told anyone what they are. Not that I've ever heard anyway."

A robot approached the table. "Your beverage," it said, handing a frosty mug to Mason. "It's on the house."

The robot turned to depart, revealing Breetar, who had used the robot's approach as cover. The alien hopped into the chair along the wall next to Nigel, where he was hidden from the view of most patrons.

"Did Peepo tell you anything new?" Breetar asked.

"No," Mason replied. "Although she did mention something cryptic about the possibility of information being obtained here for a price."

"Do you suppose she was talking about something in particular?" Nigel asked. "Or was that just her general thoughts on the transactions that occur here?"

"I don't know," Mason replied; "either is possible."

"Do you suppose she tapes conversations in here?" Nigel asked. "If she did, she may very well know what's going on."

"There are probably more cameras here than most banks or high-security prisons have," Breetar said. "Our speech is probably being recorded and continually analyzed for stress and any number of significant keywords."

"So I should watch what I say?"

"Without a doubt." Breetar's head popped up. "He's here!" he exclaimed. "The merc that hired me is here!"

"Where, damn it?" Mason asked.

"The Besquith that just walked in from the back rooms. He's headed toward the bar. Shit! Don't let it see me!"

"Fuck!" Mason barked under his breath. "Hate those motherfuckers."

"Besquith?" Nigel asked, his eyes darting back and forth from alien to alien at the bar. He didn't know what a Besquith was, but didn't like the reactions it was receiving.

"Big, hairy, wolf-looking thing headed toward the bar," Mason said. "Look toward the Oogar and to the left. Mean as all shit."

Nigel's eye's opened wide as he found the alien. "Big" didn't cover it. The alien was enormous, standing at least six feet tall with broad shoulders and long arms that ended in huge claws; it looked like something out of a nightmare. Its mouth hung open slightly, exposing a huge jaw full of the biggest teeth Nigel had seen. They probably would have been the envy of most of Earth's sharks.

"I see it," Nigel said. "It looks like it could eat granny in a single bite."

"No shit," Mason replied. "It probably would, too. Their digestive systems can break down a huge percentage of the galaxy's life forms, and there isn't a race that most of them wouldn't try. The things are ferocious; it doesn't matter if it's a fight or a trade negotiation, intimidation is one of their favorite tactics."

"I'll bet it works," Nigel said, trying to hide a shudder. He looked out of the corner of his eye and could see Breetar cowering under the lip of the table.

"Yeah, it—don't move!" Mason exclaimed.

Nigel looked back to the Besquith and saw the creature had its head held high. It sniffed the air, its nostrils wide, turning its head back and forth, looking for the source of the scent it had picked up.

The Besquith's head stopped rotating as it zeroed in on the smell and its head slowly turned to look at...Nigel. Nigel's heart missed a beat as the alien's lips pulled back from its teeth; they were even larger and sharper than he had imagined. The beast gathered itself and sprang toward him!

Events seemed to slow in Nigel's sight as the beast charged. Mason pushed away from the table, his gun already free of its holster as he rose. Nigel also rose, but bumped into the table and fell backward into his chair.

"*Pew—crack!*" Breetar was the first to fire, but his shot went high and right of the sprinting alien, and the hypervelocity slug blew a hole through the wall on the other side of the bar.

Mason realized he didn't have time to fire and dove at the Besquith, but the creature bolted to the left, vaulted an empty table, and smashed through the door of the establishment.

"Quick!" Mason yelled. "After it!"

The three raced to the door to find the Besquith already a long way ahead of them, a trail of aliens on the ground in its wake.

"*Pew—crack!*" Breetar's pistol fired again and the Besquith went down, crashing out of control into a large group of GenSha, massive creatures that resembled large bison and weighed nearly a ton in standard gravity.

They also didn't move very quickly, and Nigel's group arrived to find two of them jumbled up with the Besquith in a tangle of claws, hooves, and teeth as it tried to break free. Before Nigel could do anything, a third GenSha sat down on the Besquith's head and a fourth on one of the Besquith's legs, effectively pinning it to the ground.

"Does this creature belong to you?" roared one of the GenSha in a deep voice as it sat on the Besquith's head.

"Uh, yeah, sort of, I guess," Nigel said. The Besquith had ceased struggling and gone limp. "Maybe you should get up before you kill him."

"He has caused a number of injuries to my friends. Who is going to pay for their treatment? Are you?"

"Um, well, you see, I don't have a lot of money at the moment…"

"Oh, for the love of Golban!" Breetar squeaked, pulling a pouch from his belt. "Here! There are enough credits in here to pay for all of your bills as well as plenty left over. Just get off the stupid thing before you kill it."

Breetar handed the money pouch to the lead GenSha, who got up, then Breetar came to stand next to Nigel. "I can't believe I'm saving a Besquith's life," he said, looking up at Nigel. "You owe me for what I just paid him, plus interest. A lot of interest."

"Did you have to shoot him though?" Nigel asked. "What if he's dead?"

"Oh, he's not dead. I shot him in the leg. That's probably going to be broken, and maybe separated from his body, but I didn't kill him. He's probably just unconscious; I would be if one of those things farted in my face."

Nigel looked up. "Umm, the cow things may be gone, but we seem to be attracting a lot of other attention." Not only was everyone walking by looking at them, some of the aliens had also stopped to watch.

"Keep moving!" Mason yelled. "We're bounty hunters completing a contract!" He rolled the Besquith over, and Nigel could see the creature's leg was definitely broken; a piece of bone stuck through its hide. "Give me a hand, Nigel," Mason said with a grunt as he shifted the creature prior to lifting it. "This damn thing weighs a fucking ton, and I doubt the rodent is going to be much help."

"'The rodent' is the only reason the Besquith didn't get away," Breetar said. "Perhaps you should shut your mouth before 'the rodent' shoots you too."

"Stop it, both of you," Nigel said. He helped shoulder the body. Mason had about 200 pounds of it…which still left another 100 unwieldy pounds for Nigel. "Oof…damn thing…is heavy. Where…where do we have to go…with it?"

"There's a hotel I know nearby that doesn't ask a lot of questions. We can take it there and have the platoon's medic come meet us, along with a couple platoon members. We're going to need some gear to restrain it."

* * * * *

Chapter Fifteen

Hotel Crash and Burn, Orbital Transfer Station, Karma VI

"That's the best I can do," Corporal Cindy 'Shrewlet' Epard said. "I'm a *human medic*, not some sort of exo-species veterinarian."

The Besquith lay strapped to the bed in the ill-kept flophouse. It was the only choice; there was no other furniture in the tiny room. Faded stains covered the floor, the walls, and the bed in a variety of sizes, colors, and shapes; Nigel really didn't want to know what most of them were. The latest ones were blood stains from the Besquith on the bed. Mason had tipped the hotel staff substantially, though, and had said the staff wouldn't mind the blood stains, as long as no blood leaked through the floorboards into the room below.

Nigel didn't want to know how Mason knew that, either.

"Is it going to live?" Mason asked.

"I think so," Shrewlet said. "Most of the major damage was confined to its right leg. Whatever hit it tore out a big chunk of meat, shattered the bone, and almost tore it right off. If it had hit the bone, it probably would have. I can't fix the bone—that's going to take some reconstructive surgery or time in the regen tank—but I did set it where the shards are all mostly aligned and sprayed it with the nanite med spray. There are some other signs of trauma, although they're a lot more minor than the leg wound. What did you say it was called?"

"It's a Besquith," Mason replied.

"Well, the med spray is certified to work on over 500 species. If 'Besquith' is one of them, he should be all right in a while. He's going to hurt like a son of a bitch when he wakes up, but he isn't going to die. I don't think so, anyway."

"Okay, thanks," Mason said. "Did you give him a stimulant?"

"Yeah, he should be awake shortly."

"Great. Why don't you go join the rest of the squad outside?" Even Nigel could tell from the tone of voice it wasn't a request.

The trooper departed, leaving Nigel, Mason, and Breetar alone with the Besquith. It wasn't long before the creature started moving, and its eyes popped open.

"I look forward to eating your young," it growled.

"Hurts, don't it?" Mason asked. He sat down on the bed, and the Besquith flinched and growled as its leg shifted. "Oops, sorry." He smiled. "Here's the deal. We want to know who your employer is. If you tell us that, we'll let you go. Otherwise, I can't imagine that this conversation is going to be much fun for you." He leaned over, placing his left hand on the bandaged leg. "So, what's it going to be?"

The Besquith opened its mouth and howled.

Mason jammed his pistol into the beast's mouth, and the howl ceased.

"See now, there wasn't any need for that," Mason said as he removed the pistol and inspected it critically. "Now you've gone and gotten slobber on my pistol. Next time, I'll just shoot you and be done with it. I hate having to clean my pistol without actually getting to shoot someone with it first."

The Besquith surveyed the room as best it could while strapped to the bed, its eyes stopping on Breetar. "You're dead. When I get out of here, you're the first one I'm going to kill."

"Good luck with that," the Flatar replied. "You may not be aware, but things aren't looking so good for you at the moment."

"Things change," the Besquith said. "I'm going to eat you first."

"If you'd like, I can finish you now," Breetar said. "I'm the one who shot you; I can certainly do it again." He hopped onto the bed and drew his pistol. "It won't hurt. Much."

The Besquith shifted and lunged, its giant mouth open, but Breetar jumped back nimbly. "You're going to have to be faster than that."

"Okay, this is fun and all, but we don't have a lot of time," Nigel said. "Just tell us who hired you, and we'll be on our way."

"Yes, must go save your sister, right?"

"What do you know about that?"

"Oh, nothing. Just that your time is running out. If you're not there soon, she will be dead."

"Why is that? Why are you doing this?"

"Me? I'm not doing anything, and I have no idea. Nor do I care. I was hired to do something and I did it, unlike the Flatar here. I've changed my mind...must be the pain...if you let me go now, I won't kill you. Well, except for the Flatar. He dies. No one shoots me and gets away with it. And he broke his word, so he's going to have to die for that, too. But the rest of you can leave. If you go now."

"Tell me who hired you, and we will."

"I don't know."

Mason leaned a little harder on the bandaged leg. "I think you do," he said.

The Besquith gasped and squinted its eyes. "Okay...Mason," the creature said with a grunt, "you're dead, too."

Mason flinched backward. "You know me?"

"Of course, you stupid bastard. Both of our companies were hired to track down the F11 thief on Septan-7. I was a squad leader for the group that brought him back, or what was left of him, anyway. I believe your company was still wandering around in the forest for several days after that. I'm sure it was just because the view was good, and not due to your utter lack of competence."

"I remember you now, you sick bastard. What you guys did to him was..." his voice trailed off and Mason chewed on his lip, thinking. "Let's see....your name was… Brel-Al?"

"It still is. That was a nice contract to collect on. Too bad you didn't get any of the payout because you were lost in the jungle."

"Well, you little asshole," Mason said, slapping the bandage on the Besquith's leg, hard. "It's *so* good to see you again. I didn't recognize the pelt, but I should have recognized the smell."

"Oh, don't worry; I recognized your scent immediately. Failure. It suits you. I'm not surprised you're helping this loser." Brel-Al nodded toward Nigel.

"Enough of this shit," Nigel interrupted. "You two can discuss old times later. If you won't tell us who your employer is, how about telling us where Amanda Spivey is being held?"

"Who is that?" Brel-Al asked.

"She's the daughter of one of my employees. You have been using her as leverage to get the employee to do what you wanted."

"Oh, is that her name? When I last saw her, they were calling her something else."

"What's that?"

"Dinner."

Nigel leaned forward and put his elbow on the alien's bandaged leg and stared into Brel-Al's eyes. "By the mercy of God, if you have harmed her, I will track you down and make sure you die however she did."

"Good luck eating me. Our flesh is toxic to most of the other species in the galaxy."

Nigel stood up and leveled his pistol at the Besquith. "If you would like, I can do it right now…"

"Go ahead," the alien replied. "I don't think you have the guts."

Nigel flipped the safety off. "Oh, no?"

Mason waved a hand in Nigel's line of sight, distracting him. "If I may, sir?"

Nigel lowered the weapon. "Go ahead; I can always kill him later."

"Okay," Mason said, leaning forward again onto the alien's leg. "Here's the deal. Play time is pretty much over. Either you tell us what we want to know, or I'm going to let Breetar shoot you again. This close, it will probably tear off whatever he shoots. Maybe a foot…maybe a hand…something that gives you a little time to think while you bleed out. Just like you did to the thief on Septan-7. So, what's it going to be? Who hired you?"

The Besquith shut its mouth with an audible snap. Mason leaned down harder on the Besquith's leg with an elbow.

"I…don't…know," he ground out.

"*Who hired you?*" Nigel yelled.

"I…don't …know!"

"If you don't know who he is, describe him. What race is he?"

"I…don't …know!"

"*Hey guys,*" Turk called over the platoon's radio frequency. "*I don't know what you're doing in there, but you better hurry up. There is a pla-*

toon of Lumar forming up out here, led by a Jivool. Looks like some of the pass-ers-by are pointing you out."

"Meet us around back," Mason replied. *"We don't have time to go through a security interview."*

"Okay," Mason said; "it's going to get crowded in here fast. Time to go." He pushed down the Besquith's leg to get up, eliciting another growl.

"I know the Jivool is a giant bear-like thing, but what are Lumar?" Nigel asked.

"Big four-armed humanoids that like to brawl. They're not particularly bright or fast, but they're burly as hell and awfully tough in close quarters."

"Like here."

"Yeah."

"Should I kill him?" Breetar asked.

"Nah," Mason said. "I didn't tip the staff enough to get rid of a body or fill in the hole in the wall your pistol will make."

"Too bad," Breetar said, spinning the pistol once and sliding it into a holster on his belt. "I'll have to kill you another time." He bounced down off the bed.

"Only if the Blood Drinkers don't kill you first," the Besquith replied.

"They're entering the hotel," Turk reported. *"Better hurry!"*

"Let's go!" Mason ordered. "Follow me!"

"See you soon!" the Besquith said.

Mason ran out the door with Nigel and Breetar following close behind. As Nigel went through the door, he could hear a commotion from downstairs.

"This way!" Mason urged, going in the opposite direction. He went to the last door on the right and tried the handle. Locked.

Mason stepped back and kicked the door where it latched. It sprang inward with a crash, startling the…creatures…on the bed. There were tentacles everywhere and at least four bodies Nigel could see in the writhing mass.

"Don't stop for me," Mason said as he crossed the room to a wardrobe against the back wall, notable in that it was the only non-bed furniture Nigel had seen in the hotel. Mason gave the wardrobe a shove and it slid to the side, revealing a small door. He looked back toward the bed and shuddered, then turned back to the door. "Let's go," he said over his shoulder as he vanished into the darkness.

So'Kla's Ship, Orbital Transfer Station, Karma VI

"I'm the last," Mason said as he came onboard. They had raced back to the ship with the Lumar in pursuit. Happily, the Lumar were better barroom bouncers and brawlers than they were sprinters. "Tell the flight station to detach and get us the hell out of here."

"I told them," Corporal Vitali reported. "The Jehas want to know where we're supposed to be heading, and if Mr. Nigel agrees to our early departure."

"Yes, I agree!" Nigel exclaimed. "Tell them to get going ASAP and head for the stargate."

"The Jehas want to know what 'a sap' is. It's their understanding that sap moves slowly from trees. Especially during springtime."

"Just tell them to get going *right fucking now*, or we're all going to be in big trouble. Tell them security is coming for us, and they're going to get the foam treatment if we stay here one second longer!"

"The flight station says we are detaching now and will make for the stargate at the ship's best speed. They recommend securing all lose articles and getting strapped into your acceleration couches within the next five minutes, or you will become one with the bulkhead."

"That's better."

"Where are we going?" Mason asked. "Unless I was listening to a different conversation than you, we didn't get the info we were looking for. I hope you're not planning on heading for Moorhouse."

"No, we didn't get the info we were looking for on who hired Brel-Al. But we did get *some* info from him."

"What's that?"

"I think we know who's guarding Moorhouse."

"I'm sorry, I must have missed that while restraining my xenocidal urges to kill the bastard. When did he tell us who was guarding Moorhouse?"

"Remember when Breetar said he'd have to kill Brel-Al another time? Brel-Al said something like 'Only if the Blood Drinkers don't kill you first.' Who are the Blood Drinkers?"

"Oh, entropy," Breetar replied. "That's a Besquith merc unit. I've heard of them. They don't work or play well with others. They usually only take contracts where they're allowed to kill and dismember their enemies. The people who've worked with them say their unit's name isn't symbolic; they usually *do* drink the blood of their enemies…and often while they're still alive."

"Yeah, Breetar's right," Mason said. "That's who Brel-Al was with on Septan-7. The Blood Drinkers. What they did to the thief once they caught him…I saw pictures because the company we were working for wanted to make sure no one else got any ideas about stealing from them. They wanted everyone to see what happened to him…the pictures were everywhere; it was inescapable. I still have nightmares about that."

"So Brel-Al was a Blood Drinker?" Nigel asked.

"Yeah, he was when we were on Septan-7 anyway; I don't know if he still is."

"Huh. That complicates things."

"What do you mean?"

"Well, I thought that Brel-Al was saying the Drinkers would kill us when we attacked Moorhouse, meaning they were the ones who had killed my family and were now garrisoning it."

"What changed?"

"Well, if Brel-Al is still a member of the organization, maybe he was talking about them coming after us for revenge on what we did to him."

"We should have killed him," Breetar noted.

"Yeah, we probably should have," Mason said, nodding his head. "But we would have had a harder time leaving the station; they probably would have locked down our ship. Also, we wouldn't have been able to go back there again. As the majority of the merc contracts in this arm go through Karma VI, Nigel would have had a hard time getting work in the future."

"Either way, I wish I knew what Brel-Al meant when he said that the Drinkers would kill Breetar."

"I agree with your earlier assessment, sir," Mason said. "They must be waiting for us at Moorhouse."

"Why's that?"

"Well, first of all, there's no profit in going after Breetar. No matter how big a pain in the ass he is—"

"Pain in the ass?" Breetar squeaked. "Me?"

"Yeah, you." Mason turned back to Nigel. "No matter how big a pain in the ass he is, there isn't any money in killing him. Sure, they might put out a contract on him, maybe, but they're not going to go out of their way to find him and kill him. If they happened to be in the same place, they might kill him, but there's no business case for tracking him down. If Brel-Al thought that the Drinkers were going to kill him, he meant they'd do it on Moorhouse."

"Perfect," Nigel said; "that's just what I was hoping you'd say."

"What? You still intend to go after Moorhouse, now that you know the Drinkers are there? Are you crazy? There may be other units I want to fight less, but there aren't many of them. And even if I decided to go against them, there's no profit in hitting them on Moorhouse. They're wily; they will have a plan to kill your sister as soon as we show up. There's no way we can save your sister. There may be some merc outfits we could hit and get her back, but if it's the Drinkers? Forget it, she's dead. We might as well cut our losses and return to Earth."

"I know a way we can hit them and not get Parisa killed," Nigel stated.

"It can't be done." Mason stated flatly.

"Oh, I think it can," Nigel said with a smile.

"Please, sir, awe me with your mighty depth and breadth of merc knowledge. Show me how, on Day 1 of your merc career, you know more than I do, and you can do things I say are impossible. Please. Wow me."

"Okay, I will," Nigel's smile faded. "It all starts with the initial garrisoning of Moorhouse. How much do you know about that?"

"None. I was on another planet; I only heard about it when your father got killed."

"Not only was the garrison contract hard for Asbaran because we generally don't do much garrisoning and don't have the gear, it was also hard because of the size of the contract. The contract was for four companies of troops. I know; I looked at the contract before we left."

"So?"

"So, it was bigger than most contracts we ever take. Most merc outfits aren't bigger than a couple of companies. Asbaran is no different; we normally only have two standing companies of troops; we had to hire an additional two companies to meet the specifications of the contract. This was obviously meant to draw in all of my family; we would have wanted to save money by leading the units ourselves, but Father didn't initially send any of the family."

"So they weren't able to kill any of you," Mason added.

"No, although the garrison was lost," Nigel sighed. "I don't know how the Drinkers, if indeed it was them, were able to overwhelm them, but somehow they did. I suspect they used some sort of trickery; hell, they may have had plants in the additional two companies of mercs we had to hire. I don't know how they did it, but they did, and now they are in place to complete the contract themselves."

"Wait. The enemy in place on Moorhouse is going to get paid? You mean the Drinkers are going to fulfill the contract?"

"I suspect so. The contract was to ensure the safety of the red diamond processing plant there. The contract had verbiage in it that allowed the contract to be assumed by other parties, as long as operations at the plant weren't disrupted."

"Red diamonds?"

"After F11 and maple syrup, red diamonds are the third most valuable resource in the galaxy. They can't be reproduced in a lab, and only exist in extremely small quantities on a handful of planets. Moorhouse happens to be one of them; the plant there has a deep core miner and processes what is harvested. If the Besquith didn't destroy the plant in the assault, they could have taken over the contract in place of Asbaran and would get paid at the end of it. There's a huge price tag for completing the contract, too."

"And once they captured the planet?"

Nigel shrugged. "I'm sure it was easy after that. They would have known from Spivey how many troops were coming and what their assault plan was. They would have had defenses in place and would have been ready for them. It would have been easy to shoot them all down. Parisa must have done something unexpected, though, because she was able to make it to the planet. She always was smarter than my brother."

"Why didn't they just kill her then, too?"

"They must have been afraid I wouldn't come. After everyone else failed, I would have been tempted to write off the contract and cut our losses. Holding her for a ransom I didn't have is the only way they could get me there too."

"But why do they want you *there*? What do they hope to gain from it? There must be some business decision that this supports. Companies don't do things this big without a reason…something that will favorably affect the bottom line of their financial reports."

"I don't know. Maybe we'll find out when we get there."

"*What?* You expect to take on *four companies* of Besquith with a company of troops in older model CASPers? *Do you have a freaking death wish?*"

"No, I do not have a death wish," Nigel replied calmly. "And who said anything about taking on four companies of Besquith? Not initially anyway."

"What do you mean?"

"Remember I said that we had to hire additional troops to garrison Moorhouse?"

"Yeah."

"I'll bet they did too," Nigel said, "and that means their home base is wide open. Or at least wide open enough that a company of troops with late model CASPers can take it."

Realization dawned on Mason's face, followed by skepticism. "I see where you're going sir, but that just isn't done. Mercs don't hit other mercs' bases like that."

"They haven't before," Nigel replied, "which is why they'll never expect us to do it now."

* * * * *

Chapter Sixteen

So'Kla's Ship, Approaching the Free Trading Station, Grbow III

"How much time do we have left before they execute your sister?" Mason asked.

"Just over three weeks. Counting transit times, it's going to be close."

"If time is so short, why did we come here? Don't you think it's time to let the rest of us in on your plan?" Mason asked. "We might be able to support you better if we knew what it was we were trying to accomplish."

"Yeah, it's time," Nigel agreed; "I just needed to work some things through in my own mind before I discussed them openly."

"You mean, like how we're going to get away with hitting a merc base? That would be a good start."

"Well, I know how we're going to get away with it; it has already been done before."

"What do you mean?"

"About 20 years ago, Cartwright's Cavaliers got a contract to remove some mercs that had gone native. The other company was originally brought in to provide security, but then decided it was easier to stay and extort 'protection' fees from the local populace than it was to go find a new contract."

"That happens, sometimes," Mason allowed.

"Yeah, well the Cavaliers got called in to remove them. Thaddeus Cartwright ghosted in and killed their entire command staff. When the new staff didn't get the message, he did it again. After that, the rest of the group packed up and left. My intention is to do something similar to the Drinkers. We ghost in, wipe out whatever is at their home base, and take whatever intel we can find about their setup on Moorhouse."

"Still looking for your edge?" Mason asked.

"I am. We're still going to be way outnumbered on Moorhouse, even if we can get in there unscathed. We need something to even the odds."

"Okay, so how are we going to ghost into their base, which I believe is located *on their home planet,* and do all that shit?"

"We're going to have to…um…borrow a ship to get there."

"*Borrow* a ship?" Mason asked. "That doesn't sound completely legal."

"It's not going to be."

"I like it already!" Breetar exclaimed. "You guys were starting to bore me. Tell me more!"

"The reason we came here to Grbow is that it's the closest trading base to the Besquith's home world of Bestald. I hope to find a ship going there, take it over, and use it as our assault ship."

"A Besquith ship?" Breetar asked.

"What do you mean?" Nigel replied.

"Well, most mercenary races usually aren't traders, and vice versa. The Besquith are different. They are both mercs *and* traders. We may be able to find a Besquith ship here going to Bestald."

"It would be helpful if it were a Besquith ship," Nigel replied. "That would simplify what to do with the crew of the ship. Once we're done with it, we dump it into a star, and no one will be the wiser."

"Okay," Mason said, "I see how that *might* work, and I do mean *might*. However, there are a number of things that could go wrong. How do you intend to get aboard? They're never going to let humans aboard their ship."

"We're going to need Breetar's help with that…and we'll probably need to hire a few other mercenaries for the assault on Bestald."

"Hire a few mercenaries to hit the Besquith home world?" Mason asked. "Who'd be dumb enough to do that?"

"I don't know, Nigel said, "but judging from your reactions when we discussed them earlier, I'm betting there are a lot of folks who don't like the Besquith in general and the Drinkers in specific. Maybe a few of them would like to participate in a smash-and-grab operation. I'm not interested in stealing from the Besquith; whatever they find, they can keep."

"Awesome!" Breetar exclaimed. "An opportunity for maximum carnage, a chance for treasure, *and* we get to kill all the Besquith we want in the process? I'm in. I don't know who'll be around on Grbow, but I know a number of folks who'd be interested in an operation like that. Let's face it; who wouldn't want to kill some Besquith?"

Luscious Libations, Gravity Ring, Free Trading Station, Grbow III

"See any likely candidates?" Nigel asked, looking around the bar. Unlike the outpost at Karma VI, which was a merc guild base, Grbow-3 was a

Trader's Guild base, and the races populating the station's biggest bar were representative of that difference. Duplato and Zuparti traders took the place of human and Tortantula mercs, and the clientele were not as tough-looking, although most seemed to be armed.

Many of the groups also had at least one member who was obviously there for security, including one group that had a MinSha standing nearby. The creature looked like an oversize bipedal praying mantis with iridescent blue chitin. Nigel had never seen one in real life before, and he felt shivers down his spine every time its ruby-red compound eyes swept across him. Creepy.

"I don't see anyone I know, unfortunately," Mason replied. "The main security force for the station is another group of Lumar, and I've never served with any of them. They're not the best troops so they get the shit jobs like guarding stations. We're more likely to find someone doing personal security."

"I've never served with any of the Lumar either," Breetar said, "and I don't see anyone I recognize. We probably don't want to stay much longer though; we're starting to get some looks."

"Why's that?" Nigel asked.

"Well, we're obviously not traders, especially since Flatar and humans don't trade that much, so we look out of place. The longer we sit here, the more attention we'll attract. As we don't want anyone to remember us, we'll need to leave soon. Maybe we can check out some of the other bars. I know this one bar where—hang on, there's a Tortantula walking in I recognize. She is *just* the person we're looking for. You guys head outside and I'll go invite her to join us."

Breetar jumped down from his seat and headed in the direction of the enormous spider analogue.

"Think he's okay?" Nigel asked.

"Probably more so than either of us," Mason replied, getting up. He raised his voice a little to be heard by the neighboring tables. "C'mon, let's go. This place sucks."

Nigel followed him out of the bar and to a side alley where Breetar and the Tortantula joined them a couple of minutes later. On seeing the humans waiting, the Tortantula drew two pistols and pointed one at each. "What is the meaning of this?" the creature asked. "What are *they* doing here?"

"These are the employers I told you about," Breetar said, coming to stand in front of the alien. Even on his tip toes, he couldn't block the enormous spider's pistols. Both humans raised their hands. "They're okay," he added.

"You didn't tell me your employers were humans," the Tortantula said. The pistols didn't flinch. "I didn't think you worked with humans."

"I haven't before," the Flatar admitted, "but these two are kind of fun, despite what you hear about them. They have a proposal I think would be right up your alley."

"There's a good opportunity to make some credits on it," Nigel said.

"Even better, the operation is a chance for wholesale slaughter," Breetar added. "Kill everything that moves and take their shit. Best of all, it's killing Besquith. All the ones you can find."

The Tortantula holstered her pistols. "Wholesale slaughter?" she asked. "Name's Zzeldar. I'm in. I could probably find a few others of my kind on the station who would be interested, too."

"Don't you want to know what it pays?" Nigel asked.

"Not particularly," Zzeldar replied. "If Breetar is in, it must be a paid gig, and there must be a plan to get back out again. I'm just in it for the destruction factor. Do we get to blow shit up, as well, or just shoot every Besquith we see?"

"Does it matter?" Mason asked.

"Not really," Zzeldar said. "I just want to know what equipment to bring."

Loading Bay A-12, Free Trading Station, Grbow III

"*M*ove up!*"* Mason radioed, *"but stay under cover!"*

Nigel checked the progress of the platoon as it advanced from one stack of crates to another across the crowded loading bay. The men and women of the platoon had assembled outside the dock after transiting the station in groups of twos and threes to avoid attracting unwanted attention. They had also left their CASPers behind on their ship for the same reason. Although Nigel had been worried about the loss of combat capability, Mason had assured him they would be all right without the CASPers for this operation.

Mason had asked Nigel to remain at the back of the formation to provide overwatch for the platoon, so he had a great vantage point from which to observe the advance. While Mason's request had seemed legitimate at the time, Nigel could now see it was meant to keep him behind the lines and out of harm's way. Or to keep him from screwing things up; he wasn't sure which. Probably both.

"And no explosives either here or in the ship!" Mason ordered. *"Got that, Zzeldar?"*

"We know," the Tortantula replied. She didn't sound happy about it.

Nigel decided he liked the overwatch duty. The action was his first combat experience, and he knew he didn't have the training required to direct the tactical action of the unit. Yet. He also didn't particularly want to be in the middle of a firefight, anyway; he just wanted to be close enough to learn the tactics involved while he directed the strategic goals. This time.

The platoon followed about 50 feet behind the three Tortantulas as they navigated the maze of stacked boxes and crates on the loading bay deck. Zzeldar operated the controls of the pallet jack she walked behind while the other two marched alongside, weapons drawn, as if guarding the crate it carried.

Mason followed closest behind, no more than 30 feet behind the crate, darting from cover to cover. He was followed in turn by the other 19 members of First Platoon, then Nigel and the two new pilots. Zzeldar had been a great addition to the team; not only had she known someone in the security force who could disable the loading bay's security cameras, she had also brought the two pilots to the team.

Brown five-foot-tall humanoids, the two Pendals followed in Nigel's shadow as if planning to use him for cover. They wore matching brown capes with large hoods that hid their faces. From what Nigel had seen of their faces, he was happy to have them out of sight; with two independently-tracking eyes on either side of a gaping central mouth, and a third eye above it, they were just plain creepy. Mason had told him the Pendals were excellent pilots due in part to their second set of arms that let them manipulate several controls simultaneously. That remained to be seen.

"Hold up," Mason transmitted. *"Get ready; here we go."*

Nigel peeked around the stack of crates he was hiding behind, and he could see the Tortantulas had reached the loading ramp of the ungainly looking freighter. Built for hauling the maximum amount of cargo, it was long and blocky, with a little bit of tapering in the front to allow it to operate more efficiently in atmosphere. A guard could be seen at the bottom of the ramp leading to the cargo bay, and another at the ramp leading up to the crew compartment.

"Who are you guys?" the Besquith at the cargo bay ramp asked as the procession approached.

Nigel jumped at the voice in his ear, but then realized the Tortantulas had turned on their radios so the platoon could hear the exchange.

"We're delivering the cargo your captain purchased," Zzeldar replied, sounding bored. She worked the controls of the pallet jack, and the crate settled to the deck.

"I don't know anything about a delivery," the guard said. "I'll have to check it out."

"Okay," Zzeldar replied, "just don't use your radio. This box is full of explosives, and I really don't want you to set them off while we're still here. Please feel free to do so after we leave, though. Give us about five minutes to get clear of the blast radius."

"No radio?"

"Nah, this is a shipment of the new mines your captain ordered. These babies are sensitive to radio transmissions, so when your enemy tries to communicate nearby, boom! There's a block of K2 explosive in each of them; if they all go off at once, you're looking at an explosion that will wipe out a couple of miles of this station."

"*What?* Aren't those illegal? How did you get them aboard this station?"

"I told you; they're a new type of mine, and they don't look like mines. They're for your conflict with the humans."

"Really, I heard that was going well—Hey! What do you know about that?"

"The thing about operating cargo lifts is you always know what's going on. Logistics, you know? Who's getting the new stuff for the win and who is underprepared and going to get wiped out."

Zzeldar looked at her data pad. "Sorry, I'd love to stay and talk, but we're running behind schedule. The boss has already docked my pay once this week for being late, and I can't afford to let that happen again. Hundreds of little mouths to feed, you know? We were supposed to load these for you because they have some special handling procedures to protect them from kinetic detonation, but if it's going to be a while for authorization, we'll just leave them here." Zzeldar turned to leave. "C'mon, girls, the sooner we put a couple of miles between us and these things, the better I'll like it."

"Wait!" the Besquith guard shouted. "How do I know this is real? No one told me live ordnance was coming."

"Quiet!" Zzeldar replied in a stage whisper as the other two Tortantulas skittered away from the crate. "Too many loud noises and they'll detonate!"

"Well, I want to see them, to make sure they really are mines. Open the crate."

The two 'guard' Tortantulas jumped away from the crate again. "Not while I'm nearby," one said.

"Out here?" Zzeldar asked, overriding her companion. "Are you crazy? With all of the radio transmission going on out here, the entire *lot* of them will detonate if I open the box out here. It's probably safe enough inside to open it and show you, but there's no *way* I'm doing it out here."

The Besquith looked around for help, saw the other guard at the personnel ramp, and waved him over.

"What's going on?" the new guard growled.

The first guard pulled the newcomer away for privacy, but the Tortantula's microphones were sensitive enough to pick up the conversation.

"These cargo handlers say they're delivering a new set of mines for our operation with the humans," the first guard said.

"They're not supposed to know about that."

"I know, but somehow they've heard. Their leader says the cargo crews always know first, because they see the logistics involved."

"We're going to have to let the captain know."

"I agree…but what should we do with the mines? They say there's special loading instructions for getting them aboard without setting them off."

"Are you sure they're mines?"

"We can't open it out here or the radio transmissions will set them off. They're anti-personnel mines that are armed by radio."

The second guard turned to look back at the Tortantulas milling about by the crate for several seconds, before turning back to the first guard.

"While I wouldn't put it past the Tortantulas to develop illegal mines or sneak them aboard the station, I'd like to see them before I let them walk away. I also don't feel like having to do the work of loading them onto the ship. I'll go aboard with the loader and have him open up the crate inside. You stand guard over the two that are left behind."

The Besquith returned to where the Tortantulas waited. All three were shuffling their multitude of feet and edging away from the crate.

"Okay, we'll take it," the second Besquith said. He pointed a rifle at Zzeldar. "You're going to take it up nice and easy and stow it where I tell you, and then you're going to open it up. Your friends can wait down here. If everything's legit you can be on your way."

"Fine, fine," Zzeldar said. "Can we at least get going? I'm now late for my next delivery."

The Besquith motioned toward the ramp with his rifle. "Be my guest."

With a noise the translation device turned into a "harrumph," Zzeldar worked her control pad, and the pallet lifted and started toward the ramp into the cargo compartment.

One of the other Tortantulas moved as if to follow, and the first guard stepped in front, his rifle almost pointing at the giant spider. "You stay here with me," the Besquith said, and the Tortantula moved back to where she had been.

The Besquith's rifle remained pointed near the Tortantula; it wouldn't take much to bring it into a firing position.

Nigel looked over to Mason's position. The trooper was already easing his rifle over the top of the crate he was hiding behind.

"That's good right there," the Besquith in the cargo compartment said. "Now open it up."

Two muted shots from a laser pistol could be heard from the cargo compartment. Before the second one was heard, Mason had already fired and dropped the Besquith at the ramp.

"*Let's go!*" Mason ordered, breaking cover to lead the advance. The other Tortantulas were already halfway up the ramp, and they disappeared inside the ship before Mason could take another step. *"First Squad, cargo bay! Second Squad up the personnel ramp! Last two people grab the Besquith!"*

Nigel joined in the charge, as additional muted shots could be heard from the interior of the ship. He glanced over his shoulder; the Pendal pilots were just beginning to advance and seemed in no hurry to be part of the action. Screw them.

Nigel raced over to the personnel ramp but was caught behind the troopers struggling to lug the dead Besquith up the cargo ramp. Reaching the interior, he was faced with whether to go right toward the forward portion of the ship or left toward the cargo compartment.

"Cargo compartment clear!" Turk reported. *"Four tangos down back here."*

Nigel turned to the right.

"Clear forward!" Mason transmitted. *"Five tangos here."*

Nigel hesitated, now unsure which way to go. It sounded like the action had already ended.

"Ship's clear," Mason added confirming the assessment. *"Everyone assemble in the cargo compartment. Turk, call Second Platoon and have them move up."*

Nigel moved out of the way to let the troopers coming from the cockpit go past, then fell into trail behind Mason as the two Pendal pilots glided past him going in the opposite direction.

"Nine enemy down?" Nigel asked. "I thought there were 10 onboard."

"Nine plus the one outside *is* 10," Mason replied.

"Is combat always that fast?" Nigel's eyes swept the corridor, looking for additional enemies. He found he couldn't keep himself from talking. The adrenaline was flowing, and his body screamed at him to run…to shoot…to do *something!*

"That was hardly combat," Mason said. "Damned spiders had already killed everyone before we made it aboard. You want killing machines; that's them. Besides, this is a freighter. There aren't that many places for a Besquith to hide onboard. It's just engines, a cargo hold, and basic living quarters."

Mason sighed. "This was the easy part," he added. "The real combat comes next."

* * * * *

Chapter Seventeen

Captain's Cabin, Besquith Ship *Beheader*, Approaching Bestald

Zzeldar appeared in the doorway but didn't enter the crowded compartment. She couldn't. Nigel and Mason sat on the bed, one of the Pendals sat in the desk chair, Breetar stretched out across the desk, and several other members of the platoon's staff filled the remaining floor space of the tiny cabin.

"I take it you called us here to tell us how you're going to get into the Blood Drinkers' base?" Zzeldar asked.

"Yeah," Nigel replied. "It's really pretty simple, though. We fly in disguised as a routine transport ship, land at the Blood Drinkers' base, kill everyone there so there aren't any witnesses, download their files, and fly back out again."

"And?" Zzeldar asked from the doorway.

"What do you mean?"

"Can we get a little more detail?"

"That's pretty much it. We fly in, destroy everything, then fly out again."

Groans and expressions of disapproval filled the cabin.

"Surely you had some sort of plan when you vouched for him, right?" Zzeldar asked, turning her body toward Breetar to indicate to whom she was speaking. "If this is some kind of joke to piss off the Tortantula, I remain unamused. I was promised wholesale slaughter, not getting killed in transit. How are we supposed to get past their planetary defenses?"

Defenses? Nigel wondered how they expected him to know what the defenses would be. He could feel the tension in the air and see the combat veterans shaking their heads. As his eyes darted around the room, looking for assistance, he caught the look Mason gave Breetar. Based on Mason's expression, Nigel had erred. Badly.

"Well?" Zzeldar asked. Even through the translator, the alien sounded pissed.

Nigel leaned forward into Mason's line of sight and gave the mercenary commander a panicked look, silently begging for assistance.

After a second, Mason jumped and then nodded. "Okay," he said; "it looks like the joke has gone on long enough. Want me to brief the plan like we discussed?"

"Yes," Nigel replied, trying not to show the relief he felt. "Please go ahead."

Mason stood and scanned the room, meeting everyone's eyes in turn. "The biggest problem we have," he said, "is getting on and off the planet. Generally, they don't let foreigners onto Bestald, so we don't know what planetary defenses they have. We can probably talk our way down to the planet; the hard part is going to be getting back up to space again."

"Bioweapons," the Pendal said, his voice nothing more than a harsh whisper. Nigel realized with a shock it was the first time he had heard either of the Pendals speak. It was hard to see his mouth moving in the interior of the hood…but what he could see didn't appear to be in synch with the way the mouth was moving.

"What was that?" Mason asked.

"Bioweapons," the Pendal repeated in the same whisper. "If we claim a bioweapons accident, they will be very happy to get us off the planet."

"I don't know if they'll allow us to leave if there's an accident," Breetar disagreed. "Won't they want us to stay there until blame is assigned, and all fines paid in full?"

"Not if we have the accident on the way in," the Pendal whispered. "I have an idea."

The alien spoke for another five minutes, then the meeting broke up, with everyone much happier than they had been a few minutes previously.

"Thanks for the help," Nigel said when only Mason remained. "I had no idea what Zzeldar expected me to do about the planetary defenses."

"Happy to help," Mason said, "but most of the plan was the pilot's."

"Yeah, but he might not have spoken up if you hadn't said something first."

"Of course…but you did ask for help."

"What?"

"You stopped talking for a second, and I distinctly heard you say, 'Help.'"

"Well, I certainly wanted and needed help, but I didn't ask for it out loud."

"Huh, well, I don't know. I'm pretty sure I heard you ask me for help." He paused and then asked, "You're not psychic or something, are you, sir?"

"Not that I'm aware of." Nigel shrugged. "So, do you think the plan will work?"

"It depends on how paranoid the Besquith are."

"And how paranoid are they normally?"

"As a race? Probably more than any other."

"Damn."

Cockpit, Besquith Ship *Beheader*, Approaching Bestald

"How much longer?" Nigel asked, his eyes locked on the forward view screen. He had asked to watch the approach from the cockpit, and the Pendals had allowed him to sit in the jump seat at the back of the tiny compartment. Bestald's planetscape filled the screen, the dark green band around the planet's equator at the center.

"Soon," the copilot said without looking up from his instruments.

This was worse than his first combat, Nigel decided. Their conquest of the *Beheader* had happened quickly; there was almost no delay from inception to assault. Here, though, he had been forced to endure two long days of waiting while the planet slowly grew in the viewer…days where he had questioned everything they were about to do and his readiness to lead the mission.

Listening to his grandfather's stories as a young teenager, assaults on the enemy seemed so exciting. Death was something that happened, but usually only to the enemy. Of course he knew people died—there were plenty of stories about Uncle Jimmy's dropship failure, and the size of the crater it had made—but even that story was told from the perspective of how he had spectacularly accomplished the mission…not that he had perished doing it.

Nigel had relinquished command for this part of the mission to Mason. If he didn't know about something as basic as planetary defenses, what else didn't he know? Nigel had decided to follow the company into the command building. He was also taping every aspect of the attack so he could replay it later and hopefully learn something that would make him a better commander.

But that didn't help *now*, nor did it make the time pass any more quickly.

"*Approach, this is the* Beheader," the copilot transmitted. The Pendal's whispering voice sounded closer to normal on the radio. "*We are beginning our initial approach.*"

"*Understood,* Beheader," the approach controller confirmed. "*You are cleared to proceed to the Alpha-32 landing area.*"

"*Roger, we are proceeding to the Alpha-32 landing area.*" Having found a schematic in the cockpit of the planet's landing areas, the pilots knew where it was.

"Alpha-32?" Nigel asked, his mind suddenly drawing a blank. "Is that the one we wanted?"

"No, we asked for -17," the pilot said. "-32 puts us several hundred miles away from where we want to be."

"So what are we going to do? What *can* we do?"

"We have a backup plan," the copilot said.

"What is it?"

"No time to discuss it," the copilot replied, "and it would help us if you didn't interrupt." All four hands were a blur of motion, throwing levers, pushing buttons and inputting data into the ship's system.

"Um, okay," Nigel said. He sat back in his seat and tried to relax. Taking a few deep breaths didn't help; he found himself sitting at the edge of his seat again within moments.

The ship continued its approach to the target, marked with a triangle on the view screen. They were now close enough for Nigel to see the bare area of the Blood Drinkers' base, where it had been carved out of the jungle.

"It's time." The copilot noted.

"Agreed," the pilot said. "Proceed."

The copilot's hands stilled, and a single hand reached out to push a button on the right side of the control panel. Within seconds, a series of red lights illuminated on the instrument panel.

"*Mayday, mayday, mayday,*" the copilot transmitted. "Beheader *is declaring an emergency.*"

"*State the nature of your emergency,*" the approach controller replied.

"*Our engines are losing power, and we are unable to brake our descent. This is going to be messy.*"

"Messy?" Nigel asked from the jump seat in the back of the cockpit. "Is that some sort of aviation technical term?"

"It means we're going to crash," the pilot replied, turning slightly to look at Nigel with one eye. "Now please be quiet, sir. With the motors throttled back this far, we really *are* in danger of crashing the ship, and we need to concentrate." He turned back to his instruments and Nigel suppressed a shudder. He had no doubt that everything would work out if the Pendals were as good at piloting as they were at creeping him out.

"Beheader, *our system shows you impacting—I mean landing—near the Blood Drinkers' base. Can you confirm?*"

"*Roger, Approach, we're hoping to put it down there. Our cargo is headed there, anyway. We have some…uh, special weapons for them.*"

"Beheader, *please state the nature of the special weapons.*"

"Uh, I'm not sure what they are exactly. We're carrying five large canisters that the suppliers treated very carefully."

"What's in the canisters?"

"They are unmarked, so I don't know, but we were paid an awful lot of money to bring them here. If I were you, I'd evacuate the area surrounding the base; when we hit, it's going to contaminate a large part of the surroundings."

"Beheader, your clearance to land has been revoked. I say again, do NOT land on the planet. Return to orbit and await further instructions."

"Return to orbit!" the copilot exclaimed, his voice louder than Nigel had heard before. *"Haven't you been listening? We don't have enough power to land safely; how in the Great Rift do you expect us to abort?"*

There was a long pause before a new voice answered. *"Beheader, this is General Al-Kar. Do whatever you must, but do NOT land on the planet. You are cleared to jettison any other cargo you have or take whatever action you deem prudent, but do not land on Bestald. Do you understand?"*

"We understand, General, and will do our best to comply." The copilot reached out with a lower hand and pushed a button. Nigel caught movement and a flash of fire from one of the monitors.

"What was that?" he asked.

"We just lost the dropships," the copilot replied.

"What? I'm going to need them!"

"You need them now more," the pilot said. "It is necessary for us to survive this in order for you to need them later."

"Are they going to be recoverable?"

"No," the copilot said. "A missile system activated at the field, but it doesn't exist anymore. Nor does the starport tower at the base. Their command and control just became a lot more challenging."

"But what am I going to do for dropships?"

"You'll have to figure something else—*darn it!*"

The ship swayed alarmingly.

"What's going on?" Nigel asked, a note of fear in his voice.

"The engines aren't used to being used like this," the copilot said. He switched to the ship's intercom system. *"Everyone strap in. This is going to be messy!"*

"Wait!" Nigel said, his voice bordering on a panicked scream. "You said messy was bad!"

"It is, now *shut up!*"

Nigel watched the pilots try to save the ship, alternately amazed and scared out of his mind. Their hands flew across the instrument panel, flipping switches and pushing levers as warning and caution lights illuminated across its length. The noise from one of the engines rose alarmingly in a high-pitch shriek and then went quiet, along with the illumination of five or six more red lights on the panel. The copilot made a noise that was somewhere between a whimper and a growl.

"Two seconds," the pilot announced. *"Hold on!"*

The two seconds seemed to last an eternity, then the ship crashed, sending everything not tied down flying through the cockpit like a giant's shotgun blast. Something whizzed past Nigel's nose to hit the bulkhead next to him and fell to the floor. His helmet. Damn it; that would have been a lot more useful *on* his head.

The floor shifted and fell out from underneath him, and Nigel slammed into the starboard bulkhead, where he looked up at the front of the cockpit at a weird angle. His helmet rolled to a stop next to his chest as if in accusation.

"Nicely done," the copilot said, unstrapping with one pair of hands while the other held him in place.

"Thank you," the pilot replied. "Thanks for the help."

"What…what happened?" Nigel asked.

"We lost a motor toward the end," the pilot said. "We crashed, which destroyed the starboard struts; we lost just about everything else on the starboard side when the ship fell over onto it."

"But we can fix the struts and fly out of here, right?" Nigel asked.

"Not likely," the copilot replied. "You're lucky to be alive. The pilot did an emergency cross-connect of the motors which squeezed a little extra thrust out of the starboard motor; if it weren't for that, we'd just be stains in the ship's wreckage."

"We can't leave here?"

"Not in this ship. Not without a major shipyard overhaul. There is, however, a ship on the other side of the landing area. If you want to leave, you'd better go capture it."

"Hang on; I'll tell Mason." Nigel extricated himself from the wreckage of his seat and its surroundings. Standing on the starboard bulkhead was disorienting.

"Mason can't do it," the pilot said. "The rest of your company left the ship as soon as we landed. They are almost to the Besquith's hangars. If you want to capture the ship, *you'll* have to do it." He pointed out the cockpit canopy, and Nigel could see a frigate-sized ship about half a mile away.

"Well, I'll tell Mason after they finish the assault," Nigel replied.

"That will be fine," the pilot agreed, "unless there is a crew onboard the ship, and it takes off, leaving us stranded here."

"Could that happen?"

"Of course. I don't know if anyone is on it. The only way to find out is for someone to go over there. At the moment, that someone is you. We're not going. We're pilots, not combat troops."

Fear of attacking a ship single-handedly warred with his fear of being stuck on Bestald.

"I'll be right back," Nigel finally muttered, his desire to get off the planet finally winning out. He made it to the cockpit door, but then had a thought. "How many…umm…how large do you suppose the crew of that ship is?"

"There's no way to know," the pilot said. "It depends on how close they were to launching it. There could be anywhere from just a few guards on watch to the entire crew, along with embarked troops."

"Wonderful," Nigel said, his head down. "Here I go."

Nigel went through the troop compartment to get his weapons and found several troopers still onboard. "What's going on?"

Corporal Epard looked up from the soldier she was treating. "We had a couple of casualties from that ratfuck of a landing we were treated to." She nodded at Private Allen who was sitting off to the side. "Thunder's got a broken arm." She leaned forward to close the eyes of the soldier she'd been working on. "Watkins didn't make it."

The medic stood up and strode over to the weapons rack and snatched a rifle from it.

"Where are you going?" Nigel asked.

"I'm going to go get some payback," the medic snarled. "I can't kill the pilots until we're off this rock; I thought I'd start with killing some damn wolves." She walked toward the loading ramp, which extended out from where the ship lay on its side.

"Wait!" Nigel called, grabbing a rifle of his own. "I need you to come with me and help me capture the other ship here. Our ship is broken, and it's the only way we're going to get out of here."

Epard drew up sharply. "Capture a ship? Just the two of us?" She stared at Nigel for a few seconds and then added, "Why the fuck not?" Under her breath she added, just loud enough to be heard, "What else could go wrong today?"

"I'll come," a voice said from behind Nigel. He turned and saw Private Allen struggling to his feet. "I can still shoot a pistol."

The soldier grabbed a couple of pistols, stowing them in pockets, then turned toward Nigel. "Okay," Thunder said, "I'm ready."

Hanger Two, Blood Drinkers' Base, Bestald

"*L et's go!*" Mason transmitted as he waved his troops forward. He spared a glance at the group of Tortantulas as they skittered off to the left toward Hangar One and flinched as one of them launched a claw-held surface-to-surface missile at something it saw inside the hangar. The missile detonated with a 'wumpf' and blast of heat Mason swore he could feel from several hundred yards away. The Tortantulas chattered happily over their assigned frequency, and a second missile ravaged the interior of the hangar. The Tortantulas advanced, spraying fire indiscriminately throughout the hangar and joking happily over the radio. They seemed happiest when they were blowing things up.

"*Hey, Breetar, keep 'em somewhat under control, would you?*"

"*They were promised wholesale slaughter,*" the Flatar replied from his position on the back of Zzeldar. "*I don't think that's going to be possible.*"

"*Well, do what you can, okay?*" Mason shook his head and focused on his target, refusing to be distracted by the explosions that continued to the left. The command hangar was right in front of him. If they were going to find what they were looking for, it would be there.

"*Jammers on?*" Mason asked.

"*Since we hit the ground, Top!*" Sergeant Sam Bush reported. The platoon's intel specialist, he ran both the jammers and electronic exploitation. "*Jamming all frequencies except the ones we're using.*"

"*Good, keep it up!*" Still no movement in the hangar. Damn it. "*Murph! Horsey!*"

"*Yes, Top?*" replied Staff Sergeants Donald 'Murph' Murphy and Dean 'Horsey' Wynhorst.

"*Murph, take your squad around to the left of the hangar and look for a way in through the front. I think they must be setting up a welcoming party for us since they haven't come out to play. Horsey, take your squad around the right side of the hangar. No one goes inside the building until I say so.*"

"*Got it, Top!*" The two squads split off toward the ends of the hangar.

That left Mason with the XO and the 20 effectives from second platoon. As they approached the enormous hangar, he realized just how thin the force was and regretted sending the two squads from first platoon around to the front. He entered the shadow of the building and slowed to a walk to give the other platoon time to get into position.

"*Remember, there may be a human female here we're looking for named Amanda Spivey, so make sure you mark your targets.*"

The hangar was nearly empty, which emphasized just how vast it was. A dropship was the cavernous building's only occupant, located nearly a quarter of a mile to the left with its port engine partially disassembled on the ferrocrete next to it. Aside from the dropship, there were a few stacks of parts and some boxes scattered around, but very little other cover available. Mason could see why the Besquith weren't waiting for them out here—they would be much better able to defend themselves inside the office space portion of the building…where they could also set traps for his men.

Mason wished they'd been able to bring the CASPers; if they had, the unit could have waltzed through the hangar as if they were at a Sunday dance. All of a sudden, his laser rifle felt woefully inadequate.

A trooper to the right fired, then all hell broke loose. He dove forward behind a large crate, looking for the target. Glass shattered in a number of places as it hit the floor to the front of him and laser beams scorched in from the sides. *"What have you got?"*

"Movement up high in the windows," Sergeant Todd Salter replied. *"There's at least three or four of them up there!"*

Mason looked up from the shattered glass and saw a series of small windows about four stories up. There was no way for the humans to get up to them; however, they were also too high to make effective sniping platforms. Anyone who wanted to shoot down at them would have to lean way out the window, exposing themselves to return fire.

"Nuisance fire from the right!" Staff Sergeant Jamie Howe reported. *"Looks like two or three of them were hiding behind some pallets of shit, but they've run off."*

"About the same over on the left," Staff Sergeant Jill Cox added. *"Looks like three Besquith. Corporal Vitali is hit, but not bad. The Besquith we saw just took off; they're gone."*

Mason shook his head. He hadn't even noticed the windows up there. He had been too busy looking for ambushes in the crates that he had forgotten to keep his head on a swivel. Damn, he was getting too old for this crap. What else could go wrong?

"Top, this is Colonel Shirazi," Nigel transmitted. *"Can you send out a couple of squads when you get a chance? We need help capturing the frigate."*

Cargo Bay, Besquith Ship *Beheader*, Bestald

Nigel stared out the back of the cargo bay. With the ship lying on its side, the ramp extended straight out from the left side of the gaping hole. The ramp was useless, and it was a long way down.

"I'll go first," Corporal Epard said. Without waiting for confirmation she slung her rifle, sat down at one of the corners and slid to the edge, her feet dangling into the opening. Grabbing hold of the edge, she slid the rest of the way out and was gone.

"I'm out of the way!" she yelled back up.

"Coming," Private Allen said. He jammed the pistol he was still holding into a cargo pocket and followed the medic. Even with one hand, he still made the dismount look relatively easy.

Which left Nigel staring at the opening yawning in front of him. He hated heights, and the drop was high enough to make him really uncomfortable.

"Coming, sir?" Corporal Epard yelled, jolting Nigel from his reverie.

He had to do this, Nigel knew, or he would never have the respect of the men and women of the company. This was his big chance to show his worth. Eyes locked on the far bulkhead, he slid to the edge.

"Drop your rifle to me," the medic called.

Nigel looked down to find where she was and immediately wished he hadn't; the horizon tilted, and he had to snap his eyes back to the bulkhead. Without looking again, he held the rifle over the edge and released it.

There was no clattering noise, so he figured Corporal Epard had caught it.

Which just left him.

Without breaking his visual lock on the bulkhead, he reached out and took hold of the edge. Before he could think about it, he leaned forward and started sliding into the abyss. As his butt left the edge, he had a change of heart and tried to lean back into the ship; all he succeeded in doing was to hit the back of his head on the edge. Hard. While his helmet blocked most of the damage, it stunned him, and he didn't think about the landing. He hit with his right leg nearly straight, wrenching his knee, and he collapsed forward in a heap. At least the battle armor kept him from hyperextending it.

A hand slid into his armpit and helped lift him from the ground.

"I'd have to give that landing about a 'three,' sir," Private Allen said, helping Nigel to his feet. The pain in his knee was incredible, but Nigel thought he could walk…at least a little. "You're supposed to drop and roll," the private added helpfully.

"Yeah, thanks," Nigel replied. "The next time I have to jump out of a crashed spaceship, I'll try to remember that."

Nigel scanned his surroundings, amazed at the devastation they had already caused, and the attack had barely begun. Smoke rose from the opposite end of the field. Nigel guessed that was where the missile system had been; all that was left now was a crater and several small brushfires. The starport's tower hadn't fared much better; although the tower had too much mass for the dropship to completely crater the structure, it had been obliterated, and pieces of it lay scattered for half a mile in every direction. The platoon was entering one of the two massive hangars; the other was already burning in several places.

Nigel turned a little further to the right and saw their target. Positioned across the landing area from the tower, the spaceship had been saved from the bulk of the destruction…but it also made it a long run from where the threesome currently stood.

"Want me to take a look at your knee?" Corporal Epard asked.

"No, we don't have time. We need to capture that ship before it takes off. Let's get going!"

The two troopers started off at a jog, and Nigel was quickly left behind. "Wait up!" he yelled. "I'm hobbling as fast as I can go."

The troopers turned and waited for him to catch up. As he approached, Nigel could see a frown on the medic's face. "Are you sure this is a good idea?" she asked. "Thunder has a broken arm, and you've got at least a sprained knee, if not worse. I'm the only trooper fully combat effective, and my primary job is to *fix* our casualties, not cause the enemy more. Wouldn't it be better to wait for Top Mason and the others to get back and assault it as a company? Who knows how many troops are waiting inside that thing?"

"I'd love to," Nigel grunted as he hobbled past her. "But that's our ride home. If you can promise me that someone won't try to leave with it before Mason gets here, I'm all for it. Otherwise, I'm going to go secure it. By myself if I have to."

Epard watched as her boss staggered on, her mouth hanging open.

"Last one there buys the first round when we get back," Thunder challenged, and chased off after Nigel.

"You're both crazy!" Epard exclaimed. "But I ain't buying," she added as she leaned forward into a sprint. She was sure she could beat the colonel, but passing Thunder would be tough.

* * * * *

Chapter Eighteen

"How many of them are there?" Lieutenant Treb-Sa asked as the corporal ran into the company command post on the fourth floor of the hangar. Recently recruited to the Blood Drinkers, the lieutenant had been the most expendable of the company's officers, and therefore the one chosen to stay behind and watch the base while the rest of the company was on-mission.

"I only saw eighteen of them entering the hangar," Corporal Pres-Al replied. "They looked like humans, but they didn't have any of their big, armored suits with them. If that's all they brought, it's a pretty small force for a full-on assault."

"That isn't much of a force for an assault, and in most cases, we would eat them alive. However, they may have sent some of their soldiers around to the front and, with everyone gone, we've only got 10 people left to stop them." He turned to his communications technician. "Have you been able to recall any of the troops stationed at the tower?"

"No sir," replied the tech. "They weren't answering earlier, and now the humans appear to be jamming us."

"The slackards over in the tower are probably sleeping through all of this. Can you reach any of the other merc units close by for assistance?"

"No sir, the jamming is too strong."

"Entropy. Okay, they are here for a reason, and the only one I can think of is to get our files. With the power off, we can't erase our logs. Put all of the drives into the safe, and we will defend it with our lives, if necessary. Eventually, the planetary forces, and maybe some of the other merc units, will arrive to see what is going on. We just have to hold them off until additional forces get here."

"As directed, I placed some explosives on the entryway doors," a private said as he ran into the room. "Besides that, all we have are a few of the old lasers left in the armory; all the good weapons are with the companies. We won't be able to hold them off for long."

"What about our 'guest?'"

"I have hidden her cage," the private said. "They probably won't find it…and if they do, they will pay a price."

"Good," the lieutenant said, "We will hold them off as long as is necessary, and then we will kill them and feast on their flesh. It is the Blood Drinker way."

His troops howled their acknowledgement.

Hanger Two, Blood Drinkers' Base, Bestald

The platoon froze as a distant howl could be heard. A primal shiver went down Mason's spine.

"Well that's creepy," Private Parker said. "Reminds me of the wolves back home."

"What do you do when the wolves prey on your sheep?" Mason asked.

"You shoot 'em, Top, you know that."

"I do, and that's what we're going to do with these bastards. There must not be many of them here, or they would have met us in force." He pointed to a door. "Jernigan, get some breaching charges on that door."

"Want me to try it first and see if it's open?"

"No, it may be booby-trapped. I want to blow it open. Besides, they know we're here; stealth isn't going to get us anywhere."

Private Jernigan pulled a roll of advanced det cord out of a pocket and ran forward to the indicated entryway. Starting from the floor, he ran a double line of cord around the frame of the door, the molecular adhesive holding the cord in place. He inserted the detonator and ran back to Mason. "All set!"

"All right, everyone clear the area in front of the door. I don't want anyone hit if they've got something nasty waiting on the other side." When he saw the area was clear, he nodded to Private Jernigan. "Blow it."

Baa-boom! The det cord blew, firing through the frame of the door, where it was enveloped by a sympathetic detonation from the other side. The door, as well as thousands of pieces of shrapnel, blew outward into the area just vacated by the troops.

"How did you know it was booby-trapped?" Jernigan asked looking down at the hand he would have used to open the door. Mason could see it was shaking slightly.

"It's what I would have done to slow us up," Mason replied with a smile. Maybe he wasn't too old for this. "All right, let's go. Don't open any doors without checking with me first."

Approaching the Alien Ship, Blood Drinkers' Base, Bestald

"Holy shit!" Nigel cried, throwing himself to the side as a laser bolt hit the ferrocrete next to him.

"What?" Corporal Epard asked. "Your knee give out?"

Nigel looked up to see the two troopers had stopped and were looking back at him. "Don't stop!" he yelled, struggling to his feet. "Run! Someone just shot at me!"

The troopers turned in time to see a strangely-shaped figure retreating into the spaceship. "Run, damn it!" Epard urged. "Before they raise the ramp!"

The two soldiers dashed toward the ship with Nigel hobbling after them. Within seconds, the ramp began to rise.

"Not…gonna…make it…" Thunder grunted. Every step was torture as wave after wave of pain spread from his broken arm.

Epard dropped her rifle and pack, and she sprinted as hard as she could, leaving both of the men behind. 50 yards away. 40 yards, and the end of the ramp passed the level of her midsection. 30. The ramp appeared to be moving more quickly. 20 yards, and the end was level with her face. 10 yards. She took her last few steps and jumped, just hooking her fingers over the edge. She let her momentum swing her legs in, and as they swung back out she pulled herself up onto the edge of the ramp, and threw a leg over it.

No time to rest, she saw. The ramp was within seconds of shutting on her and cutting her in half. Rolling, she went over the edge and onto the nearly vertical ramp, falling, bouncing and rolling down to the bottom.

She came to rest on her back at the bottom of the ramp, the wind driven from her lungs and partially stunned from the fall. She looked up and met the compound eyes of what looked like a gigantic ant. The reddish-brown nightmare stood nearly six feet tall on its rearmost set of legs. The creature came complete with antennae, which twitched in apparent surprise at having her fall at its feet.

It pranced backward on spindly legs that didn't look big enough to hold it then turned to retrieve its laser rifle.

The sight of the rifle jolted her to action, and she drew her pistol from its holster without getting up. "Drop it!" she yelled as the creature turned back toward her.

If it understood her, it didn't give any indication; it brought up the rifle.

She fired, and the .40 caliber hollow point hammered the creature in its thorax. She continued firing, hitting it four more times as the bullets walked up the creature. The final bullet hit it between its eyes, and the creature fell over backward. As it fell, she could see the bullets had passed through the creature's body, leaving a splatter painting in three colors on the bulkhead behind it. Gross.

Epard got up and inspected the creature. If there was anything important in its midsection or head, it was dead.

She turned and cycled the boarding ramp back down. Thunder ran up with a pistol out, ready to shoot.

"I heard shots," he said.

"Yeah, I got it," she said, nodding toward the dead alien. "Whatever the hell it is."

Nigel handed her the rifle and pack she had dropped and examined the alien. "I think it's an Altar," Nigel said, "but that doesn't make any sense."

"What do you mean?" Corporal Epard asked, checking her rifle for damage. Finding none, she set it aside and reloaded her pistol.

"Normally the Altar and Besquith are enemies," Nigel explained. "At least they were in the Tri-V games I used to play." He nodded at the pistol. "Old school, huh?"

"Lasers don't get it done for me in close," Epard replied. "I like something with a little more stopping power for close encounters. It's big enough to hurt 'em but small enough for me to control. With hollow points, it gets the job done. Did with that thing, anyway." She toed the Altar's corpse.

"One thing makes sense," Nigel said, looking at the body. "Altars have compound eyes, like the ants back home, which is probably why it missed me with its rifle. Their eyes are good for movement detection, but pretty crappy for distance resolution." He shrugged. "Let's see if we can find the bridge or cockpit or whatever it is on this ship. The damn things are communal; if there's one, there are more. I guarantee there will be some of them on the bridge, and they'll take off with us if we don't stop them."

* * * * *

Chapter Nineteen

Hanger Two, Blood Drinkers' Base, Bestald

"*T*his *level's clear,*" Mason reported. "*Everyone move up to the second floor.*"

Corporal Jen 'Sparky' Davis gave the room a last sweep. Unlike most of the squad, she wasn't scared. Well, she was, a little, but her sense of curiosity far outweighed the feelings of terror that consumed most of her squadmates after they had heard the alien howling. *This* was the reason she had joined Asbaran Solutions in the first place—she had wanted to explore new places and see new things. The room was some sort of machine shop, but whether it was for fixing ships or APCs or something else, she didn't know. And she really wanted to know.

She picked up a strange tool from one of the workbenches, trying to figure out what it did, but Sergeant Jeremy 'Gemini' Crouch slapped it out of her hand, and it fell to the floor with a clatter.

"What the fuck are you doing?" he asked. "Don't touch anything; it could be booby-trapped. C'mon, we're moving up to the second deck."

Sparky sighed. So many new things to explore. How could she resist picking it up?

She backed out the door, watchful as always, but there were no aliens in sight. Nothing jumped up or did anything interesting.

The squad went up the stairs to the second floor, but the passageway was empty.

"I don't want 'em behind us," Mason transmitted. *"Make sure there aren't any Besquith in these rooms."*

One of the last ones up the stairs, Sparky didn't get to kick in any of the doors, which was disappointing. Each room was like an unopened Christmas present. What would be inside when it was opened?

In this case, nothing exciting. These rooms were boring, she saw as she stalked down the hallway. Mostly office space, although the desks were oddly shaped, and there were no chairs. Maybe because the Besquith had tails. That, at least, was different, if not totally 'interesting.'

"Nothing on this level, either," Turk reported.

"Stay frosty," Mason said. *"We know they're here, and they know we're here. Everyone move up to the third deck."*

As the squad retracted back to the staircase, she found herself toward the front of the formation. Even better! Maybe she would get to kick in a door!

But no, Gemini was in the lead, and he kicked in the first door. "What the *hell* is this?" he asked as he advanced into the room, rifle at the ready.

Sparky followed, sweeping the corners in the opposite direction of Gemini's advance.

This was different, but not in a fun way.

They had found a torture chamber. Or a meat processing facility. Or something.

"Is this the kitchen?" Gemini asked.

Sparky continued to sweep the room. Oh, a kitchen. That made sense. The room was full of large metal tables that shined as if recently cleaned. A variety of large knives that looked like curved butcher knives hung from hooks on the ceiling, and a selection of smaller knives waited on smaller tables next to the larger ones. Drains scattered throughout the room made for easy clean up.

"A kitchen," Sparky said. "That's funny. When I first saw it, I thought it was some sort of torture room. I guess my imagination was wandering."

"Oh, shit…" Gemini said, reexamining the equipment. "No, I think you're right. The tables have straps on them, and there are wires running to some of them. Oh, hell." He switched to his radio. *"Hey, Top, I think we just found a torture room or something. It kind of looks like a kitchen…but kind of not."*

"Be right there," Mason replied.

Sparky continued through the room. She had never seen so many knives in one place before. As she reached the back corner of the room, she came upon an oversize cabinet of cutting implements. They didn't look like any sort of kitchen utensils she had ever seen; they looked evil. As her eyes traveled down the cabinet, she saw there were six-inch skid marks on the floor leading to where it was currently positioned.

Weird, she thought. Why would the aliens have moved it to the back of the room where it was out of the way? As big as it was, most humans would have placed it in a position of greater prominence. Also, it wasn't up against the wall on the side next to the back wall; instead, it was pushed forward about three inches. She tried to push it back, but couldn't. Strange.

"What do you think?" she heard Gemini ask as someone came into the room behind her. "Kitchen?" Sparky thought she heard a note of hope in his voice.

"No, this isn't a kitchen," Mason replied after a pause. "Well not really. It's the Blood Drinkers' torture room…they just happen to eat the things they kill. Including prisoners, the sick fucks."

Sparky looked behind the cabinet and thought she could see a line, but it was too dark to tell.

"Yeah, well remind me to never get caught by them," Gemini said. "Shoot me first, would ya?"

"Yeah," Mason said. "Make sure you do the same for me." He paused and then added, "C'mon, we've got work to do. Let's get the hell out of here."

"Sparky!" Gemini called. "Let's go!"

"Just a second," Sparky said as she tugged on the cabinet. "I've got something weird over here."

"Now what are you into?" Gemini asked, sounding frustrated. "Can't you leave anything alone?"

Mason and Gemini came over to where she was. "What have you got?" Mason asked.

"It looks like they moved this cabinet," she said, pointing to the skid marks. "Also, it doesn't sit right against the wall. I'm trying to move it to see what's behind it."

"Hang on," Mason said. He pulled a mini flashlight off his belt and shined it behind the cabinet. "Wires back there," he noted. "Looks like it's booby-trapped."

"*Jernigan, I've got a trap for you,*" Mason radioed. "*First door to the right from the stairwell.*"

Private Jernigan entered the room and came over to the group.

"Looks like they may have wired this cabinet to blow if we pulled it away from the wall," Mason noted, handing him the flashlight. "Take a look under there."

"Sure, Top." Jernigan laid down on the floor and slid underneath the cabinet. Turning on the flashlight, he looked up the back of the cabinet. "Yep, it's wired to blow, all right. If you'd pulled out the cabinet about two more inches, it would have pulled the pin out of a grenade attached to a wad of plastic explosives. Bad juju."

"I always told you that curiosity killed the cat," Gemini said to Sparky. "Almost killed you this time."

"I know…but I couldn't help it!" Sparky exclaimed. "I *had* to know what was back there."

"Gimme a sec," Jernigan said, his voice muffled. He shifted around under the cabinet then slid back out. "It's safe," he said. "It was a simple trap; it looks like something they just threw together in a hurry. All I had to do was disconnect the wire from the cabinet."

"Well, let's find out what's back there," Mason said. "We're wasting time."

He grabbed the corner of the cabinet and pulled. Gemini added his strength to the other side, and they were able to walk the cabinet away from the wall.

"It's a door!" Sparky said, reaching for the handle.

"Wait!" Jernigan ordered. He removed the explosives hanging from the latch and handed them to Gemini. "It'd suck if that got caught on something and detonated." He put his hand on the door latch. "If you would all just step back a second, just in case?"

Everyone else moved away from the door and Jernigan eased it open a crack, just enough to shine the flashlight in. "Okay," he said, throwing the door open; "it's clear." Behind the door a passageway continued into the dark.

He took one step into the hallway and was met with a very human-sounding scream. He jumped back in surprise.

"Let me do it," Sparky said. She slung her rifle and pulled out a pistol. She walked past Jernigan, taking the flashlight from him as she passed. Now *this* was interesting.

Flipping on the light, she advanced into the gloom. Another scream sounded, weaker than the first. Using the sound as a reference, Sparky moved forward, noting that Jernigan had followed her. The passageway was narrow, with a low ceiling; she was okay, but knew Jernigan would have to duck to walk through it.

Nine steps down the passageway led her to the cage.

A six-foot square, the cage had been assembled in an alcove not much bigger than the enclosure. There were only two things in the cage, a cot and an extremely emaciated human woman, who cowered away from the light.

"Stay away!" the woman whimpered and then broke down sobbing.

"Amanda?" Sparky asked. "Amanda Spivey?"

"Yes," the woman said, sounding confused. "What…who are you?"

"I'm Corporal Davis, ma'am. I'm here to save you."

"Wha…what?" the woman asked.

Sparky looked around for a key and didn't see one. She turned to Jernigan. "Go back and see if you can find the key to the cage," she said. "It must be back in the other room."

"It's not—*sniff!*—it's not locked," the woman said.

"It's not?" Sparky asked.

"No," the woman replied. "It doesn't need to be. Where would I go? They'd tear me apart if I left, so I'm just sitting here, waiting to die."

Sparky grabbed the gate and pulled. Sure enough, it opened.

"Let's go, ma'am. We've got to get you out of here."

"I'm not sure I can walk."

Sparky advanced into the cage and helped the woman up from the cot.

"I'll help you, but we have to hurry," Sparky said as she assisted the woman from the cage and back to the torture room.

"Good to see you," Mason said to the woman. "Jernigan already told us who you are."

"Thank you for coming!" the woman exclaimed in her strongest voice yet. "I was *so* scared. If you hadn't come, they were going to *eat* me!"

"That's okay, ma'am," Mason replied. "Sparky here will help you out to our spaceship so we can get you out of here."

The woman looked at Corporal Davis. "Sparky?"

"It wasn't my fault!" Sparky replied. "I asked for the insulated screwdriver, and they handed me one with a magnetic tip. The thing is, nobody cares whose fault it is when you electrocute yourself on your first day at the new job. I've been Sparky ever since."

Hanger Two, Home Base, Bestald

"That should do it," Lieutenant Treb-Sa said as he shut the vault door and programmed in a new code. "The humans won't be able to get them; if nothing else, we have done our duty."

"Not a moment too soon, sir," Corporal Pres-Al replied. "The humans are advancing. They have bypassed many of my traps or blown them up. They also appear to have additional troops; it looks like there is at least a platoon coming up both stairwells."

"Any word from off-base?"

"No sir," the communications technician replied. "We're still being jammed."

"Then it is time for us to make our last stand. Corporal, take four of the privates to the east stairwell; I will take the other four to the west stairwell. Kill as many of them as you can. We will make them pay for attacking us!"

Hanger Two, Blood Drinkers' Base, Bestald

The platoon paused in the stairwell as the howl sounded again. It was much closer and louder this time, awakening the primal urge to flee.

"Damn, I wish they'd stop doing that," Private Parker whispered. "They sound like werewolves."

"Shut up, Parker," Mason ordered. "One more flight to go. Be ready; they're going to hit us soon. They've got nowhere else to go." So far, the humans had only received light harassing fire from the Besquith, but like he had told the troops, the enemy was now cornered and might do something desperate. They would either try to defend their last area in the hope that help would arrive at the last minute, or they would try to go out with a bang and kill as many of the humans as they could. He was betting on the latter; he doubted the Besquith would try to surrender…which was good because he had no intention of letting them.

The soldier in front of Mason had just stepped onto the next-to-last corner landing of the stairwell when the Besquith attacked. The only warning Mason had was a small scratching noise, and then the Besquith launched themselves into the stairwell from the floor above. Mason saw a shadow out of the corner of his eye and ducked, and a Besquith flew past him to crash into the two soldiers at the tail end of the formation. The trio went rolling down the stairwell to come to a slamming halt at the next landing.

Another Besquith dove past him, colliding with a third soldier, and they tumbled backward to land on the first Besquith, turning the pile into a tangle of claws, fur, and teeth.

A third Besquith collided with the soldier in front of Mason, slamming Private Sheila Jewell into the wall at one of the corners of the stairwell. Without pause, the Besquith straddled her, pinning her to the stair, and leaned forward to tear out her throat in a spray of blood.

Mason fired several times into the side of the alien, but the laser blasts didn't appear to have any effect. The wolf leaned forward again, grabbed the soldier's neck in its jaws and shook its head, snapping the soldier's neck.

Realizing the inadequacy of the laser rifle, Mason dropped it to its sling and drew his kirpan. He took a step, and then launched himself into the beast. Mason crashed into the alien, knocking it off its feet. The two slammed into the wall, and Mason drove the point of his weapon into the creature's chest. The Besquith roared a bestial cry of pain, and Mason stabbed it again and again until the alien collapsed to the floor. Rising to a knee, Mason chopped down with the kirpan, severing the Besquith's spine.

Turning, he found the rest of the battle was far from over. Although two of the Besquith were dead above him on the stairs, one of the Besquith straddled private Jernigan, trying to bite him. The soldier had his rifle in both hands and was using it to hold off the bigger creature. As Mason started toward them, the Besquith bit down on the rifle, saliva dripping past it to splatter on Jernigan's face mask, and then stood up, ripping the weapon from Jernigan's hands. It turned its head and spit the rifle out into the central shaft, before turning back to bite Jernigan.

Unable to defend himself, Jernigan jammed his arm crosswise as far in as he could reach, hoping his armor would be proof against the creature's bite. It wasn't, and the soldier screamed as the Besquith bit down on his arm, crushing the vambrace protecting his forearm.

The alien threw the soldier's arm out of the way and opened its mouth for the kill, but Mason dove into the Besquith from above and sent him over backwards. Mason grabbed onto the alien to protect himself from the fall, and he drove his head into the Besquith's ribs as the two crashed into the wall. Mason could hear several bones break in the creature's chest.

Mason drew his kirpan again, but the Besquith threw him to the side, and Mason fell down the stairs, rolling to the next landing where he fell on top of Corporal Jennings. The soldier didn't care; Jennings was slashed in a number of places and missing most of his right arm. If he wasn't already dead, he soon would be.

"Help!" a voice yelled from below him, and Mason rolled over to find Staff Sergeant Kirkland on top of the last Besquith. Somehow Turk had gotten behind the alien and had an arm around its throat. Choking it didn't seem to be working, and the creature was slamming itself into the stairwell wall, trying to dislodge the human. Like a cowboy on a bull, Turk was just trying to hang on at that point. With a final slam, the Besquith broke Turk's hold and ripped the human from his back.

Before the creature could finish Turk, Mason dove into it, driving it backward down the stairs. The creature's feet went out from under it and the three combatants rolled to a stop on the next landing. Mason ended up on top and tried to draw his kirpan, but found his right arm wouldn't work. The large knife was mounted where it could be drawn with either hand, though, so he grabbed it with his left instead and began stabbing the alien.

"That's...good," grunted Turk, his voice coming from far away. "Can't...breathe."

Mason rolled off the alien and found Turk's legs protruding from under the Besquith. Mason braced himself and pushed as hard as he could with his left hand. The creature rolled off Turk.

"Thanks," Turk said. "I couldn't breathe." His eyes widened, and something huge crashed into Mason from behind, knocking him down the stairs. He lost his balance and tried to curl himself into a ball to protect from any further damage, holding the kirpan away from him to keep from impaling himself. As he crashed into the stairs, the knife was ripped from his grasp.

Mason bounced again, then hit hard on the next landing. Stunned, an enormous weight landed on him before he could get up. The alien had him pinned; Top couldn't move and was too tired and sore from fighting and falling down the stairs to shift the alien off of him.

While Mason waited for the alien to kill him, he also realized how bad they smelled.

After what seemed like an eternity, the alien finally shifted, and Mason opened his eyes to find Turk offering him a hand up. Turk bent down and pulled the kirpan from where it had lodged in the Besquith's neck. He wiped it off on the alien's fur and passed it over.

"Are we clear?" Mason asked.

"Yeah. All five are dead, thanks to you."

"Have we heard from the other squad?"

"I haven't."

"Horsey, Top; what's your status?"

There was no reply.

"Horsey, Top; I repeat, what's your status?"

"Top, this is Gemini. Horsey's pretty fucked up. So are most of the rest of us that are still living. They hit us pretty hard. I can't confirm, but I think one of them got away. We've got four hostiles down, along with most of the platoon."

"Damn it." Mason changed to the command frequency. *"Is anyone outside? It looks like one of the Besquith got away."*

"My group is outside," Breetar replied. *"We had to leave the other hangar. It kind of fell down. Oops. I already shot the Besquith, and Zzeldar and her buddies finished it off. I hope you didn't want to interrogate it…there isn't much left."*

"No, that's fine. As long as it didn't get away."

A new voice joined the conversation.

"Hey Breetar, Nigel. If you are done with your objective, how about coming over to the frigate and giving us a hand? There's more killing to be done over here."

"Really? We're on our way."

Aboard the Alien Ship, Blood Drinkers' Base, Bestald

"Think we should split up?" Thunder whispered. "We might be more likely to find the bridge."

"We also might be more likely to get wiped out," Corporal Epard replied. "You've only got one arm, and the boss is lame."

"Well, not totally lame," Nigel replied, "but I'm not running a marathon any time soon. I agree; let's stick together. I don't suppose you know where you're going, do you?"

"Not exactly," Epard replied. "I've been on a frigate before though, and if this is anything like it, I at least have a general idea."

"Great," Nigel whispered. "You lead. I'll bring up the rear."

"Maybe I should take that spot," Thunder replied, "in case we get hit from the rear. I've got more experience."

"No, I want you in the middle so you can back up the corporal with your pistol if needed. Also, I have a rifle, so I can better defend the rear." Thunder nodded, and Nigel smiled inwardly. He had made a combat decision that apparently made sense to the troops. Hopefully, it would be the first of many. And he'd be alive long enough to make them. "Let's go!"

Epard led the way, staying close to the port bulkhead. The corridor intersected with a major passageway; Epard eased around the corner then jumped back out of the way. "Three ants to the left," she advised. "They're coming this way."

"Grenade?" Nigel asked.

"No," Epard said. "Quick; back up!" She pushed Nigel and Thunder back a few paces and lined them up in a firing line across the passageway. "Make sure you see the third one before you shoot."

Within seconds the three Altar rounded the corner. "Fire!" Epard ordered.

Epard's pistol was deafening in the enclosed space as Nigel squeezed the trigger on his rifle. He aimed for the center of mass on the creature in front of him, and he hit the Altar in the upper thorax. When it didn't fall, he shot it a second time, blasting chunks of exoskeleton from it and spraying its blue blood throughout the corridor. It collapsed to the floor.

Nigel swung the rifle to the side, but the others were already both down. Epard's had taken three pistol rounds in the head and most of its brains were on the passageway wall behind it; Thunder's had two in the chest and one in the head.

"We're going to need to hurry," Corporal Epard said, reloading her pistol.

"Yeah, they probably heard your cannon all the way up on the bridge," Thunder noted. "Wherever that is."

"Lead on," Nigel said. "Fast as you can; I'll try to keep up."

* * * * *

Chapter Twenty

Hanger Two, Blood Drinkers' Base, Bestald

"Damn," Mason said under his breath. Second Platoon looked like doggie chew toys; they had literally been torn apart. All of them had claw and bite marks, and three of the First Squad troopers were missing limbs. Those three were dead, as were two other Second Squad members. The ones that were still alive weren't in much better shape.

Sergeant Bush was one of the fatalities, as was the jammer. It had fallen three stories and what was left was beyond repair.

"Turk, I want you to take charge of this mess. Take what's left of First Platoon and get everyone as stable as you can and back to the ship; we're not leaving anyone behind. Especially not here. I'll take Parker and Jernigan and go look for the unit's records."

"What if you run into more of them?" Turk asked. "There's only three of you, and they're pretty tough up close."

"We already went by their main office, and I don't think there are any more around. Get moving; we don't have much time to get everyone back to the ship." Turk nodded his acceptance and Top turned back toward the Blood Drinkers' company offices. "Jernigan, Parker, you're with me."

The trio returned to the offices they had passed on the way to Second Platoon without difficulty. Several doors lined both sides of the passageway; nearly all of them were askew from where they'd been kicked in when First Platoon had gone by earlier. Just like before, they were quiet and appeared unoccupied.

"Where do we start, Top?" Private Parker asked.

"I'm going to make a guess that the one with all the writing around it is where they kept their classified information."

"Can you read Besquith?" Private Jernigan asked.

"Nope, but 'Stay the hell out!' looks pretty much the same, no matter where you go," Mason replied. The indicated door had partially closed, and he pushed it open with the barrel of his rifle. The room was dim and quiet, and the trio advanced, rifles at the ready.

"*Nigel, you are going to need to hurry,*" the Pendal pilot radioed over the common net. All three soldiers jumped at the unexpected, unnatural voice. "*The local government wants to know what's happening. I told them that we are trying to contain a potential weapon leak and to remain clear, but I don't know how long they're going to buy it. At some point, they are going to want to send cleanup crews to assess the damage.*"

"*Understood,*" Nigel replied. "*We're still working our way up to the bridge. The ship appears to be an Altar ship, and the damn ants are everywhere. They just started the motors and we're trapped just shy of the bridge. It looks like we're going to need a hand…and fast!*"

"All right," Mason said; "you heard the man. It's time to go. Grab all the drives and let's get the hell out of here."

"Sorry, Top," Private Parker said from the other side of the room, "but it looks like the Besquith took all the drives." He pointed to a number of disassembled computer systems, all of which had holes where something had been removed from them.

"Took them? Where the hell would they have taken them? The ones we fought definitely weren't carrying anything when they hit us."

"Probably right here," Private Jernigan replied, patting a 10-foot square black metal box in the back corner of the room. "Looks like they have a walk-in vault."

Mason strode over and looked at the front of the vault. A flashing light strobed across a lit keypad. "What the hell is this?" Mason asked, frustration tinging his voice. "How does this have power? It's out everywhere else."

"It's an Altar Systems 9100 model," Jernigan replied. "It's got an internal generator."

"An Altar what?" Mason asked. "How the hell do you know that?"

"I had a…non-traditional…upbringing," the private replied. "I wasn't always the fine, upstanding citizen you see before you."

"Did your non-traditional upbringing teach you how to bust into one of these things?"

"It did, and you can't." He tapped on the input screen and frowned. "Once it's locked, it won't open without the code; that's why it has the internal power source. You need the 32-digit password, in the Besquith alphabet on this one, or you're not getting into it."

"Can we blow it?"

"I don't know," the private said, lost in thought. "We didn't have enough to blow it…I mean, I think it would take an awful lot of explosives. You'd probably end up damaging whatever's inside of it. Just a guess."

"Well, fuck," Mason said. "We've got to get into the damn thing, or this whole damned assault has been for nothing."

"I don't know what to tell you, Top," Jernigan replied. "I don't think we're going to get it open. Not in the time we have left anyway."

"Damn it!" Mason exclaimed. All of his troopers dead for no reason? No. "There has to be a way to get it open." He took two steps and looked out the window into the hangar four floor below. It was as empty as when they had come through it.

"Sorry Top, there may be a way, but I don't know what it is."

Mason shook his head in annoyance. An idea struck him, and he looked out the window again. A fleeting smile crossed his face. "Suppose it would survive a four-story fall?"

"Hell if I know. I do know it's heavier than the three of us can move, though."

"It looks like it is," Mason said, "which is why I don't think we'll have to destabilize the floor very much for it to fall through on its own. What do you think?"

Jernigan came to stand at the window. The safe was up against the back edge of the office space. If they blew the back wall out and some of the floor, the safe would fall to the hangar floor. "It's worth a shot," Jernigan agreed. "I don't know if that will spring it, but it's better than anything else I've got."

"I've got two grenades and a roll of det cord," Mason said. "What have you guys got?"

"Two grenades," Private Parker replied.

Jernigan smiled. "I've got four grenades and two sticks of C-12."

"What the hell were you planning to do with all that?" Mason asked.

"What can I say?" Jernigan asked with a shrug. "I like blowing shit up."

"I take it you have the detonators for them, too?"

"Wouldn't be much good if I didn't, would it?" Jernigan reached into a pocket and pulled out the needed accessories.

"All right, let's get this wired ASAP."

"Sure thing, Top. I've never seen a safe fly…this is going to be fun."

Aboard the Altar Ship, Blood Drinkers' Base, Bestald

"I think we're at the bridge," Shrewlet said as she looked around the corner before jumping back. Several shots went past.

"How do you know?" Nigel asked.

"Because they stopped retreating and are guarding an open doorway." She ducked down and fired two shots around the corner, then her pistol locked open. She put in a new magazine and jacked in the first round. "I only have one more magazine after this one," she said, "so I hope that's where we're going."

Nigel felt a small vibration through his boots and could hear a low rumble.

"Damn it," Corporal Epard said. "They're starting the motors."

"We've got to get up there and stop them," Nigel replied.

"I'm trying," she said, firing around the corner again. "Shit. Now's there's four of them. They're getting reinforced."

Nigel ducked as a laser bolt from behind him narrowly missed his face. He fired several shots down the passageway. "They're getting braver back here."

The rumble in the floor grew.

Epard fired around the corner again, then fell back, her shoulder singed. "Too close," she said. "I think there are five of them now."

"We don't have time," Nigel said, "They've got both motors running and—" He stopped as a call came in.

"*Understood,*" Nigel replied over the radio. "*We're still working our way up to the bridge. The ship appears to be an Altar ship, and the damn ants are everywhere. They just started the motors and we're trapped just shy of the bridge. It looks like we're going to need a hand...and fast!*"

The lights flashed. "Damn!" Corporal Epard exclaimed. "They just transferred to internal power. We're seconds from liftoff."

"There's a bunch of them behind us, too," Nigel said. He fired his rifle several times to keep the Altar under cover. "Better do something quick—I can't hold them much longer!"

Hanger Two, Blood Drinkers' Base, Bestald

"Blow it," Mason ordered. The men had rigged the explosives then retreated down the hall to avoid shrapnel.

Jernigan mashed the button on the detonator, and the building shook with the force of the explosion.

"I didn't hear the safe hit the ground," Mason noted.

"Wait for it…" Jernigan urged.

They waited, but they didn't hear anything further. Mason led them back into the room, where the safe waited for them, almost unscratched.

"Damn it; I was afraid that was going to happen," Mason said. The explosives had blown out the back of the office and part of the floor; however, the force of the blast had pushed the safe away from the wall; it hadn't fallen through.

"Well, at least we have a hole now," Private Parker said. "Can't we just push it through?"

"The damn things are really heavy," Jernigan replied. "*Really* heavy. We can try, but I doubt we're going to move it."

"How about more explosives underneath it? What if we go down to the next floor and set up some more explosives on the roof?"

"Got any more explosives?" Mason asked.

"I don't, but we could radio for more."

"We don't have time," Mason explained; "we've got to get this done *now*." He looked around the office until he saw what he needed in one of the side offices. Judging by the quality of the furniture, it was probably the CO's or XO's office.

"This may work," he said, returning with two flags and their stands. He pulled the flags out of the metal bases and placed the bases next to the safe. "Take this," he said, handing Jernigan one of the flags. "The flag staffs are metal and may be strong enough to use as levers. If we can just flip the safe once, it's out the hole. Try to do it gently and not snap your pole."

The two men slid the poles under the edge of the safe and onto the flag bases. "On three," Mason said. "One…two…three!"

Both men pulled down on their poles, but the safe didn't budge. "Okay," Mason said after a couple of seconds. "Let's try it again, but make sure you pull at the end of the staff." He turned to Parker. "You could get your lazy ass over here and give us a hand, too."

"Want me to go look for another flag?"

"No, just grab the bottom of the safe and lift when I say."

"But it's—"

"Just fucking do it, Parker!"

"Sure thing, Top," Parker said, bending over. "Ready when you are."

"On three," Mason said again. "One…two…three!"

The three men strained, and the edge of the safe lifted. One inch. Two.

"*Lift!* Mason yelled. Six inches. Momentum took over and it started to rise a little easier, but the poles hit the end of their throw. "*Switch!*" Mason yelled. He dropped his pole and grabbed the bottom of the safe next to Parker. Jernigan joined him as the momentum ceased, leaving the three men holding up one side of the safe with their arms outstretched.

"*Lift!* Mason yelled. All three men strained, but the edge of the safe didn't move any higher.

"Can't hold…much longer," Jernigan said. "Going to…drop it."

"No," Mason said. "One more try. One…two…three!" Once again, the safe didn't move.

"Can't…hold…it," Parker said.

With a loud snap, the floor underneath the other edge gave way. Weakened by the explosion, it couldn't support the concentrated weight of the safe, and the floor fell away, with the safe going over after it. The three men fell forward toward the hole, and then scrabbled away from the edge. With several loud crashes, the safe fell through the third floor and second floor, before getting kicked into the main part of the hangar away from the offices. With the largest crash yet, the safe hit the hangar floor and buried itself halfway into the ground.

"It doesn't look like the door came off," Jernigan observed.

"No, it doesn't," Mason replied. "We're going to need more explosives."

"But we don't have any."

"I know," Mason said. "I guess I'll have to call the spiders."

Aboard the Altar Ship, Blood Drinkers' Base, Bestald

"Damn," Corporal Epard said as the slide locked back again. She inserted a magazine. "I'm out of ideas and almost out of ammo. I don't know how we're going to get past them, and this is my last mag."

"*Hey, Zzeldar,*" Nigel radioed. "*We sure could use your help on the ship. How long until you get here?*"

"*That depends. There is a pack of them at the entryway. Can I use rockets on them?*"

"*Negative, Zzeldar. This is our ride home, and it's a long walk if you blow it up.*"

"*Not being able to use our explosives hampers our ability to move quickly. Still, we should be there fairly soon.*"

"Fairly soon ain't gonna get it," Shrewlet said.

"That's okay," Thunder replied; "I've got a plan."

"Crap," Shrewlet said. "In the middle of this, *you've* got an idea? Now I'm scared. It's probably going to get me killed, isn't it?"

"I hope not," Thunder replied. "Just let me know when you're ready."

"I'm as ready as I'm going to be."

"Just a sec," Nigel replied. He fired several times down the hall, and the Altar there jumped back around a corner. "Ready!"

"What the hell do you think you're going to do?" Shrewlet asked.

"This," Thunder replied. He pulled a MIB ("Meal In a Box") out of a cargo pocket. The box was a six inch square and relatively flat. "Here we go!"

The private leaned around the corner and threw it sidearm like a flying disc toward the group of Altar, then he charged around the corner. "Follow me!" Thunder yelled as he ran past Corporal Epard.

A perfect toss, the flying meal packet landed on the ground about three feet in front of the group of aliens and slid into their midst. All five looked at it then dove away in different directions.

Two of the aliens threw themselves to the floor in front of Thunder as he ran down the passageway. He shot both of them in the head, then he killed a third Altar which had gone head-first into the side of the passageway and was lying in a heap, stunned.

Thunder continued on, with Shrewlet and Nigel close behind, but the other two Altar were already recovering, and he had to throw himself to the side as one of the remaining ones fired its laser pistol at him. Shrewlet and Nigel dove to the other side of the corridor as both Altar rose to their feet, already firing.

Shrewlet fired and hit one of them several times before her pistol locked back, out of ammo; Nigel killed the other with a shot through its head.

Both humans got up and Shrewlet ran over to Thunder, who was crawling slowly toward the meal packet. She grabbed the packed and handed to him, and he flipped over onto his back. He'd been hit several times in the chest. His mouth moved but Shrewlet couldn't hear what he said. He repeated it, then his head fell off to the side and stilled.

Shrewlet rose with a smile, although a tear ran down one side of her face.

"What did he say?" Nigel asked.

Shrewlet handed the meal packet to Nigel. It read, Cheese and Vegetable Omelet. "Thunder said, 'This shit's awful. I would have run from it too.'"

Her eyes widened and she grabbed for Thunder's pistol and came up firing. "Quick," she said, "Into the bridge! They're coming from behind us."

Nigel ran through the open doorway and found that the ship's 'bridge' wasn't much more than an oversize cockpit, with two pilot consoles and two other consoles in a second row behind them. Two Altar were busy at the controls.

"Don't move!" Nigel ordered.

The two aliens turned to look, and the copilot on the right reached for a pistol on top of the instrument panel.

"Don't do it!" Nigel said, sighting down the rifle at the giant ant. The claw stopped two inches shy of the pistol. "Out of the seats." He motioned with the rifle barrel to show what he wanted, and the aliens rose.

The pilot got out of the seat first, partially blocking Nigel's view, and the copilot grabbed for the pistol. Unable to get a shot at the copilot, Nigel shot the pilot in the head, and blue blood and chitin exploded throughout the cockpit.

As the pilot's body fell, the copilot brought the pistol up and Nigel dove to the side, bringing the rifle up as he fell. The alien's shot missed, passing through the space Nigel had just vacated. Nigel crashed to the deck and fired several times, hitting the copilot in the thorax.

The alien fell backward onto the instrument panel, advancing several of the levers there, and Nigel could hear the sounds of the engines go to full power. Dropping his rifle, he jumped to his feet, stepped forward, and grabbed the alien. Nigel pulled the creature off the instruments as the view outside the canopy shifted. The ship was starting to rise!

Nigel grabbed the levers and pulled them back, too fast, and the ship slammed back to the ground. The ship tilted to the left as it hit out-of-level, then it slowly righted itself.

Nigel released the breath he didn't know he'd been holding.

Shrewlet backed into the room, firing Thunder's pistol out the doorway. "Nice crash," she noted.

"Hey, we're down."

"If you say so, sir." She stopped firing long enough to spare a glance around the space. "Not much in the way of cover."

"No," Nigel said. "About all we've got is the chairs."

"If that's what we've got, then that's what we'll use," the corporal said philosophically. "The hard part's over."

"It is?"

"Yeah, we don't have to advance; all we have to do is hold what we've got."

"*Nigel, we are out of time,*" the Pendal pilot radioed. "*The local government is sending a spill response and containment unit. I cannot dissuade them. It will be here within 10 minutes.*"

"*Damn. Okay, come on over to the new ship and get up to the cockpit as soon as the Tortantulas clear the way. We'll leave once everyone's aboard.*"

"Looks like the ants are taking fire from behind," Shrewlet said, firing over the back of the copilot's seat. One of the Altar dropped, a laser hole between its eyes. "We may pull this off yet."

Nigel fired several times at the last couple of aliens facing them, but the shots went over them.

"Careful, sir," Shrewlet said. "You don't want to hit our folks on the other side of the ants. Keep your shots low." She fired and another one fell to the deck.

Nigel aimed at the last ant, but it collapsed before he could pull the trigger. It twitched as Lieutenant Seville stepped over it, and she fired a shot between its eyes with her laser pistol. She looked at the other ants piled up in the corridor and shot each of them again before looking up to see Nigel staring at her. "Just like to make sure," Mama said with a smile. "I hate ants."

She strode the rest of the way to the cockpit, with LTJG Minion right behind her. Mama nodded toward the corridor. "We came up with the spiders," Mama said. "If you two wouldn't mind vacating our cockpit, sir, we'll take it from here."

Hanger Two, Blood Drinkers' Base, Bestald

"*I*f anyone has some extra explosives," Mason radioed, "*we need some at the hangar ASAP to blow a safe that's on the hangar bay deck.*"

"*Blow up a safe?*" Zzeldar replied. "*We still have plenty of explosives. I will send someone immediately.*"

Zzeldar and Breetar were waiting for the humans when they got down to the hangar bay. Zzeldar was already inspecting the safe.

"I thought you were going to send someone?" Mason said.

"And miss out on blowing up a safe?" Zzeldar replied. "Unlikely. All we were doing was shooting at ants, anyway; this is far more fun. Besides, the rest of your troops just got there; they should be able to force an entry into the ship without me."

"Nigel, we are out of time," the Pendal pilot radioed. *"The local government is sending a spill response and containment unit. I cannot dissuade them. It will be here within 10 minutes."*

"Damn. Okay, come on over to the new ship and get up to the cockpit as soon as the Tortantulas clear the way. We'll leave once everyone's aboard."

"Shit," Mason said. "We're out of time. I need you to blow this and blow it now."

"You have partially buried the door. That will make it difficult, but there are cracks in the metal I can exploit. I have some liquid explosive I've been waiting for the right moment to try out."

"Do what you need to; just do it *now*."

"Nothing could be easier," Zzeldar replied, pulling items from off the harness she wore. "Breetar, you will want to dismount, and all of you will want to clear the area. This will have a substantial blast radius."

"Typical Tortantula response," Breetar noted. "When dealing with explosives, there's no kill like a good overkill."

Mason looked around the hangar, wondering about its structural stability. "You're not going to drop the roof, are you?"

"I hope not. That would make it difficult to get whatever's inside the safe."

"Exactly. What's inside is valuable. I don't want you to destroy it or make it impossible to get to."

The Tortantula began tapping two of her feet. "I'm not going to do anything while you continue to talk with me. If you would like me to proceed, you should leave the hangar."

"Okay, folks, clear the area," Mason said, leading the troops and Breetar outside.

Within 30 seconds, Zzeldar joined them. "Ready?" she asked.

"Do it."

Zzeldar pushed a button on a box she was holding, and the explosives detonated. Mason could see the hangar's sides bow out, but the structure remained standing.

The group raced inside to find the door of the safe lying to the side. Smoke still clouded the interior of the safe, but cleared as they approached.

"Fuck," Private Jernigan said. "That's a mess. If the drives were in one piece before, they aren't now."

"You told me to hurry. I hurried. The door is off, isn't it?"

"Yeah, the door is off," Mason said, shaking his head, "but I don't know what we'll be able to salvage out of what's left. Quick, scoop up the remains, and we'll figure it out once we get to space. We're out of time."

The group started for the frigate, but Mason had a thought. "Hey Zzeldar, there *is* one more thing I need to do, and it's right up your alley..."

* * * * *

Chapter Twenty-One

Cockpit, Asbaran Ship *Annihilation*, Bestald

"Everyone's onboard," Nigel said. "Let's get out of here." The capture of the Altar ship had gone quickly once the rest of the platoon had added its firepower to the Tortantulas. Another two humans were dead, and one of the Tortantulas had been seriously wounded, but they were finally ready to go. The cockpit was still splattered in blue, although the smell of dead Altar was more fruity than unpleasant.

"Strap in," the pilot said in his harsh whisper; "this may get ugly."

"Ugly how?" Nigel asked.

"Ugly as in they say, 'no, you cannot leave' and start firing weapons at us."

"Oh. That ugly."

The pilot advanced the throttles and Nigel hurried to strap in…wearing his helmet this time.

"*Departure control,* Annihilation *is departing for orbit.*"

"*Negative,* Annihilation, *return to your point of departure. I do not have a clearance on file for you.*"

"Missile systems coming online across the continent below us," the copilot advised.

"*We are unable to return, departure, we don't have time! We have a bioweapon onboard that is breaking containment.*"

"Is this the same weapon that was illegally brought down at the Blood Drinker's base?"

"Yes, departure, it is. The weapon was damaged in the ship's crash and containment is failing on it."

"Missile systems going active," noted the copilot.

"Do not shoot us!" the pilot transmitted. *"The weapon is spore based! If you destroy us, it will seed the entire planet. We will all be destroyed!"*

"What are your intentions, Annihilation?"

"We intend to take the weapon through the stargate to an uninhabited planet and dump it into the star there. The spores should be destroyed, but if not, at least they won't be a harm to us."

"Missile systems targeting radars have locked onto us," the copilot announced. Nigel couldn't tell, for sure, but it sounded like his voice had gone up a couple of notes. If the unflappable copilot was nervous…

"We have containment failure! It's in the ventilation system! I've got crew dying throughout the ship! I've got my suit on, but I don't know how long I'll last! If I don't leave now, we will crash back to the planet and release the toxin into the atmosphere. Entropy! My copilot is melting!"

"Annihilation, your clearance to depart is approved as is passage to the stargate. Can you make it before you run out of air?"

"I'm trying to figure that out now…yes, if I go at full speed and tap into the ship's emergency system, I should just…just, be able to make it."

"Hurry, Annihilation, and get to the stargate at your fastest speed. We will clear out all traffic in front of you."

"Best speed, aye. Direct to stargate, aye. Annihilation, out."

Cockpit, Asbaran Ship *Annihilation*, Breaking Orbit

The pilot pushed back from the console with all four hands and took several deep breaths.

"Nice job," Nigel said. "I didn't think they would buy it, but you were so convincing you almost had *me* believing we had bioweapons aboard."

"We do," the pilot said without turning around.

"We do what?"

"We do have bioweapons aboard. I saw five unmarked canisters in the hold when I did my preflight inspection of the ship. I assumed it must be something like that; the approach controller's reaction would seem to confirm their nature."

Nigel's eyes opened wide. "*What?* We've got bioweapons onboard, and you never said anything?"

"Until we took off and saw departure's reaction, we didn't know for sure," the copilot interjected.

"But, but, but what if they'd shot us or forced us to return. What if we'd crashed and one of the bioweapons had gone off?"

The Pendal's shoulders twitched. "Had we crashed," the pilot said, "all of us would have been dead. The weapons would have had little effect on us. They would only have been dangerous to the Besquith on the planet."

Nigel slumped back into his seat, relieved to still be alive. After several deep breaths of his own, he had a thought and leaned forward in his seat again.

"It was you, wasn't it?" Nigel asked quietly.

"What do you mean?" the pilot asked.

"In the strategy meeting, when I didn't know what to do. Somehow, you told Mason to help me. Didn't you?"

The Pendals looked at each other, but neither said a word.

"*Didn't you?*" Nigel repeated slightly louder.

"Please keep your voice down," The pilot said. "You are treading on very dangerous ground."

"Why is that?"

"The fact that we are empaths is a secret known only to a very few outside our race, and we make sure it stays that way."

A shiver ran down Nigel's spine at the way the Pendal made the pronouncement, but he pressed on, "You're not just empaths, though—you transmitted to Mason. You're some sort of telepath."

"Sometimes I can be heard by those not of our race," the pilot admitted. "Tortantulas are easiest, just because of the way the Creators put them together."

"What does how they're put together have to do with it?"

"They have eyes all the way around their heads," the copilot said. "They are used to processing a number of data streams simultaneously; usually, they don't notice an additional one."

"I have never tried it with a human," the pilot said; "I didn't know if Mason would hear me. While it was fortunate he did, it was unfortunate he knew someone had spoken to him; however, I didn't have time to be subtle."

"Why not?"

"Because having an angry and frustrated Tortantula onboard a spaceship is never a good thing. Zzeldar was beginning to feel betrayed and was about to start breaking things."

"Really?"

"Indeed."

Nigel shook his head. "I don't buy it. You just happened to be here? And then you risk exposing your hidden capabilities to keep

Zzeldar from breaking things? It doesn't add up." Nigel paused and then asked, "Why are you really here?"

The Pendals looked at each other again, and Nigel could tell they were communing on what to tell him. After several seconds, the Pendals broke eye contact and the copilot turned in his seat to face Nigel. The eye Nigel could see in the depths of the Pendal's hood glowed with intensity.

"Let me tell you a story," the copilot said. "Our race joined the Union almost 2,000 of your years ago. Like you, we were young and naïve."

"Hey! We're doing pretty well!" Nigel exclaimed. "Sure, our troops got crushed when we first joined the Union, but now we're winning a whole lot more than we're losing."

"True, you have adapted quite well as a provider of military forces," the pilot noted, "but you still have only the barest grasp of the political realities of the galaxy. While you might see things and think you understand the plans in motion, you have *no comprehension* of the plans within the plans that drive the outward manifestations you see. Some races can be very subtle in achieving what they desire. Additionally, while you humans seek quick gain, other races take a much longer view, happy to accept losses today that help them achieve their goals hundreds of years later."

"Are you saying that some races are letting us win?"

"Letting you win? No. Not trying as hard as they could, or employing all of their capabilities? Absolutely. You are being tested, as surely as we are sitting here."

"We can plan ahead, too."

Both Pendals made noises like steam escaping a boiler, and after a few seconds Nigel realized they were laughing at him. A flush crept up his neck and enveloped his face the longer it went on. "Are you about done?"

The Pendals stopped laughing. "We are sorry," the copilot said, "but to call your race short-sighted is one of the galaxy's greatest understatements. You can barely see beyond your nose, where races like the Besquith see to the galaxy's end."

"Okay, so maybe our race isn't as mature as some of the others," Nigel allowed, feeling put out. "What of it?"

Neither of the aliens said anything for a few seconds, and the silence stretched uncomfortably.

"I merely speak the truth," the copilot finally noted. "If it is too uncomfortable for you to hear, we can forget this conversation ever happened."

Nigel sat back. No one had made him feel so small since his grandfather, when Nigel had disappointed him in some task. The mercenary shook his head. "No, I'm sorry," he said. "Please continue."

"2,000 years ago, our race was just as naïve," the copilot started again. "Like you, we thought we were far smarter than we really were. Even though we didn't intend to divulge the fact we were empaths, somehow the word got out, and we became the focus of several of the mercenary races. They thought we would give them extra capabilities they didn't have."

"They did not understand how much we did not like killing," the pilot interjected. "The mercenary groups thought they could capture our people and force us to work for them."

"Your people?"

"Yes, they wanted to take over our entire planet and oppress the whole race. The only advantage we had was they didn't want anyone to find out about us and lose the opportunity we represented, so they jealously guarded our secret even better than we had. When we wiped out the mercenary units involved, no one else was left who knew our secret."

"Wiped out? I didn't think you were any good at killing."

"I said we didn't like it, not that we weren't good at it. Still, the cost was…significant to us, and we vowed to always keep our central eye on the mercenary races to ensure it didn't happen again."

"Is that why you are here? To watch us?"

"Several of the original mercenary units that wanted to enslave us were Besquith. We watch them especially closely. We recently received reports they were dealing with the Altar. The fact that the Besquith were interacting with their traditional enemies made us…curious. We wanted to know more about what the Besquith were doing; you just happened to be going our way."

"But you watch humans, too?"

"Are you a mercenary race?"

"Well, yeah, but we haven't tried to enslave you."

"No…not yet, anyway."

"Well, at least as far as the Besquith go, we would seem to have a common enemy. Wouldn't that make us your friends?"

"The enemy of my enemy isn't necessarily my friend, although it may be someone who I can work with. That is the only reason we're having this conversation; there may come a time where it is necessary for one of us to assist the other. We believe that having established ties ahead of time will help smooth our working relationship if that is needed. I am, however, counting on you to keep this to yourself. It is a secret we believe worth killing for, and for our race, there are none greater."

"Will you be coming with us when we reach our transport?"

"Unfortunately, no. Another ship will be waiting for us at the free trading station."

"Really? You set that up with your 'special ability?' How far can you transmit?"

"None of your business. It is also, however, irrelevant to the topic, as arranging transportation was nothing so exotic." The pilot tapped the instrument panel with one of his right arms. "The radio works very well."

"So that's how I should contact you if I need you? By radio?"

"Contact us? You don't contact us. Ever. We're empaths, though…when you need us, we'll contact *you*."

Nigel sat back in his chair, shook his head, then looked at the pilot. "Who knew that when we hired you as a pilot, you'd turn out to be some sort of master spy?"

"In this galaxy, things are rarely what they seem."

Captain's Cabin, Asbaran Ship *Annihilation*, Approaching the Stargate

"I went and checked the hold," Mason reported from the doorway. Nigel waved him in and the soldier took a seat on the desk chair, "and we've got a couple of problems."

"Yeah?" Nigel asked, sitting up on the bed.

"Well, first, it looks like the pilots weren't lying; there are five unmarked canisters down there that could very well be bioweapons. Whatever they are, we don't want to pull into somewhere with customs or an inspection process while they're still aboard. That'd be bad juju. Personally, I don't even want to have them onboard."

"Agreed. We need to get rid of them before we get back. When we're done, go talk to the pilots. When we get out of hyperspace, have them swing by the system's star so we can dump them in. What's the other problem?"

"The other problem is similar to the first. There are also two banshee bombs in the hold."

"Banshee bombs? I've never heard of them. Why are they a problem?"

"Well, they're even more illegal than Ensalaran brain slugs. First, they're built to be used from altitude. Like high altitude."

"Above the 10-mile limit."

"Exactly. That right there makes them illegal. Banshee bombs are also nuclear weapons."

"Nukes aren't illegal. Bad for business, maybe, but I don't think they're illegal. I mean, they're cheap and easy, right? So why not?"

"You're still kind of new, boss, but I've got to tell you, it goes way beyond a mere 'bad for business.' Most mercs don't like taking contracts where nukes are involved, or any type of slaughter contract for that matter. You never know when you might be on the receiving end of a slaughter contract, and it's awfully hard to surrender to an incoming nuclear warhead. Mercs take that kind of shit personal, you know? Mercs generally like to fight, but getting nuked out of existence just ain't my idea of a fair fight."

"Okay, so we don't use them. Why would the Besquith have them then? If they're illegal, what would they be doing with them? They can't use them; someone would notice if nukes started going off."

"Maybe…maybe not."

"What do you mean?"

"That's the thing about banshee bombs; they aren't your typical nukes. They're actually enhanced radiation weapons more like the ancient neutron bombs. Yes, they're low-yield thermonuclear weapons, but instead of a thick radiation case, they have a case that's wafer-thin, allowing all the neutrons to escape and radiate the people in the area of effect. The bombs don't generate anywhere near as much blast. The people die, and the structures remain standing. The victors can move right in shortly thereafter."

"For being illegal, you seem to know quite a bit about them."

"I took a contract one time where we moved into an area the Besquith had captured. There was an awful lot of radiation in the area, but not the kind that occurs naturally; most was zinc-65. One way you could get that is if you used an enhanced radiation weapon with a shell of neutron-activated zinc-64. The resulting zinc-65 scattered about would be a gamma emitter that was great for area denial. We didn't have enough evidence to prove they did it, but there have been lots of rumors for a long time that the Besquith have used banshee bombs in the past."

"But why would they do that? Wouldn't the Besquith irradiate themselves?"

Mason shrugged. "No idea. Apparently, they're fairly resistant to low levels of radiation."

Nigel's brows knitted. "Wait a minute," he said after a pause. "A banshee bomb would kill the people and leave the buildings standing?"

"Yeah, as long as they weren't really close to the detonation site."

"And the Besquith could move in right after?"

"Yeah, pretty much."

"And if they were released from greater than 10 miles' altitude, you wouldn't have to launch them from overhead; the ground forces might not even know they were under attack until it was too late."

"It would certainly be a non-standard attack that might go unnoticed…at least at the start."

Nigel snapped his fingers. "That's *it!* That's how those motherfuckers got into Moorhouse. They used banshee bombs on our base, killed our folks, and then moved in with all of their anti-air support. *Son of a bitch!* All they would have had to do is come up with a decent cover to get them fairly close. The troops would never have expected it."

"*Bastards!*" Mason added, kicking Nigel's garbage can. The thin metal crumpled under the force of his steel-toed boot. "You're right, sir, that *has* to be how they did it. *Damn it! Fuck!* Oh, if I didn't want to kill them before, I'm *so* ready to kill them all now."

When Nigel didn't say anything, Mason looked back at his leader. Nigel seemed lost in thought, his eyes unfocused.

"What are you thinking?" Mason asked. "Oh, crap, I never thought about it. We've got their bombs; we can call them out for using them."

"No," Nigel said, his voice quiet and far away. "No," he said again, a little louder and stronger. "We will *not* turn them in. Not only can't we prove the bombs are theirs, we can't prove they used them on our base. Knowing what must have happened isn't the same as proving it did."

"Besides," Nigel continued, his eyes still looking at something Mason couldn't see, "I don't *want* to turn them in. I had a Bedouin nanny who helped raise me, and she taught me the concept of 'hamasa.' This is the bravery honor code among the tribes. To have hamasa means you have the willingness to defend your tribe…whatever that takes."

Nigel's eyes regained their focus and he turned to look at Mason. The older soldier could see the fire burning in his eyes. "Hamasa demands that *I* defend our honor. Hamasa demands that *I* kill these bastards, who would seek to do harm to *my* tribe and all that I hold sacred. Hamasa demands that I kill *every one* of these worthless, honorless sons of bitches. And I'm going to do that! I will *not* turn them in; *I will bring them justice myself!*"

Nigel sprang from the bed, looking back and forth as if for something to take his anger out on…but found nothing. After a few seconds, he took a deep breath, let it out slowly, and his shoulders slumped. He sighed. "I promised myself I wasn't going to let my anger take hold of me again," Nigel said; "I promised to be more rational and work through situations, but the Besquith have driven me beyond that. I don't know how, but I can promise you two things. We *are* going to get to Moorhouse and, once there, we *are* going to kill every last one of them."

* * * * *

Chapter Twenty-Two

Captain's Cabin, *Annihilation*, Free Trading Station, Grbow III

"You said you wanted to see me once the Pendals left?"

"Yeah, thanks for coming by," Nigel said as Mason walked in. "I thought we needed to have a strategy session." He showed his senior enlisted to the chair at the desk and then sat on the bed.

"Sure thing, sir," Mason replied. "What's up?"

"I've been thinking and came up with some things that didn't make sense. I need to run this by someone, but I need you to keep this private." Mason nodded, and Nigel continued, "What do you know about the Pendals?"

"Do you mean our pilots or the race in general?"

"Either. Both."

"Well, I haven't had a lot of dealings with any of them, but I've seen them around periodically. They usually keep to themselves, though; I can't remember seeing them interacting with anyone. That's kind of weird, I guess, isn't it? I mean, I've seen them at Peepo's Pit, but I can't remember them either hiring anyone or being hired. I never thought about it before, but now that I do, I wonder what they were doing there."

"Okay, so the race is generally aloof. What do you know about our recent pilots?"

"Not a whole lot. I can't think of anything really specific."

"Yeah, me either. I don't think I even know their names."

"Now that you mention it, sir, I don't think I ever heard their names, either. Weird."

"You know what's even weirder? I think the Pendals knew ahead of time there were bioweapons on the ship."

"They did? How would they do that?"

"I don't know," Nigel said, "but if you remember, the pilot was the first person to suggest we use the term 'bioweapon' as a way to get onto the planet."

"That's right!"

"And it worked just as he suggested it would, so it's obvious the Besquith *are* using bioweapons."

"I would also have to agree with that."

"And, he's the one that suggested we attack the Besquith frigate that had the weapons onboard."

"Well, yeah, but we needed a ship to get off the planet, and that was the only one available. Are you suggesting he crashed the transport in order to make us capture that ship?"

"I don't know. I was in the cockpit when we crashed, and I don't *think* they did it on purpose. That would be a pretty dangerous stunt to crash it just hard enough to break it but not hard enough to kill everyone aboard."

"So what are you saying?"

"I don't know. Perhaps the crash was just a serendipitous event that gave them the opportunity to do what they already wanted to do. They may have wanted us to search the ship anyway, and the crash gave them the ability to do so. We'll never know. What I *do* know is that the pilot didn't seem to be very surprised when he found the weapons, and even though we were in a hurry to get off the planet, he did a thorough enough pre-flight to find them onboard."

"So what do you think that all means?"

"I don't know," Nigel said. "I'll tell you what, though…I'm looking forward to the next chance I get to talk to one."

"I'd rather meet one of them than the Besquith on Moorhouse," Top replied, handing him a data pad. "Here's the final list of casualties we took on Bestald. I don't see any way that we can continue with the original plan. We're down to only about a platoon of effectives; I've gone ahead and reorganized them as such."

Nigel took the data pad and scanned the list. He had known that some people were killed in the hangar assault, but he'd had no idea how bad it was. Almost half of the company was dead in just one battle; they were the first people killed under his leadership, and it was all his fault. His desire for retribution and hamasa evaporated like dew in the morning sun. He wasn't the right person to lead this mission, after all. He was incompetent and going to get everyone else killed when they reached Moorhouse. Obviously, Mason had been right at the start; Nigel wasn't ready for the leadership role. If his sister's life wasn't at stake, he would have dropped out of this mission and started looking for someone else to lead Asbaran Solutions. He had no idea what to do next.

"What do *you* think we should do?" Nigel finally asked.

"I think you wanted the leadership position, and we should do what you say—"

"You know as well as I do how that turned out! We lost half of our company. You want me to say it? Fine! I will. You were right; I wasn't ready to lead. There, is that what you want?"

"Easy, sir, that wasn't what I meant. You actually have done pretty well so far. You listen to advice and have shown good leadership. For example, even though you were hurt, you led the assault that captured this ship. You saw what needed to be done, gathered the available assets, and accomplished the mission. If you hadn't, we'd still be back on the planet…and I don't think they'd be treating us very well. The troops actually are starting to believe in you."

"Well, then why did you turn it around on me and say I should figure it out?"

"You interrupted me, sir. What I was going to say was that we'd do what you said, but if you wanted my advice, we need to hire more troops. We can't take Moorhouse and four companies of Besquith with what we've got. Even if we bluff our way to the surface and hit them with our CASPers, we'll still be slaughtered. You saw what the Besquith did to us on Bestald. Five of them were the equivalent to about 17 of our guys. The CASPers give us additional capabilities, but not enough to overcome 8:1 odds. It can't be done. We need more troops."

"Maybe we could hire the Tortantulas and Breetar to come with us to Moorhouse."

"I'm sorry, but that isn't going to happen," a voice said from the door. Breetar entered the room. "I've fulfilled my contract and will be leaving the ship here."

"What? You're not coming to Moorhouse with us?"

"No thanks. I told you before that airborne assaults aren't my thing. I hate spaceship crashes and they tend to do that around you a lot. Besides, I've seen enough Besquith in the last couple of weeks to last me the rest of this life and most of the next."

"What about the red diamonds? You're going to miss out on a big payday."

"I *am* sorry to miss out on that…however, a big payday isn't much good to me if I'm too dead to enjoy it."

"You don't think we'll be successful?"

"In a word? No. You're too outnumbered, even if you do get onto the planet unopposed."

"What about the Tortantulas?"

"They're out, too. They like wholesale slaughter better when they're the ones doing it, not having it done to them. Sorry. Hopefully, we can do business again in the future." Breetar turned and left.

"He's got a point," Mason said. "Even if they stayed, the psychopathic spiders wouldn't have made enough of a difference. Besides, this mission requires a little more subtlety than the Tortantulas generally possess. While they're great at blowing things up, we don't necessarily want them to drop a hangar on where the enemy is holding your sister. The chipmunk at least answered to orders, but he'd barely be a snack to one of the Besquith."

"We could have used them, though. We don't have time to go back to Earth and recruit more troops."

"Agreed; however, we don't have time *not* to. You want your sister back. I get that; I want her back too. But neither of us are getting her back if we don't get more troops. We'll be killed and so will she."

"Well, shit."

"Yeah."

Both men stared at the deck, trying to come up with an option that didn't end with their own funerals.

"Huh," Nigel said after a pause long enough to be uncomfortable.

"Got something, sir? I'm willing to discuss even a crappy idea at this point."

"Well, maybe. We need people right?"

"Uh, yeah. We *have* been discussing that."

"They don't have to be our people though, right?"

"What do you mean?"

"Well, all along, I've been thinking about going back to Earth and recruiting more people to fill out our ranks. But that means finding them, interviewing them, hiring them, and then training them to our standards. That's going to take a long time, far longer than we have. But what about if we hire a unit that's already trained?"

"What are you going to pay them with?"

"Well, we could sell So'Kla's ship and this frigate. That would give us enough credits to buy a transport."

"And then what? Try to get a group of troops to jump ship from one company en masse and come over to us? I don't think that would work too well. Besides not being terribly ethical, we probably don't want anyone who would just up and quit their company at a moment's notice. They couldn't be trusted and we'd get a pretty bad reputation, pretty quickly. There's also the fact that, even with selling the ship, the last time I looked, the company was pretty broke. Generally, mercenaries like to get paid and we're also going to have to refuel the frigate, which won't leave much left over to pay the mercs. History has shown that it's bad practice not to pay the people with the weapons once they complete the job you've hired them for."

"No, I'm not talking about trying to steal forces from another company, I'm talking about actually hiring another company…well, subcontracting our contract out to them, anyway. Look at it this way, we have a contract to provide defense for the plant on Moorhouse.

That contract is coming to an end. If we come in, wipe out the Besquith without destroying the factory, and satisfy the terms of the contract, we will get paid, and from that payment, we could pay whoever comes in with us."

"Subcontract it out. Hmmm…never thought of it that way."

"It would be a perfect solution. *If* we can find the right people, they wouldn't have to do a whole lot beyond the initial assault. Admittedly, there's going to be some danger in the assault they'd have to be compensated for, but after that, we'd just have to hold the plant for a few more days and then everyone would get paid. Not only that, we've had to fight to complete the contract, so we will collect on the combat clause, as well. If we can take it and hold it, we stand to have a pretty big payday, and one more than large enough to share with another company."

Mason's brows knit as he chewed over the plan in his mind. Finally, he looked up and said, "You know what, sir? I think you may have come up with a workable solution. There are some things that would have to be ironed out, and we would have to find the right company to subcontract to, but that just might work."

Nigel smiled.

"Before you get too big for your britches, though," Mason added, "there *are* some issues with the plan, and some of those may be showstoppers."

"Like what?"

"Like the fact we're on the ass end of the system, and there aren't a lot of opportunities. There's only one merc pit likely to have the forces we need as quickly as we'll need them."

"Okay, I defer to your judgment on that. We can head to that star system—wherever it is—as soon as we get our CASPers off the other ship."

"That isn't the problem. The problem is that, like I said, we're on the ass end of the system, and we are a *long* way from Earth. The odds of our finding humans out here will be pretty small."

"Okay, well maybe we'll have to hire an alien race to help us."

"That's going to be tricky. As we've already discussed, the Tortantulas and the Flatar are out. We're certainly *not* going to hire Besquith, and they will probably make up the bulk of the forces we find there. Hell, we may have a hard time just getting in and out of the pit if the word gets out that we were the ones that leveled the Drinkers' base. There will be Besquith that will want to avenge them."

"Let's talk about that for a moment, shall we? I heard the base went up in a nuclear explosion once we got off the planet. You wouldn't happen to know how that happened, would you?"

"Well, I didn't want the Besquith to be able to pin it on us, and we left a lot of our blood around the hangar, so I merely *suggested* to Zzeldar that some of the weapons in the hangar would do a great job of covering our tracks. What she took it upon herself to do with that information, I really can't be held accountable for."

Nigel's eyebrows rose. "Really, that's your story?"

Mason shrugged. "There wasn't time to call you, so I made a command decision to mention it to her. I didn't cause the explosion, though."

It was Nigel's turn to shrug. "Okay; whatever. I'll let it go, but next time, please clear it with me before you decide to nuke somebody, all right?"

"Yes, sir," Mason replied. "Besides, I know it wasn't a perfect solution; it was just the only thing that could be done with the time remaining."

"What do you mean?"

"I mean that it's possible some Besquith will come looking for whoever did it. They might even figure out it was us. I mean, we *are* in possession of one of their frigates, and there aren't very many humans on this side of the galaxy."

"But why would they want to search us out? There's no business reason to do so. They will just lose assets and not get paid anything for it. It doesn't make sense."

"Politicians don't make sense," Mason said, "and yet people still vote for them. Besquith don't make sense, either, and they certainly don't need a reason kill us; they just need an opportunity. I doubt they are going to want a rumor going around that someone blew up one of their bases *on their home planet*, and they didn't track down the people responsible and kill them in some horrible way. It's bad for their image."

"Okay, so we need to get rid of the frigate, and we have to be careful while we're there."

"Careful? We'll have to be *damned vigilant*. You may remember that there's only a platoon of us left, right? And the Besquith will have companies, if not *battalions*, of troops on the station?"

"I'm aware," Nigel replied. "Still, we have to go there."

"We're at least going to bring the CASPers this time, right? I understand why we had to leave them here when we went to Bestald, but the suits will help us even the odds some, too."

"Like I said, yes, we are going to get them. We should have had them last time. I shouldn't have worried about walking through the station with them. We lost a lot of good folks because I didn't bring them. That is a mistake I won't make again. We will also have the Jehas get the dropships from this ship once I purchase a transport for us; I want every advantage possible for when we get to Moorhouse."

"Bet your fucking ass," Mason said, then added, "Sir."

Gravity Ring, Free Trading Station, Grbow III

"*eople are staring,*" Turk radioed on the command frequency where only Nigel and Mason could hear.

Nigel slewed the monitor of his CASPer left and right. The corridor was fairly crowded, and all of the passers-by *were* staring.

"*Well, we have to get the CASPers to the new ship, and this is the fastest way to do it,*" Nigel replied. "*At least they're older models that had our unit insignias removed. They'll know we're human, but we could be any unit from Earth.*"

"*Can I do some misdirection, sir?*" Mason asked.

"*Go for it.*"

Mason turned on his external speakers. "Make a hole!" he broadcast as he slammed his way through the crowded ring. "Varangian Guard coming through!"

"*Varangian Guard?*" Nigel asked.

"*Always hated those stuck-up bastards,*" Mason replied. "Varangian Guard coming through!"

They made better time through the throng with Mason broadcasting, and they arrived at their destination 10 minutes later.

"There it is," Nigel said. "The *Vindicator.*"

"You actually *bought* that piece of shit?" Mason asked as he stared out Docking Bay B-17's viewing window. "With real money?"

"What do you mean?" Nigel asked. "The Jehas said it was a sound ship."

"They're hard to understand sometimes," Mason said. "What they probably said was, 'It sounds like a piece of shit.'"

"No; I had them look at it before I bought it. They said the engineering spaces were good."

"Really? Did they have their eyes open? Because I've left better-looking craps in the toilet after a hard night drinking."

"Look. We needed a transport, and this was the only one available. I was able to afford it with what I got from selling the ships we had. We wanted to blend in and look non-offensive. This ship screams 'inoffensive.'"

"And, 'It would be safer to fly anything else.'"

"Well, look at it this way. Who would be dumb enough to launch an assault using this?"

"I'd love it if you named any other merc unit *besides* Asbaran Solutions," Mason said hopefully.

"Oh, stop being such a baby. The Jehas said it would probably hold together for as long as we needed it to. It's going to work."

Mason turned away from the window. "Well, at least we won't have to worry about getting eaten by a Besquith." He shrugged. "Although I'm not sure dying in space is any better."

Captain's Cabin, Asbaran Ship *Vindicator,* Enroute to Telgar II

Nigel dropped the pen and sighed. How could there be so much paperwork while they were *on* a mission? Okay, there were probably things that needed to be documented for the bean counters back on Earth, but he needed to implement some procedures so he didn't have to authorize *every single credit* spent.

A knock on the door saved him from the stack of paperwork, and Mason and Turk shuffled into the cabin with their heads down and sat on the bed. Neither looked particularly happy when they looked up, either.

"So, what have you been able to learn from the info we gathered on Bestald?" Nigel asked.

Mason snorted. "Mostly we learned, 'Don't let Tortantulas open safes for you.' Zzeldar used way too much explosive, and the only info we got out of it is what we've been able to piece together from the remnants we gathered afterwards. It's been like putting together a jigsaw puzzle without the box to show us what it's supposed to look like."

"Did we get anything helpful?"

"A little. Turk has been spearheading the effort, so I'll let him brief you on what he found. Turk?"

The trooper cleared his throat. "I have some good news and some bad news, sir."

"All right, hit me with the good news. After playing with paperwork for the last couple of hours, I could use some good news."

"Despite the fact most of what we got was in little pieces when we recovered it, we were able to extract a few data points that will hopefully make our lives a little easier. Not only did we get some of their crypto codes, we also got some good info on their deployment data and the forces they took to Moorhouse."

"Yes?"

"Yes, sir. As you were no doubt aware, the contract called for four companies of troops. They took two companies of their own troopers and two companies of heavy air defense forces."

"They only had two companies of combat troopers?" Nigel asked. He turned to Mason. "I guess that confirms what you thought about their using banshee bombs."

"Unfortunately. There's no other way they could have evicted four companies of our guys in state-of-the-art CASPers. Especially since they would have been dug in and ready for them."

"I can't confirm that, sir," Turk said, "but I can tell you that's all the ground forces they took. Either they had traitors on the inside or they cheated somehow; I don't know. What I do know is that they lied about the air defense forces. Although they brought two companies of air defense troops, they brought *four* companies' worth of gear."

"Wait…four companies' worth of gear?"

"Yeah, in addition to the two companies of Blood Drinker troopers and two companies of anti-air forces from the Eagle Swatters, they also brought the gear from two companies of the Red Archers. All of these units are Besquith, by the way."

"The Drinkers paid to have extra equipment shipped in? That doesn't make sense. I mean, it makes sense for why we haven't been able to recapture Moorhouse…no one was prepared for that level of air defense. But that's a pretty big expense they aren't going to be reimbursed for."

"That's the interesting thing, though; they didn't pay for it. Someone else did. But here's the bad news, we don't know who as that data was lost. We searched through the pile of fragments we had three times, but no luck. Either we missed it or it was destroyed, but we don't have it. And, what's worse is there was another shipment."

"Of what?"

"I don't know. The only thing we recovered just mentioned it as 'the shipment,' but from the connotation, it had something to do with defensive material or systems, and it was *heavy*."

"So someone's helping them for some reason, although we don't know who or why. And they're sending the Besquith extra defensive material. Lovely. Well, maybe when we get to Moorhouse we can find out who they were going to pay it back to."

"Maybe…" Turk didn't sound convinced. "I don't think they are going to pay it back. One of the other fragments said something wouldn't have to be reimbursed. The Drinkers were just supposed to keep whatever it was as 'an advance against future ops.'"

"Who told them that?"

"Sorry, sir, but that info was lost, too. All we got was a callsign; it didn't explain who it was."

"Damn it! Well, thanks for putting that together. It explains part of the puzzle, even though I think it creates more questions than it answers. At least we know why our folks failed in their assaults; there were twice as many missiles headed at them as they were expecting. The good news is there aren't as many of the Drinker's combat troops as we thought there would be."

"Yeah, there are fewer," Mason said, "but we're still vastly outnumbered. Even if you only count the air defense assets as half-strength troopers, the Besquith still have the equivalent of at least

three companies of troops on the ground, and we only have a platoon of CASPers."

"I hope we find some troops at Telgar II, then."

"We'd better."

* * * * *

Chapter Twenty-Three

Gravity Ring, Free Trading Station, Telgar II

Mason put his hand on the door, then he stopped and turned around. "This pit is different than Peepo's," he said.

"What do you mean?" Nigel asked.

"I don't know…it's just different. Rougher, somehow. I've only been here once, and it was a long time ago. Don't expect Peepo's, though; if you do, you'll be disappointed."

He opened the door and walked in, followed by Nigel and Turk. Nigel could tell immediately what Mason meant by 'different.' It wasn't that the layout was different, although the establishment was smaller by about half. It also wasn't that the illumination was poor, which made things harder to see. Jingo's Jobs had a totally different feel to it that Nigel had a hard time placing.

As they walked across the pit to a table on the other side, Nigel finally figured it out. The place had a different vibe due to the undercurrent of conversation. In Peepo's, conversations were generally upbeat—positive people looking for work and finding it. When contracts couldn't be arranged or didn't go as planned, the parties usually separated peacefully or took it outside.

Business was handled differently at Jingo's. The mood seemed far more negative, with discussions usually devolving into yelling, insults, and aggression. Even though smaller and not as busy as Peepo's, the background noise was far louder, and the tone set him on edge. His eyes roamed the merc pit almost on their own, searching for the danger he could feel but not see.

"I see what you mean," Nigel said as they sat down at a table along the wall. "This place seems…I don't know. Evil isn't the right word for it, but it's not too far off."

"Yeah, I know," Mason agreed. "It feels like someone is staring at me, but I can never catch anyone doing it."

Nigel's eyes swept the room. The size of a neighborhood bar back in the United States, it could have held 200 or so humans, although there weren't any other humans there, and the various alien species tended to take up more space than the average human. As expected, there was a much higher percentage of Besquith, which didn't make Nigel feel any more comfortable. If any of them knew the humans had not only been to Bestald, but had also blown up one of the merc bases there, he doubted he would leave the establishment alive.

He didn't recognize many of the other species represented in the pit, and he realized that finding an appropriate subcontractor was going to be a lot harder than he had originally assumed. Besides the Besquith, he only recognized a couple of races he knew to be mercs.

On the opposite side of the pit, two MinSha stood at a table, recognizable as the only race that looked like oversized praying mantises. Considering mercs from that race had destroyed nearly all of his home country, including most of his ancestors, he had no desire to work with them or do anything that would advance their cause.

The other merc he recognized, a Selroth, sat a couple of tables away. A race that developed underwater, the Selroth had a rebreather unit on its tentacled head and a water tank on its back. Although he had heard they were honorable in nature, a Selroth unit would have a difficult time just staying alive in the arid climate of Moorhouse. They were out.

Before he had a chance to look further, a Veetanho appeared at the table. Nigel never saw her coming; she was just there. The Veetanho looked a great deal like Peepo, but was slightly shorter and her fur was a little darker.

The alien removed her dark glasses and sniffed several times. "You are newcomers to Jingo's," she announced. "No, one has been here before," she corrected, peering at Mason, "but the rest are new and unwelcome. We are currently not taking on new clients."

"I assume I have the honor of talking to Jingo?" Nigel asked.

"Yes, I am Jingo," the alien replied. "Why is it you are still talking to me when I have already informed you we are not taking on new clients?"

"May I at least establish my credentials?" Nigel asked. "While I may not be known to you, it would surprise me greatly if my company has not done business here before." He handed over an Asbaran Solutions coin.

Jingo took the coin and peered at it for a few moments before removing her goggles and staring at it a little longer. She handed the coin back. "I am sorry," she said, "but this company is unknown to me. As I earlier indicated, Jingo's is not taking new clients at the moment."

"It looks like business is going pretty well," Mason said, holding out a hand to indicate the busy interior; "aren't you even interested in what we're looking for?"

"No, I am not," Jingo replied. "Now, it is time for you to go."

Two Besquith appeared next to the Veetanho. Nigel had to force himself not to shrink back from them; they were the largest of their species he had seen, and saliva dripped from the open mouth of the alien on the left. Nigel wasn't sure how that many teeth could fit in one mouth.

"Are these…creatures…bothering you, Jingo?" the one on the right asked.

"No, I think they were just leaving."

"C'mon, let's go," Nigel said. Mason's mouth opened, and Nigel added, "No, let's just go."

The group walked out of Jingo's Jobs with the Besquith following one step behind. "And don't come back!" yelled the one that had previously spoken to them before slamming the door.

"What the hell?" Mason asked. "I've never heard of a merc pit closed to new customers before. Selective? Yes, Peepo's is selective and you have to have some credibility to get in. But to be told 'no' without even getting a chance to identify yourself? Never."

"It doesn't matter," Nigel said; "we weren't getting anything there, and we needed to leave. Arguing wasn't going to get us anywhere. Worse, nearly every Besquith was watching. If you'd done anything to Jingo or her pets, we'd have been torn to shreds. As it is, all of them probably now have categorized our scents for future reference."

"Well…hell," Mason said. He shook his head. "How did we get in this position?"

"Out of a job and unable to hire a subcontractor?"

"No, where you're the smart, rational one, and I'm the impatient hothead?"

"I think it's mostly because of something my grandfather used to say. He always appreciated Thaddeus Cartwright as a friend and competitor, and he used to say that Thaddeus gave him the best piece of advice he'd ever received."

"What's that?" Mason asked.

"Never trust a smiling Besquith. You couldn't see it, but the one behind you was smiling. It was time to go."

"Oh. Shit."

"Yeah, that."

"Hey," Turk interrupted, "If I can interrupt your lovefest, there's someone at that bar over there waving at you."

The three humans looked where the trooper pointed; two human males sat at an outdoor café. Judging by the uniform and their builds, they were both mercs.

"Do you know them?" Nigel asked. "Looks like an officer and a senior enlisted, but I can't place the company."

"Not me," Mason replied. "Never seen them before, and I thought I knew all the human outfits."

"Looks like they've been out for a while," Turk added. "Their uniforms are pretty beat up. I can't place them either, though."

"Well, know them or not, they're the first friendly faces I've seen here," Nigel said, "and it looks like they have beer. Let's go see what they want."

The officer introduced himself as Colonel Antonio Moretti of the White Company and the other man as his senior enlisted, First Sergeant Paolo Valenti.

"Did they let you in the merc pit?" Moretti asked after the group had been seated and ordered the closest thing the café had to a beer.

"No," Nigel said. "Jingo said they weren't taking any more clients."

"Got rather adamant about it, too," Mason added. "She even called a couple of her pet Besquith to see us out."

"One talked, and the other drooled?" First Sergeant Valenti asked.

"Yeah," Nigel said. "Somewhere between a St. Bernard and a Bloodhound."

"*Si*, we got the same treatment," Moretti replied. "The thing is, we aren't new clients. We've been there before. Hell, we got the contract we just finished in Jingo's. It was two years' ago, but still, that's where we got hired. How can she say we're not clients?"

"You just finished a contract?" Nigel asked.

"*Si*, we just finished a garrison gig. It was probably the most boring contract I've ever taken, but it was the only thing available here. In case you haven't noticed, humans aren't well-loved in these parts."

"Yeah, I've kind of noticed."

"Well, business used to at least be okay out this way, but it looks like the Besquith are trying to kick us out of this part of the arm. Or something. There were a whole lot more humans here when we left on the last job; you're the first ones we've seen since we got here two days ago."

"So what's your plan?" Nigel asked.

Moretti snorted. "I think the company's had enough of this part of the arm—"

"Got that *damn* right, sir," Valenti interrupted.

"—and I know I've had enough of it," Moretti finished. "The problem is that we are stranded here. Our first contract went bad, and we got left out here. I keep trying to negotiate a ride back to Earth as part of our contracts, but I haven't been able to find an employer that would let that clause stand. 'Too expensive,' they keep saying."

"Well, as it turns out, we've got a ride home," Nigel said.

"Anybody says something that way, there's a catch," Valenti said. "Read the fine print, sir!"

"There isn't a catch, per se, but we do have some business we have to complete prior to returning to Earth."

"What's the business?" Moretti asked.

"We have to kill a few Besquith that have claim-jumped on a contract of ours and, while we're there, get my sister back from the bastards."

"How many is a 'few' Besquith?"

"Four companies."

"I see," Moretti said, sounding considerably less enthusiastic than he had a moment previously. "How many companies do you have to kill them with?"

"How many men do you have?"

"We have two companies with Mark 7 CASPers."

"Then counting your troops, we have about two and a half companies."

"*Figlio di puttana!*" the first sergeant exclaimed. "Sir, these men are crazy. Let us leave before they infect us with their idiocy! I'll walk home first, if that's what it takes. I'd have a better chance of living through it!"

"I am afraid my first sergeant is correct. No matter how much we want to return home, to assault a planet with two-to-one odds against you is not bravery, it is lunacy. There will be none of us left when we are through to accept your ride home."

"What if I told you I knew their operational patterns? How and where they deployed their forces?"

"I believe we would still have to pass, *grazie.*"

"What if I had an operational transponder from one of their ships that would probably get us through their defenses so we could take them by surprise?"

"That might actually be something worth talking about…if we were starting from better odds. As we are not, unfortunately, we must still pass."

"What about the fact that the Besquith are holding my sister? Surely you must want to help a damsel in distress?"

"Despite our Italian heritage, we are mercenaries, not romantics. I am sorry for your sister, and I hope she has an easy death, but adding ours to it won't make it any better. Pass."

"Not even to help one of the Four Horsemen? We have long memories for those who help us…as well as for those who did not."

"Your memory will be somewhat shorter when you are all dead, which you *will* be after this assault. I have a tremendous respect for the Horsemen…but I must decline."

Nigel sighed. "I had hoped to appeal to your softer side, but what if I could pay you ten million credits for two weeks' worth of work, plus a ride home when we're done?"

"Ten mill—I'm sorry, did you say, ten *million* credits for two weeks' work?"

"I did."

"And how exactly do you intend to pay us this fee?"

"It'll be paid in red diamonds."

Valenti leaned over and whispered something into Moretti's ear. Moretti made eye contact with him afterward and nodded.

Moretti turned back to Nigel and asked, "How do I know your word is good and that these red diamonds actually exist in this quantity?"

Nigel reached into a leg pocket and pulled out a small wad of folded up papers. He unfolded them and smoothed them out on the table. "Here's the applicable pages from the initial contract. We were to be paid 20 million credits for keeping four companies of troops on garrison duty on Moorhouse while our employers mined the red diamond vein there. It was a one-year contract that ends in two weeks. We also had a combat clause of 5% per occurrence, with a maximum of 25%. Our assault on the Besquith will be the fifth combat action between us, so we stand to make another five million. All told, whoever is in possession of the garrison there will be paid 25 million credits if they can keep the red diamond mine from being damaged for the next two weeks; I will pay you 10 million credits if you help us recapture the garrison."

"Well, this certainly sheds a different light on the situation," Moretti noted. He looked around the cafe. "Please put away the papers before someone else sees them."

Nigel folded the papers and returned them to his leg pocket. "So," he asked, "are you in?"

Gravity Ring, Free Trading Station, Telgar II

"Okay," Colonel Moretti said, "you've piqued my curiosity, especially if it comes with a ride home. I'm interested enough to listen to your plan, anyway. If there's only two and a half companies of us, though, and four companies of Besquith, it's going to take a good plan or we're out. A *damn* good one."

"And hopefully the plan includes a big pre-assault bombardment to even the odds, right?" First Sergeant Valenti asked.

"Well, no," Nigel replied. "Actually, it doesn't. They are holding my sister hostage. If we bomb them, we may inadvertently kill her. They would also know we're coming, and they might kill her or try to use her against us."

"So what's your plan?" Moretti asked.

"I have a few options I'm looking at. Before I tell you what they are, how about telling me a little bit more about your forces and what their capabilities are. That way, I can incorporate them into the plan to the greatest extent possible."

"We are returning from an extended period of garrison duty—"

"*Non-combat* garrison duty," Valenti interjected.

"A period of non-combat garrison duty," Moretti finished. "On the good side, we have state-of-the-art Mark 7 CASPers that are in pretty good shape since they haven't been used much."

"Mark 7s?" Nigel asked. "How long have you guys been out here?"

"A while. Why?"

"Because the Mark 8 has been the standard for several years now."

"Really?" Moretti sighed. "It has been too long since we were home."

"How much better are the Mark 8s?" Valenti asked.

"They're a little more agile," Mason replied, "and they've got a bit better power management, but they're small as hell and chafe something fierce."

"I will look forward to seeing your Mark 8s in action then," Valenti said.

"Me too," Mason replied. "At the moment, we are using a combination of 6s and 7s."

"What?" Moretti asked. "I thought the Horsemen always had the best equipment."

"Usually, we do," Nigel replied; "however, after several failed attempts to recapture Moorhouse, we are down to our backup gear."

"If you have already tried to recapture this base 'several times,'" Moretti remarked, "what is going to make this attempt succeed, where the others did not?"

"*This* time, we know where they are," Nigel said. "We have their base schematic and know where all their fortifications are. More importantly, though, we also have one of their transponders."

"And what is that going to do for you?"

Nigel smiled. "What's that going to get us? Close."

Moretti leaned forward and put his elbows on the table. "If you can get us close, I have something that may help."

"Sir, you're not going to—" Valenti started, but Moretti cut him off.

"Yes. Yes, I am. I hate those bastards, and this will help even the odds."

"But sir, if it gets out…"

"Well then," Moretti replied, twirling one side of his mustache, "I guess we will just have to make sure the word doesn't get out, won't we?" He turned to Nigel. "What are your intentions regarding Besquith prisoners?"

"We're outnumbered, and I don't have anyone to guard them," Nigel replied. "Besides, how many times have you ever heard of a Besquith surrendering?"

"Never." He released the mustache and smiled. "In that case, I'd like to let you know we are still in possession of several thousand gallons of diethylzinc left over from our last garrison contract."

"I'm not familiar with that. What do you do with it?"

"I'm told it is an important reagent in organic chemistry; however, our use was somewhat less esoteric." The smile grew. "We have it because it is also highly pyrophoric."

"What the hell's that?" Mason asked.

"It ignites spontaneously in air," Valenti explained. "The way we have it formulated, the substance does it quite spectacularly after a few seconds."

"Would this be of assistance?" Moretti asked.

Now it was Nigel's turn to smile. "Yes, I think it might." He spoke for another 10 minutes then answered questions for another five.

Moretti sat back in his seat, frowned, then shook his head. "Even with all that, it is still going to be *very* dangerous." The smile reappeared. "Happily," he added, "that's just the way we like it. We're in."

Asbaran Ship *Vindicator,* Free Trading Station, Telgar II

Mason entered the cargo hold to find Nigel and Colonel Moretti supervising the loading of a number of 55-gallon drums. "Are they almost done?" Mason asked. "We need to get going. I just saw the Jehas, and they said we'll be late to the stargate if we don't depart soon."

"This is the last one, I think," Nigel replied as a tractor loaded a 2,000 gallon drop tank in the space next to the drums. The vehicle crawled across the deck, barely moving as it delivered its load.

"Is that the fastest it can go?" Mason asked.

"If you value your ship, yes," Moretti replied. "The diethylzinc inside those containers will self-ignite in air, and it's nearly impossible to extinguish once lit. As one little hole in any of those drums would likely result in the loss of this craft and everyone onboard, you will hopefully excuse my men for being very, *very* careful loading and securing them onboard."

"Impossible to extinguish?"

"He's correct," Nigel replied. "I looked it up. A long time ago, the space agency in the old United States of America used it as rocket fuel. Expose it to air and off you go. It's so nasty the Jehas refused to let it come aboard. I had to up their contract to get them back to the cockpit, and they refuse to go into combat with it still onboard. If there is a danger of someone shooting at us, it has to go aboard one of the dropships."

"Really?" Mason asked. "That's all it took to get a raise? Just complain a bit?"

"We need them to fly the ship. You're a grunt; you'll get nothing and like it."

* * * * *

Chapter Twenty-Four

Cockpit, Asbaran Ship *Vindicator,* Approaching Planet Moorhouse, Kepler 62 System

The ship dropped into normal space and was immediately hailed by the forces on the planet. *"Unknown ship, this is Bravo Delta Control. State your name and intentions."*

"This is the Annihilation," the Jeha pilot replied, *"with stores for the company."*

There was a brief pause before the reply, *"Roger that, Annihilation. Your signature isn't matching what we have on record for you. What type ship are you?"*

The pilot turned in his seat to look at Nigel, who was watching with Colonel Moretti from the back of the cockpit. "What type of ship are we supposed to be? You never told me that."

"The *Annihilation* was a cruiser," Nigel replied. "No wait, it was smaller. It was a frigate."

"That's the problem. This trash hauler is bigger than a frigate." The pilot switched to the radio. *"Bravo Delta Control, we are a company frigate. Don't you have our transponder?"*

"We do, but it doesn't match your radar signature. Authenticate Whiskey Tango Foxtrot."

The Jeha looked at its slate. "Well, you're in luck," it said. "That's one of the codes I have." He switched to the radio. *"I authenticate Bravo Sierra. We're also shuttling some new dropships in, too; that's probably why our shape looks off. We will appear a little larger than normal."*

"Stand by. We're looking."

"Think they bought it?" Colonel Moretti asked.

"I don't know…" Nigel said. "The codes should have been good, and the transponder is off one of their ships. I never thought about them checking our ship's size or shape…"

The seconds turned into minutes and seemed like hours.

"Annihilation, *you are cleared to proceed and land at the base.*"

"Cleared to proceed. We are starting our approach."

Nigel nodded and turned to Colonel Moretti. "See, we're in."

"Yeah, here's where the fun starts. I just hope your plan works."

"It'll work," Nigel replied. He added silently, *I hope.*

Cargo Hold, Asbaran Ship *Vindicator,* Approaching Planet Moorhouse, Kepler 62 System

"So here's the plan," Mason said, briefing the assembled troops and pilots. A diagram of the Besquith base hung from the bulkhead behind him. "My platoon is going to be in Dropship *Two*. Our mission is to assault the headquarters building here at the north end of the starport," he said, pointing to a building on the diagram. "We have to hit them hard and fast so they don't kill the hostage before we can rescue her. The White Company will deploy from the *Vindicator* as it flies across the base and will assault the Besquith barracks, which are on the west side of the starport. There are three buildings here," he tapped the diagram; "these are the barracks. Your mission is to kill any Besquith you see and ensure they are contained so my squad can recover the hostage unimpeded."

"What will Dropship *One* be doing?" First Sergeant Valenti asked.

"Dropship *One* is going to hit the barracks ahead of your assault and try to kill as many of the damn wolves as possible, right, Lieutenant?"

"Yeah," LT Seville said. "I'm not sure what it's going to look like; all I can tell you is it's going to be impressive. You'll want to make sure the *Vindi* isn't too close when I begin my attack run."

"The pilots know," Mason confirmed. "Trust me, based on their response, they will stay *way* back. After Dropship *One* hits the barracks, the White Company will jump out of the *Vindicator* and hold positions here and here." He tapped the diagram. "Once the troops in the barracks are no longer a threat, the White Company will split. First Company will come to the headquarters building to assist us, if needed, and Second Company will go capture the air defense positions here to the east of the starport."

"How many Besquith will be in the barracks?" First Sergeant Valenti asked.

"It should be most of them," Mason replied. "We'll be attacking at night. It's possible, although not probable, that there will be a patrol or two out, but most of the enemy forces should be in the barracks when the assault begins."

Valenti looked penetratingly at Lieutenant Seville. "If you miss, we will be outnumbered two to one," he said; "please try not to miss."

"That's the plan," Mama replied, "but I've got to tell you—I've never done anything quite like this before."

Second Platoon, First Company, Blood Drinkers

Sergeant Creg-An looked through his night vision glasses, surveying the countryside. Nothing.

"Why do you bother?" Corporal Stel-Ca asked. "There's nothing out here. There wasn't yesterday, there isn't tonight, nor will there be tomorrow. This place is a desert. There's no reason for us to even be out here."

Sergeant Creg-An removed the glasses from his eyes. "No, there isn't," he replied, "and if your littermate hadn't eaten one of the miners, we wouldn't be out here on this punishment detail."

"This is stupid," Stel-Ca said, head down as he picked his way through the rock-strewn path. "He's dead. I don't understand why *we* have to do this useless patrol. They could at least let us use the vehicles."

"We're being punished for the 5,000 credits it cost the company. The colonel thinks we should have been watching him better and prevented him from doing it. It's punishment. *That's* why we're walking."

"You can't really blame him; he was bored."

"We're all bored. This place is awful, and there are no creatures to amuse ourselves with except for the miners, who are off-limits. Still, our hitch is almost up. We will be out of here soon, with a lot of credits to entertain ourselves with. Assuming no one else screws up."

"Well, at least we only got one week of night patrols. First Platoon got two weeks, and they have to patrol the hills."

"See? It's not so bad, now is it?"

"*I've got lights up ahead,*" the squad's scout, Corporal Shah-Ca radioed from the front of the patrol. "*Coming toward us, moving quickly.*"

"It's probably the supply frigate. Headquarters said we had a ship coming in."

"Ah, okay. Definitely a ship coming."

Sergeant Creg-An raised his night vision glasses again. Although he could see pretty well in the dark without them, the added assistance turned the night into day. "Entropy…" he muttered.

"What is it, Sarge?" Corporal Stel-Ca asked.

"That's not one ship," he said; "that's three ships flying in formation."

"Base, this is Sergeant Creg-An. You've got three ships incoming!"

Cockpit, *Dropship One*, Approaching the Besquith Base, Planet Moorhouse

"Shit!" LT Seville exclaimed as her radar warning gear came to life with the warble of an acquisition radar going live. *"Defensive systems are lighting off in front of us!"* she announced on the command frequency. *"I don't know how, but it looks like they know we're coming."*

"We're almost there," Nigel replied. *"Go, go, go!"*

Mama jammed her throttles to the stops, accelerating past the lumbering transport. Faster and more nimble than the bigger ship, she raced ahead, quickly leaving it far behind.

"We've got a minute or two while they warm up," she said, "but then things are going to get hairy. We're going to have to get this right the first time."

"Guidance is good," LTJG 'Dark' Minion said, looking into his targeting scope. "I've got the base in front of us and am just starting to break out the barracks."

LT Seville pushed the throttles harder, willing the dropship to go faster, but the motors were already at max thrust. A third enemy acquisition radar activated, and then a fourth.

"I was hoping it would take some time for the damn wolves to get out of bed and to their positions," she said. "No such luck."

"I've got the targets," Dark said. "Come right 10 degrees so we can line them up."

"Right 10," she repeated, turning the dropship to the new heading. She shook her head. The transport, and all the troops onboard, were going to be in a world of shit by the time they arrived.

"Perfect," Dark announced. "Left five. We're on target. 20 seconds."

"Left five," Mama replied. She threw a switch in the center of the instrument panel. "Master arm is on!" The constant warble in her ear changed pitch and frequency. "Target tracker activated! Active defenses coming on!" She pushed the button on her controls that launched a spread of decoys. The flares blossomed brightly behind her, burning at over 3,000 degrees, silhouetting her ship.

"Stand by…" Dark said. "Stand by…bombs away!"

Mama pressed the release button and twenty 55-gallon drums separated from the dropship in a string several hundred yards long. As the last drum fell away from the craft, she pulled back sharply on the stick, and the dropship went into a vertical climb.

"What the hell are you doing?" Dark asked as the night sky turned to day behind them. "They'll kill us up here for sure! We'll attract all the missiles!"

"Yes, we will!" LT Seville exclaimed, the missile warning tone going crazy in her headset as the system detected multiple launches. "If the transport gets shot down we'll end up just as dead!" Passing

20,000 feet she snapped the dropship back around in a tight turn, launching another round of missile countermeasures. "Hang on; we've got a date with their antiaircraft folks."

Cargo Bay, *Dropship Two*, Approaching the Besquith Base, Planet Moorhouse

"*Stand up!*" Mason ordered as the red light came on and the back ramp of the dropship started down. The black of night yawned in front of the troopers as they turned and queued up at the end of the ramp.

"*Go!*" Mason yelled as the light went green. Troopers jumped into the void as fast as they could follow the soldier in front of them. Nigel watched from the back of the stick as the troopers shuffled toward the door. Fear of jumping into the unknown warred with the excitement of knowing the assault was finally underway. Fear seemed to be winning.

A bright light lit the night sky as the trooper in front of Nigel jumped, and the dropship was buffeted by a blast, throwing Nigel to the side as the dropship swayed out from under him. Mason, the only other trooper onboard, steadied him and pushed him out the door.

Overbalanced, he fell into the void head first and flailed his arms trying to regain his balance. After a few seconds of sheer terror while falling headfirst toward the ground, he remembered the attitude adjustment system and triggered the autocorrect. Tiny jets fired, righting the suit and stabilizing his fall. He triggered his jets as the ground came rushing up to meet him, but was a little late and ended up crashing into the ground at a higher rate of speed than the suit was rated for.

His knees were bent, preventing massive damage to the system, but he was thrown forward face-first onto the hard, bare ground.

"That did *so* not rock," he said to himself as he picked himself off the ground. The impact had stunned him, and he found himself a little wobbly as he looked around to orient himself. Several yellow warning lights had illuminated on his display, but nothing was in the red. Both his laser and his MAC were green. That was something. He armed them both.

"Are you okay?" Mason asked as he landed next to Nigel in a bust of flames. "Sorry, didn't mean to give you that much of a shove."

"Yeah, I'm okay…mostly…I think. Nothing's broken."

"Good. Let's go, sir, or we're going to miss the assault. Follow me!"

In a blast of rocket fire, he was gone.

Cargo Hold, Asbaran Ship *Vindicator,* Planet Moorhouse

The White Company stood assembled in perfect company formation on the cargo bay ramp, staring into the darkness. Not designed to deploy troops, the Jeha pilots had overridden the safety interlocks to get it to open in flight. The Company stood at a state of attention that would have been exemplary on the parade ground; the fact they did so with empty space rushing past just a few yards away was a tribute to their professionalism. Moretti couldn't have been any prouder of his men and women than he was at that moment.

"See that?" Colonel Moretti asked, pointing to the void behind him. *"You know what that is? That is your destiny! We jump tonight as a brotherhood; all of us, humans, united in one fight! Riches await those of us who survive the night, but even more important is the message we send these worthless dogs. They thought they could come here and take this planet from humans and collect on our bounty. They thought we would lie down and allow them to take humans hostage. They were* wrong! *We will crush them and burn them in their lairs, and then we will teach them* not *to fuck with humans again! By the time we are done with them, the entire Besquith race will call the White Company their masters. They will learn to* fear *humanity, and they will learn to fear us!* Who is with me?"

"We are!" the troopers screamed as the night lit up behind Moretti, giving them a look at the ground only 200 feet below them.

"Look at this! They have even turned on the lights so they can see their destinies arriving! Take care of your brothers and sisters, and don't leave a single one of those bastards alive. They want to kill humans? We'll show them who's boss!" The light went green. *"For the White Company and humanity!"* He turned and stepped off the ramp, with the rest of the White Company right behind him.

* * * * *

Chapter Twenty-Five

“Missile, two o’clock low!” Dark yelled, pointing at the weapon streaking toward the craft. It looked like the finger of God pointing at them.

“Tally,” Mama, said, turning into its path. She fired off a set of countermeasures and yanked the dropship around in a hard 8-g turn, and the missile tracked off on one of the decoys.

“Kinda busy,” Mama said. “Can you flip the Master Arm on and set it up to release the centerline store?”

“What? You’re not going to—”

“The hell I’m not! Arm it up! I’m *not* going to get hit with it still attached to us!” Mama fought the controls as she evaded another missile and then a third. The air defense techs might have started slow, but they were up to speed now, and she knew it wouldn’t be long until one wiped her from the sky. The controls were already mushy; something had broken loose in the last near miss. At least it hadn’t hit the store or it would have been ‘game over’ for them.

“Master Arm on! Centerline store ready for release.”

In a burst of flames, a missile lifted off from the left. As soon as it cleared the launch rails, it turned and began tracking the dropship. Fuck.

“Missile, three o’clock low!” Dark yelled. “Break right!”

"Can't!" Mama exclaimed, pushing the controls forward until the planet filled the cockpit window. "Got one over here, too." She risked a glance to the right and saw the missile Dark had called. She winced; they were screwed. She might beat one of them, but the other would get them. It was higher than she wanted to drop the non-aerodynamic store, but she was out of time. Mama nudged the controls, putting the reticle in the center of the missile complex and mashed the release button. She felt the dropship jump as the 2,000 gallon tank fell away from the craft, after which she yanked the ejection lever with her left hand. Her seat was still going up the rails when the first missile hit.

The White Company, Barracks, Besquith Base

"Top, take First Company down to the furthest building, and I will send one of my platoons to the second building," Colonel Moretti said.

The three-story barracks buildings were burning nicely. Each of them had been hit with at least two of the 55-gallon drums of diethylzinc, and it looked like the middle building had been hit by no less than four; the barrels ruptured as they hit, spraying diethylzinc all over the building, which then immediately caught fire as it was exposed to the air.

100 years before, people might have confused it with napalm, but it was much, much worse; unlike napalm, it was a liquid. It ran into cracks, under doors, and anywhere else the enemy might be hiding. The screams when he had first arrived had been horrific. Several of the Besquith had stumbled out of the building on fire, trying to escape the flames. They had been shot down like dogs.

It was an awful way to die, but it was evening the odds nicely. And if the Besquith had nuked Asbaran, they deserved it. As another Besquith stumbled out of the building on fire, Moretti changed his mind. No. No one 'deserved' to die like that, even the Besquith.

With a roar, a missile lifted off across the starport. Moretti watched it go, thankful he was on the ground. That was at least the third that had launched. The missile exploded, illuminating the dropship it had just hit.

"*Looks like they just bagged one of the dropships,*" First Sergeant Valenti radioed.

"*I saw it,*" Moretti replied. "*Obviously there are mutts over at the air defense positions.*"

"*Want me to send a squad? I saw at least one parachute; we might be able to recover the pilot.*"

"*No, we need to make sure we clean out the barracks first. Anyone that got out will have to—*"

The night turned to day as an enormous fireball covered the entire air defense site.

"*That ought to suppress the air defenses some,*" Valenti noted.

"*No shit. Okay, let's concentrate on the barracks, and then we'll see if we can find the pilots.*"

"Movement!" Corporal Rick 'Waldo' Ewald shouted. "Here they come!"

Moretti turned in time to see the pack come around the end of the building. Already in an arrowhead formation, the group of 10 Besquith fired light lasers as they raced toward his men.

"*Platoon, fire!*" he ordered, sending the location of the enemy via a push to the other troopers still in company with him. "*Light 'em up, Waldo!*"

Moretti lifted his right arm, braced himself and began firing his arm-mounted .70 caliber machine gun. *"Chunk! Chunk! Chunk!"* The rifle fired three-round bursts, and two of his first three shots hit the lead Besquith as it charged straight toward him. The rounds could pass through a quarter-inch steel plate, and the first round had no problem going through the creature's helmet, skull, and back out the other side. The alien looked like it had run into a wall; its head snapped down, breaking its neck, and its rush turned into a tumble. In a bit of overkill, the second bullet tore out the Besquith's lungs.

Ewald opened up with his minigun, sweeping the six-barrel rotary machine gun back and forth across the oncoming force. Thousands of .50 caliber hyper-fragmentation bullets scythed through the formation, and most of the aliens dropped. The rest of the platoon joined in, and the attack was destroyed. Only one Besquith remained alive. Shot through the spine, it continued to crawl toward Moretti using only its arms, saliva and blood dripping from the corners of its snarling mouth, its back legs useless.

Moretti took two steps forward, flipped the alien over, and pinned it to the ground. One round through the head, and the Besquith stilled.

"Hey, does anyone smell barbeque?" Corporal Hicks asked.

Moretti turned to look at him. Even through the suit, his body language indicated displeasure.

"Too soon, sir?" Hicks asked.

"Yeah."

Second Platoon, First Company, Blood Drinkers

*"T*he base is under attack," Sergeant Creg-An reported.

"Is that what is happening?" Staff Sergeant Cahl-Ga, the First Platoon leader asked. *"We saw the sky light up and thought there had been an accident. Where are you currently? Can you see who is attacking?"*

"We are approaching the starport from the north, but we haven't made contact with any of the enemy yet. I suspect it is the humans but can't confirm."

"That makes sense," Staff Sergeant Cahl-Ga noted. *"We are approaching from the east. I saw several missile launches, so it looks like the missile folks are active."*

"They were. *It looks like they just got hit with some kind of fire bomb. I don't know how many of them survived. The humans also hit the barracks with fire bombs. They are on fire, and I do not believe we will receive much support."*

"Understood. It is up to us to hold the base. Search out opportunities to hit them where you can do so without losing many troops. We don't know how many troops they have, and until we do, we will want to minimize our losses."

"Yes, Staff Sergeant; I will do as you instruct."

"Good. We will be there soon. Out."

"First platoon is on their way," Sergeant Creg-An said as the platoon approached one of the outlying buildings. "We are to look for opportunities to hit the enemy." He pulled out his night vision glasses and surveyed the surrounding area. "There is a ship on the starport," he noted.

"Why do you suppose it's there?" Corporal Stel-Ca asked.

"I don't know," Sergeant Creg-An replied. *"Corporal Shah-Ca, are you in position to see the starport?"*

"Yes. A ship just landed."

"Can you see what's going on around it?"

"It doesn't look like anything is going on. No one is offloading. The ship is just sitting there."

"The ship is our opportunity," Sergeant Creg-An noted. He nodded to the vehicles surrounding them. "This is how we're going to exploit it."

Asbaran Force, HQ Building, Besquith Base

Mason was already giving orders when Nigel landed next to him at the side of the headquarters building. "Glad you could make it, sir," he said. "I took the liberty of assigning some duties in your absence; here's what I'd like to do. I'm not a big fan of opening doors when people know I'm coming, so I'd like to take Otter and Lucky with me and enter through the second floor. I sent Corporal Sparks and Privates Lewis and Freese to watch the back door, and I'd like it if you'd stay here to shoot any Besquith that tries to escape through the front."

"So, basically, I stay out of the way and let you do your job?"

"I guess you could look at it that way, sir, if you had to. I'd prefer if you'd look at it like you were controlling the fight from a place where you could see the whole battlefield."

An enormous fireball engulfed the missile revetments to the southeast, adding to the light of the burning barracks buildings to the southwest.

"See sir?" Mason added. "A good commander would want to know what just happened over there, since that wasn't part of the plan. While you do that, we'll just go take a look around inside."

"Damn it, Mason," Nigel said. A second blast came from just north of the antiaircraft position, and Nigel sighed. "Okay, go ahead. But be careful, all right?"

Mason smiled. "Vigilance is my middle name." He turned to Corporal Melissa Otero and Corporal Jim Day. "Let's go." Without a further word, he jumped, rocketing upward to smash headfirst through a window on the second floor of the building. The corporals launched themselves through the air and crashed through windows on either side of Mason's point of entry.

East of the Starport, Besquith Base, Planet Moorhouse

LT Seville checked her parachute. Good canopy. Well, at least one thing went right tonight. She looked down to check her landing area and found the whole area lit up from the fire burning at the air defense site. From what she could see, the drop tank had landed a little short of her aim point, but it had then burst and coated most of the area in whatever the hell the substance was. Most of the missile emplacements were burning merrily as their ammunition cooked off under the ferocious heat of the fire. The dropship had come down a little further north on one of the revetments. She smiled. Those were good things, too.

The smile was fleeting. The fires lit the area so well she could see that there were still a number of Besquith soldiers running around. Some were trying to extinguish the flames in various places, to little avail. Others were trying to move ammunition away from the spreading flames. Unfortunately, there were still others who appeared to have decided to look for the people who attacked them and continue the fight. She could see them quite clearly as she rocked slightly in her chute…and if she could see the Besquith, they could see her.

She tried to draw her pistol, and nearly passed out as a wave of pain lanced through her arm. Looking down, she could see that her arm bent unnaturally at the wrist; it must have been broken in the ejection and she hadn't noticed it until then.

She wouldn't be able to fire or to even draw her pistol with her right hand.

Damn it.

She tried to reach over with her left hand, but the parachute straps were in the way. All she did was cause the parachute to sway, aggravating her arm. *Damn it!*

She looked down, dreading what she'd see, but none of the Besquith seemed to have noticed her. They were all firing at something to the south of her. Holding her right arm as close to her chest as she could to protect it, she reached up with her left hand and grabbed the handle on the parachute risers. Slowly, the parachute turned, her right arm on fire with the effort.

Finally she could see what they were aiming at. As she had feared, they were firing at LTJG Minion in his parachute. She strained to get her pistol again, but once again the risers kept her from reaching it. She drew a breath to scream and draw their attention, but saw she was too late. Dark had been riddled with both laser fire and some kind of MAC-like weapon. The Besquith continued to fire at the copilot, even though he was now slumped in his chute, laughing as they fired. One of the MAC rounds severed his left riser and that half of the canopy flew up, turning the parachute into a streamer. Dark fell the remaining 30 feet to crash into the ground where he lay unmoving.

Bastards. They'd pay for that.

* * * *

Chapter Twenty-Six

The White Company, Barracks, Besquith Base

ovement from the east!" someone radioed. *"Holy shit! Armor! I've got armor coming from the east!"*

The radio went wild.

"When did the mutts get armor?"

"No one told me we were going up against armor!"

"This ain't happening, man!"

"Everyone knock that shit off! Moretti ordered, using his command suit to override everyone else's transmissions. *"So they've got armor. We've faced armor before. Now shut the hell up so we can deal with it. Valenti, what have you got?"*

"We've got at least one tank and three APCs headed our way. We're going to need assistance."

"Copy. The northern barracks building is pretty done. Everyone, head to First Company's position on the double. Let's go—shag ass!"

Inside his suit Moretti shook his head as he activated his jets and jumped. Where *had* the Besquith gotten the armor? If they had it here, did they have more of it somewhere else? He shrugged off the thought; he'd deal with the approaching forces first and would worry about any additional forces afterward. If there was an afterward.

Asbaran Force, HQ Building, Besquith Base

Head down, Mason crashed through the window, pieces of acrylate splintering in all directions. Smashing the pseudo-glass didn't make as much noise as real glass would have, but the slamming sounds of three half-ton suits landing above them was sure to be loud enough for any Besquith below to know the humans had arrived.

Mason knew their time was limited.

The interior of the room was much darker than outside, and Mason activated the suit's low-light monitor. Nothing worthwhile. It was some sort of office space and the middle of the night; no one was there.

"Follow me," Mason said, heading to the door. He threw it open; the hallway beyond the door was just as dark; no light showed from underneath the other seven doors. The floor seemed quiet…except for the Besquith at the end of the hall. The enemy soldier had been aiming a weapon out a window on the front of the building; as Mason opened the door, it turned and fired back down the hallway.

Mason dove back into the room. The Besquith was a split-second too slow; the cannon rounds narrowly missed the human and destroyed the wall at the end of the corridor.

"Grenade, right," Mason said as he picked himself off the floor. "One Besquith, 50 feet down the corridor."

"You got it, Top," Otter said. She stepped to the doorway, pulled the pin from a grenade, and lobbed it down the hallway without looking. The grenade detonated, and she stepped into the passageway. The Besquith was already down, trying to hold its stomach together. She shot it through the head with her laser. "Clear!" she exclaimed.

"Good job," Mason said, coming out of the room behind her and heading toward the staircase. "Let's go."

Asbaran Command, HQ Building, Besquith Base

"*D*ropship One, *Asbaran Command*," Nigel radioed. "*Come in!*" He had tried a couple of times, but hadn't received an answer. Hopefully, the fireball at the missile revetments hadn't been the dropship. They only had two.

"*Command, this is Dropship* Two. *Dropship* One *is down. There may have been a chute; it was hard to see.*" Fuck, fuck, fuck. The White Company was facing armor, and Nigel had no idea if they had the weapons to deal with them. He felt completely worthless standing in front of the headquarters building waiting for Besquith that might try to escape. He didn't have any help to send the White Company nor could he go look for the pilots. They were already spread too thin. Moretti would have to deal with the armor on his own, and the pilots, if they had even made it out in time, would have to take care of themselves. What else could go wrong?

"*Command, this is the* Vindicator. *We are having problems with one of our engines. We had to land on the south side of the starport and shut it down before it blew up.*"

Fuck.

East of the Starport, Besquith Base

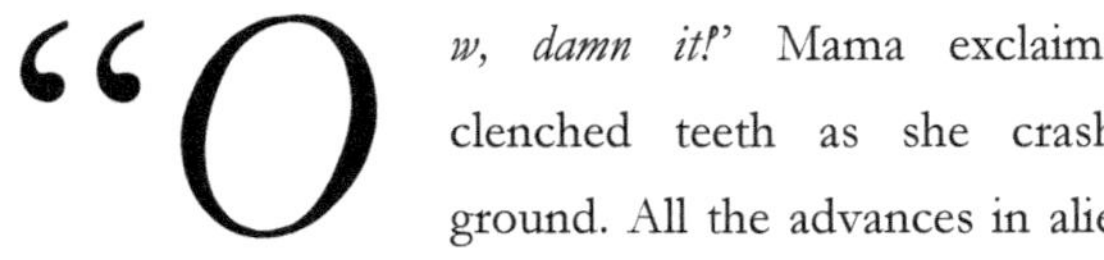

"*Ow, damn it!*" Mama exclaimed through clenched teeth as she crashed to the ground. All the advances in alien technology, and parachutes still drop you like a ton of shit. A light breeze filled her chute and began pulling her along the ground, jarring her arm and making her feel like she was being dragged along a cheese grater.

"Damn it!" she exclaimed again, trying to work the attachment holding her to the chute. "Better," she gasped as the left riser came loose. Without it, the chute lost its ability to hold air and she collapsed to the ground. She would have loved to lay there until a medic arrived, but she knew the only medics on her side of the starport were Besquith…and they probably weren't going to have the kind of bedside manner she was hoping for.

Holding her arm close, she struggled to her feet and released the other parachute connection. The parachute tried to blow off in the breeze, but she stepped on it to hold it in place. She might need some of it.

The terrain was rocky, with 15-foot hills of stone sticking up everywhere. She wouldn't be able to see the Besquith until they were close, but they also wouldn't be able to find her as easily. Hopefully, they didn't have a good sense of smell.

"Okay, think," she muttered. "What have I got?" Not much. One laser pistol, which, in a combat environment where the enemy was armored, was more likely to annoy the opposing soldiers than seriously damage them. She also had the two grenades she had talked the White Company supply sergeant out of, but they weren't going to be as helpful with her throwing arm broken.

Maybe she could make a trap that would stop pursuit. She could cut some of her parachute cords to make a tripwire that would pull the pin out of one of her grenades. Tying it would be a bitch, but possible. She had sawed through two of the cords when she heard the sounds of someone coming.

Well, shit. Tucking the cords under her bad arm, she pulled one of the grenades out of a cargo pocket and pulled the pin. The noises were closer, boots on rocks. She raced to the next outcropping and lobbed the grenade underhanded back toward where she'd been. The throw wasn't going to win any distance competitions, but it was on target, landing near the outcropping where the noises had been coming from.

She had just rounded the next corner when it detonated.

* * * * *

Chapter Twenty-Seven

The White Company, Barracks, Besquith Base

Colonel Moretti paused at the top of his jump to survey the battlefield. The tank was easy to spot on the starport pad in front of the last barracks building—its muzzle flash indicated its position. Unfortunately, the flash also indicated the tank mounted what looked to be a good size particle accelerator cannon (PAC), or at least some kind of energy weapon. The PAC was certainly doing a good job on the last barracks building; the last third of it had collapsed into a pile of bricks and ferrocrete.

Madonna! He recognized the vehicle. New enough he hadn't seen one yet on the Rim, he had certainly heard of them. The Besquith had a Zuul heavy tank! Almost 50 feet long, the massive war machine not only mounted the enormous PAC but also six smaller lasers and four missile launchers for close-in defense. The vehicle ran on a fusion power plant, so even if you presented it with enough targets for it to run out of missiles, its lasers and PAC had the power necessary to operate for *years*.

The weapons on the APCs alongside the tank began winking at him, and shells filled the sky where his troopers were advancing. Great. There were *five* APCs, and it appeared *all* of them had an anti-air capability. One of the APCs began firing at him, and he willed gravity to work faster so he could get below the shelter of the rooftop. As he touched down, several of the men with him crashed and tumbled to a stop.

"White Company, stay below the tops of the barrack on your jumps," he ordered. *"The APCs have anti-air."*

"Too late sir," Sergeant Bianchi replied. *"I'm hit. Looks like Corporal Colombo is dead."*

"I'm hit, too," Corporal Rossi added. *"I will require a medic behind the middle barracks building."*

Figlio di puttana! Where had the Besquith gotten *anti-air APCs?* A Zuul heavy and anti-air APCs? It was almost as if they had known humans, with their jumping suits, would be coming.

With a couple of smaller jumps that stayed below the rooftops, he made it to the back of the last barracks building and found First Sergeant Valenti.

"Status?" Moretti asked.

"Our status is we're pinned here behind this building for the moment. Normally, I'd just jump over them and hit them from behind, but with the anti-air APCs, we're going to lose a lot of troops doing it that way. Also, the tank is a Zuul heavy. It's going to have shields that will defeat the majority of our weapons, so attacking it is going to be problematic."

"You said 'for the moment.' What's going to change?"

"At some point, the tank is going to slag enough of the building that we won't be able to hide behind it any more. When that happens, we will have to do something else. They might also have the armor come around to this side of the building. That would also force us into action."

"Really, First Sergeant? You can't do any better than that?"

"I assume you saw what was out there, right? We can't shoot at the tank from a distance, because it has shields. We can't fly up to it, because of the APCs. We can't attack it on the ground because it's a damn *tank*. I'm open to suggestions, because going out there is pretty much a death trap."

The south end of the barracks building collapsed, leaving only a portion in the center at its full height.

"Well, we better think of something, because there isn't going to be anything to hide behind soon."

Second Platoon, First Company, Blood Drinkers

"*I got one!*" Corporal Stel-Ca reported.

"*I got two of them!*" Corporal Shah-Ca added.

Sergeant Creg-An didn't doubt the scout's claim; in addition to being one of the stealthiest people the sergeant knew, he was also the best gunner they had. He had painted a picture of a human in one of their suits on the side of his APC from their last battle. He'd get to add some victory slashes to it when they were done.

Unfortunately, the humans weren't as stupid as he would have liked. After shooting several of them down, they stopped jumping high enough to be seen. Pity. Still, the ones behind the barracks building wouldn't be going anywhere fast.

"*We have captured the humans' ship, and I have a major concentration of them pinned down behind the southern barracks building,*" Sergeant Creg-An reported. "*There is at least one company of soldiers in their suits here, and I believe it is closer to two. We await your assistance to finish them off.*"

"*We will be there shortly,*" Staff Sergeant Cahl-Ga replied. "*We are almost to the field. Don't do anything rash.*"

"*I don't intend to. I have five APCs and the tank, but I am not going to take them into a confined area without infantry support.*"

"That is a good plan. Keep them pinned down, and we will be there soon. Feel free to kill as many of them as you can in the interim."

"Understood."

Entropy. Creg-An doubted the humans would wait for the infantry to show up. Humans rarely waited for anything, especially if there was something rash they could do instead. They were here, weren't they, even though being here didn't make any sense? They would do something stupid, no doubt, and he'd be ready.

"Fire!" he ordered, and the right end of the barracks building collapsed. A smile crossed his face; he'd always hated living there.

If there was one thing he knew, it was that he was *not* going to go drive between the buildings or get tied up in the terrain behind the barracks. His armored force had the advantage in the open. If any of the humans tried to assault them, they would die, no matter whether they came in on the ground or in the air. And the shorter he made the buildings, the easier it would be to swat them from the skies.

There would be plenty of blood to drink out of their silly metal suits by the time the sun came up.

Asbaran Force, HQ Building, Besquith Base

Mason led the troopers down the stairs to the first floor. Although the stairs were fairly wide, walking down *any* stairs in a suit was a challenge.

"Look out—" was all the warning he received, and then a massive weight crashed into him from behind, overbalancing him. He fell forward, head first, and his face slammed into the front of his suit as he hit the stairs. Stunned, he was unable to break his fall; he slid the

rest of the way to the landing and across the hallway to crash into the opposite wall.

"Sorry, Top," Otter said as the weight lifted from his back.

Mason climbed to his feet. Damn it. Several yellow lights were illuminated on his suit.

"Hey Top," Lucky said as he picked his way down the last stairs, "if you're all done doing…whatever it is you're doing with Otter, there's a light on at the end of the hall."

Mason shook his head inside his suit. If there were any Besquith that *hadn't* heard the humans' second floor entry, even *they* had to be aware the humans were in the building now.

Still, there was no sign of a response to their intrusion. The hallway he was in ended at the building's front door, with four doors along the sides and the door with the light showing from underneath it at the opposite end of the passage. The stairway also continued down to a basement.

"No reason for stealth now," Mason said. He kicked in the closest door. Some sort of administrative facility. The other doors along the hallway led to similar rooms.

"Okay, let's see who's home." He positioned himself to one side of the door at the end of the hallway, and Otter and Lucky took the other. Another well-placed kick gained entry to the room. Beyond a small outer office lay a larger executive-style office with a massive desk in the center of the room and an oversized armoire along one wall.

Like the rest of the floor, the office was empty, although it appeared to have been recently occupied.

Lucky ripped one of the doors off the room's armoire.

"You know this is going to be the boss' office, right?" Mason asked.

"I wanted to make sure there weren't any Besquith hiding inside it."

"You couldn't have just opened it?"

"I guess I could…but there might have been a Besquith in it!"

"And that's why we don't get nice toys, isn't it, Top?" Otter asked.

"Damn right." Mason surveyed the room. "All right, there aren't any other places for them to hide, or for us to destroy, so they must be down in the basement."

The troopers returned to the stairs. "Hey, Otter, try not to tackle me this time, okay?" Mason asked.

"You got it, Top."

Mason crept down the stairs, or as much as he could creep in a half-ton suit. The building was eerily quiet, which amplified the noise the suits made on the stairs. The hairs on the back of his neck were rigid; whatever was going to happen would happen down here.

Reaching the landing, Mason eased out to look both ways before stepping out. Nothing in either direction, aside from a few holographic pictures of places Mason didn't recognize hanging on the walls. There was a door at each end of the hallway, about 20 feet away in each direction, and a third on the opposite wall.

Mason crossed to the opposite door and waved the other troopers over. Pulling out a grenade, he kicked in the door and threw the grenade into the room. The weapon detonated and the troopers poured into the room to find it empty; instead of Besquith, the room was full of mostly destroyed monitors. The room appeared to be a command center, and the monitors that weren't destroyed showed portions of the base. Most of the scenes were peaceful, except for one of a large building that had fallen down on one end; some sort of beam weapon was working to level the other end of it.

A large conference table dominated the center of the room; it sagged on the right where the grenade had blown off two of its legs.

"Damn it," Mason said. "There has to be some sort of duty section here, or they wouldn't have all of this gear on. Let's go."

He led them back to the hallway and down the hall to the right. They stacked at the door, and Mason kicked it in.

The soldiers charged into the room to find yet another empty room. "What the hell?" Mason asked. The room was a communications center, with a large number of radios, laser uplinks, and other devices.

Without warning, Otter blew up.

Cockpit, Dropship *Two*, Besquith Base, Planet Moorhouse

"*Colonel Shirazi, we need your assistance at the starport. There are several tanks here that appear to object to our presence.*"

"What?" LT Tom 'Harv' Walsh asked. "Who's that? And where the hell did they get tanks?"

"Sounds like one of the *Vindi's* pilots," his copilot, LTJG Michael 'Salty' Morton, replied. "No idea on the tanks...but why would the *Vindi* care? Aren't they supposed to have returned to space?"

"I thought so," Harv replied. "They've got that civilian girl onboard. They were supposed to return to space to keep her safe. How about giving them a call to find out what's going on."

"Vindi, *Dropship* Two," Salty radioed. *"Say your position and condi-tion."*

"We are in the southern portion of the starport landing area. We had an engine malfunction and were forced to land."

"They chose to land in the middle of a battle?" Harv asked. "With a civilian onboard? What the hell were they thinking?"

"Who knows? Have you ever talked to the Jehas? They make my head hurt." He switched to the radio. *"What is your status?"*

"Our status is not good. Our right engine needs repairs, and there are three tanks on the landing area next to the ship preventing us from going outside to work on it."

"Can you see anything on the starport?" Harv asked.

"No, and I can't use the night vision equipment with all that shit burning down there."

"All right, then, we'll have to go a little lower to find it." Harv snapped the dropship over in a hard turn. "Tell him or her, or whatever it is, that we're coming," he said.

"We are?"

"You bet we are," Harv said. "We have to; that's our ride home."

East of the Starport, Besquith Base

The force of the blast pushed LT Seville forward, adding speed to her steps. She thought she had seen a Besquith come around the outcropping just before the grenade exploded; hopefully, the weapon would slow them down a bit, although she doubted it would stop them entirely from chasing her.

She needed a plan. She couldn't go west, as she would end up on the starport ferrocrete where she would be exposed and an easy target for the Besquith gunners. To the south and east, the rocky hillocks grew smaller and more infrequent, ultimately turning into a flat, arid plain…where she would also be exposed and an easy target.

That left heading north, which was perhaps the most dangerous of all; it led back toward the missile batteries. If she could get past them, though, she ought to be able to make it to the headquarters building at the north end of the field where the rest of Asbaran was currently located. She shrugged. At least the stupid wolves probably wouldn't expect her to do that; maybe it would buy her some extra time.

She looped around a little further to the east then proceeded north. Most of the fires were going out, so there wasn't as much light to navigate by; hopefully, that would also make her harder to track.

Something flipping around caught the corner of her eye. She still had the two pieces of parachute cord she had cut to make the grenade into a trap. Making a trap with her other grenade didn't seem necessary at the moment, so she measured the cords, tied them into circles, and threw them over her head, fashioning a makeshift sling for her arm. The sling held her arm a little better, reducing the pain slightly. At least she didn't feel like she was going to throw up *all* the time now.

She stayed to the east of the little hills, hoping to keep as many as possible between herself and the missileers, and passed the missile revetments which still had enough little fires burning inside them to indicate where they were. As she passed the last one, she froze.

A platoon of Besquith raced in from the east. She held her breath, worried that a single noise or smell would give her away, but they were moving so quickly none of them noticed her. Heavily-armed, they took up positions in the last missile revetment. Mama looked at her pistol. Inadequate before, it was completely unsuitable for going up against a platoon of frontline troops who were armed to the teeth. When she had been given the pistol, the armorer had told her the only reason for having it in combat was as a means to acquire a rifle. Judging by the Besquith platoon's obvious competence and professionalism, she doubted she was getting one of theirs.

Without warning, an aircraft screamed overhead, no more than 50 feet above her head. She recognized the other dropship as it vanished into the night. What the hell was Harv doing?

With a roar, a surface-to-air missile lifted off from the revetment. A handheld one from its size, she doubted the missileer had been able to get a good lock on the ship before firing. She lost the missile in the dark once its motor burned out, but didn't see an explosion. Lucky.

She hoped Harv wouldn't come back so she wouldn't feel obligated to do something about the missileer.

* * * * *

Chapter Twenty-Eight

Asbaran Force, HQ Building, Besquith Base

Mason and Lucky were thrown to the side as the blast enveloped Otter. Lucky was the first up, and he made it to the doorway in time to see a Besquith go into the stairwell.

"Besquith!" he yelled, running down the hallway in pursuit. The door at the other end of the passage stood open. The enemy must have been hiding there.

He reached the stairwell in time to see the Besquith going around the corner above, but couldn't get a shot. He charged up the stairs and rounded the corner.

Three Besquith waited at the top of the stairs. They fired and Lucky was hit; one of the MAC rounds pierced his armor and went through his stomach. Staggered, Lucky paused and was hit again in the shoulder, losing control of his left arm.

"*Arrr!*" Lucky yelled, summoning his strength. He started up the stairs and was hit two more times, but the rounds missed his human body inside the suit.

He reached the top of the stairs and clubbed the Besquith on the right with his rifle, slamming it to the floor. Turning, he swung the rifle like a machete, crushing a second alien's chest.

The remaining Besquith shot him again with its MAC, the round passing through the center of his chest. He collapsed to the floor, and the Besquith ran off down the hall.

Lucky lay on the floor, trying to catch his breath, but failed. He turned up his suit's heater, but grew colder and colder as the blood flowed out of his body.

Motion caught his eye as Mason ran up the stairs to join him.

"One…more," Lucky said, gasping. "Ran…into that room." His right hand reached out to point down the hall, then it fell to the floor as he lost the strength to hold it up.

Mason ran to the indicated door. Although he had shattered the locking mechanism on his last visit, someone had pushed the door shut and braced something against it. He stepped back and kicked the door with the full force of the suit, and the door shattered as did the chair holding it shut; pieces flew like shrapnel into the room. Mason crossed the anteroom to the office and found the Besquith. The alien stood behind the desk, and it looked up and snarled as he entered. The Besquith held a mini-torch in one hand and a sheaf of papers in the other; judging from the smoke curling from a small metal garbage can on the edge of the desk, the alien had already burned several documents.

"Don't move!" Mason ordered as he walked through the door. He gestured with his rifle. "Come out from behind the desk."

The Besquith stepped to the side, still holding the torch and papers.

Mason recognized the limp. "Well, Brel-Al, it's *so* nice to see you again."

"Did you bring the Flatar with you?" the Besquith asked. "When I'm finished with you, I'm going to eat him for dessert."

"And how exactly do you intend to do that? You're my prisoner."

"Prisoner? I don't think so." The Besquith dropped both papers and torch into the can and dove behind the desk. Mason fired several rounds, but they went over the alien.

Mason ran to the desk and swatted the can off it. He rounded the corner of the desk; the Besquith was already rolling over, a laser pistol in his hand. Mason shot him twice in the chest, and the Besquith's shot went high. He aimed and fired another bolt between the Besquith's eyes, and the creature stilled.

Turning, Mason saw the torch up against a wall, which was starting to char. He picked up the torch, extinguished it, then reached down to pat out the embers on the papers scattered about.

"I need a medic in the first floor hallway ASAP," Mason radioed. *"The entranceway should be free of Besquith. Also, Colonel Shirazi, can you come into the building? I've got something for you."*

Corporal Epard was in the hallway in seconds, and Nigel shortly thereafter. "What is it?" he asked.

Mason handed him the stack of papers. "I can't read these, but your good buddy Brel-Al was destroying them, so I figured you'd want 'em."

"I'm sure I do."

Cockpit, Dropship *Two*, Besquith Base, Planet Moorhouse

"**M**issile, right 5:00 low!" Salty called. "Never mind," he added a couple of seconds later as the missile flew off to the side; "it's not guiding."

"Do you see the *Vindi*?" Harv asked, scanning the field as he roared across it at 50 feet. "*Shit!*" he exclaimed as he yanked the stick to the left. The dropship slid past the *Vindicator* with only a few feet to spare.

"Some lights would have been nice," Salty said when his heart started to beat normally again.

"No shit." Harv pulled back and left and the ship banked in a climbing left-hand turn. "I'm going to take it around again. I didn't see much last time."

"Except the ship."

"Except *way* more of the ship than I wanted." Harv paused, then added, "I'll be a little higher and slower; keep a good scan for missiles."

"Wilco," Salty agreed. "I think the last one came from the revetments. Mama must have missed one of them with her fireball from hell."

"It must have been a heat seeker; I never got any indications from the warning gear. They're small, and the best time to see them is when they lift off. Keep a good eye out."

"You got it."

The White Company, Barracks, Besquith Base

"What do you think, First Sergeant?" Colonel Moretti asked.

"At some point, they will have destroyed all of our cover, and we're either going to have to flee or charge them head-on," the senior enlisted man said. "Of note, I do not believe the latter course of action is survivable."

"I agree, charging them is suicide, but we're going to have to deal with them at some point. Do you think we can draw them in where we can take them with missiles from the side?"

"If you were in the tanks, would you want to come in here where your maneuverability would be restricted?"

"No, I wouldn't, and I don't think they will, either. We've got other problems. I just heard on the command net that this isn't all of the armor; there's more over where the spaceship landed."

"*Merda!* More armor? Where did it come from?"

"No idea. I'm more worried about the ones trying to kill me at the moment, and I don't see any way we can do this without some assistance."

"Nor do I."

"Well, let's see what our illustrious leader can do for us." Moretti switched to his radio. "*Colonel Shirazi, Colonel Moretti. We're going to need some support. We've got a full-fledged Zuul tank and five anti-air APCs down here at the barracks.*"

East of the Starport, Besquith Base

Without warning, the Besquith evacuated the revetment, exiting on the far side of the facility from where Mama looked down on them from the top of a small hill. As much as running with a broken arm had hurt, it was nothing compared to how much it had hurt while crawling up the backside of the hill.

She couldn't see the whole position, but it appeared all the aliens had left the area around the missiles. They still remained close, though, taking up defensive positions in the hills to the west where they could watch the starport.

Why would they leave the cover of the revetment? It was a great place to launch their handheld missiles.

Her unspoken question was answered moments later when, with a whirring noise, the missile system in the revetment came to life and spun around to point to the west. How could the system launch, though? It needed guidance info, and she had killed all their radars, hadn't she?

The fires Mama had started had mostly gone out, so she scanned the area as best she could in the gathering gloom. Finally, she saw a flash of light as a small, dancing flame was reflected by a spinning radar. The missiles *had* guidance…and if the aliens had left the pit, they intended to launch.

She had to stop it.

Her laser pistol was useless from this range and there was no way she was throwing a grenade that far with her left hand. With her right, maybe, but that wasn't an option. She pushed back one-handed from the crest then slid down the rest of the hill on her backside, her urgency causing her to go faster than she should have.

The last three feet of her slide was vertical, and she tried to stop or at least slow herself before she got to it. Without both hands, she couldn't, and she dropped off the ledge to fall the remaining distance. Pain blinded her with a white hot flash, and she may have passed out momentarily, then she was up and running as best she could in the near dark.

The tiny hillocks were maze-like; despite being close to her objective, they kept angling her off to the side. Using a hillock slightly larger than the rest as a guide, she finally made it to her destination, only to find the revetment wasn't where she had thought it was.

A missile lifted off to her right and she saw had missed the revetment by one small hill. The missile was a small one, a handheld one; there was still time. She could see the tips of the missile in the revetment and ran toward them.

The first missile lifted off the launcher while she was still 20 yards away.

* * * * *

Chapter Twenty-Nine

"Mama's fireball has died out so I'm going to bring on the night vision gear," Harv said. He flipped a switch, and the screen enhanced the night's ambient light.

"There it is," Salty said, pointing. "Over there to the left."

"Got it." Harv maneuvered the craft to fly past the larger spaceship, high enough to go safely over it. "See anything?"

"Yeah, I got them," Salty replied. "It's not three tanks; it's three APCs. Stupid Jehas don't know tanks from APCs."

"Even APCs will mess up the ship pretty badly if we let them."

"True. How 'bout this? Let's not let them. If you come back around and run in from the north, I ought to be able to shoot them without hitting the *Vindi*."

"You got it," Harv replied, extending out away from the ship so he could loop around and come back in from the north.

"The tanks are calling us on the radio," one of the Jehas called. *"They say if we don't surrender the ship in three minutes, they will destroy it. What should we do?"*

"Don't do anything," Salty replied. *"We will be there in two."*

"I heard," Harv said. "We're only going to get one pass at this before they destroy our ship, so make it good, would you?"

"Hey, you just get us there and let me take care of blowing shit up, all right?"

"Inbound, here we go." He flipped a switch. "Master arm is on, gun is hot."

Salty moved the joystick around and watched the gun tracking. He'd have to shoot quickly and switch targets even faster as the ship roared across the field at 500 miles an hour. He took a deep breath and let it out slowly. He could do this. Just like in the simulator.

He found the *Vindicator* in the targeting scope and followed it down to the three dots nearby. The Besquith armor. "Got 'em," he said. "Stand by for in-range…"

"I got missile radar," Harv said. "Launching countermeasures."

Salty didn't look up; he didn't want to be blinded by the flashes. The range counted down…he squeezed the trigger…

Harv yanked the dropship to the left and up, causing the gun to lose the target.

"Damn it!" Salty said; "I had them. Get back on target or we're going to miss them!"

"We had a missile I had to evade!"

"Long walk home, remember? Get us back on target!"

The range continued to count down. It was going to be close.

Harv rolled the dropship upside down in the turn and then flipped it back right-side up. Right on target.

Morton squeezed the trigger and the first APC came apart under the hammering of the dropship's 50mm cannon.

"One down, shifting targets." Salty moved to the next one in line.

Harv saw the flash from the left at the same time the warning system went into a constant warble. "Radar missile launch! Evading!"

"No damn it; keep us still! Firing at the second!" On target. He squeezed the trigger and watched the cannon shells walk up the ferrocrete to the APC. It blew up after a couple of hits.

"Cycling to the third!"

Wham! The missile hit, the ship lurched, and the cockpit went black.

"Engines out!" Harv yelled. "We lost both electrical busses."

"Get 'em back! My gun's dead, and we're out of time!"

"I know," Harv said. He looked out the cockpit window. From this angle, he could see the *Vindicator* and, by the light of the two burning APCs, the remaining APC sitting just long of them. He bit his lip as he sighed, and a tear glistened at the corner of one eye. He would have liked to have seen his daughter one more time. "I've got this."

They were already below 200 feet of altitude. It didn't take much…just a little push forward on the stick…

The dropship impacted just short of the last APC, and the rolling fireball of debris swept across the armored vehicle at 500 miles an hour, blotting it out of existence.

East of the Starport, Besquith Base

Its right motor out, Mama watched in horror as Dropship *Two* fell like a rock. Only 100 feet above the ground when the ship had been hit, it looked like Harv hadn't had a chance to pull it out of the dive he had been in. The ship impacted the starport in a titanic blossom of flame.

Mama had failed. Worse, she could hear the Besquith on the other side of the revetment laughing and cheering the demise of the dropship. Bastards. If she only had her ship back, she'd…

It didn't matter what she'd do with a ship; she didn't have one. She did have her last grenade, though, and maybe the Besquith troopers would think the launcher had blown up on its own. As the missile system cycled back to its 'ready' position with a whirr of hydraulics, she pulled the pin with her teeth and rolled the grenade into the revetment. It came to a stop underneath the missile launcher and she began running to the north.

She ran as fast as she could, her pain driving her on through the fatigue. The grenade exploded behind her, with several smaller detonations as some of the ordnance cooked off.

As the sounds of the explosions ceased, she heard a number of howls; obviously the Besquith didn't believe the system had blown up on its own. They had her scent and were coming after her.

Mama knew the Besquith had all the advantages. They had better weapons and weren't wounded; she was already running on her last reserves of energy. It was only a matter of time until they caught her.

Second Platoon, First Company, Blood Drinkers

"*W*e succeeded in shooting down the last of the humans' ships," Staff Sergeant Cahl-Ga advised. "*I am leading some of the antiaircraft crews to find a saboteur, but I will send my platoon there immediately to assist you.*"

"*I believe the dropship crashed on members of my platoon,*" Sergeant Creg-An replied. "*I have not had contact with the APCs guarding the human spaceship in some time.*"

"*Let's worry about the human soldiers first. Their ship doesn't appear to be going anywhere. My platoon is on its way to your position; when it arrives, use it to kill them all.*"

Asbaran Command, HQ Building, Besquith Base

"*Colonel Shirazi…Handley. I have…laser fire…southeast.*"

"*This is Colonel Shirazi.*" Nigel replied as he ran out of the headquarters building to get better reception. "*Who is this and what do you have?*"

"*Private Handley, sir. I've got flashes of light down to the southeast in some little hills there. It looks like someone's shooting down there.*"

"*There aren't any Asbaran forces there,*" Mason said as he followed Nigel out of the building.

"What do you think?" Nigel asked. "Is it a trick to draw us into the hills?"

"It could be, I guess…" Mason replied. "You got anything else, Handley?"

"No sir." The private pointed to the southeast. "There was an explosion over there where the missile launchers were, then I saw what looked like laser fire a little further to the north of it."

Nigel looked where the trooper was pointing and saw a flash.

"*There!*" Handley exclaimed. "*Did you see it?*"

"Yes, I saw it, and no I don't think it's a trick."

"Then what is it?" Turk asked as he joined the group.

"I don't…" Nigel said. "No, wait I *do* know who that is—it's got to be one or more of our pilots. We've got to go help them."

With a blast of jet fire, Nigel jumped toward the flash.

The two senior enlisted turned toward each other, but before either could say anything, a voice came over the radio.

"*Colonel Shirazi, Colonel Moretti. We're going to need some support. We've got a full-fledged Zuul tank and five anti-air APCs down here at the barracks.*"

"I'll take Second Squad and go help the White Company," Turk offered. "I've got experience dealing with tanks. Go help the Colonel get the pilot."

"Makes sense," Mason said. *"First Squad, you're with me!"* He turned and jumped in the direction Nigel had taken.

"Second Squad, let's go kill a tank!"

East of the Starport, Besquith Base

Mama came to a sudden halt as the passage between the hills ended suddenly. Dead end; she was trapped. If she'd had two good arms, she probably could have climbed one of the hills and escaped the cul-de-sac…but she didn't.

One of the Besquith howled; they were close.

There was nowhere to hide, although the cul-de-sac did have a rocky outcropping that would afford a little protection. She nestled down behind it and used it to steady her arm. She was spent, and her arm was twitching uncontrollably. Without the rock to brace her, she doubted she could have hit anything smaller than the house she grew up in.

Motion! She fired and was rewarded with a yelp, but then the alien jumped back behind cover. Several laser beams came from where the Besquith were hiding, but they weren't close to her. She didn't want to give her position away, so she held her fire, waiting for a target she could see.

The Besquith fired several more shots, then a small object landed in the center of the open area. She dropped behind the rock, snuggling down as far as she could. The grenade detonated. Although she was protected from the shrapnel, the concussion was amplified in the enclosed area, and everything became fuzzy as a high-pitched squeal filled her ears.

Trying to fight off the effects of the blast, she struggled to get to her feet, but a heavy weight hit her from behind, knocking her from behind the rock. One of the Besquith had climbed the hill behind her and had jumped on her from above.

She sprawled forward, her pistol flying free as she tried to use her good hand to break her fall. It didn't help; she crashed down on her broken arm and darkness fell across her vision as an overwhelming wave of pain hit her. When she could see again, she found she was trapped. Not only was the alien that had hit her from behind holding a rifle on her, but several more Besquith had entered the cul-de-sac, and one was already picking up her pistol.

She tried to rise, but the enemy behind her kicked her arm out from under her and she collapsed on her broken arm again. The Besquith flipped her over onto her back, and the alien with her pistol came to stand over her.

"You have caused us some problems," it said. "Do you know what we do to people who cause us problems?"

"Bore them to death threatening them?" Mama asked.

The Besquith kicked her, sending new waves of pain across her body. "No, your death will be much more…exquisite. I will kill you with your own weapon, but not until after you watch us drink your blood."

He looked up, suddenly. "*Entropy!*" He pointed the weapon at Mama and pulled the trigger.

East of the Starport, Besquith Base

Light flashed in the cul-de-sac, illuminating the area, and Nigel gave his jumpjets a touch more power to adjust his landing. He saw a flash of dark fur, adjusted again, and the thousand pounds of suit and human came crashing down on the Besquith holding the laser pistol on the human. The alien's armor deformed, no match for the force applied, and the Besquith exploded like a pumpkin hit with a sledgehammer.

Nigel didn't need to look to see if the alien was dead; instead, he spun to face the other Besquith in the group, but Top and several other troopers came down on top of them. Those that didn't land on top of the aliens used their swords or knives to kill the creatures, or simply hammered down on them with armored fists. The fight was over almost before it started; most of the aliens hadn't even seen the humans coming.

Nigel turned to the human who was laying on the ground. It was Mama, and she had been shot through the chest. She wasn't quite dead yet; her chest was still rising and falling.

"*Medic!*" he radioed.

"Almost…made it," the aviator said.

"Stay still," Nigel said. "There's a medic coming."

"Killed a…bunch of the bastards." The light went out of her eyes.

"Move!" Shrewlet ordered. She had already taken off her suit, and she ran up with a first aid kit. She checked out the pilot and shook her head. "I'm sorry, sir; she's gone."

No! He had only been a couple of seconds too late; he had *seen* the laser blast that killed her. *Damn it!* He turned and kicked a rock outcropping nearby, causing two yellow lights to illuminate in his display. *It wasn't fair!* If he'd just been a little quicker or sent someone earlier, she'd still be alive. *Damn it!*

* * * * *

Chapter Thirty

Second Platoon, First Company, Blood Drinkers

"**S**ergeant, I have contacts approaching from the northeast," the radar operator, Corporal Sep-Ga, reported.

"Is it the humans?" Sergeant Creg-An asked.

"I don't know," the corporal replied. "I don't think so. They aren't jumping like the humans do."

"Then it is our First Platoon. Hold your fire; Staff Sergeant Cahl-Ga said he was sending it to assist in finishing off the humans."

Second Squad, Asbaran Solutions

"*I*'ve got movement on the left," Sergeant Marin radioed as the platoon continued its run toward the Besquith armor. With five anti-air APCs in the force, it was a little slower to run than jump, but ultimately it was probably safer as it didn't highlight them. "*They're on the ground, and they look like they're converging with us.*"

"*Does it look like the Colonel and the other squad?*" Turk asked. "*They should be coming from that direction.*"

"*I can't tell.*"

Turk shook his head. Something didn't feel right. First Squad had already recovered the pilot and were rejoining them for the assault? He shrugged. There weren't any Besquith in that direction; they'd all been wiped out by the dropships. First Squad had been able to use their jumpjets to get the pilots; that must be how they had moved faster than his squad. That had to be it.

He refocused on his objective. He could see the enemy armor illuminated in his thermal sights. He didn't want to question *why* they hadn't taken any fire, for fear of jinxing himself; the Besquith were obviously tied up with the White Company and simply hadn't seen his platoon yet.

"The group to our left is Besquith!"

"Shit! Fire!"

Second Platoon, First Company, Blood Drinkers

"Sergeant, I have weapons firing in the force to the northeast," Corporal Sep-Ga reported.

"Who are they shooting at?" Sergeant Creg-An asked.

"They are…*yes!* They are shooting at each other!"

"What? Why would they do that?"

"I don't know," the corporal replied. "Wait a minute…Some of them are jumping now. There are humans in that group!"

"Don't talk! Shoot them! Shoot them now!"

"But Sergeant, they are intermingled with our troops. How will we separate them?"

"Don't try to separate them. Kill them all!"

The White Company, Barracks, Besquith Base

"Colonel Moretti, it appears the Asbaran troops are attacking the armor!"

The colonel risked a glance; sure enough, most of the armor had turned and was firing in the opposite direction at a battle occurring to the northeast. What a cluster! There appeared to be several groups, all firing at each other indiscriminately.

Although the situation to the northeast was confused, at best, there was one force he knew incontrovertibly to be the enemy, and this was the opportunity he had been waiting for.

"Asbaran won't last long in the open," he radioed. *"This is our chance."* He rose to his feet and triggered his jumpjets, launching himself toward the enemy armor. *"Attack!"*

* * * * *

Chapter Thirty-One

Second Squad, Asbaran Solutions

Not only were there more humans than Besquith, Turk saw, his force was also better armed and armored than the aliens. They should be able to—

Sergeant Cohen blew up as the green beam of the particle accelerator cannon enveloped him, the molecules of his suit and body unable to contain the energy unleashed on them. The tank was firing on his force!

"Go to close quarters with the Besquith!" Turk radioed. *"We've got to use them as a shield from the armor!"*

Turk jumped, landing in the middle of the Besquith platoon, and immediately had several of the enemy grappling with his suit, trying to bring him down. Although more survivable than the tank's main weapon, dead was dead, and he fought furiously to break out of their grasp.

He fired a laser blast to the face of the attacker on the right that burned through the enemy's face shield. The Besquith dropped away, freeing his arm. He kicked the alien in front of him as his sword blade snapped into place; the enemy came back at him, and Turk eviscerated the creature. Turing to the left, he thrust out again with the blade. Besquith armor was no match for the polysteel blade, and his weapon easily pierced the alien's chest piece; pulling down and away, he gutted the alien, and it collapsed in a lifeless, bloody heap.

Having achieved some space to work, he turned to find another Besquith approaching him, but it was shredded by the antiaircraft shells from one of the APCs.

Fuck! The armor was *still* firing on them! As close as they already were to the enemy vehicles, they couldn't run; they'd be shot down from behind.

"*Disengage and attack the armor!*" he ordered, "*It's our—*"

The tank's beam weapon passed through him, and he exploded.

Asbaran First Squad, East of the Starport, Besquith Base

"Damn it!" Nigel yelled, kicking the side of the rocky outcropping again.

Mason strode over and grabbed the officer. "Sir! We need to help Second Squad." He spun the officer around and pointed to the southwest. The sky glowed with a variety of green, red, and blue flashes. "Turk took Second Squad to help the White Company. I was listening to their net, and they need help."

It took a few seconds for Nigel to process the information, and the moments went by agonizingly slowly for Mason. "You're right," Nigel finally said. "Let's go."

"*First Squad, follow me!*" Mason ordered. If the night sky was any indication, the battle was more intense than ever. "*Now!*" Mason said, triggering his jumpjets. The squad jumped nearly as one to aid their comrades.

The White Company, Starport, Besquith Base

Colonel Moretti landed on the deck of the Zuul tank with a grenade already in his hand. Arming the weapon, he looked for an open port to drop it into the vehicle. Before he could find one, the APC next to the tank turned and fired. He was swept off the tank, dead before he hit the ground.

"No!" First Sergeant Valenti yelled, inbound to the tank. He altered his jump and landed on the deck of the APC instead. The turret of the APC spun toward him, but he avoided the barrels of the antiaircraft system. Seeing the vision slit in the turret was too small for a grenade, he pulled out a smaller flash-bang charge. Arming it, he slid it through the port. There was a shout and then a flash of light through the slit. The concussion would have been deafening in the close environment, if not deadly, and the magnesium-based charge caught something on the interior on fire. Smoke began pouring from the vision slit, and Valenti jumped from the vehicle just before it exploded.

Corporal Ewald landed behind another of the APCs and swept the back of the vehicle with his minigun. Designed for personnel, the hyper-fragmentation bullets didn't penetrate; instead, they shattered and ricocheted, sending thousands of pieces of mini-shrapnel to rain down on the battle area.

"Piece of shit," Ewald muttered, switching to the anti-armor reservoir. The turret started to turn so he changed his aim point and triggered the rotary machine gun. The armor-piercing bullets penetrated the side of the turret, scything through the Besquith unlucky enough to be inside it. He aimed lower and fired the weapon through the back of the APC. One of the bullets hit something explosive inside, and the sides of the APC bulged outward as it detonated.

Turning, Ewald fired into the back of another APC. He had fired another 100 rounds, destroying it, when one of the close-in lasers from the tank speared through his head, killing him.

Second Squad, Asbaran Solutions

"*Disengage and attack the armor! It's our—*"

Private Handley saw the beam weapon in the corner of his monitor, and then the explosion of metal and red as Turk exploded. He dove to the left to evade the beam, and rolled back to his feet in time to see his squad leader, Staff Sergeant Jill Cox, similarly destroyed.

The tank's lasers and the APCs' antiaircraft MACs chewed through both Besquith and human troopers, and Private Handley saw his comrades falling like wheat before the scythe.

"*Jump!*" Staff Sergeant Elizabeth Kaine screamed, and all of the remaining humans went airborne.

Optimized for anti-air, the APCs reached out to swat the humans from the sky. 12 humans launched themselves into the teeth of the enemy armor; five were still alive to land among the vehicles.

One of the few soldiers with missiles, Private Handley landed to the left of the formation. Too close for the missiles' safeties, he removed them, and set the missiles to arm upon emergence from their tubes. Touching down, he fired a volley of three into the closest APC, and was blown backward when it exploded in his face.

The White Company, Starport, Besquith Base

"*Vaffanculo!*" Private Bianchi yelled, diving to the side as one of the tank's lasers targeted him. He rolled to the side and came up on one knee. Triggering his missile launcher, he fired one at the tank. Although it blew off the laser, it barely scratched the paint on the massive vehicle.

"Kill the APC," First Sergeant Valenti ordered, grabbing the private and turning him toward the remaining antiaircraft vehicle.

The private fired his last two missiles. One glanced off the glacis and spun off to explode harmlessly; the second hit the joint between the turret and the main body, blowing the turret from the vehicle.

"*Everyone attack the tank!*" Valenti used the emergency override to push his order to the force, and the remaining members of the force fired everything they had at the tank.

The commander of the tank obviously realized the danger he was in. With a lurch, the tank accelerated from its position, causing many of the troopers' shots to miss. As it broke free from the remaining humans, its turret spun and began firing its beam weapon back at the Asbaran force. Private Emma Holt and Sergeant Charles Tucker disappeared as the beam played through the group.

Valenti dove to the side as the beam settled on Private Ricci. As it moved on, only Ricci's armored legs remained. Valenti charged the tank, knowing he had to do something to stop it, but dodged to the side as another armored figure landed in front of him.

Sergeant Carlos Marin pulled out a grenade, armed it, and triggered his jumpjets again. He flew up to the barrel of the tank and threw the grenade in as the weapon fired. The turret and Sergeant Marin were both atomized in the resulting explosion.

Asbaran First Squad, East of the Starport, Besquith Base

"*F*uck," a voice said as First Squad landed at the site of the armored battle. The pieces of the vehicles were readily identifiable; those of the people who had been killed were not. A handful of White Company soldiers were performing coups de grâce on the wounded Besquith troops.

Nigel landed next to one of the two Asbaran soldiers he could see on the battlefield. "Where is the rest of Second Squad?" he asked.

"You're looking at them sir," Private 'JR' Handley said. "Staff Sergeant Howe and I are the only ones left." He picked up a small piece of metal from the ferrocrete. "I think this was Sergeant Marin."

Tears brimmed in Nigel's eyes. He had been too late. Again. Too late to save the pilot, and now too late to save the platoon. He should have come here first. Inside his suit, tears trickled down his cheeks as he went to find Colonel Moretti, but could only find First Sergeant Valenti.

"Where's Colonel Moretti?" Nigel asked.

"He didn't make it, sir. He died attacking the tank. We were victorious, but at great cost."

"I'm going to make this worthwhile," Nigel said. "I don't know how, but I'm going to make it right."

Nigel dove to the right as something went past the side of his head. He readied his rifle as he spun through the air, and found himself aiming at a small stream of water emanating from the ground. He safed his weapon again, taking in the irony; the sprinkler was watering a patch of ground where the grass had been completely burned off in the earlier firebombing.

* * * * *

Chapter Thirty-Two

Commander's Office, HQ Building, Asbaran Base, Moorhouse

Corporal Cindy 'Shrewlet' Epard knocked tentatively on the open door, interrupting the conversation Mason and Nigel were having on how best to deal with their employers. "Come in," Nigel ordered.

"Hi, sir," Shrewlet said as she entered the cabin. "I've been working on translating the papers we found in the Besquith headquarters building."

"What did you find?" Nigel asked.

"Well, Sergeant Bush was our intel guy, and he had a lot more training on the translation software than I do, but I have been able to figure out a few things. I've got to tell you, though, it hasn't been easy, and I may have missed some things. The Besquith leader was burning a number of documents, and they were all mixed up. I don't even know why he was burning most of them, as they referenced pretty boring stuff. Duty details, requisitions, supply shipments. That kind of stuff."

"Most? Does that imply there's something else?"

"Yes, sir. There were several other sheets that were…interesting, although I don't know what to make of them."

"What were they?"

"Well, see, that's the problem; I don't know exactly *what* they are, and the condition of the files didn't help. They were burned in a few places, charred in a few more, and had several holes in them as well."

"So stop telling us what they aren't and tell us what they are."

"Well, sir, if I didn't know any better, I'd say it looks like some sort of money laundering scheme."

"What?"

"See? That was what I thought as well. Aliens doing money laundering…what? But that's what it appears to be." She held up a piece of paper. "This letter is the deployment order for the leader of the Besquith forces. It instructs him to bring his troops here and includes a detailed battle plan for defeating the Asbaran Solutions force. After the battle, the Besquith leader was supposed to meet up with somebody named Tranayl to get paid."

"I don't see how that's money laundering."

"Apparently, there was a second contract, beyond the one that brought us here. The Besquith were going to be paid 40 million credits for their participation."

"What? That's a lot more than we're getting paid."

"Correct. They were to take the extra money after the end of this mission and recruit additional troops that were to be used for 'future operations.'"

"That sounds ominous. Does it say what those operations were or when they are supposed to occur?"

"No, sir. If that was included in the file, it's been lost or destroyed."

"Damn."

"Yes, sir."

Nigel turned to Mason. "I think it's time to go see our employer and get paid for our efforts."

"And maybe find out who this 'Tranayl' person is?" Mason asked.

"You can count on it."

* * * * *

Chapter Thirty-Three

Caroon Outpost, Planet Moorhouse

"This place is almost as big a shithole as the base is," Mason noted. Nigel and seven of the troopers had driven the three miles to the mining outpost in an armored personnel carrier one of the platoon had found in the motor pool, and then had dismounted to walk into town. Mason had said the alien Caroons were somewhat skittish around military hardware, and the CASPers would intimidate them enough; an APC rolling through the town would make them head for their holes, never to be seen again. The "town" looked like a frontier town from the American Wild West; buildings lined the street for about three blocks, with no other signs of habitation in the area. The town appeared in poor shape; the buildings looked ready to fall over in the first breeze.

The road into town, such as it was, only extended into the wilderness about 200 feet from the first building before petering out. Beyond the town on the far side, the land disappeared into a giant strip mine. At over six miles across and three miles deep, the mine dwarfed the largest mine on Earth, the Bingham Canyon Mine, and was the reason for the town's existence.

As the group approached the settlement, Nigel could see some of the aliens hurrying between buildings. Generally mammalian in appearance with long noses and droopy ears, the Caroons looked like oversized anteaters. The aliens had long sharp claws and were adapted for life underground; they had a reputation for being excellent diggers and miners.

"The base got hit with a major assault that destroyed most of it," Corporal Davis said, looking at the ramshackle buildings. "The outpost didn't, and it looks worse off than the base."

"It smells pretty bad, too," Nigel said. As the only soldier not wearing a CASPer, he was exposed to the brunt of the aliens' unique scent; he decided it was somewhere between vulture vomit and a trash dump at noon on the hottest day of the year.

Without any vehicular traffic to avoid, the humans walked down the middle of the street. Led by Nigel and Mason, the force spread out from one side of the street to the other. Nigel carried a laser rifle, his eyes constantly in motion; the CASPers were fully armed, and their operators swept the town with their sensors, looking for trouble.

None of the Caroons bothered them as they walked into town; most of them ran shrieking in terror, and those that stayed tended to give the combat suits a wide berth, scampering into buildings as the humans approached.

The march through town was uneventful, and the group was soon in front of the last building before the mine. Labeled Peskall's Pretties, it was the local office of the company that had hired Asbaran Solutions to protect the mine. The building was enormous, extending another two blocks beyond the town, with a processing facility behind it. Large pieces of earth-moving equipment rumbled back and forth from the pit to the processing plant.

A number of Caroons entered and exited the building through a giant entryway located halfway along the building. Nigel used a small slate and translated the sign over a normal-sized doorway at the end of the building as "Company Offices."

Nigel led the group to the smaller door, which he would have to bend down to enter. He inspected it for a couple of seconds, then turned to look at the group of CASPers. "I don't think you're going to fit," he noted.

Mason approached the doorway and looked down on it. "Not unless it opens up a bunch behind it." He reached down and pressed the entry stud. The door opened, and he bent down to scan the interior. "Nope. It's going to be difficult to get the suits in there." He paused and then asked hopefully, "Unless I can knock down a wall or something?"

"No. No breaking the Caroon's stuff. We don't know if they had anything to do with it yet."

"Well, I can't let you go in there alone, sir, especially since we *don't* know whether they had anything to do with it or not."

"Well, I have to go in so we can get paid, if nothing else. They may also have information on where Parisa is. I'll tell you what; I will maintain radio comms. If anything goes wrong, you are authorized to knock down walls or whatever else you need to do to get me out."

"I don't like it, sir, but I also don't like not getting paid even more, and I'd surely like to see your sister again. I'll let you go in there, but I'm going to spread the men out around the building. If you call, we'll be in there ASAP, from a variety of directions."

Cell Block, Planet Moorhouse, Kepler 62 System

"I'm happy to tell you your end is near," Tranayl said.

"I've known you for quite some time now," Parisa replied; "I wouldn't say you look or sound very happy."

"Of course I'm happy; your life is measured in days. As soon as your brother leaves this world, I get to kill you. I'll probably eat you afterwards. Or perhaps I will capture him and make him watch…Yes, making him watch as I devour you would be much more fun."

"Wait a minute…if my usefulness is at an end, that means my brother must be here. *That's why you're mad!* He came and recaptured the base and killed off all your little troopers, didn't he! Hahahaha! I told you he was smarter than you!"

"Yes, he is here, and yes, they recaptured the base. They won't, however, find this place. I suspect they will search for you a bit near the base and then give up, collect their payment, and leave. When they go, you will die."

"I thought I was the bait to get him here. If he's here, why don't you just kill me now?"

"Are you in that much of a hurry to die?"

"I'm not in a hurry to die; in fact, I hope I'm still alive when he gets here as I can't wait to see what he does to you. Still, you told me I was only useful as a means to bring him to the planet; now that he's here, what you said doesn't add up."

"Maybe he's not really even here, or perhaps everything I've told you is a lie. Have you ever considered that?"

"Repeatedly, however, there's no point in it. The only reason you'd lie to me is to give me false information I would act on when I got out of here, and we both know you can't let me out of here alive. Therefore, I doubt what you've told me is a lie." She nodded a couple of times then added, "He's here all right, and I doubt you will outlive me by more than a handful of minutes."

Tranayl drew a pistol from his belt. "I could shoot you right now!"

"I'm sure you could, and there's nothing I could do to stop it. But nothing's changed since this discussion started. I still have value for some reason, so I doubt you'll kill me now while my brother's so close—that's it! You don't want to kill me now because you're afraid my brother will figure out your plan. I'll bet you're just keeping me alive because you know he's going to find you, and you want to have something available to trade him for sparing your life."

Tranayl's antennae dipped and Parisa could tell she'd scored a point. The alien stepped closer to her cell and put his head up against the bars. "Why I'm keeping you alive is none of your business," he said slowly, "but I can tell you one thing—you will *never* leave here alive."

Manager's Office, Peskall's Pretties, Planet Moorhouse

Nigel walked into the building, hunched over to keep from hitting his head. Although the lights turned on automatically, they were dimmer than what would typically be seen in a human building. The hallway led off into the gloom, and he took several steps along the passageway. The door shut behind him, completely blotting out any trace of sunlight, and the hallway dimmed further.

"Assistant Manager for Exploration," read the first door on the left as translated by his slate. "I'm not looking for the flunkies," he muttered. He looked at the door on the right. "Assistant Manager for Maintenance."

Another 10 paces brought him to the end of the hallway and three additional doors. "Administration," on the left, "Assistant Manager for Operations" on the right, and finally, "Manager," on the door at the end of the passage.

He opened the Manager's door and walked into a small anteroom. The space was dominated by a desk, behind which a Caroon sat, working on a slate. Several chairs in a variety of shapes lined the two side walls, and a door sat behind the Caroon at the desk.

"May I help you?" the Caroon asked, looking up from the slate.

"Yes, I am Nigel Shirazi, the head of Asbaran Solutions. I am here to speak to the Manager and collect our terminal payment for the completion of the contract."

The Caroon looked back down at its slate. "I don't see an appointment for you?" he asked as he looked up again.

"No, I don't have an appointment; however, the contract ended several hours ago. As such, I would have thought you'd be expecting me."

"Please wait here."

The Caroon got up and went through the door. After a few minutes, it came back and took its seat at the desk. "If you will wait a few minutes, the manager will be happy to meet with you."

"*How's it going?*" Mason radioed.

"Okay so far," Nigel replied. "*The manager has agreed to meet with me.*"

"*Let me know if you need me…I'll be right there.*"

Nigel sat in a chair that worked for his human physiology. After another five minutes, the door opened and a Caroon wearing a large amount of jewelry, including a red diamond necklace, came out. "Mr. Shirazi," the Caroon said, "if you would come in please?"

"Please leave your rifle here," the secretary said.

Nigel laid the rifle on the secretary's desk. "I will be back for this," Nigel replied. "And I will hold you personally accountable if anything happens to it."

"I'm going into the manager's office," Nigel radioed. "I have to leave my rifle in the outer office. If anything's going to happen, it will happen now. Be ready."

Nigel followed the manager into the office. The interior reeked of opulence, with an immaculately polished, burled bubinga wood desk, a variety of over-stuffed chairs, and paintings framed in precious metals. The ceiling in the office was tall enough for him to stand upright, and he stretched his back gratefully.

"Please have a seat," the Caroon said. "I am Ka-Tal, the manager of this facility. I understand you are here to collect payment on your contract."

"That is correct," Nigel said. He remained standing, having noted the chairs on his side of the desk were significantly shorter than the manager's; if he sat, he would have been looking up at the manager.

The manager looked at Nigel. When Nigel didn't sit, he said, "As you prefer; you may stand if you wish." He pulled a jeweled box from a desk drawer. "I have here the payment for successfully completing your contract. 20 million credits." He pushed the box across the desk toward Nigel.

The human didn't move to take it. "You're forgetting something, I believe," Nigel noted. "There was also a combat clause of 5% per occurrence, with a maximum of 25%. Over the course of the past year, there have been five combat actions, for a total of an additional five million credits."

"Can you prove there actually were five separate combat occurrences?"

Nigel walked around the desk to stand next to the manager. "I would be happy to show you the dead bodies of my troops from their latest round of combat a couple of days ago if you would like." He reached over and grabbed a handful of the manager's cloak at the shoulder. "Come on; I'll take you there right now. We had to move the dead Besquith's bodies as they had begun to stink like the backside of a Blorph during the rut."

"No, no, that will be all right," the manager said, trying to pull away. "I will take your word for it."

Nigel released the manager, who smoothed his cloak, and then opened another drawer and removed a smaller box. He handed it to Nigel. "Here is another five million credits."

Nigel opened the box. It was full of what *looked* like red diamonds, but he wasn't a gemologist and really had no idea what he was supposed to look for in them. He set the box down on the desk and opened the larger box. It was full of larger red gems.

"How do I know this really is 25 million credits?"

"Well, the value of gems *does* vary over time, and even though it's 25 million credits today, it might not still be when you go to sell them."

Nigel took a step back toward the manager. "Perhaps, then, you might want to make sure they're going to be worth 25 million when we get them to market. You wouldn't want us to think you shortchanged us, *now would you?*"

"No, no, we definitely wouldn't want that. On second thought, perhaps you should have a few more." He opened the center drawer, pulled out a few loose diamonds, and dropped them into the larger box. "Here, that should ensure you come out on the right side of 25 million."

"Thank you," Nigel replied. "You know we can find you if this is short, right?"

"I'm sure you can," the manager acknowledged. "Now, if we have everything concluded, I have a lot of details to attend to regarding the transshipment of the rest of the gems back to our corporate offices."

"Thank you very much," Nigel said, picking up both boxes. "It's been a pleasure doing business with you. Please think of Asbaran for all your future security needs."

Nigel walked to the door, but then turned back around. "Oh," he said, "I had one last question."

"Yes?"

"Where's Parisa?"

"Who?"

"Nothing," Nigel said. "Sorry to have bothered you." He went back into the outer office, ducking back down as he exited the manager's office. His rifle was still on the desk; Nigel retrieved the weapon and left the office.

"I've got the diamonds," he radioed, *"and I'm on my way out."*

* * * * *

Chapter Thirty-Four

Cell Block, Planet Moorhouse, Kepler 62 System

"Well, human, it doesn't seem that your brother is as smart as you thought, after all," Tranayl noted. "He's taken his payment, and the humans have gone back to their ship."

"He was here?" Parisa asked. "Just now?"

"Yes, he was just here, but there is no reason to start yelling. Besides, he won't be able to hear you; he's already left."

"Where did he go?"

"I expect he's heading back to your miserable planet, and when he leaves, your usefulness to me will be at an end."

"You're wrong," Parisa Shirazi replied. "I told you; he's much smarter than you give him credit for. Worse, he's a stubborn son of a bitch." She chuckled in spite of her situation. "I should know that better than most."

"Obviously, he is *not* smart enough, for he took his payment and left."

A slapping sound came from up the tunnel, and the head of the outpost ran up. "The humans—" it said, out of breath. Like the rest of its kind, the Caroon was not built for sustained athletic endeavors.

"Yes," Tranayl said. "I know. The humans came and got their pay. It is unfortunate, but will ultimately not make any difference; we've killed a lot of their troops and destroyed an enormous amount of their equipment. What they collected won't begin to replace what they've lost."

"They *will* find you," Parisa said, "I told you, Nigel is smarter than you know. He's smarter than even *he* knows. He's going to figure it out, and he's going to find you. He won't be very forgiving when he does."

"I rather doubt that," the MinSha commander said. "We—"

"*But that's what I was trying to tell you!*" the manager interrupted, earning a glare. "They left, but they have returned! My secretary is stalling them, but they must know something! They won't leave!"

"They? There was only one last time."

"There are three this time and two of them are in the combat suits the humans wear. If I do anything to their leader, the humans in the suits are sure to kill me!"

"Then you must go and deal with them. Tell them they accomplished their contract, and their presence is no longer required. Just tell them you're too busy to talk with them as you have to attend to the details of the diamond transfer."

"But I don't like conflict!" the manager cried.

The MinSha commander stalked across the tunnel to the manager and leaned over to look down on the Caroon from directly above. "You have not yet begun to experience conflict," Tranayl whispered ominously. He sniffed. "Perhaps you are unaware that you smell particularly tasty when your pheromones are raging…it's your choice. Conflict with the humans or conflict with me. I know which one *I* hope you choose."

The manager started to back away, but the MinSha was faster; it struck like a cobra and bit a small chunk out of the manager's left ear. The manager fled down the hall, faster than he had come.

"Pity," Tranayl said as he watched the Caroon scurry away. The manager disappeared into the gloom, and the MinSha turned back to Parisa, who smiled.

"Told you so," the human said.

"Just because he came back doesn't mean he knows or suspects anything," Tranayl said. "Perhaps the idiot manager didn't pay them correctly."

"We shall see," Parisa said, her smile larger than ever.

"Yes, I think I *shall* go see." Tranayl turned and stalked up the tunnel in the direction the manager had taken. He stopped after a few steps and looked over his shoulder. "Regardless of how this turns out," he said, "you will soon be dead."

Caroon Outpost, Planet Moorhouse

"So, we got paid, sir?" Sergeant Jeremy 'Gemini' Crouch asked.

"Yeah, I think so," Nigel replied. "I don't know a whole lot about gems, but they look pretty." He started walking back to where they left the APC. "I think I intimidated him enough that he wouldn't intentionally rip us off."

"Did he have any information on your sister?" Mason asked.

"No," Nigel replied. "He said he didn't know her."

"And you believe him?"

"Well, yeah, he seemed legitimately surprised when I asked him; I don't think he was hiding anything. He honestly didn't seem to know her."

"Damn." After a pause, Mason asked, "So, where do you think she is? How are we going to find her?"

"I don't know," Nigel said. "I thought he would have some information…" His words trailed off and he came to a stop in the middle of the road. "That's it!" he exclaimed as the rest of the group came to a stop around him.

"Uh, sir, most of us can't read minds," Mason noted. "Can you give us a little more to go on?"

"Yes I can," Nigel replied. "When I asked the manager where Parisa was, he asked, 'Who's that?'"

"So? You already said he didn't know."

"Right, but I didn't tell him Parisa was a person. I just asked, 'Where's Parisa?' It could have been a thing as well as a person. He didn't ask what a Parisa was, though; he *knew* it was a name."

"I don't know, sir; that seems kinda thin. Maybe he just assumed you were looking for a person."

"No. I'm sure he knew it was a person; he's just a better liar than I thought. I believed he didn't know who she was, but he absolutely knew what I meant."

"So what are we going to do about it?"

"We're going to go back and kick his ass until he tells us what he knows."

"Now you're talking, sir! That's finally a plan I'm excited to be a part of. Can I come with you when you go back in?"

"Yes, First Sergeant, I believe you can."

The humans returned to Peskall's Pretties, and Nigel walked up to the door. "The ceiling is pretty low until we get to the manager's office," he said. "You'll have to go on your hands and knees until we get there, but then you ought to be able to stand up."

"That's fine," Mason said. "I can shoot from my knees if I need to. I've got the armor, so I'll go first, then you, sir, and Private Handley will bring up the rear."

Mason turned to the other troops. "Lewis and Gibson, go around back behind the building," he ordered. "Freese and Davis, keep an eye on the front of the building. Kennedy and Crouch, take a look inside the building once the others are in position and see what the Caroons are doing. Maybe you'll spook them into giving away something they're hiding."

"Yes, Top," the troops replied as they left for their patrol areas.

"Good plan," Nigel replied with a smile. "I would hate for the manager to run out a back door and miss out on our talk."

"Me, too." Mason walked to the door. "Ready, sir?"

"I am."

"All right, let's go have a chat." Mason kicked in the door.

Hangar Bay, Peskall's Pretties, Planet Moorhouse

A giant earthmover as big as a two-story house rumbled past as Sergeant Kennedy and Sergeant Crouch approached the entrance to the building. Like an oversized hangar, the facility had rolling doors that expanded to close the huge entranceway; however, all of them were retracted, and the bay yawned open in front of them.

Kennedy paused and scanned the gigantic space. A beehive of activity, there was something happening across most of the interior. Five of the enormous earthmovers were parked on the left side of the hangar in various stages of disassembly; three of them had scaffolding set up alongside, with aliens conducting maintenance on them. Although mostly Caroons, flashes of other colors indicated the presence of additional races as well.

A number of activities were underway on the right side of the bay. Some Caroons performed maintenance on smaller vehicles and moved stores on pallets from pile to pile, according to some plan of which only they were aware.

"What are we supposed to be looking for?" Sergeant Crouch asked.

"No idea," Sergeant Kennedy replied. "Anything out of the ordinary." He indicated the left side of the bay with his MAC rifle. "For example, that looks like routine maintenance to me."

"Except for the fact the trucks are bigger than my freakin' house back home. That part is out of *my* ordinary…but yeah, it looks pretty routine to me."

The workers continued about their business as the humans walked through, coming and going through doors on either side of the hangar. In most cases, the aliens generally ignored them unless the humans got in their way.

A flash of blue as a door opened on the right caught Sergeant Kennedy's eye. "Holy shit!" he exclaimed. "Down!"

* * * * *

Chapter Thirty-Five

Caroon Outpost, Planet Moorhouse

Mason kicked the door; it shattered and flew inward in a number of smaller pieces. "Oops. Looks like their door malfunctioned." He got down on his knees and entered the hallway beyond. "Kind of dim in here." He turned on an external light, illuminating the space as if it were a sunny summer day on Earth. "Here we go."

Mason crawled further into the building, stopping at the first set of doors.

"The manager is at the end of the hall," Nigel noted from behind him.

"Yes sir. I'm just not a fan of leaving armed aliens behind me. Or armed humans, for that matter." Bracing himself, he punched in the door on the right with a single blow.

"You could have seen if it was unlocked," Nigel said.

"I could have," Mason replied; "I just didn't want to." He looked into the office. "Empty."

Mason turned back to the door on the other side of the hallway. "Just for you, sir," he said as he pushed the handle that opened the door. "Locked." He punched it in. "Oops."

The second set of offices were also found to be empty once Mason punched in the doors. He opened the door at the end of the hallway, and Nigel heard a scream from the room.

Nigel squeezed past the Mason. The room was empty. "Where did the secretary go?" Nigel asked.

"It's hiding behind the desk, I believe."

Nigel walked around the desk to find the Caroon secretary huddling under it. "Come out!" Nigel ordered. "Where's your boss?"

The alien said something inaudible and neither moved nor looked up.

"I said, where is your boss?"

The secretary mumbled something again, but didn't come out.

"This is getting us nowhere," Mason said. He entered the room and walked across the room on his knees. "If I may, sir?"

Nigel shrugged. "Be my guest. He doesn't seem to want to talk to me."

Mason leaned forward, lifted the desk off the alien, and threw it to the side. It crashed into the wall, splintering the desk and making a hole in the wall. He grabbed the Caroon by its cloak and lifted it to its feet, spinning the alien around to look into the 'face' of the CAS-Per. "Colonel Shirazi is speaking to you," he said. "I suggest you answer him, or I'll get angry." Mason spun the alien back around to face Nigel.

"Thanks, First Sergeant." Nigel looked down at the Caroon and didn't need to be an exobiologist to see the creature was terrified...or a really good actor. "So, what's it going to be? Are you going to tell us where your boss is, or are we going to have to take you back to our base with us?"

The alien didn't say anything for a few seconds, then he pointed toward the door to the manager's office. "In there," the secretary said, its voice barely more than a whisper.

Nigel walked to the door and put his hand on the latching mechanism.

"Sir, that's my job," Mason said. "I'm the one with the armor." He guided the alien toward one of the corners of the room with a light push that sent him sprawling. "Stay there, and Private Handley, make sure he does."

"Yes Top!" Private Handley replied.

Nigel moved to the side, allowing Mason to open the door. It was unlocked and Mason threw it open. A laser bolt reflected off his chest, the pistol it came from not powerful enough to penetrate the armor.

Mason crawled into the room, then stood up and walked over to the manager, who stood looking up at where the CASPer's head would be, its mouth half open and the pistol hanging loosely in his hand. Mason grabbed the pistol and pushed him back into his chair.

"You can come in now, sir," Mason called. "The little bastard would have shot you if you had opened the door."

"Why would you want to do that?" Nigel asked, entering the room.

"I…I didn't mean to…," the manager cried. "I just heard the commotion…the crashing…and thought you had come back to steal all our gems. When this…this thing…opened the door, I thought it was some kind of monster and shot it."

"Some kind of monster?" Nigel asked. "You're telling me you've never seen a CASPer before?"

"A CAS—, CASP—, what did you call it?"

"A CASPer. Never mind, I don't care if you've seen one. All I care about is the location of my sister."

"Your sister? Why would I know where your sister was? I have only just seen you for the first time and do not know who your sister is. My contact with your kind has been limited to you and the members of your company who signed the contract to defend the plant."

"My sister's name is Parisa Shirazi, and I believe you *do* know where she is. When I was here earlier, I asked where Parisa was and you asked who that was. If you didn't know her and, as you say, your contact with humans has been limited, how would you know she was a person rather than a place or a thing?"

"I wouldn't know that. Nor do I know it now. I imagine that what you are asking about is nothing more than a figment of the universal translator. In my language, we use the same word for who, what, and where; the only difference is the thing being asked about. If it is a person, the word translates as "who." I'm afraid that is the cause of the confusion. I simply do not know who, what, or where a Parisa Shirazi is and therefore, the universal translator cannot render my speech correctly into your language."

"Huh. What do you think, Top?"

"I think he's full of shit and making this up as he goes along, sir. I've never heard of anything like that with the translator."

"Just because you haven't heard of it," the manager said, "doesn't make it any less true. You say Parisa Shirazi is your sister. I do not know who she is."

Nigel walked over and spun the manager's chair around to face him. Nigel bent over to look the Caroon in the eye. "I'm only going to ask this one more time, and then things are going to get ugly. Where. Is. My. Sister?"

"I don't know."

Nigel's brows knitted as he stared at the manager. Finally, he straightened and turned to Mason. "First Sergeant, did you injure him?"

"I pushed him into the chair, sir, but I don't think I hurt him."

"He's missing part of his ear. You didn't do that?"

"No, sir, I didn't."

"Well, he didn't have time to go somewhere else, so if you didn't do that, who did?"

"Uhhh," the manager said, "it must have happened when I…when I fired my pistol. It must have ricocheted and hit me."

"Right," Nigel replied. "I'm not buying that. First Sergeant, does that look like a laser wound to you?"

"No, sir, it doesn't."

"I didn't think so either. So, Ka-Tal, either you cut part of your ear off doing your administrative work here, or you went somewhere else while we were gone. As we didn't see you on the street, and you didn't pass us coming back in, there's another exit from this office. Would you like to tell us where it is, or would you like my first sergeant to bounce you off the walls for a while first?"

The manager's mouth moved, but nothing came out.

Before Nigel could say anything else, a voice came over the radio. *"I've got bugs in the hangar bay!"* Sergeant Kennedy reported. *"Looks like the better part of a squad of MinSha! We could use a little assistance or we're going to be overrun."* He paused. *"No! Don't—"*

An explosion that could be felt in the manager's office rocked the building.

"All patrols go to the hangar bay to assist Sergeant Kennedy," Mason ordered. He took two steps forward and grabbed the lapels of the manager's tunic in an armored gauntlet. Setting his feet, he lifted the

alien off the floor and shook him. "MinSha? Where did the *hell* did MinSha come from?"

"They've…they've been here all along," the manager said with a squeal. "They arrived here a year ago, right after the Besquith took over your base. They…they had weapons! We had to obey them or they would have killed us all!"

He struggled to break free from Mason's grasp, but the armored suit was far stronger. Nigel stepped forward and slapped the Caroon across its muzzle.

"I've heard enough," Nigel said. "Where's the other door out of here?"

The manager stilled, going limp in Mason's grasp. Without a word the alien pointed at a bookcase on the back wall of the office.

Mason dropped the manager, who landed in a heap, and strode to the bookshelf. The trooper ripped the bookshelf away from the wall with his augmented strength, and Nigel ducked as books flew across the room.

The bookcase crashed to the floor, revealing a door with a number of peepholes behind it. Without waiting to be told, Mason stepped forward and yanked open the door.

An armed grenade spun slowly to a stop on the floor in the narrow passageway beyond.

Hangar Bay, Peskall's Pretties, Planet Moorhouse

"**D**own!" Sergeant Kennedy screamed. He pushed the other soldier behind a pallet of tires and dove back out of the way as the first MinSha fired its laser rifle. The bolt glanced off his leg armor, doing no damage. Kennedy crashed to the ground and rolled behind another of the pallets.

Lifting his MAC above the stack of tires, he fired a spray of rounds in the direction of where he had last seen the MinSha. Judging by the wet, squelching noise he heard, at least one of the rounds struck home; several others whined off as ricochets.

He checked Sergeant Crouch; the trooper was already shooting his laser rifle at the MinSha.

The other creatures in the hangar bay all seemed to be running away. Hopefully, they weren't going for their weapons or this was going to well and truly suck. They were pinned down behind the pallets by an unknown force of bugs, with no way to get to a more defensible position. They needed help.

"I've got bugs in the hangar bay!" Sergeant Kennedy radioed. He took a peek over the pallet then ducked back down as several MinSha fired at him. *"Looks like the better part of a squad of MinSha! We could use a little assistance or we're going to be overrun."*

He looked to Sergeant Crouch for confirmation the trooper had heard his transmission; the soldier was unlimbering the flamethrower attached to his right arm.

Kennedy rose and fired several more rounds over the top of the pallet. One of the MinSha went down as the MAC round struck it in the neck and nearly tore off its head. A laser round struck his right shoulder, partially melting his armor.

As he ducked back down, he saw the drums on one of the pallets the MinSha were using as cover. At least one bore the universal symbols for "flammable" and "explosive," and that drum was spraying its contents out from a pair of MAC-round holes in its side. If Sergeant Crouch hit that with the flamethrower…

"*No!*" Kennedy yelled, his mike still set to radio. He rose to run to Sergeant Crouch and took a hit in his torso that spun him around. He reoriented as Sergeant Crouch stood up and activated his weapon. "*Don't—*"

The hangar erupted in a cataclysmic detonation.

* * * * *

Chapter Thirty-Six

Manager's Office, Peskall's Pretties, Planet Moorhouse

Mason threw the door shut, but the grenade detonated before he could latch it. The door blew in, slamming into Mason. Pieces of door and shrapnel peppered his suit, and the force of the explosion staggered him backward several steps. Although Mason's suit saved Nigel from the blast and shrapnel, the explosion was deafening in the small space, and he had a hard time hearing through the ringing in his ears.

"Damn it," Mason said, flailing one of his suit's legs. "I've got a bunch of yellow lights on my suit, and my right knee is out. Private Handley, get in here! You've got point. Go find whoever threw that grenade and kick his ass!"

"Sure thing, Top." The manager scurried out from the path of the trooper as he marched to the door. He held his MAC out the door and fired a burst. When he didn't receive any return fire, he stepped into the corridor.

"No one out here," Private Handley said.

"You mean the grenade just threw itself?" Mason asked.

"No; whoever threw it must have run away. The passageway turns after about 30 feet."

Nigel saw movement; the manager was scurrying toward the door. Nigel ran over and grabbed the manager's collar. "Where are you going?" he asked. "I'm not done talking with you. You still haven't told me where my sister is."

"If she is still alive, she is down that passage," the manager whined, trembling all over like a frightened Chihuahua.

"Good," Nigel said. "We're finally getting somewhere. Now you're going to take us to her." He began dragging the Caroon to the back door out.

"*No!*" the manager exclaimed, digging his claws into the bookshelf as they passed it. "I will not go! He will kill me!"

"Who?"

"Tranayl, the MinSha commander. He's down there and he'll kill me!"

"Sir, we don't have time for this bullshit. If both your sister and the MinSha are down there, we need to *go!*"

"You're right," Nigel said. "Let's go." He started toward the door but turned back around. "And if anything's happened to her," he added, "I'll be back."

Cell Block, Planet Moorhouse, Kepler 62 System

Parisa sat on her small bunk, her head in her hands. She had to break out while her brother was close, but how?

She heard a swishing noise and looked up. Tranayl hurried past her cell without stopping.

"Hey!" Parisa cried out. "Where are you going? You look like you're running away. What? Is my brother kicking your troops' asses?"

The MinSha commander stopped as if he had hit a wall. "I almost forgot about you," he said as he turned and approached the cell.

"So you *were* running!" Parisa laughed. "I should have guessed. For the record, I told you my brother would come."

"I wasn't running. I was withdrawing to a better location to regroup. And, as far as your brother goes, you'll never see him." The MinSha drew his pistol. "You have now outlived your usefulness, as *I* told *you* would happen."

He fired twice, striking her in the chest with both shots. Parisa fell to the floor.

Hangar Bay, Peskall's Pretties, Planet Moorhouse

Clang, clang, clang. "Hey, you okay?" It sounded like someone was talking through a foot of water. Indistinct and barely audible. *Clang, clang, clang.* That was loud and clear.

Sergeant Kennedy managed to open an eye. Sergeant Stephanie Freese looked down at him and tapped his suit with her armored gauntlet. *Clang, clang, clang.*

"I'm awake," Kennedy said. It took a lot more effort to say those words than he would have thought possible. As his vision focused he saw his control panel looked like a Christmas tree of red and green lights, with a few yellows thrown in for variety. Most of the systems below his waist still worked, but everything above it was either non-functional or only partly operational.

"Man, you should see the dent in your armor right by your head," Sergeant Freese added.

"'S okay," Kennedy replied. That explained why everything was going in and out of focus. Concussion. "I think I have the same dent in my head." He tried to roll over to get up, but had a hard time with several of the suit's motors not working.

Sergeant Freese helped him to his feet.

"Any more…MinSha?"

"Naw, man. Whatever you guys blew up in here killed them good. All we saw were a few pieces."

"What about Sergeant Crouch?"

"He didn't make it. A piece of pipe got blown all the way through his suit. He's dead."

"Shit." Kennedy surveyed the hangar. It was trashed. Everything near ground zero for the blast was just *gone*, including the concrete flooring in a radius of about 20 feet. The pallet of tires he had been behind had slowed the majority of the pieces headed at him. If he hadn't stood up, he'd probably have been okay. He could see the pipe that impaled Sergeant Crouch. Yeah, he was dead. Damn it.

"So, now what, Sergeant?" Corporal Davis asked. She looked nervous; she kept turning as if she were trying to watch in all directions at once.

"I don't know," Sergeant Kennedy said. He was having a hard time thinking, but there was one thing he knew about the MinSha. "If there were some of those damn MinSha here, there are probably more close by. Damn bugs." He tried his radio even though it was one of his "red" systems. Nope. "Any of you guys got comms with Top or the Colonel? I think I remember telling them we had MinSha here, but I'm kinda fuzzy after that."

"Stand by," Sergeant Freese replied. After a brief pause she reported, "They're going after the MinSha commander down in some tunnels underneath here. Top got hit by a grenade and his suit's messed up."

"They're going to need help," Kennedy decided as Sergeant Lewis and Corporal Gibson ran up. "Their damn commander isn't going to be alone, and the Colonel's only got two CASPers with him, one of which is fucked up. They're going to need us. Let's go."

"Dude," Corporal Gibson said. "Your suit looks pretty fucked up, too. What are you going to do if we come across any of the insects?"

Kennedy ran a scan of his weaponry. Corporal Gibson was right; all of it was inop except for one system. He activated the switch, and the giant spring-loaded sword blade extended and snapped into place on his right arm, extending over two feet beyond his fist. He looked at Sergeant Crouch's body and stood a little taller.

"What am I going to do if we run into any of the bugs? I'm going to kill the motherfuckers."

Manager's Office, Peskall's Pretties, Planet Moorhouse

"**A**ll right, Handley," Mason said. "Move out."

Nigel started to follow the trooper, but Mason stepped in front of him. "My suit may be messed up, sir, but it's still better protection than what you've got." Mason entered the corridor and Nigel followed the senior enlisted.

The passageway wasn't much to speak of. Although there was a flat area next to the door, the passageway immediately sloped down into the ground at a steep angle. Hewn from the rock, it had been braced periodically to keep it from caving in, but wasn't much larger than a CASPer in either height or width. Nigel had a great view of Top's back as he limped along, dragging his right foot, but not a lot else.

As Private Handley had noted, the passageway ran for about 30 feet then made a turn to the left as it continued down. After another 20 feet, the passageway leveled out; it also widened and grew taller, and Mason moved forward to limp alongside Handley. Nigel could finally see a little of the way ahead, although the two CASPers still blocked most of his view.

After another 100 feet, they came to the cells, barren squares about 10 feet by 10 feet, with bars that ran from floor to ceiling on all sides. The first several were empty, aside from small bunks or piles of some sort of straw.

"Damn it," Mason said, stopping suddenly in front of one of the cells. He reached over and ripped the door from off its hinges with a single pull, but he was too large to make it through the small door-way in his suit. He stepped back, allowing Nigel access. "Is that who I think it is?"

Nigel stepped forward, dreading what he would see. A body lay in the middle of the cell, not moving. His heart skipped a beat as he recognized who it was. The clothing was tattered and the hair a rat's nest, but it was his sister. Parisa. He dropped his rifle in the passage-way and ran forward.

"Oh shit. Parisa!" Nigel fell to his knees next to her. She'd been shot at least twice, and her chest was a mess. Something important had been hit; there was blood everywhere, and it pooled around her. Judging by the bubbles that continued to form, she was still alive…and shot in the lung.

He took her hand. "Parisa, can you hear me?" She didn't move.

"Is she alive?" Mason asked.

Nigel looked up. "Just barely. She's been shot a couple of times, and one is through the lung. *I don't know what to do for her!*"

"Without a hospital, there isn't much you can do," Private Handley said.

Nigel looked back down. Parisa's eyes were open, and she was looking at him. Her lips moved, but Nigel couldn't hear what she said. He leaned forward to where his ear was next to her lips.

"Bastard said…wouldn't see you. Was wrong." She coughed out a glob of blood. "Knew…you'd figure…out. Something else…need to…do."

"Whatever it is, we'll do it together."

"Not possible." Her hand reached up and pulled Nigel closer. "*Avenge me!*"

The hand fell away, and her head rolled to the side. She was dead.

"Fuuuuuuuck!" Nigel yelled.

Mason screamed something inaudible and ripped the door off the next cell and began beating the bars with it. Several snapped out of their frames under the assault and rattled as they hit the ground. "Damn it," he chanted with every blow. "Damn it." *Crash.* "Damn it!" *Crash.* "*God fucking damn it!*" *Crash. Crash! CRASH!*

"Hey uh, Top, Colonel," Private Handley said, "I've got movement up front."

Locked in their grief, neither man responded.

"*Top, Colonel!*" Private Handley yelled. "I've got movement up front! *MinSha!*"

Mason threw the door through the hole he had made in the bars, and it clattered loudly as it hit the floor inside. He turned to find Nigel retrieving his laser rifle from the passageway. "Stay back, sir," Mason said. He gave Nigel a push that threw him backwards down the hall. "These motherfuckers are mine."

The last cell had a solid metal frame and door, which Mason ripped from its hinges as easily as he had the others. Holding it as a shield in front of him, he advanced down the hallway, and rounds immediately began hitting it.

"What are you doing, Top?" Private Handley called as he fired to the side of the advancing trooper.

Mason half-turned as a MAC round penetrated the shield, but bounced off his armor, having spent most of its energy penetrating the cell door. "Isn't it obvious?" he asked. "You can come with me or not, but I'm getting some revenge."

* * * * *

Chapter Thirty-Seven

Manager's Office, Peskall's Pretties, Planet Moorhouse

Sergeant Kennedy led the group down the tunnel out of the manager's office. They had caught the manager removing a box from a hidden safe when they arrived, and Sergeant Kennedy had appropriated it as spoils of war.

The manager had pointed out where the other humans had gone when asked; having five CASPers crowded around you aiming weapons in your vicinity *could* be somewhat intimidating.

It wouldn't have been hard to find their direction of travel in any event; the path of destruction led from the bookcase on the floor, through the shattered door and into the tunnel.

They followed the passage as it turned and widened, and then reached the cell block.

It looked like a major battle had occurred; some of the cells were completely trashed, although Sergeant Kennedy didn't see any evidence of weapons impacts that would have caused the damage.

The colonel sat in one of the cells with his back to the door, a woman's head in his lap. The only blood was the red of humanity, and Kennedy could see enough of it to know that the woman was dead. Judging by the scene, the woman was Parisa Shirazi, former head of Asbaran Solutions and sister to Nigel.

Despite all of their efforts and travel halfway around the galaxy, they had failed to save her.

The colonel was obviously taking it hard; his head was down, and he didn't give any indication he had heard them approach.

"Sorry, sir," Kennedy said.

If Colonel Shirazi heard him, he didn't give any indication.

"Where are Top and Handley?"

This time the colonel did move; he waved a hand further down the tunnel. "Go away," the colonel finally muttered.

Sergeant Kennedy turned toward the rest of the group. "C'mon," he said. "Let's go find Top."

The group had only taken a few steps down the tunnel when they heard the unmistakable sounds of a heavy weapon. "Hurry," Kennedy added. "Before it's too late."

Tunnels Under Peskall's Pretties, Planet Moorhouse

Private Handley watched Mason advance down the tunnel, holding the door in front of him. Some of the bigger rounds staggered him, but then he would regroup and press onward. Private Handley glanced at the colonel, who sat in the center of the passageway where Mason had thrown him, looking stunned. As the colonel gave no indication he needed help or that he was even going to get up, Handley fell in behind Mason as he strode down the passage.

The private caught up with Mason, and he could hear the senior enlisted muttering something as he proceeded down the tunnel. Handley turned up the gain on his receivers, and after a few seconds he realized Mason was repeating the same mantra as he advanced. "Gonna kill them," he said as he stepped out with his left foot, followed by "Gonna kill them all," as he dragged his non-functional right foot up.

Mason kept repeating it, over and over, and Handley began to doubt Mason's sanity; he also started to rethink his decision to follow the senior trooper. Handley was safe following behind him, though, or at least relatively so; leaving the safety of Mason's shadow would put him at risk from the fusillade of MAC rounds and laser bolts passing by him.

Handley realized with a start their progress was slowing; the further they traveled, the more Mason had to lean forward into his shield to absorb the impacts of the MAC rounds, and maintaining his balance was taking more and more of his time.

But the litany continued, "Gonna kill them; gonna kill them all."

Handley risked a glance around the side of the shield and saw the problem. With no one returning fire, the MinSha had become bold. The passageway widened into some kind of chamber after another 100 feet, and the MinSha had formed a firing line across it; at least six of the bugs were in the open, shooting at the humans.

That would never do.

He attached his rifle to the mounting clip on his leg and pulled out two grenades. He pulled the pin from one and threw it as hard as he could over the top of Mason's shield, then armed and threw the second as quickly as he could.

The bugs yelled something untranslatable by his suit, and they scattered like cockroaches when the lights come on.

The grenades detonated and, as the pressure on the shield diminished, Mason ran forward, moving the remains of the cell door to the side so he could see as he sprinted. Increasing his speed to keep up with Mason, Handley got a better look ahead as they advanced.

There was a large, open area at the end of the tunnel, and then nothing. The mining pit, with its three mile drop off, lay beyond the chamber.

Handley didn't have time for more than a glance; the MinSha were climbing back to their feet. Mason reached them just in time and shielded himself as the first one fired. He caught the laser bolt on the cell door, and then he was upon the enemy, swinging the door like a giant fly swatter.

The shield came down on the alien that had shot at him, and chitin and fluids sprayed as the Minsha's body disintegrated under the blow. Mason threw the door like a flying disc at a second MinSha, decapitating it. Mason's giant knife blade sprang out as he turned left and advanced on a third.

A laser bolt flashed off Mason's shoulder, and Handley turned to find several more MinSha on the right that had survived the grenade blasts. One was already firing; Handley shot it first, and a string of MAC rounds crossed the alien's chest, penetrating armor and chitin with enough force to pass all the way through.

A second MinSha leveled its weapon at him, and Handley stepped forward. Holding his rifle across his body with both hands, Handley knocked the weapon out of the alien's claws with the butt of his rifle, then reversed the stroke and drove the rifle butt between the MinSha's eyes, shattering its skull. The alien dropped, and Handley stepped forward to fire point-blank at a third MinSha that was struggling to its feet, leaking blue blood from a number of wounds. The alien was hit twice in the head and fell to the ground.

Handley turned back to find Mason standing over the remains of several more MinSha. Blue viscera and blood dripped from his knife and looked like paintball splatters across his armor from head to toe.

The senior trooper wasn't moving; he just appeared to be looking down at the disemboweled MinSha.

Handley walked over to Mason's side and waved a hand in front of his camera pickups. "Are you okay?" he asked.

No response.

"Hey, Top," he said, trying again. "Are you all right?"

Again, no response. This was creepier than when Mason had been repeating his chant.

A metallic noise reverberated through Handley's speakers. Damn, he had forgotten to turn the gain back down. He spun to see what had made the noise; another squad of MinSha were setting up a crew-served weapon on the other side of the large, open bay. The noise he'd heard was the click of the heavy MAC snapping into the tripod.

And it wasn't just a large, open bay—it was a hangar bay. Some sort of MinSha courier ship sat on the other side of the alien troopers.

"Get down!" Handley yelled, diving behind a nearby pallet of equipment. He hit the ground and rolled to look back. Mason hadn't moved.

"Mason! Get down!" Nothing. Handley didn't know what Mason was doing in his suit, but he appeared to be completely detached from the outside world.

Swearing under his breath, Handley rose and raced across the intervening distance to slam into Mason, knocking both of them to the ground as the first rounds flew past over them. On his knees, Handley struggled to drag Mason to the safety of another equipment pallet.

He had just reached the pallet when Mason slapped his hand away. "Stop!" the senior enlisted said simply, then he started to rise.

"Stay down!" Handley ordered, planting a hand on Mason's chest to pin him down.

Mason struggled against him for several seconds as rounds began impacting the pallet, then he stilled. "Where are we?" he finally asked.

"We're in a MinSha hangar, and there is a squad on the other side of the bay with a heavy weapon."

"Who else is with us?"

"No one."

"So what's our status?"

Handley risked a glance above the pallet, then ducked back down as the heavy MAC began firing again. He had seen enough, though. As he had feared, the MinSha squad was advancing on them. Using the crew-served weapon for cover, the squad had split and a group of three MinSha was flanking them on both sides.

"Our status?" Handley asked. "We're pretty fucked."

* * * * *

Chapter Thirty-Eight

Hangar Bay Under Peskall's Pretties, Planet Moorhouse

"Hurry up and kill them before more of their damned suits show up," Commander Tranayl urged.

"I need them to stand up," the MAC gunner replied. "The tires in that pallet are stopping our rounds. I don't want to move the weapon; it would give them a chance to attack. Besides, the squad should force them from cover shortly. They almost have the humans flanked on both sides."

"You want them to stand up?" Tranayl asked. "I can do that. Just be ready." He mounted the courier ship's ramp and selected the hangar's intercom system.

Tunnels Under Peskall's Pretties, Planet Moorhouse

A voice came over the hangar's speakers. "Nigel Shirazi, if you can hear me, I wanted to compliment you on how close you came to saving your sister. Had you arrived a few minutes earlier, she might still be alive. Too bad, really, just like it's too bad we didn't get a chance to meet. Unfortunately, I have places to go and humans to kill, so I have to be going. I look forward to our next meeting, for I am sure we *will* meet again."

A red haze covered Mason's vision, and it took all of his control not to charge into the teeth of the heavy weapon just to kill a few more of them. His soul ached; they had only been a few minutes too late…

Handley peeked around the side of the pallet. "Brave bug," he said, dropping back into cover again. "The little bastard is on the boarding ladder to the ship. It's almost as if he were daring us to shoot at him."

"He's here?" The tenuous hold Mason had on his emotions snapped. He stood up, yelling a feral cry of rage and fired at his tormentor.

Mason's first few rounds went high, and then an alien MAC round hit his weapon, destroying it. He continued firing, pulling and releasing the trigger, unable to comprehend why his rounds weren't having an effect. Oblivious to everything except the urge to kill, Mason also failed to notice when a second round removed most of his suit's right hand and lower arm. He continued pointing the stub of his arm at the MinSha on the boarding ladder, firing the weapon that was no longer attached, while lighter weapons from the other MinSha riddled his suit.

"*Top!*" Handley screamed. "*Get down!*" When Mason didn't flinch, Handley chopped at his leg, trying to bring the senior enlisted down, but the leg of Mason's suit had locked fully extended when it failed. It didn't budge.

"Damn it," Handley said, realizing his error. He climbed to his feet and tackled Mason to the ground.

Tunnels Under Peskall's Pretties, Planet Moorhouse

Sergeant Kennedy held up a fist as he approached the end of the tunnel, and the group behind him stopped in place, scanning for danger.

"I see Top and Handley," Kennedy reported. *"They're laying down behind a pile of shit. Someone must be shootin' at them. Weird; one's on top of the other. It almost looks like they're trying to have sex in their suits."*

"Are they moving?" Corporal Davis asked.

"No, but I see movement beyond them. Looks like some MinSha are sneaking up on them. Top and Handley must be injured. Shit! There's another group on this side of them. Stand by; I'm going to call Top on the command net."

Tunnels Under Peskall's Pretties, Planet Moorhouse

A voice called Mason back from the depths of wherever his sanity had gone. *"Top! Top! Are you there? You're about to get attacked."*

"Yeah," Mason replied, recognizing Sergeant Kennedy's voice; *"I'm here, although my suit's pretty messed up. All the cameras seem to be out and everything from the waist up has either a yellow or red light."*

"Your cameras are probably just blocked as you're either on top of Handley, or vice versa. He may be blocking your inputs."

Mason rolled back and forth. He was underneath Handley. He pushed the other suit off and, as he achieved some separation, got a look at Handley's suit. One of the big MAC rounds had gone through the suit at the level of Handley's head. Everything he could see was splattered in red and gray. He had no recollection of that happening, but Handley was on top of him; the trooper must have tried to pull him down and had gotten killed for his effort. Damn it.

"Top! Don't move. You've got bugs on both sides of you."

Tunnels Under Peskall's Pretties, Planet Moorhouse

"**I** got Top and he's okay, but he's about to get overrun," Sergeant Kennedy transmitted, switching back to the group's net. *"There are two groups of bugs; looks like three in each. We'll have to shoot them off of him."*

"Any other enemy present?" Sergeant Freese asked.

"Not that I see. Form a firing line, and we'll take out the ones on the far side of him first, then hit the ones close to us."

As the group formed a line abreast, Sergeant Hannah Lewis' shoulder dragged across the side of the tunnel, producing a loud screeching noise.

Everything stopped, and the two groups of MinSha turned toward the noise.

"Fire!" Kennedy yelled. Lacking a weapon, he charged the closer group. In a blast of jet fire, he jumped into their midst, the sword blade on his right arm coming down as he landed to behead the MinSha on the right. Spinning, he cut the arm off a second, and slashed through its thorax in an explosion of blue on the return stroke. Turning further, he slapped the laser rifle out of the third alien's claws and stabbed his sword into the alien's thorax all the way up to his fist.

He pulled down and out, eviscerating the MinSha, and turned to look for additional targets.

The heavy MAC round hit him in the chest, knocking him backward five feet and driving him from his feet. It killed him instantly.

* * * * *

Chapter Thirty-Nine

Tunnels Under Peskall's Pretties, Planet Moorhouse

From his vantage point behind the pallet, Mason saw Kennedy get hit by the MAC round, and he knew the trooper was dead. *"Get back!"* he radioed to the rest of the troopers and they scattered back into the tunnel. *"Can anyone see any more MinSha?"*

"Nope."

"No."

"Looks like we got 'em all."

"None here."

Mason couldn't see any of the aliens, either. The three Kennedy had attacked were either dead or soon would be, lying in large pools of blood and entrails. The troopers were safe, as was he, at least for the moment, although he was still trapped. With his suit as messed up as it was, there was no telling what was going to work if he stood up.

He went through the systems quickly, one by one, to determine what capability he still had to wage war. What the hell? Where had his right hand gone? Crap! Six inches higher and he would have lost his real hand. His weapons, what he had left, were inop across the board. His secondary weapon, a hypervelocity pistol like the one Breetar used had taken a hit from something during the fight. The barrel remained in the holster, somehow, but the handle was missing.

The knife blade on his left hand was jammed and wouldn't come down.

From a personal standpoint, he was exhausted and beaten up. His armor had stopped anything from physically damaging his human body, but he felt like he'd gone twelve rounds with one of the heavyweight fighters of old.

He was also mentally and emotionally spent. Although he didn't know for sure, he was pretty sure he was responsible for Handley's death, and he knew Kennedy had died trying to save him. He wasn't sure how he could feel any worse.

One of the courier ship's motors came to life with a backfire that echoed throughout the hangar.

The only way he could feel worse than he did right now was if he let the head bug, Tranayl or whatever its name was, escape. He could *not* allow that to happen. He would avenge Parisa, even if he had to throw himself into one of the ship's engines to destroy it and crash the ship.

Hopefully, it wouldn't come to that, but for the life of him he had no idea how he was going to get past the heavy MAC.

With a roar, the ship's second engine started.

"Do any of you have missiles?" Mason asked. *"The head of the MinSha is on that ship and we can't allow him to get away. He is also the one who killed Parisa Shirazi."*

"I've got missiles," Corporal Jen 'Sparky' Davis said. *"Want me to step out and tag it with one?"*

"Not yet. If you step out, you're going to eat one of the MAC rounds like Kennedy did. Besides, the motors aren't facing you; you'll have a hard time hitting anything important. We'll have to wait for the ship to take off, then I'll distract the MAC crew while you shoot down the ship."

"How are you going to distract the crew?"

"You leave that to me; you just be ready to shoot down the damn ship. How many missiles do you have?"

"Six, why?"

"Fire them all, as fast as you can. The ship is sure to have some sort of countermeasures and we've got to bring it down."

The roar from the ship's engines increased as the pilot brought them to full power. Mason risked a glance around the side of the pallet and saw the ship lifting. He ducked back behind the pallet as a MAC round went past him and slammed into a pallet behind him.

The engine noise shifted as the ship began to move. *"Here we go!"* Mason transmitted. He pulled a tire off the pile in front of him and threw it to the right. The MAC fired at the motion and tracked the tire as it flew; Mason rose to his feet and hobbled off to the left, dragging his right foot.

The MAC turned back to Mason and fired. The first round missed, but the second round caught him in the shoulder of his suit, spinning him around and throwing him to the ground. As badly damaged as his suit was, he didn't lose any other systems, and he struggled back to his feet and lurched toward the MAC.

With a roar, the first missile launched at the courier ship as it cleared the hangar bay and began accelerating. The MAC crew spun to target the new threat, and Sergeant Freese pushed Sparky out of the way as it fired. The round hit Freese in the chest, killing her instantly and throwing her to the side.

Sparky's second missile misfired as she stumbled, blasting the contents of a nearby pallet to shreds, but she reoriented herself and the third flew true.

The remaining troopers, Sergeant Lewis and Corporal Gibson, charged the MAC, firing as they went. One of the MAC loaders went down, shot through the head, and the MAC gunner shifted its aim. Lewis and Gibson both took rounds to the chest as the fourth missile raced after the courier ship.

A fifth missile roared out of its tube as the MAC reoriented on Sparky. The weapon fired, removing the suit's right leg at the knee, and the last six inches of Sparky's leg.

Sparky was spun around and thrown to the hangar bay floor. She tried to get up, but found her right leg wouldn't respond. Looking down, she was amazed to find the bottom portion of her suit gone, along with her foot and the bottom of her leg; there was no pain, but the loss of the limb was interesting…and inconvenient. She still had a missile remaining, but she couldn't stand up. Grabbing onto one of the pallets, she used her arms to pull herself up onto the top of it as the gun crew reloaded.

Mason staggered as quickly as he could toward the gun, but was forced to watch as the gunner charged the weapon and fired. Sparky's last missile launched half a second before the round hit her in the chest, killing her.

The MAC gunner tried to spin the weapon toward Mason, but the trooper slapped away the barrel with the stump of his right arm and slammed his left fist down on the gunner's head. The chitin shattered and blood sprayed across Mason's dented suit as the gunner went down. The other loader scooped up a laser rifle, but Mason was on the creature before it could fire. He knocked the weapon out of the alien's claws and grabbed the creature by the throat. Lifting it off the ground, Mason squeezed until the MinSha's head popped off.

The creature's legs continued to kick sporadically, and he threw the corpse to the side.

Turning, he was just in time to see the sixth missile hit the courier ship's right engine. The left engine had already been hit at least once, and that side of the ship was already engulfed in flames. The right engine erupted in a ball of fire, and the craft flipped over and drove into the ground, exploding on impact.

Mason turned away from the devastation outside and found the destruction inside the hangar, if anything, to be worse. Several small fires burned across the nightmarish scene, and human and MinSha bodies covered the area, surrounded by pools of red and blue.

Mason collapsed to the floor and threw up in his suit.

Cell Block, Planet Moorhouse, Kepler 62 System

Nigel's tear dripped onto the top of Parisa's head. Too late. Nigel had been too late. Again. He had been too late to save Lieutenant Seville, he had been too late to save Second Squad, and now he was too late to save his sister. After all he had been through, it hadn't been good enough. Like Mason had once told him, *he* hadn't been good enough.

Was that all there was? To go back to Earth a failure, having been unable to save his sister? *It wasn't fair!* The deck had been stacked against him the whole time. He had been shuffled off to the side of the fight while his family had been killed off. He'd never had a chance. His equipment was second-rate, the troops he led were under-trained, and he'd never had time to actually *plan* for anything; the Asbaran forces had been playing catch-up the entire time. Not only that, but he'd had to fight two races, not just one. If he'd had any advantage whatsoever, he might have pulled it off.

It wasn't fair.

He leaned over to kiss Parisa's brow one last time, and a flash of red fell out of his breast pocket. One of the red diamonds. He shook his head. If he'd had a few of those, he could have bought some of the newer Model 8 CASPers. Maybe they would have been successful with 8s.

It wasn't fair.

He hadn't had the diamonds before, or they might have made a difference…but he had them now. In fact, the more he thought about it, the more he realized he now had *everything*. He had lost Parisa, but now the enemy no longer had any control over him…he was free to do whatever he wanted. To go where he wanted and to kill everyone responsible for this debacle. And with all the red diamonds he was coming home with, he could buy some new equipment. New CASPers, new dropships…maybe even something to replace the *Vindicator*.

He could re-equip, hire new troops, and then…and then he could do whatever the hell he wanted. For the first time in his life, all the doors were open to him. He was in charge, and he would make the decisions, and the first thing he was going to do would be to make the last year of his life worthwhile. He would make his entire *life* worthwhile. And just like Mason had shown him the way in telling him he wasn't ready before, Mason had also shown him what he needed to do now.

Revenge.

He would find out who had done this to his family, and he would make them pay. The Besquith were dead. All of them. They wanted to nuke humans? He'd see how they liked having it done to them. Their planet would *burn*. But they were only pawns. The MinSha had been running the whole thing. He would kill the MinSha, too; in fact, he would start with the MinSha. Maybe there was someone above them; if so, he'd find out who and kill them as well. Anyone involved in the destruction of his family was going to die, and he would be the one to to avenge their deaths. Hamasa demanded it. He *would* kill every alien involved. And he would start with the MinSha.

Mason limped into the cell, and Nigel looked up from smoothing Parisa's hair. Despite the armor Mason had been wearing earlier, he was bleeding in a number of places and had more contusions than Nigel was able to count. He also looked like he had had thrown up on himself. Mason looked like shit.

"It's done," Mason said, his voice flat. "They're all dead."

"All of them?" Nigel asked, his voice equally devoid of emotion. He looked back down and resumed his task.

"Yes sir, all of them." After the silence grew longer than was comfortable, Mason finally asked, "So, what's next?"

"Next, we bury our dead, round up the living, and go back home. Oh yeah. First, we go see the Caroons and make them pay us more. They violated the terms of the contract in not telling us enemies were here; therefore, they owe us an additional 10 million credits."

"That's it?"

"Yeah, that's it. It's all we can do at the moment. Most of our folks are dead, and I want to take Parisa home to bury her in the family plot." He sighed heavily. He hated Chabahar, but he would go there one last time for Parisa.

"But…but sir, what are we going to do about the MinSha?"

Nigel looked up, and Mason could see that although his voice had been flat, Nigel was anything but non-emotional. The anger was there, burning in his eyes, but it was on a leash, held back, his face set in a scowl. "The MinSha?" Nigel asked, his control finally slipping. "I'll tell you what we're going to do with the MinSha. We're going to do what humanity *should* have done with them a *long* time ago. We're going to pay those motherfuckers back for what they did to our planet and what they've now done to my family. We're going to wipe those bastards out, just like they did to Iran during first contact. What are we going to do about the MinSha? We're going to kill them all! *This is war!*"

* * * * *

Epilogue

Fleet Maintenance Yard "B," Golara Prime Orbit, Golara System

The figure watched the battered warship ease into the space dock, surprised it still held together. Holed in more places than it was whole, even making it back to the shipyard was a supreme testament to the competence of its crew.

The figure removed its goggles so it could see some of the damage in a different light and shook its head. It didn't make any difference; the ship was nothing more than scrap for the recyclers.

The ship's crew was obviously aware they wouldn't be returning; heads down and tentacles hanging limp, they shuffled down the gangway, their sea bags stuffed with all their worldly possessions. The last person off the ship was the captain, and the figure moved from the shadows to fall into step with her.

"Tell me about the battle," the figure said.

"What is there to tell?" the captain asked. "We lost, and our fleet was destroyed. We alone made it back from the debacle."

"Tell me about the humans," the figure urged. "I want to know more about them."

"They were crazy," the captain said. "We were unprepared for their unpredictability. They were everywhere and nowhere at the same time. We studied their doctrine and knew what they were going to do…but they didn't follow their own doctrine. At all." She stopped to stare at the figure. "If you've come with an offer of employment, it will be quite some time before I'm ready to listen."

"I come for information only," the figure replied, "although employment will not be long in coming. Something must be done soon, and war is coming." It replaced the darkened goggles over its large jade eyes, careful not to catch the strap on its whiskers. Equipment on the harness it wore jangled as the alien turned and began walking again. "Now," it repeated, "tell me about the humans."

# # # # #

ABOUT THE AUTHOR

A bestselling Science Fiction/Fantasy author and speaker, Chris Kennedy is a former school principal and naval aviator with over 3,000 hours flying attack and reconnaissance aircraft. Chris is also a member of the SFWA and the SCBWI.

Chris' full-length novels on Amazon include the "Occupied Seattle" military fiction duology, the "Theogony" and "Codex Regius" science fiction trilogies and the "War for Dominance" fantasy trilogy. Chris is also the author of the #1 Amazon self-help book, "Self-Publishing for Profit: How to Get Your Book Out of Your Head and Into the Stores."

Titles by Chris Kennedy

"Red Tide: The Chinese Invasion of Seattle"
– Available Now

"Occupied Seattle"
– Available Now

"Janissaries: Book One of The Theogony"
– Available Now

"When the Gods Aren't Gods: Book Two of The Theogony"
– Available Now

"Terra Stands Alone: Book Three of The Theogony"
– Available Now

"The Search for Gram: Book One of the Codex Regius"
– Available Now

"Beyond the Shroud of the Universe: Book Two of the Codex Regius" – Available Now

"The Dark Star War: Book Three of the Codex Regius"
– Available Now

"Can't Look Back: Book One of the War for Dominance"
– Available Now

"Self-Publishing for Profit"
– Available Now

"Leadership from the Darkside"
– Available Now

* * * * *

The following is an
Excerpt from Book 3 of the Revelations Cycle:

Winged Hussars

Mark Wandrey

Available from Seventh Seal Press

Spring, 2017

eBook, Paperback, and Audio Book

Excerpt from "Winged Hussars:"

"Shields are failing!" Tactical yelled over the blaring alarms. The bridge shuddered as the ship absorbed one titanic impact after another. Alexis hung onto the arms of her command chair; despite the strap around her waist and the other two crossed over her chest, the blasts were threatening to wrench her free and fling her across the CIC.

"Captain," Paka implored her, "*Pegasus* is coming apart at the seams!" The ship shuddered and jumped like a wounded animal as another particle beam slammed into her shields. The Veetanho XO was clinging to a control console as was usual in a fight; it allowed him to be more flexible in combat. A big white rodent, flexibility suited him.

"Patience, Mr. Paka," Alexis said, "patience." She glanced at him and could see the panic despite his alien features. You didn't serve with another being for decades and not pick up the clues—his goggles were back on his narrow head revealing wide eyes, his whiskers flicked crazily, and his eyes darted from the tactical board to the captain and back. "Trust me," she said.

"Do I have a choice?" he said, but not loud enough for the rest of the combat crew to hear him.

"Clear solution on battlecruiser bearing 165 mark 223!" Flipper bubbled, the words transmitted to Alexis from the mask that allowed her aquatic Selroth sensor tech to operate in an oxygen atmosphere.

"Target spinal mount and *fire!*" Alexis barked without hesitation.

The bridge crew hung on as *Pegasus* skewed from the powerful attitude reaction thrusters, her nose coming around with shocking speed. The CIC was in the center of the ship, minimizing the gravitational forces on the combat crew. Other crew in the ship, especially those near the front and back, held on for dear life as the crazy maneuver induced as much as nine gravities of force on them. Several thousand miles away, the battlecruiser that had been trying to get into a position to fire on the *Pegasus'* weakened ventral shields was surprised to find the enemy ship spin much faster than seemed possible. Instead of facing roughly away, its nose flashed around and they were staring down the maw of a huge spinal-mounted particle beam cannon.

The *Pegasus'* main gun fired, the ship's fusion plants pumping terawatts of pure energy into the weapon, which lanced out at the speed of light. The beam struck the enemy battlecruiser firmly amidships. The other ship tried to alter course to avoid the worst of it and largely failed. The beam sliced though the shields and into the ship's hull like a 14-terawatt scalpel. The enemy craft's attempt to spin and maneuver away from the blast only succeeded in the beam carving a corkscrew pattern deep into its hull. The weapon cut off, and an instant later the battlecruiser blossomed into an iridescent cloud of fiery death.

"Clean kill!" Flipper burbled.

"Use the blast debris cloud," Alexis ordered, and the ship thrust in the direction of the dead battlecruiser. At their speed, it only took a minute before the expanding cloud was between them and the bulk of the enemy force. Maybe they could escape in the confusion. "Resume heading toward the objective."

Paka looked at her in consternation. She set her jaw and nodded.

"Gravitational waves," SitCon said. "New ships entering the system." Alexis sat in the moment's calm and thought. A wave of fear flowed through her. Fear and desperation. If it didn't happen soon, it wouldn't happen at all. *<I must get there,>* the voice whispered to her being.

"Mr. Paka," she said as the bridge crew turned to look at her, "give me your best speed to the objective."

* * * * *

Find out more about Mark Wandrey and the Revelations Cycle at: http://chriskennedypublishing.com/

* * * * *

The following is an
Excerpt from Book 1 of The Kin Wars Saga:

Wraithkin

Jason Cordova

Available Now from Theogony Books

eBook, Paperback, and (soon) Audio Book

Excerpt from "Wraithkin:"

Prologue

The lifeless body of his fellow agent on the bed confirmed the undercover operation was thoroughly busted.

"Crap," Agent Andrew Espinoza, Dominion Intelligence Bureau, said as he stepped fully into the dimly lit room and carefully made his way to the filthy bed in which his fellow agent lay. He turned away from the ruined body of his friend and scanned the room for any sign of danger. Seeing none, he quickly walked back out of the room to where the slaves he had rescued earlier were waiting.

"Okay, let's keep quiet now," he reminded them. "I'll go first, and you follow me. I don't think there are any more slavers in the warehouse. Understand?"

They all nodded. He offered them a smile of confidence, though he had lied. He knew there was one more slaver in the warehouse, hiding near the side exit they were about to use. He had a plan to deal with that person, however. First he had to get the slaves to safety.

He led the way, his pistol up and ready as he guided the women through the dank and musty halls of the old, rundown building. It had been abandoned years before, and the slaver ring had managed to get it for a song. In fact, they had even qualified for a tax-exempt purchase due to the condition of the neighborhood around it. The local constable had wanted the property sold, and the slaver ring had stepped in and offered him a cut if he gave it to them. The constable had readily agreed, and the slavers had turned the warehouse into the processing plant for the sex slaves they sold throughout the Dominion. Andrew knew all this because he had been the one to help set up the purchase in the first place.

Now, though, he wished he had chosen another locale.

He stopped the following slaves as he came to the opening which led into one of the warehouse's spacious storage areas. Beyond that lay their final destination, and he was dreading the confrontation with the last slaver. He checked his gun and grunted in surprise as he saw he had two fewer rounds left than he had thought. He shook his head and charged the pistol.

"Stay here and wait for my signal," he told the rescued slaves. They nodded in unison.

He took a deep, calming breath. No matter what happened, he had to get the slaves to safety. He owed them that much. His sworn duty was to protect the Dominion from people like the slavers, and someone along the way had failed these poor women. He exhaled slowly, crossed himself and prayed to God, the Emperor and any other person who might have been paying attention.

He charged into the room, his footsteps loud on the concrete flooring. He had his gun up as he ducked behind a small, empty crate. He peeked over the top and snarled; he had been hoping against hope the slaver was facing the other direction.

Apparently Murphy is still a stronger presence in my life than God, he thought as he locked eyes with the last slaver. The woman's eyes widened in recognition and shock, and he knew he would only have one chance before she killed them all.

He dove to the right of the crate and rolled, letting his momentum drag him out of the slaver's immediate line of fire. He struggled to his feet as her gun swung up and began to track him, but he was already moving, sprinting back to the left while closing in on her. She fired twice, both shots ricocheting off the floor and embedding themselves in the wall behind him.

Andrew skid to a stop and took careful aim. It was a race, the slaver bringing her gun around as his own came to bear upon her. The muzzles of both guns flashed simultaneously, and Andrew grunted as pain flared in his shoulder.

A second shot punched him in the gut and he fell, shocked the woman had managed to get him. He lifted his head and saw that while he had hit her, her wound wasn't nearly as bad as his. He had merely clipped her collarbone and, while it would smart, it was in no way fatal. She took aim on him and smiled coldly.

Andrew swiftly brought his gun up with his working arm and fired one final time. The round struck true, burrowing itself right between the slaver's eyes. She fell backwards and lay still, dead. He groaned and dropped the gun, pain blossoming in his stomach. He rolled onto his back and stared at the old warehouse's ceiling.

That sucked, he groused. He closed his eyes and let out a long, painful breath.

* * * * *

Find out more about Jason Cordova and "Wraithkin" at:
http://chriskennedypublishing.com/imprints-authors/jason-cordova/

* * * * *

www.ingramcontent.com/pod-product-compliance
Lightning Source LLC
Chambersburg PA
CBHW070735190726
48292CB00002B/272